OVER THE
EDGE

LAURIE GIFFORD ADAMS

Laurie Gifford Adams

Over the Edge

Windswept Publishing
4590 State Route 247
Stanley, New York 14561

windsweptpublishing@gmail.com
Printed in the United States of America
Windswept Publishing 6/18/2014

Author photo by Christine A. Church – KJ Photography of CT
Christine.Church@sbcglobal.net

Cover Design and Interior format by The Killion Group
http://thekilliongroupinc.com

OTHER BOOKS BY LAURIE GIFFORD ADAMS

FINDING ATTICUS

and

www.RUinDanger.net
co-written with Scott Driscoll
An Internet and technology safety guide

For more information about autism and assistance dogs:
Autism Speaks
Autism Support Network -
http://www.autismsupportnetwork.com/
4PawsforAbility.org

The Adventures of Robbie the Raindrop by John Carroll, the children's book about weather and the rain cycle mentioned in this book, is available from any on-line retailer.

DEDICATION

To: Robin, Curtis, Sr., Curtis, Jr, Aaron and Cadbury Cottengim

Thank you for your insight in regard to living with autism and the value of assistance dogs.

And To: Troy Furst
(holding his little brother, Brody)

My wish for you is to be accepted for the wonderful person you are.

ACKNOWLEDGEMENTS

Thank you to Jim, Carrie Beth, Nick, and Mollie, my parents, Ed and Barb Gifford, my mother-in-law, Janet Adams and the rest of my huge extended family for being so supportive.

A huge thanks for all of your feedback during the draft stages of the novel to:

Dorothy Callahan, Lorraine Lander, Zita Christian, Brooke Baker, Mary Buckham, Holly Gustafson, Patricia Loftus, Robin Cottengim, Joel Waldron: Academy of Martial Arts and Personal Development, John Carroll, author of *The Adventures of Robbie the Raindrop*, and Dalan Zartman: President, Rescue Methods.

Thank you, too, to Carolyn McElravy, Donna Swarr, Kate Benson, Kendra Rugg, Emily Gifford, Jacob Gifford, Amanda Wright, Tyler Smith, Laurie Angel, and McKayla, Troy and Stephen Smith for your help in making a difficult decision. And to Christopher Robbins, owner and chef at The Robbins' Nest (for letting me use part of the name).

Because kids are my inspiration for writing these stories, and "a promise is a promise":

To my former student, who is now a teacher herself, Alyson Raabe, and her 4B class in Costa Rica: Carlos, Vonn, Ana Catalina, Brianna, Paulina, Katie, Isabella, Geovanny, Raaina, Gabriel, Gabriel, Viviana, Mariana, Antonio, Gabriela, Camila, Camila, Alberto, Jose, Nicolás, Lucía, Gabriel, Sofia

Please visit my website:
www.lauriegiffordadams.com,
Facebook: Laurie Gifford Adams – Author
Twitter: Laurie G Adams

Please send letters to:
windsweptpublishing@gmail.com

CHAPTER ONE

Gonna Fly Now. The theme song from "Rocky" startled me awake. It took me a couple of seconds to orient myself and realize it was the ringtone on my cell phone. And it was coming from somewhere in my bed. I thrashed around, patting the sheets and blanket. I finally found the phone tangled in the middle of my dark blue sheet. Once I freed it, I glanced at the caller ID - my best friend, Blake - then looked at the clock on my nightstand. What the heck could be so important that he had to call me this early?

I jabbed the screen to answer. "Dude, it's summer. Do you know what time it is?"

"Yup. Almost 8:00." He sounded happy and like he'd been awake for hours. He added a ridiculously fake southern drawl. "I thought you farm boys rise with the sun."

"Shut up!" I snapped.

I rubbed my eyes. Blake had started calling me farm boy as soon as he knew my family was moving from Manhattan to the country in western New York. I hated it.

The nickname and the move.

"Did you call just to harass me?" I growled.

"Nope, that's just a bonus." He laughed, as usual. It seemed like he was never in a bad mood.

"Hey, I'm calling because Coach Richards posted the roster for the All Star team."

I was unable to mask my irritation. "And this matters to me because?"

"Sam Reid got pitcher."

My body tensed. That got my attention. My position. My spot. I sat up and jammed my pillow against the headboard, imagined Sam's face in the middle of it, and slammed back against it.

"So what?"

"So, you're the best pitcher, man. Sucks you're stuck in farm country and can't play ball."

"They have baseball here," I countered, although I had no idea where the nearest league was.

Every swear word I could think of bounced inside my skull, and if it hadn't been for my six year old brother, Erik, asleep down the hall, I probably would have let every one of them fly. And loud! Stuck was right. I ground my teeth together.

"Timing sucks," Blake said.

I stared at the stack of baseball cards on my nightstand. Every guy in our league had his own card with stats from the spring season. I had collected almost all of them. Mine was sitting on top. Reminders of the best times of my life.

Blake was still talking, giving me the rundown on who made the team and who didn't, but I hardly registered anything he said. *I* should have been the starting pitcher for The Chargers not Sam Reid. Me! With one hard swipe of my hand, I sent the baseball cards flying across the room.

At the same time, a blood-curdling shriek split the air. The phone jumped in my fingers. I was sure someone had screamed, "Help!" but it wasn't a normal voice and it wasn't clear. Random screams weren't unusual back in the city, but I had been living in the country with my mom and Erik for exactly ten days, and I'd never heard more than a barking dog barking or mooing cow.

"Hey, farm boy, you still there?" Blake asked.

"Hold on." I focused my attention on the sounds outside.

"I'm going to beat the crap out of you."

Now *that* I heard very clearly, and some guy was pretty pissed.

"Get away from him," a female voice yelled.

Another screech pierced the air and the hairs on the back of my neck stood at attention. That sound was too close.

"Dude, I gotta go. Something's going on outside my house."

Blake laughed. "What? Pig races?"

"Yeah, whatever." I pressed the end button then army man rolled across the bed toward the window.

I separated the curtains just enough to see out. Morning sun momentarily blinded me. With the back of my other hand I rubbed my eyes until they adjusted and I could focus. In my mind I expected to see the normal skyscrapers at the entrance to Central Park, but except for a part of the huge tree outside the window, all I saw was the rundown farm about a city block across the big field. And, luckily, despite the screaming, no murder in progress.

If I'd been in our apartment, I would have ignored the screams. Not my problem. Let the cops handle it. But out here in the middle of nowhere, I didn't even know if they had cops.

I started toward my door, but within seconds, the pounding of feet in the hallway was my only warning. My bedroom door burst open like a tornado had slammed into it. A ghost-like blur of motion hurtled toward me. Before I could react, Erik vaulted into the air and landed squarely on my stomach and chest, his arms, legs and feet in motion, even after we connected. The force of his body threw us both back onto my bed. Every molecule of air in my lungs whooshed out.

"Monthtuh! Monthtuh! Monthtuh!" Missing his top two front teeth gave him a temporary speech impediment. He gasped for breath as he kicked his way past me and burrowed under my pillow, pulling the sides of it tight around his head so only a small patch of light blonde hair showed.

Worried that he'd suffocate, I snatched at the pillow, but he must have read my mind. His fingers clamped on, and I couldn't budge it.

"Dude, there aren't monsters here," I reassured him.

I continued yanking at the pillow. His skinny body shook. I'd learned long ago that there were times when he'd accept a calming hand on his back and times when physical contact of any kind would freak him out. Without a doubt, this would be a freak out time, and I didn't need to spend the next hour trying to bring him back from a major meltdown.

"Erik, take a deep breath." I spoke softly, just the way Mom and Dad sounded when they wanted to quiet him.

His muffled reply was high-pitched, like a typical panicked little kid. "Thcared! Thcared! Thcared!"

No kidding. Jeez!

"You don't need to be scared, *Oopster*." I thought using his nickname would make it sound like I was in control, but the truth was, I was a little freaked out myself. "I won't let anything hurt you." I glanced toward my window, wondering if I could keep that promise. As Erik's older brother, I wanted to believe I could, but as a city guy plopped out in the country, I wasn't so confident. Even though I'd studied Tae Kwon Do for a little over four years, I didn't know if those skills would help if someone was being murdered in my yard.

The yelling outside picked up again, so obviously this situation wasn't going away.

"Here's the deal," I said, making another half-hearted attempt to pull the pillow off his head. "You stay here, and I'll check it out. I'm sure there's nothing." I hoped the angle from the window in Erik's room would be better.

In my head I heard our twenty-year old brother's voice. *Dylan, you're such a wuss! Just go out and take care of it.*

My muscles tensed. Damn it! Trent was 350 miles away, and I was letting him get to me. But he was right. If someone outside was hurt, or being hurt, I had to suck it up and help. With Mom at work and Dad and Trent still in the city, I was the man of the house. And not for just this moment. But, I also wanted to know what I was getting into before I charged into the situation. My dad, the cop, had given me that advice.

I wiped Trent's chiding voice from my thoughts. Before the summer was over, I would prove to him - no, to my whole family - that I wasn't a little kid anymore and I was up to the responsibility of keeping my little brother safe. Besides, Mom and Dad had promised I could go

back to the city for the last two weeks of summer
if I'd help with Erik.

Right now the end of the summer was decades
away.

Wearing only boxers, I hopped over a week's
worth of dirty laundry that littered my floor and
dashed down the hall, still clutching my phone like
a security blanket. I entered Erik's room,
impressed by how neat a six year old could be. But
then, that was part of who he was. Nothing could
be out of its proper place.

I crossed to the window. The ends of the
curtains floated in the warm breeze. I caught one
end in my fingers and pulled it back to peer out
from the side. Everything appeared clear. I
scanned the tree's thick trunk, searching for
hanging bodies or whatever else my imagination
was sure was there. Sweat beaded on my upper lip,
and I backhanded it. So much for being cool under
pressure.

"Leave Einstein alone," a girl ordered.

I glanced in the direction of her voice, but I
saw no one.

"I'm killin' him," the deep voice threatened.
"I'm sick of 'im wakin' me up every day."

THWACK! An outer, leaf-filled branch of the
tree shook.

Our tree was so huge that I couldn't see the
ground under it. I leaned forward to press my face
against the screen. Two beady eyes peered through
a little opening between the leaves. What was
that? I pressed harder, and the screen bowed out
with an indentation of my nose. Because every one
of my senses was on high alert, I noticed a
metallic-like dust smell on the mesh. Who knew
screens had a smell?

There was another loud thump against the branch and whatever was in the tree screeched again.

"Monthtuh! Monthtuh! Monthtuh!"

I jumped, slamming the back of my head against the lower sash of the window. "Ow!" I whirled from the window, my heart pounding like a runaway subway.

My instinct was to yell at Erik, but I reined in my frustration. I'd never been "in charge" of him until this summer and had a new appreciation for Mom and Dad's patience level. After only four long days on the job, I was already questioning my ability to keep it together all summer.

Christina, our older sister, also knew how to handle Erik. But, if it hadn't been for her, we'd still be in Manhattan and she'd still be doing her amazing job of watching him this summer while Mom and Dad were at work. That was until the incident six months ago.

Now, the responsibility became mine by default, and it included a move away from everything I'd known.

Whatever was in the tree screeched again, and surprise launched me straight up in the air. In one quick move I plastered myself against the wall. So much for being the brave brother.

"Dylan! Dylan! Dylan!" Erik cried. His wide-eyed panic pulled me back. I was torn between comforting him and finding out what was in the tree.

"Einstein, where are you?" It was the girl's voice again. Whatever was in the tree screeched a response.

I grabbed the window sash and slammed it closed before Erik panicked any more. Who was I kidding? My heart was rattling so fast that I couldn't catch my breath. I snapped the lock across the top of the window and turned back toward Erik. All color had drained from his face. He wrung his hands together, working the fabric cat ear torn from a stuffed toy he'd had as a toddler between his fingers. Over the last couple of years he'd pulled on the ear so much that eventually it had come off. The rest of the cat had been laid to rest in the bottom drawer of his dresser, but the ear went everywhere with him.

"It's okay, buddy." I hoped my calm voice would soothe him.

Out of my peripheral vision, I caught movement in the yard. A cute girl about my age paced in the middle of our scraggly lawn - the lawn Mom had been asking me for more than a week to mow. This had to be the girl from the farm next door that Mom had mentioned. A long, brown ponytail swung against her back as she shook her fist toward the tree. Although her mouth was moving, with the window closed, I couldn't hear her. It didn't matter. I could see her very clearly and my heart kicked into high gear. This girl might be the first good thing to happen since we moved here.

If I'd known what, or rather *who*, was living on that farm, I might have felt a whole lot different about making the effort to go down the road to meet the neighbors when Mom had suggested it. Now opportunity was knocking, as my mother often said, and I was going to answer that door.

I darted across Erik's room. "Come on!" His monster didn't

matter to me anymore. My focus was on the girl. My bare feet slid at the top of the wooden stairs, but I snagged the railing before I flew head first. Erik's feet pounded behind me.

"Careful on these stairs," I said, out of breath.

We dashed through the foyer, and I flipped the deadbolt on the front door. As soon as I stepped onto the porch I stopped and glanced down. At my boxers. Really? That would make a great impression on a girl I was going to meet for the first time.

"Get back inside." I tugged Erik just inside the door then raced back up the stairs to grab clothes. A black *Dave Matthews Band* T-shirt was stuck under the corner of my bedroom door and the rug. I yanked it out and kicked aside the pile of dirty T-shirts and socks I'd heaped near my desk until I found a pair of navy blue shorts. I pulled them both on as I charged down the stairs. At the landing I threw open the door and launched over the three front steps and into the grass.

The sound of wood on wood echoed, and I rounded the corner of the house in time to see a very muscular guy, who looked to be in his late teens, taking a swing with a wooden baseball bat at a low, thick branch. The bat bounced, nearly hitting him in the head. He swore. Loudly.

I jogged in the girl's direction. My eyes hadn't deceived me when I'd first spotted her from Erik's room. This girl was seriously hot, and by the way she was standing up to the guy with the bat, she had guts, too. At least one aspect of this summer looked brighter. I was staring at her, but she only glanced quickly at Erik and me. She clenched her hands at her sides as she turned back to glare at Batboy.

"You're scaring the little kid," she said through gritted teeth. "Get out of here."

I glanced at Erik who had followed me out but stood with his shoulder pressed against the corner of the house. His eyes were bigger than quarters, and his hands were plastered against his ears, his fingers buried in his hair. The piece of cat ear stuck out between his fingers.

"I'm not leaving until I get that stupid thing out of the tree," Batboy snarled. His lips curled back to reveal a murderous expression; Harlem street gangs looked friendlier.

More squawking. Eric stomped his feet and mumbled incoherently but loud enough that it drew the attention of Batboy. The guy wheeled around, narrowed his eyes then pointed the bat at Erik.

"What's with the freak?"

All thoughts of making a good impression with the girl evaporated. Even though there were several meters separating Erik and Batboy, I took a few steps to come between them.

"He's not a freak," I growled. "He's just freaked out by you."

An evil laugh erupted from Batboy as he returned his attention to whatever was in the tree. I didn't want to be near the swinging bat, so I stepped closer to the girl.

Wham! The bat hit the tree again, and the shriek from the branches sent a shudder down my spine. "Whoa!" I muttered, impressed by the guy's homerun-worthy swing.

The girl ignored me and focused her attention on Batboy, whom I assumed was her brother. They looked a lot alike, except she was pretty and petite. Especially compared to him.

"Knock it off, idiot" she screamed. "Just go home."

I bent a little, trying to see up inside the tree. "What's up there?"

The look she gave me made me feel like a pesky mosquito she'd like to swat. "Einstein."

I took a step back. Okay. Was she putting me down or was that the name of whatever was in the tree?

Returning her attention to her brother, who was now climbing the tree, she screamed, "I'll get him. Leave him alone!"

Erik reacted to her raised voice and started running in tight circles. At least in a circle he probably wouldn't bolt, so I left him alone for the moment.

"Who's Einstein?" I asked, wishing there was a way to get a closer look without having my head smashed in by the maniac with the bat.

"My peacock." She moved even closer to her brother who now was almost up to the first big branch. I'd only seen peacocks in books and the zoo. What was one doing in our tree?

I crouched down, wondering if peacocks attack. "Is there anything I can do to help?"

Batboy twisted and sneered. "Yeah, tell the freak over there to shut up."

Erik's mumblings turned into all-out wailing. At warp speed, the faces of bullies who had taunted Erik back home flashed through my mind. Trent and Christina had always handled them while I stood on the sidelines watching. But we weren't in the city, and they weren't here.

There was no way I was letting some country jerk bully my brother, too. Erik couldn't help the way he was.

I rushed under the tree. In one swift movement, I reached up and grabbed Batboy's leg just above his Nike sneaker, yanking him hard. I ducked to the side as he plummeted. When his back connected with the ground, the air in his lungs exploded out.

The Earth stopped moving.

Time stood still.

For a moment, my life flashed before my eyes just the way I'd always heard it happened when a person thought his life was ending.

When Batboy rolled over, all of my muscles tensed. In an instant I formed an escape plan that included saving the life of Erik and this girl I didn't even know.

The bully snatched the bat and slowly got to his feet. He shook himself then raised the bat high over his head. "I'm gonna kill that stupid-ass bird." He twisted toward me. "Then you."

As if sensing the threat, the peacock leaped from the branch and aimed its massive feathered body directly at the guy. Its feet clipped the top of his head and the tail slapped his face before it landed on the ground 10 feet away. The bird walked in a circle and slowly spread its plume of feathers to reveal what looked like dozens of eyes staring blankly. From feather tip to feather tip, the tail looked six feet wide.

Batboy stalked toward the peacock, holding the bat over his head.

Images from when I was eleven popped into my head. My best friends and I had accidentally wandered into a bad neighborhood in Harlem and into the middle of a gang fight. Baseball bats were the weapon of choice. I'd never forget the sound of a bat connecting with the jaw of a scrawny kid who worked hard to appear tough. He had dropped to the ground, writhing and flopping like a worm that had been cut in two. Erik would be traumatized to witness this peacock, or me, meeting the same fate.

"Don't do it!" the girl yelled.

Behind us, Erik's wail reached siren proportions. The girl shot toward her brother, her arms stretched toward the bat. He pulled it behind his head, out of her reach, to gain more momentum. A low growl rumbled from him as he stepped closer to the peacock.

Anger and fear propelled me. I lurched past the girl and reached for the bat at the mid-point just as the guy was on the upswing to go over his head. I heard a crack inside my skull then saw the stars everyone claims are a myth. My knees crumpled like wet noodles and my back slammed against the ground.

With my eyes closed, I waited for the death blow.

CHAPTER TWO

"You idiot! Look what you've done."

I recognized the girl's voice, but I couldn't open my eyes. The tip of the bat had caught me just above my left eyebrow where the skin now pulsed. Although it hadn't knocked me out, the hit had stunned me enough so I couldn't pull myself together. I could hear Erik's feet pounding the hard ground not too far away. His wails mixed with the girl's voice, but I had no desire to look. My first coherent thought was that I didn't need to come to the country to get my head bashed in; there were plenty of opportunities in the city where I should have been right now.

Someone shook my shoulders. "Hey, you okay?" I squinted open my right eye to see the girl leaning close. Nice, pink lips. "Oh, shoot! You're bleeding," she announced.

I touched my forehead just as moisture dripped across my eye lid and trickled in a few different directions down my cheek. When I pulled my hand away to inspect the damage, it was streaked with blood.

"Yeah, there's a little blood," I mumbled. After a second, I squinted. "I thought blood freaks girls out."

The girl rocked back on her knees. "Maybe other girls, but I've taken care of plenty of hurt animals and helped even more be born. Besides, I'm going to be a veterinarian, so I better not get freaked out by blood."

"I'm impressed." My voice was weak but through the fog that swirled in my brain I meant it.

Erik's crying wound down to a whimper, which was amazing considering he didn't handle injuries well, his or anyone else's. It was another one of the weird things that no one understood, especially strangers. Instead, they made rude comments or gave our family evil stares when we were in public and Erik had meltdowns.

The peacock screeched again. Somewhere in the distance Erik's whimper escalated to a high-pitched howl again. I tried to get up so I could go and reassure him, but my head spun and throbbed. I snapped my eyes shut and dropped back to the ground with a ridiculous thud.

The girl pressed down on my chest. "You better lie here until I can take care of that cut."

As badly as I wanted to get up to comfort my brother, my head pounded when I moved. And, okay, a take charge, pretty girl wasn't hard to deal with, either.

"Brock, get a wet washcloth and a towel at the house," the girl ordered.

So, Batboy had a name. The knowledge didn't make him less threatening.

"Kiss my—"

"Brock!" she screeched. "Watch your mouth and just get that stuff."

"Get it yourself!" Brock bellowed back, his voice getting closer. "I'm not your servant, and I'm sure not helping that moron."

I managed to open my eyes a bit again so I could watch the brute as he stalked toward us. Before I thought he was a lot older than me, but now I could see he looked like he was my age. Muscles not usually associated with fourteen year olds bulged below his t-shirt sleeves. The dude had to work out because that much muscle just wasn't natural. His mouth was open as he approached me, and I swore fangs hung behind his curled back lips. The bat swung from his hand like a pendulum. Cringing to brace myself, I fully expected him to take another swing at me. That's how it worked that time when my friends and I had stumbled onto that gang fight. Even the guy who was face planted in the sidewalk had been fair game.

Instead, Brock growled and spit on the ground, narrowly missing my head. Nice guy.

I suspected he and I were not destined to be buddies.

"You're a creep!" the girl yelled.

"Thank you," he retorted.

I couldn't believe how relieved I was that he was lumbering away.

The girl stuck her tongue out at his retreating back then turned her attention back to me. "Ignore him. He's the moron. You need help. Who should I call?"

She pulled a cell phone from her jean shorts. For some reason that surprised me.

"Uh, my mother." I swiped at the sticky mess that tickled my eyebrow. When my fingers brushed across the wound, I nearly jumped out of my skin. I sucked in a deep breath, willing the throbbing to stop.

With the phone in her palm and her finger poised over the keypad, she waited.

After a few seconds, I rattled off my mother's cell phone number since I had no clue what the number was at the vet clinic where she worked. The girl tapped in the number then tucked the phone under the strands of brown hair that floated around her ear and swept across her shoulders.

"Do you wanna talk or do you want me to?"

I waved a hand in the air. "You. My mom is Dr. Westcott. Julie Westcott. Just tell her —"

"Shh!" The girl held up her palm. "Hi, is this Dr. Westcott?" There was a pause. "This is Willow from down the road." Another pause.

Willow. Her name was Willow? What kind of a name was that? It sounded like a tree or bush or something. But, then, as quickly as I questioned it, I decided the name fit. There was something different about this girl, but a good different, like her name.

"Yes, I live in the farmhouse. I'm at your house. Your son -" She abruptly stopped talking, lifted the phone away from her mouth and looked at me with her eyebrows arched.

Did she think I could read her mind? "What?"

"What's your name?" she whispered.

"Oh, Dylan."

"I'm here with O'Dylan," she said.

I popped up at the shoulders and regretted the quick move. "What? No, not O'Dylan," I corrected. "Dylan. My name is Dylan."

She held the phone away again and gave me a look that said, *Duh!* "Well, *you* said O'Dylan, didn't you?"

I started to smile, but smiling hurt, too, so I stopped. "Yeah, I did. Just get on with the call, okay?"

There was brightness in her brown eyes that made her look intelligent and fun at the same time. For a second I considered playing this injury up if it kept her attention on me. Maybe I could get her to lean in really close again to look at the cut and then I could –

What was I thinking? Any sister of Brock the Batboy would probably bash me in the other eye if I put a move on her.

"Anyway," Willow said back into the phone, "I'm with Dylan. He got hit above his eye with a baseball bat."

Although it wasn't distinguishable, I heard the pitch of my mother's voice rise. Typically, she was calm, even in the worst situations. But I'm sure hearing over the phone that your kid has been hit in the face with a baseball bat could conjure gruesome images in a mother's mind.

"No, no. It is bleeding," Willow continued, "but, no, I don't think he lost consciousness. I had to have stitches in my forehead once, and this cut looks like that did."

Like a magnet had drawn me, my attention was pulled to her forehead. A thin white line cut a jagged streak diagonally from the middle of her hairline down toward her eyebrow reminding me of Harry Potter's scar. The scar wasn't something you noticed until you looked for it. My fingers twitched in the grass while I wondered if I ran my finger along it if it would feel raised.

"Uh-huh," she said, bobbing her head and staring at my eyebrow. "Okay, I'll stay with him until you get here." She listened again. "Okay, thanks. Bye." She pressed the END button and shoved the phone back in her pocket. "Wow! Your mom's a doctor?" Her eyes widened so the brown sparkled in the sun.

"Yeah, she's a vet. My grandfather, too."

"Oh." Her expression suddenly darkened and she looked away.

I pushed my palm against the side of my head to try and stop the throbbing. "I thought you'd think that was cool since you want to be a vet."

"Yeah, it's cool." Her lack of enthusiasm was the exact opposite of her energy just moments before. I didn't get it. She stood and wiped the dirt and grass off her bare knees. "Anyway, your mom was already on her way home. She'll be here in ten minutes. She said she has a surprise for you and Erik."

Erik! All of a sudden I realized I didn't hear him anymore. Despite the pain, I pushed myself up and squinted in the direction where I'd last seen him. "Where's Erik? Where's my brother?" Panic squeezed my chest, holding my breath hostage. This couldn't be happening. It just couldn't. I couldn't fail after just four days.

Willow glanced behind her. "He was there a minute ago."

She gave me a look that said *what's the big deal?* But she didn't know his history – that the last time he'd taken off like that he'd almost been killed.

"Damn it!" I struggled to my knees and then to my feet. "Erik!" The ground spun, making it difficult for me to stand straight, so I bent over and put my hands on my knees. "He's a bolter." Pain stabbed through my left eye, and I had to cover it with my bloody hand, but that was the least of my worries.

"A what?"

"A bolter. That's what my family calls it. He takes off if he gets over stimulated." As if I was in slow motion, I pulled my shoulders up so I was standing straight then struggled to keep my head from rolling around on my shoulders. I couldn't remember ever being this dizzy in my life. "We have to find him before he gets hurt or finds some weird hiding spot."

Willow tipped her head and arched the eyebrow at the end of the scar. "Why would he do that?"

"You wouldn't understand."

I tried to run, but it was more like a drunk's stagger. "Erik, it's okay," I yelled as I moved toward the corner of the house
where he'd been running in circles. How would I live down losing him the first week I was responsible for his safety? And now Mom was on her way here, and I didn't know where he was. She thought she had a surprise for me? Well, if I didn't find Erik, I had a *bigger* surprise for her, and she wasn't going to like it.

Willow followed me. "I'll help look. How far could he get?"

"Far." Man how I wished this wasn't the way she and I were getting to know each other. "And fast," I added. I knew I must look uncoordinated running, but with one eye covered, I could hardly run in a straight line. "Unfortunately, another one of those things we learned the hard way was how fast Erik can disappear."

I stopped and checked under the bushes at the side of the house, but they were clear. My breathing was labored from moving so fast, so I had to take breaths between every couple of words in order to finish my story. "One time he hid in our apartment. I thought my mother would have a stroke before we found him hiding under the sheets in the linen closet. That was after searching for three hours."

Willow grabbed my free arm and yanked me around toward her, causing another shard of pain to shoot across my forehead. "Three hours?"

As much as I liked her touching me, I pulled my arm free so I could continue toward the front of the house. "Yeah, and now I only have ten minutes to find him unless I want to figure out how to explain to my mother that I lost my little brother."

"We'll find him," Willow said with a confidence I didn't feel.

"We better. Erik," I called. "Come on, buddy. I'm okay. You don't have to be scared." He wasn't at the front of the house, but the front door was open. I hoped it was a clue to where he was and not just open because we hadn't closed it on our way out to investigate the noise. If he'd run off into the woods past our house, there was no telling where he could be right now. I dropped my hand from my eye long enough to leap over the three front steps to the landing at the top.

"Where are you, Oopster?"

"Oopster?" I could hear the laugh in Willow's voice.

Blood gushed from my injury. I'd bleed to death before we found Erik, but I had to find him. I hurried into the bathroom off the foyer, leaving a splotchy trail of blood like Hansel and Gretel's crumbs. With my free hand, I snatched the small towel from the rack on the sink and pressed it to my brow. When I turned to go back into the hall, I nearly collided with Willow, who stood in the bathroom with me. That was awkward.

"Why do you call him Oopster?" she asked, not the least bit flustered to be in the bathroom with some strange guy.

Really? The origin of his nickname was important right now? But, as I stepped past her and ran down the hall, I answered over my shoulder. "My parents thought I was going to be their last kid. Then, oops, along came Erik eight years later. So, the nickname stuck. I've gotta find him."

As I ducked into each room to do a preliminary sweep, I heard her giggling. It was the usual response.

"Erik, we can have Lucky Charms if you come out." I hoped offering his favorite cereal would lure him.

"What can I do?" Willow asked. "It's stupid for me to follow you or stand and watch."

I thought for a second. We could cover twice the area if she was doing her own search. "Okay, you finish checking down here, and I'll check the bedrooms."

We started off in opposite directions, then I stopped abruptly. "Wait!" She turned toward me. "You, uh, you-" The words stuck in my throat. My parents kept telling me I was girl crazy, especially after I had three girlfriends in the last school year. I think now I got what they meant. It was hard for me to put together a coherent sentence around Willow. She blinked in her questioning stare and it brought me out of my trance. "If you find him, don't yell for me. And whatever you do, *don't* touch him."

"Huh?"

I couldn't blame her for thinking that was an odd request. "Erik is sensitive to loud noises and being touched. Just come and get me if you find him. Okay?"

She narrowed those mesmerizing eyes in a curious expression, shrugged and said, "Okay," and then set off on her search.

I wondered if, when we found him, she'd run out the front door and swear to never come near us again. I couldn't blame her if she did. She wouldn't be the first person to be scared off before having the opportunity to understand. But, other than finding Erik, there was nothing I wanted more right now than to get to know Willow. Something told me she could be the salvation in what was shaping up to be a horrible summer.

This house was so new to us that I didn't have a clue if there were secret passageways Erik might find. And, if anyone could find them, he would. It seemed the smaller the space, the more likely he'd be squeezed into it when he went into hiding mode. I started by looking under beds. Not original, and considering Erik and the way he thought, not likely, either.

"Erik!" I called. "I'm going to end up with more cloverleaves than you. You'll be stuck with the hearts, moons and stars."

Another one of his obsessions was counting and categorizing things. One time he poured the entire box of Lucky Charms out so he could count how many of each shape there were in the box, and he kept a tally sheet. Then, when he'd have the cereal for breakfast, he'd count how many of each shape he ate that day and subtract it from the total. His math skills were amazing for a six year old. Once I made the mistake of eating some of the Lucky Charms for a snack. A full scale meltdown resulted when he discovered he was short six moons, seven hearts and two cloverleaves. I had hurried to Harley's Convenience Store three blocks from our apartment to buy another box of cereal. When I'd returned, I counted out exactly how many Erik said he was missing, threw them in the box, shook it up, and suggested he count again because maybe he'd miscounted.

It worked that time, but Erik's disability also made him smarter than the average six year old, so I knew it wouldn't work again. It took a lot of energy on our family's part to stay ahead of his meltdowns. They were nightmares once they started.

I was so lost in my thoughts when Willow stepped up behind me in my parents' bedroom and tapped me on the shoulder that I nearly jumped out of my skin. She leaned in close to my ear and whispered.

"Found him."

"Really? Where?"

Her eyes widened. "I thought we had to be really quiet?"

"No, he just gets set off by shouting. Where is he?"

"Behind the couch in the living room," she said. I pivoted and hurried toward the door as she continued explaining. "He must have crawled in there like a snake or something because there's hardly any space. I don't know how he fit. Here, I'll show you."

Willow grabbed my hand and pulled me toward the stairs. My skin tingled, and I knew instantly if I was smart, I'd slow down so I could hold her hand longer. After all, Erik wasn't going anywhere. I decided to just go along with whatever was happening, because this girl's hand felt good in mine.

"Come on. Let's get down there before he hides somewhere else." The urgency in her voice was adorable. She had no clue that once hidden, Erik was unlikely to budge.

We were moving so fast down the stairs, still holding hands, that it was awkward. She safely rounded the corner at the landing in the foyer just before the front door swung open. There was no time to yell or warn anyone I was there. The edge of the door slammed into me.

Right into the *other* side of my face.

I thought I heard something crack in my cheek, but there was no mistaking the thud my body made when I hit the wood floor. The only thing that bothered me was that Willow and I were no longer holding hands.

"Dylan!" It was my mother's voice, but it sounded really far away.

She leaned over one side of me and Willow leaned over the other. Mom's eyes darted between the gash I'd gotten from the bat and the point of impact with the door. "Oh my goodness. Are you all right? I'm so sorry. I didn't know you were behind the door."

"It's okay," I mumbled.

"Can you get ice from the freezer?" she asked Willow. "Grab the towel next to the sink and you can put it in that."

Willow jumped up and jogged toward the kitchen at the end of the hall. I rolled my head to watch her, mesmerized by her long legs. Yeah, I could get used to looking at those legs.

Mom must have read my mind, because she grabbed my chin to force me to look at her.

"Get a grip on your hormones, lover boy."

I wanted to get a grip, alright, but my hormones were not what I was imagining.

Mom grabbed the blood-soaked towel I'd been holding against my head. "You're a mess." She dabbed around the open wound. "Stitches are definitely in order."

I groaned. When I was eight, I'd gotten stitches after I fell off the playscape in Central Park. The excruciating pain of the Novocain injection going directly into my wound would live in my memory forever.

Mom grimaced then touched my forehead like she thought it was going to be painful for *her* to touch my injuries. "Looks like you're going to have a nice welt on your cheek, too, but at least there's not a cut." She then put her fingers under my neck and lightly pressed. "Does anything hurt here?" Besides being a vet, she was an Emergency Medical Technician, so whenever we were hurt she'd check us out more thoroughly than our regular doctor. I shook my head, embarrassed by appearing to be such a klutz. Neither of these injuries were my fault, but here I was with a double whammy. Literally.

Willow reappeared and knelt next to me again. She handed the ice and towel to my mother.

"It might take both of us to take care of this guy," Mom said. "Put some ice in the towel and hold it against his cheek, and I'll take care of the cut."

I winced as their hands neared me, but, to use my brother, Trent's, words, I didn't want to look like a *wuss* in front of Willow, so I bit my lip and pretended the pain wasn't affecting me.

Mom glanced around quickly. "Where's Erik?"

"Behind the couch," Willow and I answered in unison. As silly as the response sounded, it was actually a relief to have an answer for her.

Mom scowled and looked toward the living room. "Okay. Is he all right?"

"Sure thing," Willow said cheerily. "I think he just likes it back there."

I looked up at Willow, amazed. Erik had put on a pretty good show, yet she acted like there was nothing unusual about his behavior. This girl was really something. My muscles relaxed and I closed my eyes, thankful that, for the first time in a long time, I didn't have to stick up for Erik and try to explain him. I was so used to being on the defensive that I wasn't sure how to react to someone who might accept him. But then, she'd only had about twenty minutes around him. There was still time for her attitude to change.

I was lost in the thought when a dog started barking and Willow's peacock squawked like it was under attack again.

"Einstein!" she yelled. As if realizing her mistake in shouting out and possibly frightening Erik, she lowered her voice and added, "I have to check on him." She grabbed my hand, laid it on the ice pack on my cheek then jumped up and dashed out the door.

"Who's Einstein?" Mom asked.

"Her peacock. It was in our tree. Erik thought it was a monster." It was hard to believe the situation with the peacock, Erik's temporary disappearance and my two injuries had happened in a matter of minutes. I struggled to sit up. "Can I get off the floor?"

"Sure, but let me know if your neck bothers you or you have a headache." She put her arm under my shoulders and helped me sit up. "Are you okay?" I nodded. "Dizzy? Headache?" I shook my head. My head and cheek hurt, but I'd had worse injuries from skateboarding and playing baseball. At least those injuries were earned in a more noble way.

Outside, the dog continued to bark. I wondered if the dog
was Willow's, too. The peacock wasn't screeching anymore, so at least it was one less noise that would keep Erik hiding behind the couch.

My mother again inspected both the gash and the lump on my forehead and, apparently
satisfied, once again gave me the duty of holding the towel against my cut.

"Well, do you want that surprise before I take you for stitches?" Mom asked.

The surprise. I'd forgotten she'd told Willow she was bringing a "surprise" for us. For a moment the idea of my mom bringing a surprise embarrassed me. It made me sound like a little kid in front of this hot girl. Then, suddenly I remembered the only thing I'd requested when Mom and Dad told us we were moving to the country: a dirt bike. I figured it was the least they could do for yanking me away from Manhattan.

"Well?" Mom asked.

"Sure, I'll take the surprise." What else was I supposed to say? No, don't give me a surprise? And, maybe my guess was right.

She walked to the doorway of the living room. "Erik, come out here, please." Her voice took on a sing-songy quality when she spoke to him. "I have something you're going to love."

I tossed the melting ice cubes out the open door then dabbed the cloth against my wound. The blood flow had pretty much subsided, but I continued to sit on the floor. Erik wriggled his way out from behind the couch and came into the hallway.

"Thurprithe? I don't like thurpritheth." He glanced toward my injuries while asking the question, but thankfully he was unaffected now. I could never grasp how one minute he could be babbling incoherently and out of control like a baby then the next minute sound like he was six going on sixty.

"You'll like this one. Wait right here with Dylan," Mom instructed. She moved to the door. "Jamie, you can bring her in now."

Now *that* caught my attention. Bring *her* in? I'd hardly had time to consider who the *her* could be when a big ball of golden fur bounded up the front stairs and skidded across the wood floor and into my legs. The dog kicked her feet in the air and flailed around as she tried to right herself on the slippery floor. Her leash bounced around her, sometimes getting wrapped around her legs.

"Meet Scout." Mom beamed.

Scout wasn't a little puppy, but she looked young. In the midst of my appraisal she licked at the drops of water on my cheek that were left from the melting ice. She squirmed against my arm and pushed her nose up under my elbow in an attempt to get me to pet her.

Erik stood just behind Mom and peeked around her waist to watch Scout lick me to death.

I liked dogs, but it was apparent that I hadn't made my true desires clear. As cute as Scout was, I had the sinking feeling that instead of a hot motor and two tires, my *dirt bike* had a cold, wet nose and four paws.

CHAPTER THREE

I lifted my chin to avoid more licks from the wriggling mass and saw Willow standing in the doorway next to another teenage girl and a woman about Mom's age. They both had silly grins, obviously in love with the cuddly fur ball pressed into my body.

"Dylan, Erik, this is Jamie Reston," Mom said, indicating the girl I hadn't met yet. "And this is Charlotte Taylor." She nodded toward the woman. "She's Scout's trainer. Jamie owns Atticus, Scout's father, and she helped foster Scout until she was old enough to begin training."

The dog rammed her skull under my chin and my teeth snapped together. What was a little more pain at this point?

"Charlotte runs a kennel and is also a professional assistance dog trainer. I've hired her to work with us to assimilate Scout into our home for Erik."

I wasn't sure if it was the throbbing over my eye that made it hard for me to understand or the fact that I couldn't figure out how a dog could make a difference with Erik. Either way, I was still processing it when Charlotte answered my unspoken question.

"By assimilate, your mother means I'll help all of you learn cues and commands to use with Scout, and Scout will learn how to be a part of your family and read Erik's moods."

Charlotte sounded smart, but I wondered what she really knew about Erik and how challenging it was when he was worked up. I'd lived with his autism for six years, and I still didn't fully understand.

Willow knelt next to me and rubbed Scout's head. "Aw, she's so sweet," she cooed in baby talk. I wondered why so many people talked like that when they talked to animals or little kids. "Oh, you're so pretty." Scout wiggled around as Willow scratched her back near her tail. A look of pure pleasure filled the young dog's brown eyes. The harder Willow scratched, the more the dog's backside pressed into my chest. I struggled to stay in a sitting position and keep the cloth pressed to my bleeding eyebrow at the same time.

Willow looked at me with the softest expression I've ever seen on anyone. "You're so lucky, O'Dylan." I wanted to protest her messing with my name again, but I'd barely opened my mouth before she rambled on. "I'd love a puppy, but Granny Annie has a very spoiled dog, so we can't get another one."

"Who's Granny Annie?" I asked.

"My mother's mom. We live with her." Scout lifted her muzzle and licked Willow's lips. "Ah, puppy kisses. I can never get enough of them."

I almost gagged at the thought of a dog licking my lips. Didn't Willow think about where that tongue had licked before?

It obviously didn't matter. Willow closed her eyes and pressed her forehead against Scout's. The dog suddenly looked different to me. Before, I thought if I had a dirt bike I'd look cool and get a girl's attention. It didn't take a genius to figure out that I was going to have better luck using this bundle of fur. I wrapped my free arm around Scout's neck and hugged her, which conveniently brought my cheek close to Willow's.

"Scout will actually be Erik's dog," Mom pointed out as if reading my mind. "Technically, she'll belong to the family, but we got her to do a job."

"And that's a misunderstanding that many people have," Charlotte said. "Scout looks like every other dog, but she is a worker before she's a pet."

For the first time, Jamie spoke. "One of the things Charlotte taught me was that Scout, like any other potential service dog, went through temperament testing. Lots of people don't understand that not every dog makes a good service dog. Personality is just as important as training."

Jamie looked like she wasn't that much older than us, maybe fifteen or sixteen, but she talked like a professional in the dog training field. I was impressed.

Willow leaned back and rubbed Scout's ears, causing the dog to tip her head and groan appreciatively. "What kind of job could a dog have, besides being a guard or herding dog?"

"When Erik's frightened, he runs and hides," Mom said.

I glanced toward the living room couch where he'd been hiding minutes before. "Willow experienced that first hand."

Mom tousled Erik's hair and continued. She was the only one who could get away with touching him sometimes, and it looked like this was one of those times.

"Scout's job will be to keep Erik from bolting," she explained. "If, heaven forbid, he does get away and hides, it will be Scout's job to find him. She'll also calm him when he's overwhelmed."

Referring to Erik's meltdowns as "being overwhelmed" was generous. I looked at the dog skeptically. "This dog knows how to do that? She acts like every other dog I've seen."

Charlotte stepped forward. "She *is* like any other dog until she has to work." She patted her thigh. "Scout, here."

As if a switch had been flipped, Scout leaped away from me and turned her attention to Charlotte, who added a command. "Sit." The dog obeyed. "Good girl." Charlotte squatted next to Scout and looked at my brother. "Erik, would you like to meet Scout?"Erik stood with his back pressed to the woodwork at the doorway between the hall and living room. We'd never had a dog, so I wondered how he would react. His green eyes were wide open, staring. He pressed the stuffed cat ear against his lips.

Mom moved to Scout and stroked the top of the dog's head. In a soft voice she said, "Erik, come over next to me and meet Scout. She wants to be friends with you."

If anyone could get Erik to do something, it was Mom, but even that wasn't consistent. His shoulders relaxed and he took one step forward. "Come on," she coaxed while she continued to stroke Scout's head.

Scout's full attention was on Charlotte, but then an amazing thing happened. With one circular motion of Charlotte's hand, Scout shifted to face Erik and Mom. The dog focused on Erik as if she knew this was "her person".

In order to show Erik what to do, Mom made a fist with one hand and held it out for Scout to sniff. "Let Scout meet you, Erik. Hold your hand like this and your fingers will be safe."

Erik stood like a statue, his eyes still wide. Then he slowly shook his head.

As if she understood his fear, Scout lowered her head and stretched her nose just the tiniest amount in his direction. She waited patiently, her stare never wavering. The tip of her tongue slipped between her lips and she panted, making it look like a smile. I couldn't figure out how Erik could resist her because, for me, it was tough to not reach out to pet her.

"I think she likes you, Erik," Mom said. "Can you let her sniff you?"

He didn't respond to her question. It seemed like hours passed, with none of us moving or breathing, before Erik slowly stretched his fist toward her. With each of Scout's sniffs, Erik shuffled closer, his body rigid, reminding me of the Buzz Lightyear toy I got from my best friend Luke for my seventh birthday. None of us moved. History told me this situation could go one of two ways, and none of us wanted to experience the negative possibility. I think we were all worried that Erik would reject Scout.

Our world shifted into slow motion.

The grandfather clock in the hallway ticked.

We waited.

The central air whirred to life.

We waited.

Erik shuffled closer.

We waited.

He took another step until he was just inches from Scout.

The silence in the room hurt my ears as I anticipated the inevitable outburst.

To my amazement, it didn't happen. Instead, Erik knelt in front of Scout and stared into her face. Straight into her eyes. In six years, I'd never seen him make direct eye contact with anyone or anything! What pull did this dog have that humans didn't?

Mom took a deep breath that filled the quiet. When I looked up, her lips curved in a tight smile and tears danced on her eyelids. No one dared move for fear of breaking the magical moment. Even Willow, who knew almost nothing of Erik's history, beamed.

Scout understood instinctively how to respond. Instead of moving closer, the Golden Retriever waited for Erik to make another move. And, finally, he did.

With one finger he touched Scout's ear. Although Erik was expressionless, I sensed that inside a smile was trapped and fighting to escape. After a few moments, his lips twitched and a breath of air carried her name. "Thcout."

The dog's ears lifted. Erik said her name again, this time a little louder. Scout tipped her head, her gaze connected with Erik's. I realized then that maybe this dog really did understand.

It was as if we were all frozen in place. Erik laid his hand on the top of Scout's head and just stood there. No one wanted to move, so we stayed that way for a few minutes.

Mom finally broke the spell. "I think you have a new friend, Erik."

Erik nodded. I wondered if the same thought popped into his head that had popped into mine. Forget a new friend; Erik had never really had *any* friends.

"Thcout can thleep in my room," Erik mumbled.

We glanced at Charlotte to see what she thought of that. "I'm sure she'll like that, Erik. Scout's your dog."

"Thcout'th my good dog."

"That's right," Charlotte said.

It was so quiet in the house that I heard it when Mom took a funny breath like she was trying not to cry. She laid her hand on Scout's shoulder and looked up at Charlotte. "I think this is going to work," she said, her voice choked.

Charlotte smiled. "It's a great start. Hopefully the training will go as smoothly."

I didn't know how long we all watched Erik and Scout before Mom finally spoke again, looking at me.

"Well, I had thought this would be a nice welcoming party, but I guess we better get you to a clinic for stitches."

I struggled to stand while still holding the cloth to my face. "No, I'm okay, Mom."

"You'll end up with an ugly scar if we don't get that gash taken care of."

"But we can't leave Erik," I protested.

She pulled her cell phone from the pocket of her vet coat. "I'll call Grandma to come over. It will give Erik more time to get to know Scout before Charlotte starts the training sessions tomorrow."

I still wasn't used to having my grandparents

living close. For my entire life we'd lived in Manhattan and made the six hour drive to visit my grandparents every two or three months. Now, having them so close was inconvenient for my argument.

Before I launched my next objection, Mom tapped the numbers on her cell. Decision made.

Later, when we were on our way home from the walk-in medical clinic, I couldn't resist looking in the mirror on the back of the car visor. The bright late morning sun bounced off the car's hood and directly into my face. I stretched my neck to move into the shadow. At first I only saw the shiny puffed skin on my forehead and the red spot on my cheek, but then the real badge of honor came into view. A dark purple bruise leaked from around the edges of a thin white bandage that protected my nine stitches. The area was still numb from the anesthetic, so it didn't hurt when I arched my eyebrows to see what my skin would do.

"Do you think I'll have a massive scar when the stitches come out?"

Mom chuckled. "No. I suspect once it heals you'll have a thin white line that will be barely noticeable."

I touched the swollen area with the tip of my finger. "Man, I was sure I'd have a chick magnet there."

"A chick magnet?" Mom repeated and smiled. "You've been hanging out with your father too much."

"Yeah, he says the gray hair near his ears is a chick magnet because it makes him look distinguished."

Mom laughed. "Heaven knows you shouldn't repeat everything your father says, especially if he brings it home from the precinct."

Dad was always coming home with funny "guy" stories from the police station. One time, when my sister, Christina, got mad because he made a joke about a murder he was investigating, he said finding a shred of humor in the ugly situations helped him get through the bad stuff he had to deal with on a regular basis. I guessed discovering that his dark hair was turning gray was an ugly situation.

I tipped my chin and looked at different angles of the bruise. "Well, the girls will probably think it's a mysterious injury from a big fight where I saved someone's life."

Mom laughed out loud. "I'm sure that thought will cross the mind of every girl you meet, Dylan."

I considered that for a moment. I knew a few girls in Keuka Shores from visits to my grandparents' house, but since this morning, there was just one girl who I wanted to take notice of my battle wound.

"What do you know about Willow's family?" I asked.

"I met her grandmother briefly the day we closed on the house. She came over and brought us fresh, homemade bread. Her name's Ann."

I waited for more details, but Mom stared at the road and didn't appear to plan to say more. "That's it? Where are Willow's parents?" I suddenly realized I was pretending Batboy, who would forever be that to me, didn't even exist. The numbness above my eye reminded me he was very real. "Are there more than the two kids?"

Mom shrugged. "Ann only mentioned the twins."

"Twins?" My voice squeaked like I was going through puberty again. "Willow and Brock are twins? He's gotta be twice as big as her. And twenty times as mean. How can they be the same age?"

I tried to wrap my head around that when I blurted out, "How can something so pretty and something so ugly come from the same mother at the same time?"

Mom's head whipped toward me. "Dylan! What an awful thing to say."

"Mom, you haven't seen her brother. He's like the Incredible Hulk, just not green."

She turned her attention back to the road, but there were lines across her forehead and her lips were a bit puckered, so I knew that answer didn't satisfy her. I pointed to my stitched eyebrow. "Look what he did!"

"From what I understand, you stepped too close to the bat when he was swinging it," she countered.

"Yeah, just as he was ready to pulverize Willow's peacock in front of Erik. There was no way I was letting him kill that thing and traumatize my little brother."

Her shoulders dropped, the wrinkles in her forehead melted away and she smiled. "I'm proud of you. You put concern for Erik above concern for yourself."

The shift from her being annoyed by my comment to her being proud of my actions threw me off.

"Yeah, well —" I let my voice trail off because I didn't know what to say. Finally I just blurted out, "Thanks," then turned and looked out my side window. I wondered if Dad and Trent and Christina would be proud, too. It made me feel good that Mom was proud, but for some stupid reason it embarrassed me, too.

While I stared at the corn fields with the perfectly straight rows of young corn plants, my mind drifted to the new dog and the way Willow cuddled it. Yup! That dog would be my secret weapon for getting to know Willow. When we'd left for the clinic, Charlotte, Jamie and Willow were still at the house with Erik and my grandmother. Charlotte was showing Erik some of the commands to use with Scout. According to Mom, we'd have ten days of intense training from Charlotte because there was so much for us to learn.

When we rolled in the driveway a few minutes later, Grandma, Erik, Charlotte and Jamie were sitting at the picnic table under the maple tree and sipping what looked like lemonade. Scout was sprawled in the grass, panting, next to Erik. I wondered if the dog had chosen to lay there or if Charlotte had made her. A tinge of disappointment went through me when I didn't see Willow.

Mom pointed toward the group like I hadn't seen them. "Aww, look at that Norman Rockwell moment."

I had to admit, she was right. This scene looked like it had walked right out of one of his paintings. We'd taken a family vacation to Massachusetts when I was eleven, and one of our stops had been at the Norman Rockwell Museum in Stockbridge. His paintings were all really old-fashioned-looking to me, and for a second I wondered if we had time traveled to the 1950's. I'd never seen my grandmother wear an apron, and there she sat with a flowery apron tied around her waist.

When Erik realized we were pulling in the driveway, he rocketed off the bench and ran toward us, his hand waving in an excited greeting. Just as fast, Charlotte and Scout jumped up and ran toward him. Within seconds, Scout had overtaken Erik and was putting herself between him and our car, bringing him to an abrupt stop because there was nowhere else for him to go, except over the dog. Mom gasped and slammed on the brakes, jerking us both forward. I snapped my head back up, thankful I hadn't heard a loud thump at the front of the car.

I glanced toward Grandma who was hurrying from the table, her hand over her heart and her eyes wide. I felt sorry for her, but she'd just gotten a taste of what brought us to Keuka Shores and why my older sister was gone. Once Erik decided to bolt, he was as fast as lightning.

Even though we weren't all the way in the driveway, Mom threw the Trailblazer into park and climbed from the vehicle, heading straight to Erik. I'm sure images of the past winter's trauma flashed through her mind, too.

She kept her voice even, but I could hear the bit of fear in it. "Erik, you know you never run toward a moving car. Ever. Do you understand me?"

Instead of acknowledging that Mom had spoken, Erik dropped to his knees and hugged the dog. How many times had I wished I could just ignore Mom and Dad when they were yelling at me about something I'd done? Even though I knew it was one of those "differences" with Erik, it still drove me crazy that he could get away with it but if roles were reversed, I'd be grounded for life.

Charlotte moved next to Erik and the dog. "Good girl, Scout. You did your job." Scout's tail wagged and she leaned into Erik's small arms. "We have a lot of training in the next couple of weeks," Charlotte said, "but I'm pretty impressed that Scout has already figured out that Erik is her boy."

I walked around the front of the SUV and glanced toward the farm down the road. "Did Willow go home?"

"Yes, shortly after you left," Grandma said. She came over and put her arm around my waist. "That's quite a bruiser you have there."

I glanced down at her. My mind flashed back to the past Christmas when she and Grandpa had come to Manhattan to celebrate the holiday with us. Grandpa had made a big deal over Grandma and me being the same height. Now, just a little over six months later, I had grown enough so that she had to look up at me. I straightened my shoulders and lifted my chest so I was at my full height.

"I made haystack cookies for Willow to thank her for helping with you and Erik today," she continued. "Come inside and you can have a couple before I drop the rest off to her on my way home."

The mention of the fudge-like coconut and oatmeal cookies grabbed my attention, but it was the second part of Grandma's comment about delivering them to Willow that really interested me.

"You know," I said, "I should probably go down and thank Willow myself. I could take the cookies then." I hoped my real motive wasn't obvious.

"Oh, I'm driving right by, and you should probably rest," she argued.

We were almost to the side door to the kitchen, and I felt like I was losing the battle. I had to think fast. "It would probably be better if Willow sees for herself that I'm okay. And, honest, Grandma, I feel fine."

Grandma looked up at my eyebrow and scowled then patted my arm. "Maybe you're right. Of course, it's up to your mom."

I glanced back. Mom, Erik, Charlotte, Jamie and the dog were not far behind us, and I was sure Mom could hear our conversation. "Mom, I'm fine. Anyway, I need fresh air after being cooped up in that prompt care place for over two hours waiting for stitches."

When she arched her eyebrow the way she always did when she was skeptical, I figured she'd say no. But she didn't. "I suppose it's fine. There's no concussion. Maybe Grandma can drop you off at Willow's."

I caught myself before I fist pumped the air. I'd kind of won.

"That's okay. I haven't had my bike out since we moved. This is a good time to do it." I couldn't wait to see Willow again and hopefully make a better impression than this morning.

Just as I opened the screen door, Erik wedged himself between Grandma and me and stopped on the step leading into the kitchen so we couldn't go in. "Me, too!"

My neck and chest muscles tensed. "You, too, what?"

"Ride my bike. Ride. Ride. Ride."

His bike still had training wheels. I could just imagine Batboy's reaction to that. I dropped my arm from Grandma's shoulder and whirled toward Mom. "That's a bad idea."

I knew I didn't have to say more. I'd be ticked if she made me take Erik. Since we'd only lived here for less than two weeks, this situation hadn't come up yet. Would Mom make me take Erik everywhere I went now that we were out in the country? Her expression softened, telling me everything I needed to know, and I relaxed.

"Erik," she said, holding her hand out to him, "Scout needs to go out and learn where our yard ends. How about if we go and do that?"

Unlike Mom's expression, Erik's grew hard and stubborn. He batted at her hand but came up short. "I want to ride my bike."

"I understand that, but right now we have to show Scout her boundaries."

Erik clapped his hands over his ears and squeezed his eyes shut. "Ride! Ride! Ride!"

"Please don't give in," I mumbled under my breath, knowing I couldn't be heard over Erik's wailing. "Please don't give in."

Mom tipped her head toward the yard and spoke softly. "Grandma will bring the cookies out for you to take to Willow. Get your bike and wear the helmet."

"The helmet? I'm just going down the road."

She narrowed her eyes. "Wear the helmet or don't go. You could suddenly get light-headed."

I felt fine, but history had taught me arguing was futile. I pushed past everyone on the steps and hurried across the yard before she could change her mind. My bike hadn't been out of the shed since the day we'd moved in, but I knew Dad had made sure it was easy to get to. My helmet hung from the handlebars. I set it on my head without snapping the chin strap and wheeled the bike out the door and across the yard. My forehead was swollen enough that it made the helmet uncomfortable, but I kept it on. I made sure to keep away from the side door.

After a minute, Grandma came out holding a small shoebox. "Keep this flat or the cookies will all crumble." I positioned myself on the bike so I could hold the box then kick off without a problem. For the first few feet the bike wobbled as I tried to control the handlebars with one hand and keep the box steady with the other. Stones crunched under my tires as I turned onto the gravel road. Finally I steadied myself and pumped the pedals hard. A warm breeze slid across my face, and for the first time since moving to Keuka Shores, I felt free.

Ahead of me, dark clouds gathered. From this angle it looked like they were coming up out of Willow's house and barn. I glanced over my shoulder toward our house to see a patchwork of blue sky being taken over by more clouds. If a thunderstorm was going to hit, I was glad Mom was home with Erik. There hadn't been one since we'd arrived, and I'd been dreading the inevitable. If there was loud thunder and cracks of lightning, chaos would break out in our house. Unlike the interior halls in our high rise building, or the elevators, there was nowhere here to take Erik to block out the sound. And if he got outside and started running – I shuddered. I couldn't let my mind go there.

To ease my tension, I pedaled even harder while I concentrated on keeping the box of cookies flat and safe. I envisioned Willow and me sitting side by side on their front porch enjoying this treat together.

It only took a few minutes to get to their farm. I maneuvered carefully into the dirt driveway that had more potholes than level ground. About ten feet of badly chipped and broken cement sidewalk led to the porch stairs, where I stopped my bike. I used my toe to push down the kickstand then climbed off. After perching my helmet on the seat, I glanced around.

A bunch of chickens pecked at the ground near the side of the house. A dented blue tractor sat along a wooden fence that had boards falling down and needed to be painted. There were a couple of furry animals in the pasture that reminded me of camels, but I was pretty sure people in New York, or anywhere in the United States, for that matter, didn't have camel farms. Whatever they were, if they were part of Willow's life, they were worth some Internet research time later so I didn't look like a complete idiot from the city. Based on the fact that they appeared to be the only animals, my guess was that this was not a real farm with the typical animals.

I'd taken three steps toward the house when I noticed movement in a window above the porch. Batboy's attention was completely on me. Again. A chill shot through my body, freezing me from the inside out.

In an effort to repair our relationship, I held up my hand, smiled and called, "Hey, man!"

My attempt at friendliness was wasted.

He shoved his hand through a rip in the window screen and gave me the finger.

CHAPTER FOUR

I resisted returning Batboy's welcoming gesture and instead shrugged and continued up the broken sidewalk. If he and I were going to be neighbors, and if there was any possibility that his sister was going to be my friend, we had to learn to coexist. In theory that plan sounded good, but based on my brief experience, I knew reality would probably be very different.

The worn porch stairs creaked and sagged when I stepped on them. Not that it was my plan, but there was no sneaking up on anyone here. Almost immediately I heard a deep bark inside the house.

"Napoleon, shush!" a woman scolded.

I guessed Napoleon was the dog I heard and hoped he was friendlier than Batboy. There were two doors, an outside screen door and then the inside door that was solid. Because there was no doorbell, I wondered whether I needed to bang on the screen door to be heard or if I should open that and knock on the inside wooden door. Before I decided, the inside door swung open and a woman stepped in front of the screen.

Unlike Batboy, this woman's smile was so wide that I could have counted almost all of her

teeth. I couldn't guess whether she was Willow's
mother or grandmother because she looked
younger than I thought a grandmother should look.
Based on her clothing, I would have guessed she
had just stepped out of the 60's or 70's. A wide,
multi-colored headband held her shoulder-length
brown hair back, and her flowered dress-like outfit
swirled around her legs as if she'd run to the door.
The image fit perfectly with someone who would
name their kid after a tree.

"Well, hello. Can I help you?" she asked.

I knew when she spotted the band aid on my
eye brow because she leaned toward the screen.
"Oh, dear, you're hurt." She pushed open the door.
"Do you need ice?"

"No, thanks. I'm okay. I just got back from
getting stitches."

"Stitches! You're going to have quite a shiner.
You already do. What happened?"

Even though I couldn't see the upstairs window
and Batboy from here, I glanced up, worried he
could hear us. "Just an accident. Really, it's no big
deal."

She scrunched her nose and continued to study
my forehead. I couldn't help but focus on her
wire-rimmed glasses. The lenses were big and
round like they'd been made from the bottoms of
clear drinking glasses. They made me think of
John Lennon from The Beatles.

"Willow is always getting cuts and bruises, too.
I don't think a day goes by without something new
with her." A big brownish-red dachshund waddled
to the woman's side, distracting her. His floppy
ears were twice as long as his face. He "woofed"
once when he saw me.

"Napoleon, be nice to our visitor." She leaned
over and strained to scoop the overweight dog into

her arms. Because he was so big, she grunted when she lifted him but somehow managed to cradle him like a baby. "Give Mama big kisses." The dog flicked his rosy tongue against her face, and she laughed and rolled her head to allow him to slobber on her chin and cheeks. "Oh, you're such a good boy."

Now I knew where Willow got the dog kisses thing from. I hated to interrupt the lovefest, but I really wanted to see Willow. I held up the shoe box from my grandmother to get the lady's attention again. "I have haystack cookies for Willow. My grandmother made them to thank her for helping me this morning. Is she here?"

The woman continued to cuddle the dog as she half-heartedly glanced around the yard. "I'm not sure. That girl disappears all the time. I can't keep track of her." The dachshund started wiggling and the woman struggled to put him down safely. As soon as she freed Napoleon, he waddled toward me and sniffed my legs all the way around, probably smelling Scout.

"That girl is so easy she's practically raising herself."

"Easy?" I hoped my definition for "easy" was different from hers, because I didn't want Willow to be that kind of girl.

"You know, she doesn't demand much from me. Just goes on her way and takes care of herself. She's pretty mature for a girl that age."

"Are you Willow's mother?"

She pressed her hand to her chest and laughed. "Aren't you a charmer! Do I look young enough to be her mother?"

I knew right away that I'd made a mistake, but there was nothing I could do but go along with it and hope she was flattered, not offended.

"Yeah, you do."

"Bless you child. Where are you on those days when I feel as old as dirt?"

All I could do was smile and shrug. What I wanted more than anything was to get out of this awkward conversation. "Are you related?"

She glanced around as if what she was about to tell me was a big secret. "I'm the grandmother, but I don't shout that to the world. Makes me sound old. The twins have lived with me for almost a year now."

I wanted to ask if their parents were on vacation or where they were, but that seemed rude. And that would be a pretty long vacation.

Willow's grandmother reached for the shoe box. "If you want to leave that, I'll make sure she gets it."

I pulled it closer to my stomach. "Thanks, but I was hoping to thank her in person."

Her eyes narrowed and a smirk moved across her face. I wasn't fooling her. "That's fine. You can check the barn, if you like. She spends most of her time out there in her zoo."

I looked toward the barn. I'd spent plenty of time at the Central Park Zoo, so visions of exotic animals popped into my head. I couldn't imagine what kind of a zoo Willow could have in a barn.

"Okay, thanks. I'll go there." I started off the porch, eager to see Willow and her zoo.

"Did you tell me your name?" Willow's grandmother asked.

I turned around. "Oh, Dylan." I recalled Willow's mistake when I'd answered that way earlier. "Actually, I'm Dylan Westcott. We just moved here from Manhattan."

"You're Julie's son?" I nodded. "Lovely woman," she added.

"Thanks." The compliment hung in the air between us for a few seconds. I'd never known anyone who didn't like my mom, including my friends who used to tell me how cool she was. And usually I agreed with them, except for when she was pissed off about something I'd done.

"Well, I'll take these cookies to Willow. It was nice to meet you." I hurried down the three porch steps.

"Likewise. I hope you'll come back again."

I looked over my shoulder. "I'm sure I will."

When she winked, I was startled. "I have no doubt," she said.

I smiled and decided to leave her comment at that. She was onto my motives, for sure, but the good thing about it was, apparently she didn't mind.

The barn was a short walk across the driveway and yard then down a dirt path wide enough to get a vehicle through. There were about ten trees lining it in two perfectly straight rows. As I approached the barn, I heard chords from a guitar, then a few seconds later Willow started to sing. I stopped outside of the huge, dull red and gray barn doors that were wide open. Instead of going in, I stepped off to the side and listened.

I didn't recognize the song she was singing, but it reminded me of a mix of country and easy listening. The lyrics told the story of a girl lost in a maze and how she wondered if she would ever find her way out. I didn't know if the girl ever got out, though, because Willow suddenly stopped. I wondered if she sensed I was outside. I walked through the doorway so she wouldn't think I was spying on her.

As soon as I stepped inside, the odor left me with no doubt that there were many animals here. I squinted as my eyes adjusted to the interior lighting provided by the open doors and two large square openings at either end of the barn near the roof. Several large cages were tucked against the wall to my right, and to my left were wooden animal pens, but I didn't see Willow. There was a mixture of quiet animal noises all around me, but nothing I could identify. Scratching to my left. Sniffing to my right. An animal squeaked somewhere in the shadows in front of me. Curious, I stepped toward the large metal cage closest to me and leaned forward just as a voice overpowered those sounds.

"Hey, there, O'Dylan!"

I wheeled toward the middle aisle of the barn but didn't see Willow.

"Up here." When I looked up, all I could see was the bottom of boots. I had to take a few steps back before I could finally see all of her. She sat on the edge of the overhead floor leaning across a guitar so she could see me. Her legs dangled over the side. Worn cowboy boots reached halfway up her calves, and from there all I could see was long, tanned legs that ended at her blue jean shorts.

"Oh, hey." Heat shot through my face despite the coolness in the barn.

"Whatcha doin' here?" she asked.

I held up the shoe box. "My grandmother made cookies to thank you for your help this morning."

"Cool. Be right down." She pulled her legs back from the edge and disappeared. Pieces of dried hay drifted like leaves from the ledge above. A moment later, her boots emerged from a big square hole in the overheard floor as she climbed down a wooden ladder attached to the wall.

"Where's your guitar?" I asked.

"Up there. It's usually where I play it, so I just leave it in the hay mow."

"In the barn?"

"Yup. Privacy. No one to bug me out here, if you know what I mean."

Her brother's mean-looking face came to mind. "Yeah, I'm pickin' up what you're layin' down."

"Huh?" She tipped her head in question.

"You've never heard that expression? My friends and I say it all the time."

She lifted an eyebrow, silently encouraging me to continue.

"It means I get what you're saying." I shrugged. "Guess it's a city saying."

"Anyway," she continued as if we hadn't had a mini conversation in between, "I think it calms my animals when I play guitar."

My eyes had finally adjusted to the light inside the barn so I could see better. Some kind of nose stuck out of one of the wooden pens, and I saw what looked like a raccoon in one of the smaller cages. The others were still in enough shadow to make the occupants unclear. As curious as I was to check out the animals she had, I decided I'd wait until she offered to show me.

"Hey, your song sounded great."

"Thanks. I wrote it."

Willow was definitely different than any girl I knew in Manhattan. "You play guitar *and* write songs?"

She nodded. "I love music. Taught myself to play lots of instruments. Guitar, flute, saxophone, trumpet and some others. Do you play anything?"

I shrugged. "Sports. Does that count?"

She rolled her eyes and smiled. "Hilarious. Not!"

"It was worth a try." I handed her the box. "I hope you like chocolate, coconut and oatmeal, because that's how my grandmother makes these cookies."

She lifted the lid and looked inside. "Yum! Haystacks. One of my favorites. Want one?"

"Not right now, thanks." My stomach did a flip. The truth was, I couldn't put anything in my mouth with all of the animal smells in the barn.

She set the box on top of a big, upright dirty white barrel. "We'll have some in a few minutes. Do you want to see my animals?"

"Sure. Your grandmother calls it your zoo, you know."

"You met Granny Annie?"

"Yeah, she's —" I struggled for a good word to describe her.

"Eccentric," Willow supplied matter-of-factly. "I think a part of her never got out of the flower child stage. She's always telling stories about living through the sixties. She was at Woodstock, you know."

"Uh, no, I didn't know that. What's Woodstock?"

"Are you serious?" The incredulous expression on Willow's face made me want to crawl into a hole.

"I've heard of it, but I guess I never asked what it was."

"All of the hippies went to this big weekend music festival on a farm in the Catskill Mountains. They were drinking, doing drugs and all kinds of other things I'm not even going to mention. Google it. You'll see what I'm talking about."

"Okay." Now I was curious, but I also got the sense that I didn't want to learn about all of those other "things" from a girl I just met. "So, let's get back to your zoo."

Willow grabbed my arm and pulled me toward the animal pens behind us. "I prefer to think of it as a sanctuary."

I almost laughed at how formal her response sounded. "Okay. Why?"

She flipped a switch and lights came on over a row of five or six wooden pens that looked like they were about ten feet square each. "Because I won't let anything happen to the animals as long as they're here. If they're hurt, I take care of them until they're better. If they're not hurt, I make sure they get all they need to eat and drink. Come 'ere, and I'll show you."

She guided me toward some cages in the far corner opposite the pens. As soon as we stepped in that direction, many of the animals moved to the front of their cages and started making noises. They acted like they all knew her. I couldn't believe what I was seeing.

"Who are you, Dr. Doolittle? They're acting like you're their friend."

"They trust me and know they can count on me," she said. "What living thing doesn't want that?"

We stopped in front of a tall cage that had a bird perch in it, but otherwise it looked empty. Until I looked in the corner.

Pressed back in, as far as it could go, was a bird almost the size of a crow, but instead of being all black, it had a black body and wings, some white on its neck and face and bright red feathers that stood like a Mohawk on top of its head. It looked like an exotic bird from the rainforest.

"What the heck is that?" I wanted to put my face closer to the cage to get a better look, but I was afraid the bird might attack me.

"A pileated woodpecker."

"That's cool. What are *you* doing with it?"

"I found it yesterday along the road." Willow leaned across the top of the cage and made a soft kissing noise. The bird tucked its long beak closer to its chest. "I think it might have been hit by a car."

"But, what are you going to do with it? Are you going to keep it?"

"I'll make it better then set it free."

Since it hadn't moved when Willow leaned against the cage, I braved a closer inspection. Its face was all white except for a black stripe that ran straight across its cheek and across the eye. The only other color was a hint of red under its chin. It looked scared having us so close, so I backed away.

"How do you know what to feed it and how to take care of it?"

"Internet."

"My mom could probably help. I mean, I don't know if she's ever had to treat a bird before, but I bet she'd know something."

"Thanks, but I'm doing okay with it." She moved past me toward the other cages. "In here is a baby raccoon whose mother was hit by a car. I call it Shadow since its face always looks like it's in a shadow. There was another one, but it died right after I brought them home."

The raccoon stretched its nose toward us and made a sound that was a cross between a cat purring and a pigeon cooing. When I jumped back, it hunched its back and didn't make another sound, but its beady black eyes stared straight at me.

Willow pressed her hand against the front of the cage. "It's okay, Shadow," she said softly.

The baby animal was cute, but this didn't seem right. "I don't think you should pick up raccoons, Willow. What about rabies?"

"Oh, they're safe. I'm up to date on my rabies vaccines."

"You get rabies shots? I mean, my mom has to because she's a vet, but I didn't think regular people did."

She poked her finger into the side of the cage and rubbed the raccoon's paw. "No, silly, I don't really get rabies shots. It was a joke."

"Then it probably is dangerous for you to pick up stray animals."

She spun toward me, and the look on her face told me I'd hit on a sensitive subject. "What are you, animal control? I'm careful," she snapped. "I always wear gloves."

My heart pounded. This was the first opportunity to be alone with Willow and I was totally blowing it. I opted to not point out that she'd just touched the raccoon without wearing gloves.

"Sorry. I didn't mean anything by that. Show me the rest of the animals."

She tipped her head and stared at me with a skeptical expression. To break the tension, I moved to the next cage. "Come on. I'm not done with the tour of your sanctuary."

Three small rabbits – one white, one black and white and the other a reddish brown color – occupied different areas. The black and white one was stretched completely out, one was munching on pellets in a silver bowl and the other, just a small baby, lay on its stomach watching us.

"These don't look like wild rabbits."

"They aren't. They're dwarfs, so they're smaller than regular rabbits." She opened the door on the front of the cage, reached in and scooped the white rabbit into her arms. "This is Chloe — short for Clorox because she's so white she looks bleached. Here." Willow pressed the rabbit against my chest, and I had no choice but to cradle her like a baby.

The rabbit's nose twitched, and instead of struggling to get out of my arms, Chloe snuggled against me. Her soft fur hid my arm. "Wow! She's friendly."

"Most of my animals are domestic. I've had Chloe, Cinnamon and Patch for a couple of years."

I jumped when a loud rumble of thunder shook the ground. Willow saw my reaction.

"Are you afraid of thunderstorms?" she asked.

"No, but Erik is. Actually, the word afraid doesn't even come close to describing his terror. A bad thunderstorm sends him over the edge."

"I see." Willow took Chloe from my arms and put her back in her cage. "If you don't mind me asking, what exactly is going on with your brother? He's definitely ——" It was clear that she wanted to choose her words carefully. She snapped the hooks on the cage door then turned toward me. "He's different."

"Yeah, he is different. Erik has autism. That's why he acts the way he does." Willow didn't say anything, but rather, her expression was a mixture of curiosity and encouragement. I'd never trusted a girl with the truth about Erik this early in a relationship, but Willow seemed genuinely interested. "There are certain things that trigger strong reactions in him. Loud noises is one, so your peacock in the tree this morning, and Brock yelling at it, and now the thunderstorm, well, they're all triggers that cause episodes. With that thunder, I can only imagine where he ran when he heard it. He's gotten into some pretty dangerous situations because of it."

"I've heard of autism before," Willow said, "but I never really knew what it was." She laughed. "Heck, I still don't know. Is everyone with autism afraid of thunder?"

"I suppose some probably are, but every case is different. When Erik gets upset or scared, he runs. That's why Mom got Scout. I guess a trained dog knows how to calm a kid who starts to melt down, or if Erik takes off, Scout will be trained to track him."

My mind flashed back several months to the day when Erik
bolted away from our sister, Christina, after she'd taken him to Central Park. It was the day when our family's world unraveled.

"Things might have been different if we'd had a dog like Scout when we lived in the city. Maybe we never would have moved up here."

"Why? What happened?"

A lump popped into my throat, and suddenly I wasn't sure that I could tell Willow about the horrible day or the weeks that followed. The fact that the memory still choked me up was embarrassing – especially in front of a girl I liked. We'd felt so lucky that Erik lived through it, I think our whole family tried to forget just how different the outcome could have been.

I swallowed hard. I'd come this far. Willow deserved to hear the rest.

"Our sister, Christina, had taken Erik to Central Park because he wanted to see the place where they filmed the scene from the *Home Alone* movie where the bird lady is under the bridge. It was an

unusually warm day in February after it had been cold for a long time. Because of the sudden change in temperature, a thunderstorm moved in really fast. When he
heard it, Erik took off and started running through the park. A couple of times when it thundered, he got away from Christina and tried to hide. Luckily he never got too far from her.

They had just gotten out of the park and my sister was hailing a taxi when it started to rain, and then there was a really loud thunder. Erik bolted and ran right in front of the taxi."

Willow gasped, just like everyone who heard this story. It didn't take a genius to know what came next.

"He almost died. He was in the hospital for over two months."Willow's eyes were wide and round. "That's horrible. Is he okay? I mean, is there any permanent problem now?"

"He's just more sensitive to sounds and light than ever before. It was a nightmare with him in the hospital because there were so many noises and people touching him, two of the worst things for him. My parents took turns staying with him 24/7. They were so exhausted, and I hardly ever saw them. If they were home, they were sleeping. But, other than that, the broken bones healed, and Erik's okay now." I wasn't sure how much I dared to share, but I added, "The whole thing actually messed up my sister more than Erik."

Willow's eyes flew wide open. "She got hit, too?"

"No, it messed her up mentally because she blamed herself for him getting hurt."

"Did your parents blame her?"

"Never. They felt horrible that it happened when she was just helping them out."

"How's your sister now?" Willow's voice was soft. Comforting. I wanted badly to put my arm around her and pull her against me because I could tell she really cared.

"We're not really sure. As soon as we knew that Erik would recover, she bought a plane ticket and went overseas. My parents think she may be working in an orphanage in Africa. She sent a postcard about two months ago and said that she went where she could save kids."

"Wow!"

I stared at Willow. Wow pretty much summed up how I felt about all of it, too.

"So, here we are, out in the country where it's less likely that Erik can get hurt by running in front of cars."

"Wow!" Willow said the word softer this time.

Another clap of thunder split the air, sharper, closer and a lot louder.

"I better go. That storm sounds like it's moving in fast, and I don't want to ride my bike through lightning." I also wasn't sure I wanted to reveal anything more to Willow.

"You might be too late." Willow put her hands in the middle of my back and pushed me toward the door. "Go. Go. Don't leave Erik home alone in a storm."

"My mom and grandmother are there. I'm just glad I'm not the one who's with him right now."

Big, fat raindrops fell on my face as we stepped out the barn door. Willow ran back in, grabbed the box of cookies, then came back out and slid the heavy barn doors closed.

We jogged toward the house and my bike. "I'd like to come back and see the rest of your animals," I said. I hated leaving

Willow right now before I'd really had a chance to spend time with her, but I also worried about how Mom was doing with Erik.

"Cool. Whenever you want." She turned away.

"Hey, Willow?" She turned back toward me. "Do you think I could have your cell phone number? You know, so I can text to see if you want to hang out."

She hesitated.

I worried that I'd crossed a line, so I hurried to cover myself. "I mean, if you don't want to give it to me, that's okay."

"No, it's not that. It's just – well, I can't text. My phone only does calls."

"That's okay. I can just call."

"It would have to be a quick call. I can't afford to put too many minutes on my phone each month, so I really only use it for emergencies."

My mind flashed to the call she'd made to my mother when I was hurt earlier. "You have to pay for it yourself?"

She nodded. "But it's okay if you want to call." Willow bounded up the porch stairs, using only one step to get to the top. She threw her hand in the air. "See ya around, O'Dylan."

Her deliberate misuse of my name made me smile. "Yeah, see ya." The screen door slammed shut behind her, and Napoleon barked inside.

I went the few extra feet to my bike and plopped my helmet on my head. Immediately I heard cracking and felt wet goo dripping down my face and over my ears.

"What the —" When I whipped the helmet off, pieces of eggshells tumbled around me. I looked toward the chickens pecking at the ground on the other side of the porch steps. I thought I'd left my helmet on the bike seat, but apparently not, and a chicken had found it and laid an egg. I wiped as much of the slimy stuff off my head as I could, then hung the helmet back on my handlebar. That would have to be cleaned when I got home.

I flipped up the kickstand, turned the bike around and jumped onto the seat. For some reason, I had to push extra hard on the pedals to get the bike to move because there was so much drag, but it only took a few feet before I realized why. I stopped and hopped off to check the tires. Both the front and back were completely flat.

All of a sudden I realized the chickens weren't to blame for the eggs in my helmet. I turned and looked up toward the window on the second floor where I'd seen Batboy earlier. Sure enough, he stood there with an evil grin.

And his farewell wave was exactly the same as his greeting.

Even though I'd been lucky enough in my life to never be on the bad end of bullying, it was clear that Brock was eager to change that.

It was also clear to me that I needed a plan of action to survive living next door to him, especially if I planned to hang out with Willow.

The rain drops became a downpour. I pushed my bike toward the road, forcing myself to look forward and not back. There was no way I was letting Brock come between Willow and me. Somehow, I would put that guy, with his childish games, in his place.

CHAPTER FIVE

"You want me to put Cheez Whiz on my hand?" I stared at Charlotte, Scout's trainer. This was the fourth day of training, but she'd never asked me to do something like this. The last time I'd used Cheez Whiz, my friends and I were having a fight with several cans and it was all over us. It had been a blast when we were twelve, but now with Willow standing here, I'd look stupid with a pile of Cheez Whiz on my hand.

Willow grabbed my hand and turned it over so my palm was open to Charlotte. "Just do it, O'Dylan. What's the issue?"

I loved that Willow was holding my hand, but when Charlotte squirted a little orange pile onto my palm, I just stared at the cool, wet goop. It was tempting to wipe it in the grass, but that would make me look like a little kid. I didn't get how this was going to teach Scout anything.

Charlotte interrupted my thoughts. "Remember, it's important to say Scout's name in connection to the command so that she knows you're talking to her," she explained.

Scout's ears perked up and her tongue dropped out of her mouth, but she still sat just inches from Erik's leg.

"Now," Charlotte said, "start walking and ask Scout to heel, but don't let her have the Cheez Whiz yet."

Even though it was only 10:00 in the morning, the sun was already baking us. Sweat popped up on my palm around the edges of the Cheez Whiz. I held my hand out and started walking, but Scout didn't move.

"Don't forget the command," Mom reminded me.

I glanced back at Scout. "Come 'ere."

Scout stared at me. I could tell by the look in her eyes that she really wanted the Cheez Whiz, but she wasn't moving. I looked at Charlotte. "What did I do?"

"It's not what you *did*, it's what you *didn't* do. Say her name because that's her cue that you want her undivided attention, then say the command."

I looked at Willow. Her hand was propped on her hip, and her head was angled as if to say, 'Really? You couldn't figure that out?'

I started to walk again. "Scout, heel."

Scout's attention flicked to Charlotte for a second, and then she was up, trotting to my side. Magic! Drool rolled off the end of her tongue, and I imagined how sloppy it would be when she licked the Cheez Whiz off my palm. The dog stayed by my side as I zigzagged across the yard to test what she'd do. Finally I made a wide circle and returned to where everyone else was standing.

"Ask her to sit, praise her for following directions, and let her have the Cheez Whiz," Charlotte instructed.

I followed her orders, and Scout responded perfectly. When she licked the treat from my hand, her rough tongue flicked around the outside of the pile, tickling my skin. She rolled her brown eyes to look up at me while she was getting the last bit off. I felt like a hero.

The lesson continued, and like every other day, even Willow practiced. It was obvious how much time she spent with animals because everything she did with Scout looked natural, like they did it every day. We'd already been told the first couple of days would be basic training, and Charlotte said by week's end, we would practice hiding Erik so Scout could find him.

Whether it was from the heat or the fact that we'd been going through the drills for a while, one by one we faded back under the big maple tree until only Mom and Charlotte were still working with Scout. Erik stood under the tree, too, but as usual, distanced himself from us. His attention was fixed on Scout.

Willow hoisted herself up to the first thick branch and wedged back against the main trunk of the tree. I lay down in the grass where I could stare up at her and crossed my hands behind my head. In that position, my biceps pushed against the sleeves of my t-shirt, making the muscles look bigger than when my arms were just hanging down.

I wanted to come across as cool with Willow, but the truth was my insides were twisting and rolling. Willow and Erik watched Mom and Charlotte work with Scout. I watched Willow. When she suddenly looked at me and caught me staring, my brain scrambled to think of something to say to break the awkwardness.

"If I was back home, my buddies and I would be hitting the pool right now." I closed my eyes and imagined myself diving into the deep end of the clear, blue water. "Man, the girls in their bikinis are so hot."

I snapped my eyes open. What? Did I really just say that out loud to the girl I was trying to impress? Willow tipped her head and her thin eyebrows lifted in an *'I can't believe you just said that'* look. I rushed to cover my stupid statement. "You know, hot, because it gets so hot in the city compared to the country." Lame. Totally lame, and of course Willow wasn't buying my attempt to backtrack. "So, is there a pool anywhere around here?"

"Nope." She stretched and snagged a twig full of leaves from a nearby branch. "We swim in the pond in the woods behind Fosters' barn."

"A pond?"

"Yeah, a pond." She shook the twig at me. "What, are you a city slicker pool snob, O'Dylan?"

"No, I – um – "

She interrupted my stammering. "Why is it you guys always think what we have out here in the country isn't as good as what you have there?"

Whoa! Where did that come from? "I didn't say that."

"You didn't have to. It was the way you screwed up your face when I mentioned the pond."

"I didn't know I screwed up my face. It's just that I've never gone swimming in a pond."

Willow pushed herself off the tree limb and dropped to the ground. "Then it's about time you did." She held the twig with leaves high above me and let it drop onto my stomach. "Go get some shorts on. We're going swimming."

I jumped up. "Sounds great."

"What sounds great?" Mom asked as she, Charlotte and Scout came up behind me.

"Willow said there's a pond around here where we can go swimming."

"Not you," Mom said.

"Why not?"

"Until those stitches come out, you're out of the water."

My shoulders slumped. "Oh, man!" This was supposed to be my next big chance with Willow.

"You don't have to swim," Willow said. "You can sit on the dock and hang your legs into the water. That would cool you off a little bit." She turned to Mom. "That would be okay, wouldn't it?"

Score! Willow wanted me to spend time with her.

Mom looked at my eye. The swelling had disappeared over the past few days, but when I'd looked in the mirror this morning, the bruise was still dark. I held my hand up like I was taking an oath in court.

"I swear I won't get it wet."

"You'll have to take Erik and Scout with you, because I have to get back to work."

Erik erupted with a cheer. "Yay! Yay! Yay!"

I erupted, too. "What about Grandma? Can't Erik go there?"

His face crinkled into a look of confusion. Since I was old enough to go and do things on my own, I'd always been able to come and go with my friends whenever I wanted. I never had anything, or anyone, tying me down.

Mom shook her head. "No. He'll be with her tomorrow. This afternoon he's your responsibility."

I quietly groaned. I liked that Mom and Dad paid me for taking care of him, but visions of being alone with Willow didn't include Erik.

Willow dropped to her knees to throw her arms around Scout's neck. "Awesome! Scout can swim with me." She snuggled her face into the fur around Scout's ear, and in a muffled voice added, "I'll run home and change then I'll meet you at the end of my driveway."

Happiness crept back into my soul. I hoped Willow was the bikini type. When she stood and walked away, her narrow hips sashaying back and forth, I easily imagined that bikini on her.

"Come on, *Oops*," I said, using Erik's nickname. "Let's dig a couple of tennis balls out of a box in the garage and we'll take those for Scout to go after in the water."

Fifteen minutes later when Erik and I approached Willow's house, I peered toward the window where I last saw Brock. Only the sun's reflection bounced back at me. Scout tugged on the leash, and it almost slid out of my hand. She stretched toward Erik who had wandered down the road a few feet. He hadn't gone far, but still, considering how fast he was when he bolted, I couldn't take a chance. I transferred the plastic bag with three tennis balls into my hand holding the leash.

"Erik, get back here."

He kept walking. Scout kept tugging.

"Erik."

No response. Scout pulled so hard I nearly lost my balance. I knew she was just trying to do her job and protect Erik, but I couldn't let her go. I dug my sneakers into the dirt road and leaned back. "Scout, stay. Erik, come here." Still no response.

The screen door slammed behind me and I whirled around, prepared to face off with Brock. But it was Willow. Instead of a bikini she was wearing a pink tank top and cut off jean shorts.

She had a striped, multi-colored beach towel draped over her shoulder.

"Too bad you can't go swimming," she said as she approached. "It's 90 out here."

With the sweat dripping down my back under my t-shirt, I didn't need a weather report to tell me it was hot. "Next time," I said. "Probably today I'll have all I can do to keep Erik under control. He's not listening too great." I pointed at her clothes. "Where's your swim suit?"

She looked at me like I'd asked a ridiculous question. It seemed I was good at that.

"This is it. Works for the pond – and for going through the woods. It'll dry before I get back home."

I hoped my disappointment didn't show. "A girl wouldn't be allowed to wear that in the pool back home. That's why I thought —"

"Different world, O'Dylan. Better get used to it."

I didn't think Willow intended her comment to sound mean, and she was so right. Almost everything in my world was different now. Thank you for the reality check, I thought.

Erik squatted on the edge of the road poking at something in the weeds. In his left hand was a green tin box that my grandmother had found at a yard sale. After Erik had learned to walk, we'd been visiting my grandparents and he found that box on a shelf. Because he screamed like he was being murdered when someone tried to take away, it became his box. Eventually he named it his treasure tin, and when he'd find something he considered a treasure, it went in the tin box. He'd insisted on bringing it with us to the pond in case he found sea shells. I didn't want to risk a meltdown, so I didn't tell him it was unlikely that he'd find sea shells at a pond. He was the one who had to carry it, not me, so it didn't matter.

"Come on, Erik," I said, moving toward him. That made Scout happier. "Let's take Scout swimming." Erik didn't acknowledge that I'd said anything. I looked at Willow. "We could be here a while if his attention is totally focused on whatever he's found."

"Oh, yeah," she said, and snapped her fingers. "Come on, Erik, let's head to the pond," Willow said, walking past him. Like there was a spring attached to him, he bounced up and followed.

"Really?" I said. "I've been standing here for five minutes trying to get him to respond to me, and you walk up and say 'Let's go' and he's moving?"

Willow flipped her hand in the air, bumped her left hip way out and said, "What can I say? I have the power."

"Must be nice." Even Scout was happy to fall in line behind her as we crossed a ditch then followed the edge of a corn field. "Where is this pond, anyway?"

"On the other side of the woods."

The corn field ended and we moved onto a worn dirt path that wasn't quite wide enough for a vehicle to go down. There were high weeds on either side, and every now and then Willow stopped to grab a wild daisy. She pushed it through her hair until the stem was lodged behind her ear. Eventually she had a mini bouquet embedded there. I loved that she was girly but not a sissy. And, I had to admit I liked bringing up the rear of our line because it meant I could look at her without her knowing it. She swung her arms to swat at bugs that were circling her head like a halo. It was when she was doing that one time that I noticed the bruises.

Not far below her shoulder on the right arm, a dark purple strip made a ring on her skin. I looked closer. Two or three other dark spots dotted the tanned skin on her bicep. On her other arm, there were more bruises, but these were scattered up and down on the underside. I glanced down at her legs and there were even more, some as small as fifty cent pieces and a couple that were purple and yellow and almost the size of the palm of my hand. How could I have missed them before this?

A lump formed in my throat. I'd seen bruises like that before. When I was in sixth grade, a girl in my class, Kelly Barker, had lots of bruises. In the middle of the school year the teacher held us in from recess one day to tell us that she had been diagnosed with leukemia. It wasn't long before she lost her hair and was wearing baseball hats to school. By the end of seventh grade, she had died.

I looked at Willow's long hair blowing back in the hot breeze and tried to imagine her bald. I couldn't, and I really didn't want to. She looked healthy. I could only hope that maybe she was just a klutz and fell and banged into things a lot and that's why she had so many bruises. There was no way I could ask her after only knowing her a week.

Suddenly she stopped and pointed in the air. "Look at that, Erik. It's a hawk."

I followed where she was pointing and saw the big brown bird struggling to fly with a chipmunk in its talons. I sucked in a breath, worried about Erik's reaction. I didn't appear that it registered with him what was happening because he jumped and laughed as the poor rodent hung limply from the bird's feet.

"Maybe we should keep walking," I suggested before he figured it out.

Willow glanced at me, and it seemed she understood my point. "Yeah," she said, "let's get into the woods so we're out of the sun. Besides, I want to show you guys something really cool."

That was enough to distract Erik. I breathed a sigh of relief. If he'd realized that chipmunk was the hawk's dinner, we would have been dealing with a meltdown for sure.

The woods were just a two minutes farther. As soon as we stepped into the dense area of trees, the temperature dropped several degrees. Sun rays that made it past the trees sliced created dapples on the leaf-covered ground. The path here was much narrower and it wound around trees and up a hill. Dried leaves crunched under our feet. Squirrels and chipmunks scurried up trees all around us. Scout's ears perked up and her head swiveled back and forth as she tried to keep up with which squirrel to watch.

Willow and Erik were at least fifty feet ahead of me now. They both stopped and I saw Erik grab hold of a small tree trunk and stretch out, looking over his shoulder. Willow, too, was staring at something.

"Come on, O'Dylan. Get up here and check this out. You're gonna think this is cool."

Scout tugged at the lead, so I jogged toward them. My attention was focused on the ground in order to avoid the dead tree limbs that criss-crossed the path. When I finally looked up, my heart almost stopped.

Willow and Erik stood just feet from a huge grassy ledge that dropped hundreds, or maybe even thousands, of feet straight down. I looked across the chasm that was probably a quarter mile wide. My brain whirred with the possibility of falling over the edge and I back stepped as quickly as I could.

"Erik, get away from there." My voice rose with my panic.

"He's all right," Willow said. "We're still almost ten feet
from the ravine's edge." Erik was only a yard or so from her, but if he moved suddenly, there was no way her arms were long enough to grab him.

My legs shook. I willed my brain to make my feet move forward to get him, but every muscle was paralyzed.

Erik took one arm away from the tree and pointed toward the drop off. "Look, Dylan. There'th a river."

"Erik, no! Don't let go of that tree."

Willow turned and stared at me. "You're afraid of heights, aren't you?"

It didn't sound like she was judging me, but I still hated to admit my fear. Ever since I was stuck at the top of a roller coaster with my cousin when I was ten, anything higher than fifteen feet totally freaked me out. And right now my heart was pounding so hard I thought my ribs would crack.

"I don't know what Scout would do if we were near the edge," I said, hoping she believed that was my reason for staying back.

"Want me to hold her so you can look?"

"No!" I didn't mean for my response to be so sharp, but there was no way I was going closer to the edge of that ravine. "Let's just get Erik away from here."

Now sweat rolled down my face and back. It hadn't seemed hot here in the woods when we first came in.

"Okay." She moved and stepped between Erik and the ravine. "We can come and see this another time, buddy. I think Scout wants to go swimming."

Again, as if she were charmed, Erik didn't argue like he would have with me. With each step away from the edge that they took, my body relaxed more. Finally, when they were both on the path in front of me, I drew in a full breath, thankful to have air back in my lungs. If I never saw that ravine again, it would be too soon.

"There's one more thing I want to show you before we go to the pond," Willow said. She continued up the hill on the path.

I quietly groaned. "Is it dangerous?"

She laughed. "No. It's just cool. It's up here a little ways."

While we walked, Erik picked up a stick and used it to whack every tree he passed. Little bits of it splintered off each time until it was a small nub of a stick in his hand. I loved these times when he acted like a normal kid. Following behind, Scout picked up the pieces and held each one in her mouth until we came to the next one. Then she'd drop the old and pick up the new.

"There's an old hunters' cabin up here," Willow explained. "It always makes me think of the pioneers."

She'd no sooner said that than a weathered wooden cabin that was no bigger than my bedroom came into view beyond the trees. I could see that this, too, was only feet from the edge of the ravine.

I halted Scout, and she tipped her head in apparent confusion.

"What the heck!" I called to Willow. "You said what we were going to see wasn't dangerous." I hoped I sounded more irritated than worried so she wouldn't think I was a total chicken.

She stopped and turned toward me, which luckily also caused Erik to stop.

"We're going into the cabin, not to the edge of the ravine," she said.

"The edge looks like it's just a few feet past it," I countered.

"So we'll stay on this side of it. Come on," she said and turned to continue toward it. "It's really cool."

When Erik saw it he darted ahead of Willow.

"Erik, stop!" I yelled. I felt like an over-protective parent. Besides the fear of falling over the side, I also wondered what animals might have taken up residence in there.

He didn't listen, but fortunately he went for the front away from the ravine. The wooden door barely clung to one rusty hinge at the top of the door frame. Erik grabbed the handle and pulled the door toward him. It swung

awkwardly then came to rest at an odd angle.

"Is there anything in there that could hurt him?" I asked Willow.

"Not the last time I was here," she called as she followed him inside.

I approached slowly, sure that a bear or wolf would lunge out at any second. I never knew the world could be so dangerous – and people complained about the streets of the big cities! I didn't know one person who had been eaten on the streets of Manhattan. I doubted the same could be said about these woods. I decided somewhere on the New York State Thruway on our way here I'd lost my sense of adventure. I hesitated a few feet away. The drop off to the ravine wasn't more than ten or fifteen feet past the cabin. At least Erik was inside. But considering how run down the little building was, for all I knew the back of it could have been missing and Erik could run right through.

Willow poked her head back out of the cabin. "Come in and check it out."

Erik hadn't screamed when he went in, so I supposed it was safe. I stepped up onto the wood floor and studied the interior. The air smelled of stale wood smoke and urine. I could only imagine what the hunters had chosen to christen. There was a window on each side of the cabin providing a decent amount of light. I was amazed that all of the glass was intact except for one window pane that had a long jagged crack running from corner to corner. The wall under the window had a charred area where a campfire apparently had gotten too close to the wood.

Scout sniffed around the entire inside perimeter while I took in the relics left behind. After the initial shock of its proximity to the edge of the ravine, I had to admit Willow was right. This was cool.

"I wonder how long this place has been here." I couldn't imagine how many years it had been since it was last used, but it was obvious that kids came in because there were initials carved in all the walls. *D.N. hearts S.W. KT & ALZ 4-ever* In my opinion, this didn't seem like a very romantic place to bring a girl.

"Some of my relatives from way back used to come up here to hunt," Willow said. "We had deer heads hanging on the walls in the barn, so I guess they must have had good luck."

Two partly rusted metal folding chairs leaned against one wall. A cot was tipped over near another wall and its mattress lay in a heap, the dirty stuffing poking out in dozens of places. Willow kicked at a corner of it and a mouse scurried from the cloud-like mess and disappeared through a small hole in the corner of the floor. An old kerosene lantern hung from a hook near the door and two long coils of thick, tan rope hung on big nails.

"Did these guys hunt anything besides deer?" I asked. I saw something on a small shelf on the far side and went to investigate. I was shocked to see two very large rusty butcher knives laid tip to tip.

"Bear. Coyote. Turkeys. Rabbits," Willow said. "But nobody's used it in a while."

"No kidding. And they aren't very safety conscious with their weapons, either." I pointed at the knives. "They just left stuff laying around like this?"

"They probably planned to come back. Then someone died."

I pivoted toward her. "Someone died in here?"

"No. I'm guessing that maybe that's why they quit coming up here. Maybe it was my great grandfather's and after he died no one used it again. I don't know."

I was relieved to hear that no one had died in the cabin, but I also thought it was interesting that Willow took a morbid route to explain why it was abandoned.

Erik laid his hand on the metal frame of the cot. When he pulled his hand back, his imprint was left in some of the thick dust and his palm and fingers were covered with the rest. He turned his hand to look at it then screwed up his face in a look of disgust.

He started shaking his hand hard as if the dust would fly off. "Uh – uh – uh."

My nerves jumped. I had to catch this before an all out meltdown hit. If he suddenly bolted out the door he could run in the wrong direction and right toward the edge of the ravine.

I stepped next to him. "Wipe your hand on my shirt," I said quickly. He looked at his hand once more then slammed it against my side, rubbing as hard as he could on my Yankees t-shirt. When he pulled his hand back, the majority of the dust stayed on the navy blue cloth. Like a switch had been flipped, he darted from the cabin.

"Hey, where you goin'?" I yanked Scout away from the mattress and we ran out after Erik.

He'd stopped in the opposite direction of the edge next to a circle of rocks that were charred from campfires long ago.

His nose wrinkled and he gagged. "It thtinkth in there."

"Yeah, I have to agree with you, Oopster." The urine and smoke smell were pretty strong.

Scout pressed up against Erik and he absently rubbed her ears with the hand that wasn't holding his treasure box. Willow emerged from the cabin and did her best to set the door back in place. While I watched her, I caught sight of something out of the corner of my eye. I turned toward the thicker wooded area just in time to see a dark shadow dip behind the trees.

"Hey, did you see that?" I asked as Willow approached me.

"See what?"

I pointed up the hill. "I think someone or something ran behind those trees up there."

Willow shrugged. "Probably just your imagination. You seem kind of jumpy in these woods, O'Dylan."

She turned and started down the path, Erik again at her heels.

"Maybe it was Bigfoot," she yelled, clearly trying not to laugh.

I looked back in the direction where I thought I'd seen something. This was worse than some of the alleys in the city. At least those didn't go on forever like these woods did, and they had fewer places for someone to hide. Maybe she was right. This whole country thing would take getting used to. I pivoted to follow Willow, but when I pulled on Scout's leash, she didn't give in and follow.

"Scout, heel," I commanded as I looked over my shoulder at her.

The dog stood straight as a statue, her ears up and alert and her brown eyes staring in the direction where I thought I'd seen something. The hair on her back was raised up.

I squinted, trying to see farther into the woods but saw nothing.

"Come on, Scout. There's nothing there." I pulled her toward the trail. We'd taken two steps when I heard something whiz past me just a few feet away then hit a solid mass.

I ducked at the same time as I looked up at a tree to my left. A long, yellow and blue arrow stuck out from the bark, still vibrating from the impact.

"Hey! There are people over here!" I shouted. I twisted to look behind me and swallowed against a hard lump in my throat. That was way too close. I tightened my grip on the plastic bag with the tennis balls in it, tempted to whirl it around my head and throw it like a bolas at whatever was out there.

It didn't take a genius to figure out that the shadow hadn't been in my imagination. And, it didn't take a genius to figure out whose shadow it was. At this point, it didn't matter. If there were arrows flying, I had to get Erik and Willow out of these woods.

Scout sprinted at my side as we raced down the path. "We need to get out of here!" I called ahead to Willow. "Someone's shooting arrows at us. I almost got hit."

Willow and Erik were already at the edge of the woods by the time I caught up to them.

"I'm sure it was just jerky Brock," Willow said. She stopped so I could catch up.

I stifled the urge to yell, and instead I nearly growled. "He could have killed me!"

"Trust me," Willow said, "as stupid as it was for him to shoot it in your direction, his aim is dead on, so he hit exactly what he intended to hit."

My eyes widened. "'Dead on'? Bad choice of words, Willow. What if he missed his mark?"

"Nah, he got second place in the regional competition for accuracy in archery. He knew exactly where he was aiming."

That did little to ease my concern. "What an idiot! Too bad the first place winner couldn't come out and hit a target near him," I sputtered.

"Can't. I don't have a bow and arrow with me," Willow said matter-of-factly.

My jaw had to have dropped. "Are you saying —"

She smirked. "Yep. I won first place. Katniss from *The Hunger Games* has nothing on me."

This girl was full of surprises.

"And trust me," she continued, "the fact that I'm better than him only makes him meaner. Just watch your back, O'Dylan. He's not a very good loser."

I whipped around toward the woods. Every tree was an enemy, a potential hiding spot for Brock. I was already unhappy about spending my summer out here in the country. And now, Willow was basically telling me that with Brock around, my summer had the potential to be a reenactment of *The Hunger Games*. I couldn't imagine where he'd pop up next.

CHAPTER SIX

Willow kicked off her sneakers, tossed her towel onto a bush and jogged toward the old wooden dock that jutted out over the water. The dock swayed wildly with each step, but she kept her balance, even when hopping over missing or broken slats. When she reached the end, she jumped high into the air, kicking her legs like she was on a bicycle before she splashed into the water.

Scout jerked on the leash, eager to join her, but I planted my feet.

"Scout, here." Scout turned toward me. I took a tennis ball from the plastic bag I'd brought from home and that distracted her. She took a step back and stared at the lime green ball, one front paw shaking.

Erik stared at the water, his treasure tin pressed against his side. I didn't know if he would dart toward the water. Unlike most kids his age, he didn't comprehend the boundaries of danger, but at least he looked content to just watch from a distance.

Willow popped up out of the water and laughed, an awesome laugh that made me smile. "Feels great in here. Too bad you can't join me."

"Thanks for the reminder," I said, holding the ball just a few inches from Scout's nose. Scout stretched her neck but didn't touch it.

Willow splashed then went back under water, resurfacing even farther out. Unlike a pool, I couldn't see through the water in the pond and that was disconcerting.

"Can you touch bottom?"

Water dripped down her face as she kicked to stay afloat. "Not here, but a few feet in I can. I'd rather keep moving so my feet don't sink into the gooey stuff."

I wondered what the gooey stuff was but figured I'd find out at some point when I could finally join her. The concrete on the bottom of a pool was a much more appealing thought, but there was no way I was saying that out loud after Willow had gone off on me earlier because I'd said I like pools better.

"Throw the ball and let Scout swim to me," Willow shouted.

I glanced at the dog whose bright eyes were fixed on the ball. Her tongue hung out with drops of saliva rolling off the end while her tail wagged so hard her back end swayed. "I don't dare take her off the leash. What if she runs away?"

The plastic bag crinkled and I glanced down in time to catch Erik pulling out another ball. Scout's eyes darted back and forth between the one he held and the one I had.

"You worry too much," Willow said. "She'll be fine. Trust me. You throw it and she's going after it. Retrievers love to swim."

I squeezed the ball, imagining every horrible scenario possible. What if Scout couldn't swim and she sank to the bottom of the murky pond? What if a wild animal ran out of the woods next to the pond and attacked her when she was going after the ball? What if —

In my hesitation, Erik took the lead. He dashed toward the pond and flung the ball he'd taken from the bag. Scout yanked the end of the leash from my hand and charged into the water.

"Ow!" I grabbed my hand where the nylon had burned the skin when the leash pulled across my fingers.

The leash bounced on the ground like a dead snake as Scout raced to the water. She only had to run in a couple of feet because Erik couldn't throw far. She snatched the ball and brought it back, dropping it at his feet. Her tongue hung out and she danced in anticipation of him throwing the ball again.

Feeling more confident that she wouldn't run off, I stepped up next to Erik. "Let me throw one for her, Oops." I raised the ball in the air to get Scout's attention. "Fetch." I hurled the ball and it whizzed past Willow to the middle of the pond. Grass flew as Scout whirled on shore then leaped into the water.

"Whoa! You have quite an arm, O'Dylan." Willow swam in a half circle to watch Scout doggy paddle past her.

"Yeah, too bad it's wasted," I grumbled. She probably couldn't hear me, but her compliment caused my frustration to bubble inside me again at not being in Manhattan playing for my All Star team. I'd video chatted with a couple of the guys last night and all I'd heard about was how great practices were going. I'd been trying to forget what I was missing.

Weighed down by the water in her thick fur, Scout plodded to shore with her prize in her mouth. She stopped, dropped the ball, and shook just a few feet from Erik and me, soaking us both. I expected Erik to freak, but instead, he laughed and threw the first ball back into the water.

Scout whirled and bounded back into the water. Erik had thrown it farther this time so she had to swim to retrieve it. This time instead of coming back into shore with it, she swam farther out toward Willow. When Scout was a few feet from her, Willow dove under the water and out of sight. Scout paddled in a small circle, her chin in the air to keep the ball out of the water, but her eyes scanned the water's surface looking for Willow. I expected Willow to come back up right away, but she didn't. I squinted, trying to see under the water's surface, but the reflection of the sun blinded me.

Panic prickled at the back of my neck. I walked closer to the shore. Scout still paddled in a circle where she'd last seen Willow.

"Come 'ere, Scout," I called. "It's okay. She'll surface."

Scout must have sensed my half-hearted command, because she stayed in the area where Willow had gone down.

I looked for air bubbles or ripples on the water's surface – any sign of where she might be. Had she been sucked down into the gooey stuff on the bottom of the pond that she'd described?

Erik moved closer to the water's edge. He'd taken his favorite treasure from his treasure box, an old subway token, and was squeezing it in the stuffed cat ear. He stretched his neck and stared across the pond.

"Where'th Willow?"

"She's swimming under the water. I'm sure she'll surface soon." I hoped she would, anyway. The prickly feeling was working its way down my arms. I figured it had to be close to a minute since she went under. I started out onto the dock, and it swayed as soon as I was a third of the way across. I looked down into the cloudy water. I knew I shouldn't get my stitches wet, but I also couldn't wait much longer before going in to find her. My heart started beating faster and I was taking quick breaths like I was trying to breathe for Willow, too.

"Scout, here," I commanded again, wanting to feel like I could control something. This time she responded and paddled back toward shore. I took a couple of more steps down the dock, being careful to avoid stepping on slats that looked weak. While Scout swam toward me, I peered into the water.

"Where's Willow, Scout?" I asked, as if she would answer me.

As if on cue, Willow broke the surface and grabbed onto one of the wooden corner posts of the dock, causing it to sway even more. I had to hold my arms straight out and move back and forth like a surfer to keep my balance, but I couldn't hold back my sigh of relief.

Water cascaded from the top of Willow's head to her face, and she sputtered to get it out of her mouth. She wiped the long strands of wet hair off her face and smiled. The water on her eyelashes sparkled in the sun. It made her look like a model.

"I th-think that's my n-new record," she said, gasping. "I've ne-never been a-able to s-swim from the middle o-of the p-pond to the dock with-without surfacing before."

I squeezed the tennis ball to release the leftover tension. "I was getting kinda worried," I confessed. "You were under a long time."

She continued to hold onto the wooden post but kicked her legs out behind her so it looked like she was floating on the water. "I s-swim for the school team," she said. "Keeps me in shape."

"Baseball keeps me in shape. Or, at least it used to."

Annoyed to be reminded about missing out on my baseball season, I raised the ball I'd been squeezing and took aim at a stick bobbing in the little waves out toward the middle. The ball nailed the stick, propelling it several feet.

"Impressive," Willow said. She swam to retrieve the ball then returned part way toward shore until I could tell she had reached a spot where her feet touched. "But how do I know you didn't just get lucky when you hit that stick. Bet you can't hit it again," she challenged. She tossed the ball at me, but it fell short, bounced off the dock and landed a few feet from shore.

I kicked off my sneakers, tossed them onto land and jumped into the water just a foot from shore. In an instant, Erik was at my side grabbing my wrist. He leaned over so he could keep his feet on the dry ground.

"Mom thaid no thwimming," he said. Worry creased his little forehead.

I tried to shake off his hand. For a kid who didn't like physical contact, he sure had a grip on me right now. "I'm not going swimming. I'm just going to walk in far enough to get the ball."

His fingers tightened on my wrist, and he added his other hand to the grip. "No. You can't go in the water."

"Erik, I know Mom told me to stay out of the water, but I'm not going to put my head under. My stitches are safe."

Willow splashed the water to stay afloat. "He's really into following rules, huh?"

"Yeah. He takes everything literally." I used my fingers to try and pry his off my arm.

Willow said, "That can be good, too. You know you can trust him to do what he's told to do, right?"

"I guess. But it also means whatever you tell him, he's going to hold you to it. Like if I tell him I'll play with him later, I'm stuck, even if I don't feel like it later." I finally peeled his hands off me. "Erik, I'm only going into the water far enough to get the ball. Mom would be okay with that."

I continued into the water, turning my attention back to Willow. "About that bet you just made."

She smiled and paddled in a small circle. "Yeah, what about it?"

"You think I can't hit that stick twice?"

"Nope," she challenged again.

"Bet's on. What do I get if I hit it?" I bent to grab the ball.

"A kiss."

I jerked up without even getting the ball. "What?"

"Make it pop out of the water and I'll give you a kiss."

I turned around to see if Erik was listening. Fortunately, he had gone back to his own little world, tossing the other ball a few feet into the water for Scout to get. The day was already hot so I was surprised when my face heated up even more. I snagged the ball and looked at her.

"What makes you think I want a kiss?"

She laughed and pushed her fingers through her wet hair. "Ha! It was obvious the first day we met."

Behind me Erik babbled to Scout while I struggled to think of a coherent comeback. But there was no comeback. She was right.

"Bet's on," I said.

I tossed the ball in the air a couple of times while I stared at the target. The ripples in the water settled so the stick barely moved now. I imagined a batter standing next to home plate, wound up and pitched. The ball buzzed past Willow and splintered the stick.

Her eyes popped open wide and she whooped like a cheerleader.

"You're amazing!" She swam toward shore then walked as soon as she could touch. The soaked tank top clung to her body, accenting every curve. Water raced down her arms and off her fingertips. This moment was the stuff dreams were made of.

Did she really say I was amazing? A lump the size of a baseball clogged my throat and I swallowed hard to make it move so I could breathe. I shot a look toward Erik, relieved to see he was now squatting with his back to us, using a stick to draw in the moist loose dirt near the water.

As Willow came closer, my heart hammered against my chest. Was she really going to kiss me? I felt like an idiot standing like a statue, but the warring emotions of fear and anticipation froze my muscles and I couldn't have moved even if someone had set me on fire.

She stopped inches from me, looked up into my eyes and announced, "A bet's a bet. Can't welch on a bet and not pay up."

She lifted on her tiptoes and I closed my eyes and leaned toward her. Her soft, moist mouth connected with mine, and the water from the pond that had clung to her upper lip was suddenly on mine. It wasn't salty like the ocean or chemical-flavored like the pool. It tasted like the rainwater that had landed on my tongue when I was a little kid trying to catch drops during a summer storm.

Willow pulled back, but I didn't want to open my eyes in case this was only a dream.

"Wow!" I said. "Want to make any more bets?"

She smacked my chest with the back of her hand. I snapped open my eyes, shocked at my boldness and her reaction. But she was grinning, so I relaxed. The water dripping down her face and over her eye lids sparkled in the sun and magnified her eyelashes even more up close. This was the closest I'd been to Willow since we'd met so I'd had no idea just how brown her eyes were.

"Hey, it was your idea," I said.

Willow took a step back, grabbed her hair and twisted it to wring out some of the water. "Doesn't matter. You didn't argue."

With her arms raised, some of the bruises were more visible, but I was distracted by the outline of her bra under her tank top. Suddenly my concern about not being able to move even if I was on fire was forgotten. Internal heat warred with the heat from the sun, and I thought if I didn't move or look away now that my clothes really might catch on fire.

Although I wanted to keep staring at Willow, I forced myself to turn around to check on Erik.

And he was gone.

I didn't want to panic, but my heart didn't get the message. It instantly quadrupled its beats per second. I turned in a full circle, hoping he'd moved behind me. Scout stood in the water dipping her head in and coming up with rocks that she then dropped to retrieve again.

"Erik?" The tightness in my chest caused the pitch of my voice to go up. "Where are you, buddy?"

I looked toward the dense bushes and the woods beyond, but saw nothing. When I pivoted back toward the water, except for where Scout was dropping the rocks, the surface was smooth as glass. The stick Erik had been using to draw in the dirt had been poked in so it stood like a tiny wooden pole on the shore.

"How could he disappear that fast?" Willow asked.

"You have no idea how fast he is. That's the problem." I took deep breaths to slow my heart while I turned again, trying to formulate a search plan before he could get too far. "He obviously didn't fall in the water because we would have heard a splash." Which left the woods to the left of the pond.

"Let's start over there," I suggested, pointing toward the bushes.

"You better hope he's not in there," Willow said. "That's full of poison ivy."

"Oh, man." I stared at it. I didn't know what the plant poison ivy looked like, but I sure knew what it looked like when someone broke out in a rash. "My brother, Trevor, is really allergic to it, which means Erik and I might be, too, if it runs in the family." It was the only dense area, and I feared that's where he'd gone. I started to run in that direction then remembered Scout.

"Scout, here." I called. Scout picked up her head and looked at me but didn't move. I patted my leg. "Here, Scout. Come on, girl." Still she wouldn't move.

Willow started to jog toward the woods. "You get Scout. I'll go into the woods."

I had no choice, so I ran to the water's edge and grabbed the water-logged leash from the water. "Let's go, Scout." She continued to resist. My panic turned to annoyance. "Damn it, dog. Let's go!" I pulled on her leash but she planted her body.

"Damn it! Damn it! Damn it!"

I snapped around toward the voice.

"Eric?" I took a couple of steps into the water and bent to look under the part of the dock that was anchored into the ground at the edge of the pond. There he sat, squeezed in so tight I didn't know how he even got under there. He was creating a tiny tower with a bunch of flat rocks.

No wonder Scout wouldn't move. She already knew her job was to stick by him no matter what. I wanted to yell at Erik for swearing but then realized how ridiculous that idea was since he had mimicked me.

A spider web that would make Charlotte and Wilbur jealous was suspended just over his head, and Charlotte's much bigger cousin was perched on it just inches away. In a calm voice I said, "You need to come out of there."

Erik continued to carefully stack the rocks as if he didn't hear me. The spider scooted a along the web until I couldn't see it. Was it getting ready to jump on him? A shiver ran up my spine. I had to get him out of there, but I knew I couldn't touch him.

"You can bring the rocks and build your tower out here."

"It'th not a tower." I recognized the stubborn tone. He was hearing me, but the storyline going on in his head was louder than my voice. The pediatrician explained that concept to us once. Raising my voice wouldn't change what he heard.

My back was starting to hurt because of the way I was twisted to look under the dock. "Well, then, whatever it is that you're building you can build out here. Scout can't see it under there. She wants you to build it out here, too."

Two more stones were carefully placed then re-placed as if I hadn't said anything.

Out of the corner of my eye I saw Willow coming back out of the woods.

"Hey, O'Dylan, are you —"

I held up my hand to stop her from saying more. She pointed and mouthed, *"Is he there?"*

I nodded. "He's building something out of flat stones. I can't get him to come out."

She stepped up to the other side of the dock and peeked under. "Wow! Those stones would be perfect for skipping across the water."

It was my turn to mouth back to her. *"What?"* Forget the stones. I just wanted to get Erik out of there and away from the spider in case it was poisonous.

"Yep, if Erik came out of there and brought those stones, I'd be able to teach him how to skip them across the water. It's the coolest thing you've ever seen."

He stopped stacking and stared at his tower that wasn't a tower. Was he listening to Willow?

She stood up. "Come on, O'Dylan. Let's find our own flat rocks to skip." She came around the end of the dock rather than jumping up on it in order to keep it from sagging and hitting Erik in the head. Seizing my wrist, she said, "Come on. I'm sure there are good ones right over here. It's okay if Erik doesn't want to learn."

"I want to get him out of there," I whispered. "There's a huge spider hanging over his head."

She tugged on my arm. "I guess I'll show you first. If Erik wants to learn, he'll come out."

I understood what she was trying to do, but reverse psychology never worked on Erik.

We took a few steps then she bent over and picked up three stones. "Perfect," she said, handing one to me. "Have you ever skipped rocks?"

"Of course, I have," I said. "There are ponds in Central Park. My dad taught me how a long time ago."

"Show me," she said.

I smiled. "Is this like a bet?"

"Just skip the rock." I could tell she was trying hard not to smile or laugh.

I turned the rock around in my hand until I had a comfortable grip. I angled my body so I could side arm it. It skipped across the water three times before it sank. I looked back toward the dock and saw that Erik was watching us but still from underneath.

"Not bad," she said. "Here's mine."

She put the stone in the palm of her hand and blew on it before rearranging it between her fingers. When she let it fly, it sailed across the water. She counted out loud as it skipped across. "One. Two. Three. Four. Five!" She threw her hands in the air and cheered. "Try to beat that, O'Dylan."

I was pretty sure I'd been able to get at least five skips out of a rock before. She held one out to me, but I decided to choose my own. When I bent to search, I noticed Erik was out from underneath the dock and watching us, his hands full with several of his stones. I quickly picked up a rock that was not perfectly flat, wound up and threw it into the water, not even caring how many times it skipped.

"Aw, man, I'm no good at this. Probably Erik could beat me."

Willow looked back at him. "Erik, come 'ere and see if you can beat your brother. He's really terrible at this."

Erik dropped his attention to his rocks. He'd looked at Willow longer than he'd look at most people. He took a few steps away from the dock and laid his stones on the beach in front of Scout like he thought she would guard them. It was obvious that Willow had magic in her voice or something. It was the second time today she'd been able to get him to do something when he wouldn't listen to me.

Willow stepped closer to me and took my right hand in hers. "So, the key to getting the rock to skip multiple times is all in the angle when you let go of it." She manipulated my fingers until I was holding the stone just the way she wanted me to.

"I know how to hold the rock," I said.

She gave me one of her looks that made me feel like I'd just said something stupid. "No kidding!" she whispered. "I'm describing this so Erik can hear. Now make sure you get this thing to skip lots of times."

"That's a lot of pressure," I joked.

I got the look again.

"Okay. Thanks for the tips," I said for Erik's benefit. Once again I positioned myself and sent the rock flying. It only skipped twice this time, but it was enough to get Erik's attention.

He picked up a rock and threw it toward the water. It hit and sank. His face started to crumple. But it was Willow to the rescue.

"Yup. That's exactly what happened to me my first few times. You just have to practice, Erik." She stepped over to his little pile of rocks and picked one up. "Try this one, and hold it like this." She put it in her hand first to demonstrate then held it until Erik took it.

He turned it over in his fingers several times then turned his body slightly and tossed it. This time it did skip once before it sank. That was all he needed. He picked up one rock after another and tossed them toward the water. He had no reaction, whether it skipped once or twice, or if it hit the water and sank. But he seemed happy, and that's all I cared about.

While Erik tried to skip stones, I decided to throw the tennis ball for Scout a few more times. At first Willow's attention was completely on Erik, but then at some point I noticed she had moved to sit on the dock and her attention had shifted to me.

"You're really good," she said. "Have you played baseball a long time?"

"Since I was four and in a T-ball league," I said. "And I was supposed to be on the All Stars for my team again this year. Then we moved."

Scout dropped the last ball I'd thrown, and it rolled toward my feet. I kicked it with my bare toe.

"There's a league in Keuka Shores," Willow said. "Maybe you could get on a team. Brock plays on one."

"He plays baseball?" I couldn't imagine that Brock and I would have anything in common.

"Yeah. He's actually pretty good."

I pointed at the stitches above my eye. "I know he has a strong swing."

She stretched then stood up. "Yeah, I'm really sorry about that."

"You're not the one who should be apologizing," I said, walking over to her. Erik was still tossing rocks toward the water.

"Well, I am." She hopped from the dock. "I bet Granny Annie will know who to call to get you on a team. I swear she knows everyone in town. Let's go and ask. You're wasted talent."

I smiled. It was pretty sweet getting compliments from Willow. "Thanks. It's worth a shot, I guess."

She turned toward Erik. "Erik, it's time to go back now. Can you take Scout's leash and bring her?" Again, the girl with the golden voice spoke. Without hesitation, after tucking some flat rocks in his pocket, Erik walked over and picked up Scout's leash. He started to walk and the dog followed.

Willow took my hand like it was the most natural thing to do and started to walk, leading me like I was a puppy, too. What had started out looking like the worst summer ever was getting better by the day. A girl to walk with and hold my hand and the possibility of playing baseball after all? Yeah, life was good.

I'd hardly had ten seconds to enjoy the thought before the quiet of the woods was broken by the sound of whooping and hollering. Three mountain bikes crashed through a narrow path in the brush and barreled toward us. I wasn't surprised to see Brock was the leader. He was up off the seat and pedaling hard, aiming for us.

"Brock!" Willow screamed, but his attention was fixed on me. I dropped Willow's hand and pushed her off to the side then jumped toward Erik to shield him. He tumbled against Scout and fell, then I tripped over him and landed inches from him. Brock skidded his bike next to us, throwing dirt up into my face. The other two guys with him ripped past, roaring with laughter.

I jumped to my feet, my vision blurred with rage. My eyes came back into focus just in time to see all three guys ride their bikes off the end of the dock and flip them into the air away from them as they splashed down into the water.

"Ugh!" Willow spouted behind me. I turned to see her fists clenched and her face tight with fury. "He's the biggest jerk!"

Erik got to his knees, his eyes wide in confusion. Scout pressed against him and he laid his arm across her neck and pulled her tighter.

"We can't let them get away with that," I growled. I'd never been on the receiving end of bullying, and now I wished I'd stood up for all the kids I'd watched being bullied back in our neighborhood.

Willow stalked away toward the path. "There's nothing we can do."

I hated the sound of defeat in her voice. I glanced back toward the pond. The guys had rolled their bikes out of the water, left them next to the dock and were swimming toward a tree that hung over the pond on the other side where a rope hung down into the water.

"Erik, take Scout and go with Willow," I said. I was amazed when he did what I asked. Willow stopped and looked at me.

"You two go ahead. I'll catch up to you."

Willow narrowed her eyes. "What are you going to do?"

"It's time for Brock and his buddies to get a taste of their own medicine, as my grandmother would say." I didn't exactly know what I would do, but I figured a plan would hit me. Willow opened her mouth, but I shushed her. "Just start walking. Keep Erik with you. I'll follow the path and catch up."

I walked with them until they were on the path in the woods so it looked like I was leaving, too. Then, I doubled back. Brock and his friends couldn't have left those bikes in a more convenient place. They were laying just feet from the thick bushes Willow had warned me about. I crouched as I moved closer to the bikes, then watched to make sure the three guys were distracted. When I was sure it was safe, I struck. One at a time I threw the three bikes into the bushes.

And the poison ivy.

CHAPTER SEVEN

I turned the key in the lawnmower ignition and cringed when it roared to life. Its uneven sputters echoed off the inside walls of our big shed. I threw it in reverse and backed down the low angle ramp. There were so many things I'd rather be doing right now than mowing a lawn that was more than a couple of acres. In Manhattan we'd lived fourteen stories above the city streets, and any patches of grass, so having to mow a lawn never interfered with hanging out with my friends.

I steered toward the long patch of grass between the driveway and the white picket fence next to the yard then threw the lever to engage the mowing blade. I hadn't even started and I was already bored of the tedious task of mowing in strips, wishing just once I could mow a design into the lawn to make the job more interesting. I let my imagination wander. I could cut a replica of the Empire State Building into it. Or maybe create my own miniature version of the playing field at Yankee Stadium or the Yankees logo. But Mom was adamant that the rows had to be mowed straight and even because that's how she'd had to do it when she was growing up, so I pushed my musings aside. Besides, thinking about anything connected to my old life usually gave me a kick in the gut that made me feel down for hours.

The sun ducked in and out behind the clouds, so at least I wasn't sweating. I absently scratched at a small red spot on the back of my hand then yanked my fingers back. It had been almost twenty four hours since I'd thrown the bikes into the bushes at the pond. Was this red spot the beginning of an outbreak of poison ivy? I hoped not, but it did make me smile when I pictured Brock and his goons trying to pluck their bikes from the bushes without coming in contact with the poisonous plant. I figured by the next practice, I'd know how they'd made out.

I gripped the steering wheel of the John Deere lawnmower and took the corner tighter than I should have. The blade guard gouged into the grass, leaving a thin half-circle strip of dirt that no doubt would be proof to Mom that I was mowing too fast – her common complaint. But it was the speed that made mowing at least a little entertaining. The way I saw it, I was getting the work done, having some fun, and getting a driving lesson all at once. According to my countdown calendar in the kitchen, in eighteen months, three weeks and two days I'd be getting my driver's permit. I had to start practicing sometime.

I steered toward the fence that enclosed the back yard, aiming for a strip of high weeds that apparently Mom hadn't noticed growing out of control in the back. The mower chewed them up and spit them out, leaving the pungent smell of broken stems behind. When I came around for the second swipe at them, I slammed on the brakes, jerking to a stop, and groaned. Now that I looked closer, it looked like there were orange and yellow tinged specks among the mutilated leaves and stems. Remnants of flower buds. No doubt Mom knew the "weeds" were there.

At the same time, out of the corner of my eye, I noticed Grandma scurrying out onto the deck. She was waving her arms for me to stop.

I pressed the brake and turned off the mower, but she started talking before my ears had time to adjust to the lack of engine roar.

"— day lilies."

"What?"

She leaned on the deck railing and pointed her finger in a sweeping motion. "You just mowed down all of your mother's day lilies."

Yup, I was right. "I know. I didn't see any flowers on them until it was too late. I thought they were weeds."

She shook her head. "What is it with you men? Your grandfather is constantly mowing or chopping down my flowers, claiming they look like weeds."

You men. I dropped my chin to hide my smile. Grandma didn't view me as a kid anymore. I looked back up at her. "It was my first time mowing back there. I didn't know."

Erik and Scout stepped through the open sliding door. Scout was so close to Erik's hip that they looked joined.

"Maybe it'd be better if you slowed down," Grandma said. "It's not a race."

"Yeah, I know," I said.

She waved her hand toward the other side of the yard. "Just watch out for the rest of her flowers." She turned and herded Erik and Scout back into the air conditioned house.

I restarted the lawnmower and shifted it down one gear. Okay, so maybe fourth gear on full throttle was a little fast. Mowing was less tedious when I went faster because then it was a challenge to get as close to the base of the trees as possible without ending up riding up the trunk. One time the mower did tip a little too much when the front tire caught in a jumble of roots at a tree's base, so I had to throw my weight to make the save, and I managed to keep it upright. No rollover with this mower today.

I'd been at it for over two hours when I glanced around the yard, looking for any spot I might have missed, but it all looked good. Even with stopping to pick up Scout's tennis balls and moving Erik's trucks back onto his roads in the sandbox, I'd managed to finish in record time. I spun the steering wheel toward the shed to hook on the small wooden trailer so I could pick up the little piles of sticks I'd gathered before mowing. At the front of the shed I put the lawnmower in neutral and set the brake. The trailer was inside the shed and I'd need to pull it out by hand.

I started up the ramp but stopped abruptly when I heard banging against the side of the shed. I had left the wide, roll-up door open, so I took a step back and peered inside. We didn't have much in the shed yet, and I couldn't see anything making the noise. I ventured in a few more steps, and again there was more banging accompanied by some kind of snorting noise. The sound was coming from outside.

I whirled around and grabbed a pointed shovel hanging in the rack on the wall. My weapon gave me confidence to creep back to the opening. The banging continued, and it rattled the small window in the side wall of the shed. I stopped and looked through the glass but saw nothing despite the continued banging and snorting.

At the door, I put the shovel out in front of me and hit the metal against the ground to see if anything would attack. It seemed to have no effect on whatever was out there. I poked my head around the corner.

The banging and snorting stopped, but I was confronted with two sets of black beady eyes. "This is like Wild Kingdom," I mumbled so I wouldn't startle them.

Two pinkish white pigs that weren't any taller than my knees stared at me like they expected me to attack any second. I didn't move. And it took a good half minute before they did. Apparently satisfied that they weren't becoming bacon any time soon, they returned to digging their snouts into the vegetable garden that ran along the side of the shed. They had already torn up a good portion of it. Remnants of leafy plants, tomatoes and cucumbers were strewn all over the dirt. My grandparents had planted it for us as soon as we had the closing on the house so the vegetables would be ready when we got here. Now it was all destroyed, and the pigs were after something under the small opening beneath the shed. The banging was from their heads hitting the wall.

I held the shovel out in front of me and poked one of them. "Get out of here!" I yelled.

The pig rammed its partner in crime and squealed, trying to bash it out of the way. Its corkscrew tail twitched nervously. I lightly poked the other pig, too, which caused them both to spin toward me then back toward each other like they didn't know which way to go. With the shovel to protect me, I prodded more.

"Go home!"

The pigs split up and raced past me, one squeezing between me and the shed, almost toppling me, and the other rushing past my other leg. They squealed and snorted as they dashed down our driveway toward the road. I panicked, imagining a car or truck coming down the road and flattening them.

When I sprinted after them Grandma must have seen the commotion because she came out the side door. "Where the devil did those come from?" she asked.

"Willow's, I think. They tore up the vegetable garden," I yelled. "I'm going to try and herd them back to her house."

"All right," Grandma answered. She stepped back inside but stood in the doorway watching me through the window.

I ran past the pigs so I could get in front of them at the end of the driveway. They ran in tiny circles, bumping into each other, before they suddenly split up again. One ran back toward the shed and the other one ran toward the big field that separated our property from Willow's.

"Hey, pigs!" I yelled, as if that would make them stop and listen. The one that had run back toward the shed was squealing and snorting as it zigzagged from the grassy area of the yard to the driveway. I was winded from running down the driveway and torn about whether to chase after the pig by the shed or the one in the field.

The lawnmower still idled next to the shed, and that gave me an idea. I hurried toward it and leapt onto the seat. Ignoring Grandma's request to drive slower, I threw it into the highest gear I could with full throttle up and used it to round up the panicked pig that had lost sight of its friend. I circled around it and managed to get it to run in the same direction.

I was shocked by how fast they ran. The lawnmower bounced across the rough field as the two pigs reunited and continued running toward home, making a little path by knocking down the weeds in their way. A couple of times I bounced around the lawnmower seat and almost lost my grip on the steering wheel, but my adrenaline was pumping. I never had this kind of excitement in the city. When one of the pigs veered off, I wheeled the lawnmower over to force it back with the other.

Laughter bubbled inside me as I envisioned round-up scenes from old western movies I used to watch with my grandfather when I was little. My "horse" had a loud motor – and I was pretty sure the cowboys had never been chasing pigs. As ridiculous as this scene was, I continued the chase, caught up in the thrill.

When we reached the end of the field, the pigs careened around some trees and past an old shed. For a moment I considered stopping the chase and turning back for home. But the lure of possibly seeing Willow won out over the concern regarding running into Brock. Besides, I had to make sure the pigs were safe.

I pushed the throttle lever down to slow the lawnmower then grabbed the shift handle at the side and knocked it from fourth gear to third. It lurched when it kicked into the slower speed, snapping my head back and forth. I glanced around and was relieved to see that I didn't have witnesses.

By the time I came past the shed where I'd last seen the pigs, Willow was coming out of the big chicken coop in the pasture. She carried a couple of light blue Styrofoam egg cartons, but that didn't stop her from throwing a hand in the air to wave.

I waved back, silently thanking the pigs for giving me another opportunity to see her.

The pigs paced in front of the wooden gate to the pasture, squealing and snorting like they were being murdered. I parked the lawnmower under the tree near the barn, cut the engine and pulled the key from the ignition. As soon as I tucked the key into the pocket of my shorts, I realized what I'd done. My city mentality had caused that automatic reaction. No sooner had I chided myself than I remembered the fate of my bike tires. Yeah, if I ended up out of sight of the lawnmower, a key in the ignition was nothing more than an invitation for Brock.

I crossed the driveway toward the pasture but kept a safe distance from the pigs. They were digging their snouts in the dirt under the gate when Willow came back into view from the side of the barn. She bent to look at the pigs through the gate slats.

"Hey, O'Dylan. Where'd you get the pigs?" She reached over the top of the gate and pulled up on a latch to open it.

"They were pulverizing my mother's garden, so I brought them home."

Willow opened the gate just enough so she could squeeze through, one foot lightly kicking at the pigs so they couldn't get into the pasture. She cradled the egg cartons against her stomach and laughed.

"You didn't bring them *home*. We don't have pigs."

My jaw dropped. "What? You're like Noah or Dr. Doolittle. You have every kind of animal in your sanctuary." I was careful to use her term to describe her collection of beasts.

She ignored the pigs and walked toward me. "It only seems that way. Those pigs probably belong to Charlie Peck down the road. He has a whole bunch, and they're always coming up here."

"Great! So what do we do with them now?"

"He'll come and get them."

"Maybe he can explain to my mom why there aren't any vegetables left to pick."

"He'll deny they did it 'til the cows come home." She started toward the house. "Only problem is, Charlie doesn't have any cows. C'mon, I'll go in and call him."

As we walked up the driveway side by side she bumped her elbow against mine and hitched her thumb over her shoulder toward the lawnmower. "By the way, sweet ride there, O'Dylan."

I bumped her back, thrilled to have an excuse to touch her. "Hey, it got the job done."

"As in the lawn mowed?"

"No, as in I rounded up the pigs and drove them home." I shrugged. "At least I thought I was driving them home."

She laughed and her eyes sparkled. For the first time I noticed a hint of dimples. "You rounded up pigs with a lawnmower? Ride 'em, cowboy!"

I walked a little closer until my arm continuously rubbed against hers. "Hey, I was going to offer to take you for a ride, but I may have to change my mind due to your lack of respect."

"I'll one up you on that, cowboy. I'll take you up on that ride, but I say we take your trusty steed out into the field and set up an obstacle course and see which one of us can handle that hot machine the best."

We reached the bottom of the porch stairs and I pivoted to look at the lawnmower then back at

Willow. "Is that what y'all do for fun out here in the country?" I couldn't resist using the twang in the sentence as I picked on her.

She took my arm and turned me toward her before lifting up on her toes and poking her finger into my chest. "Country kids are the most creative people you'll ever meet, O'Dylan, because we have to make our own fun. Use your imagination. I'm going to show you what you've been missing."

Warmth spread across my chest and up my neck. With her touching me, my imagination was in overdrive. The challenge for me was to keep it in check.

"I can't wait." My throat was so tight the three words came out more like a croak.

She nodded and winked. "This is going to be a great summer, O'Dylan." She ran her tongue across her lower lip then poked her finger into my chest. In a soft voice she said, "I'll be right back."

She bumped her shoulder against my arm as she moved past me to go up the steps and into the house. I'm sure she knew I'd do it, and I did. My eyes followed her sashaying body until she walked into the house and the screen door slammed behind her. Now my imagination was smoking! At least this part of the summer was going to be great.

I slipped my phone from my pocket and called my grandmother to let her know I'd be staying at Willow's for a while so she wouldn't worry. While I tucked the phone back in my pocket, I leaned against the supporting post at the bottom of the porch railing and stared toward the lean green machine. If I'd known the effect that would have on her, I would have been riding up and down the road and offering to mow Granny Annie's lawn, too.

Lost in my imagination, I jumped when the screen door slammed behind me and Napoleon barked. I whirled around, prepared to face Brock, but it was Willow's grandmother.

"Napoleon, hush!" she scolded. "Hello, Dylan. Willow told me you were out here."

She obviously wasn't a mind reader, because if she'd been reading my thoughts just before she came out, right now instead of greeting me sweetly she'd be slapping me hard across the face and telling me to stay away from her granddaughter.

I cleared my throat. "Yeah, I brought the pigs home." For an instant I imagined making a statement like that back in the city and almost laughed out loud.

"We don't have pigs," she said.

I leaned my arm on the post. "Yeah, that's what I found out. Willow's in calling the owner now."

"Well, I came out to tell you I had a chat with a couple of people I know who run the baseball league, and if you're interested, there's an opening for you."

I ran up the three steps to get on her level. "Are you kidding me? I'm in."

"I figured you'd feel that way." She handed me a slip of paper. "Here's the contact information for the coach who can take you on. He said to give him a call tonight because he wants to get you squared away for the next practice."

I looked at the paper. Rick Gordon. Coach Gordon. "This is great. Thank you."

"You're welcome." She pushed a piece of her short wavy hair off her forehead. I still couldn't believe she was a grandmother. "We want you to feel at home here in Keuka Shores and that means making friends. There's no better way to get to know people than playing on a team."

Willow came through the door and stepped next to me. "So, Granny Annie gave you the good news?"

I held up the paper. "Yeah, this is great. I can't wait to call him." I couldn't believe how awesome this day was turning out to be. I'd only thought of the city twice all day – which beat the usual hundreds of times daily, and I had a feeling the way things were going, it wouldn't enter my thoughts again today.

"Charlie will be up in a while to get his pigs," Willow said.
Then she shocked me when she hooked her arm around my elbow and added, "Granny, O'Dylan's taking me for a ride on the Deere."

Granny Annie nodded and with a sly smile said, "Don't do anything I wouldn't do."

Willow squeezed my arm and looked up at me. "That statement just gave us a whole lot of leeway, O'Dylan. Nobody's wilder than Granny Annie."

I actually thought I saw pink pop out on Granny Annie's cheeks. "Oh, you stop that, Willow. I just know how to have fun."

Willow grinned and pulled on my arm to start down the stairs, "Like I said —"

Granny Annie laughed behind us and the screen door slapped against the wood frame.

And once again, my imagination revved up.

Willow should have added the word resourceful to her earlier comment about being creative. The obstacle course she set up in the field included buckets, a bale of hay, two weathered 2 x 4 boards and a large, thick rope. The five buckets were set in a line with ten big paces in between each one. The boards were laid down parallel to each other after the buckets and they created an entrance to the rope that was laid down on the ground so it created a large circle. Willow called it a "keyhole" – a term she said she'd learned at horse shows. It was fun to see what she'd created out of whatever she could pick up around the barn.

After making sure the course was set exactly as she wanted it, we went back to the lawnmower next to the bale of hay.

"Do you have a timer on your phone?" she asked.

I nodded. I pulled my phone from my pocket and scrolled through my apps to find it. I held the phone to face her. "Okay, got it."

She looked at it and nodded. "Okay, then here are the rules. As soon as the front tires go past the bale of hay, the timer starts. You have to weave in and out between the buckets, then at the end you have to go into that keyhole without touching the 2 x 4s leading into it, turn the lawnmower around without driving onto the rope anywhere, weave your way back through the buckets and time stops when the back tires pass the bale of hay. Got it?"

"Yup." I couldn't believe how excited I was about this competition. I felt like a little kid again. "What happens if we hit a bucket or go outside the circle?"

"Five seconds is added to your time for hitting a bucket. Ten seconds added if you knock anything over or crush anything."

I ran my fingers through my hair like that would help me think. "Fair enough. Who goes first?"

Willow tipped her head and squinted her eyes. "Let's go by I.Q."

"What? I don't know –"

"Oh, never mind," she interrupted, waving her hand in the air. "That suggestion was stacked in my favor."

I was ready to protest again when her smirk widened. I fought the smile that tugged at my cheeks and finally gave up. I loved her personality. Adorable wasn't a strong enough word to describe her appeal.

"Yeah, yeah. And I suppose next you're going to say 'girls rule and boys drool'?" I said as I climbed onto the John Deere and started the engine.

"Hadn't planned on it, but now that you mention it."

I handed her my phone so she could time me then put the lawnmower into the highest gear and turned up the throttle. "Prepare yourself for defeat."

Willow rolled her eyes then stepped to the other side of the hay bale. I eased the lawnmower into the starting position to await her signal to go. My shoulders and legs tensed as I gripped the steering wheel and pressed the clutch down as hard as I could. With her attention on the timer, Willow raised her hand like she was holding a race starting flag. She licked her lip, concentrating hard then suddenly snapped her arm down to signal me to go. I jerked my knee up to release the clutch and the lawnmower sprang forward, whipping me back and forth.

I careened around the buckets, at first swinging way too wide and then narrowly missing the ones on the end. I straightened the wheels and made it through the parallel boards without a problem. Once in the rope circle, I had to maneuver back and forth several times before I had the lawnmower turned completely around and headed back out of the "keyhole" and toward the buckets again. On my second weave I nicked one and it rocked back and forth. When I looked over my shoulder to see if it had fallen over, I ran straight into another one in front of me. Bam! Just like that fifteen seconds were added to my time. I yanked the steering wheel back toward the next one and managed to regain control and not hit anything else.

When I crossed the finish line next to the hay bale, I slammed on the brake and threw my hands in the air. "Yee ha! This cowboy scored a great ride."

Willow stepped next to me and held the phone so we could both look at the timer. I realized I was breathing heavily as if I'd just run the obstacle course instead of riding on the mower.

"Let's see," she said, "forty-eight seconds but you need to add fifteen for hitting one bucket and running over another one."

"Sixty-three," we said at the same time.

I took the lawnmower out of gear and set the parking brake. "This probably isn't the right time to ask, but have you ever driven a riding lawnmower before?"

Willow scowled. "We're in the country, O'Dylan. We learn to drive practically before we learn to walk."

My mother had told me stories like that from when she was growing up in the country, but I thought that was just the olden days. I didn't think it still happened.

I climbed off the lawnmower and made a sweeping motion toward it. "Prove it. You've gotta beat sixty-three."

She purposely bumped into me on her way past. "No problem." Once on the seat, she reached up and tucked her hair into the back of her shirt.

I laughed. "You think your hair is going to create drag?"

"No, I *know* my hair is going to fly into my face if I don't put it back. Go ahead and make fun of me. We'll see who's laughing in the end." She reached down and moved the gear lever to the highest position then pushed up the throttle. The engine roared as she moved it into the starting position. Mimicking her actions from when it was my turn, I stepped to the other side of the bale of hay and reset the timer. I raised my hand and sliced it through the air to signal her to start.

She zipped within inches of the buckets as she wound around them. Her arms worked furiously as she turned the steering wheel back and forth. At the end when she was in the rope keyhole and had to turn her head back and forth in order to maneuver, her hair came untucked and flew into her face. She whipped her head around to clear the strands from her eyes without taking her hands off the steering wheel. When she did, the wheels jerked and she rode up onto one of the 2 x 4s.

"Dang!" she yelled, straightening out the lawnmower. She worked her way back through the buckets without hitting any and crossed the finish line at full throttle.

I pressed stop and held the timer up in the air as if that would maintain the integrity of the timekeeping. She parked the lawnmower, and I met her where she'd stopped.

"How many seconds get added for running over the board?" I asked.

"Ten." She craned her neck to see the final time on my phone.

"I've got fifty-five here plus ten is—"

Willow slapped the steering wheel with her palm. "Aw, two seconds? Really? I lost by two seconds."

If she'd been a guy, I would have rubbed it in that I won, but somehow it didn't seem right to do that to her. "Hey, you had a good run. Just bad luck on the boards, that's all."

"Yeah, I guess." She threw her legs over the seat like she was going to get off the lawnmower, then stopped. A big smile filled her face. "That was a blast, wasn't it? Ready for a rematch?"

I pushed my phone into my pocket then put one hand on the back of the yellow seat and the other on the steering wheel and leaned forward so I was only inches away from her. "I think I should collect my prize for winning the first heat before we talk about a second round."

She frowned. "We didn't discuss prizes."

I moved one hand so I could tuck a strand of her loose hair behind her ear. I'd never noticed the reddish highlights that reflected the sun.

"No, but I liked what I won out at the pond when I threw the tennis ball and hit the stick in the water. I'll take the same prize, if that's all right with you." I moved a couple of inches closer. The engine made the lawnmower vibrate, and the vibration went up through my arms to my neck, easing a little of the tension there.

Willow pursed her lips and pink rose on her cheeks. "I guess it would be all right." She closed her eyes and lifted her lips toward mine.

Before I closed my eyes, I looked up to make sure we weren't within view of her grandmother's house. Feeling comfortable, I lowered my mouth to intertwine with her lips. They were even softer and sweeter than I remembered. I angled my head a little and moved one of my hands to the back of her head to press our lips even closer together. A little moan escaped her lips and she wrapped her arms around my waist to pull my hips in between her knees. Heat shot through my core. I was sure Heaven had just come down to Earth.

I reluctantly released her lips because I needed to catch my breath but only leaned back a few inches. "You're pretty good at this," I said.

Her eyes fluttered open and a tiny, crooked smile played on her lips. "You're not too bad yourself."

I ran my finger from the bridge of her nose to the tip. "And you know what? You have a great smile and it reaches right down to your heart. I could get used to this winning thing."

Her gaze trailed from my lips up to my eyes. "And I could get used to letting you win just so I have to pay up."

I narrowed my eyes. "What? *Letting me win?* I beat you fair and square."

She stroked my arm with the tips of her fingers. "I suppose, but if this is how it's always going to end, then my competitive spirit has been broken. I don't need to win the competition, because in the end we both win, anyway."

I showed her that I agreed by moving back in to press my lips to hers. I caressed her cheek with my thumb, loving the feel of her skin. I never needed to leave this spot – or this moment. We were totally lost, exploring the depth of our attraction when my phone rang. At first I ignored it and it stopped, but when it rang again, I groaned and released Willow. She licked her lips like she'd just enjoyed a sweet treat. I knew I had.

I glanced at my phone and saw it was my mother calling. I reached down and switched off the lawnmower key to cut the engine so I could hear without having to step away from Willow.

"My mom. Guess she must be serious if she dialed it twice." I pressed the button and answered, turning my attention back to Willow as soon as I could. "Hey, Mom. What's up?" I wondered if I sounded as breathless as I felt.

"Charlotte and Jamie are going to be here in ten minutes for our training session with Scout. Where are you?"

"I'm at Willow's. Did Grandma tell you about the pigs?"

"Yes, but that was quite a while ago."

I tried to think fast through my fuzzy haze. "I've been giving Willow tips on how to use the riding lawnmower." I let my hand slide down her arm until I was holding her hand. I couldn't believe how this day was turning out.

"You'll have to finish the lesson later," Mom said. "I need you to head home."

"Okay. I'll be right there. Bye."

I hung up and put the phone back in my pocket. "Charlotte's coming for another training session with Scout. We all have to be there."

"Oh, Scout." She dragged out the dog's name like it was four or five syllables. "Love that dog."

"Me, too. She's making a huge difference with Erik. If he starts to freak out, she goes over and lays down on him until he's under control. The kicking and screaming stop in half the time compared to what it was like before we got her."

"She's so awesome," Willow cooed.

Seeing her reaction gave me an idea. "Hey, wanna come and do the training session with us again? I'm sure Mom wouldn't mind. And, you're hanging around enough that it would probably be good for you to know this handling stuff, too."

Willow hopped off the lawnmower. "Maybe we should ask your mother anyway. I don't want to intrude."

"Okay." I took my phone back out and dialed home. When Mom answered, instead of asking permission, I explained that I had invited Willow. As I figured, she was fine with it.

I hit the end button on the phone and looked at Willow. "She says come on down."

Willow grinned. "Awesome."

I moved onto the seat and started the engine. Once I had it in gear, I patted my thigh. "Here, I'll give you a ride."

Without hesitation, she scooted onto my lap. It was awkward trying to steer with my arms wrapped around her, but it was a great problem to have. I kept the speed lower so she wouldn't bounce off and we made our way across the field toward my house. I was relieved that we didn't need to go back toward her house and risk seeing Brock. For now, I was just as happy to keep Willow's and my budding relationship to ourselves.

After we passed through the hedgerow and just before we were within view of my house, I stopped the lawnmower but kept it running. "I think it probably wouldn't look so good to ride in with you on my lap. I'll let you drive the rest of the way."

"Okay." She surprised me by giving me another kiss before she moved off my lap.

She kept it in a lower gear so I wouldn't have trouble walking next to her through the high, weed-infested field. I tucked one hand in my pocket and felt the slip of paper in there from Granny Annie. I pulled it out and looked at it again while I walked. I'd call Coach Gordon as soon as our training session with Scout was over.

Oh, yeah! Everything was going my way today.

Charlotte's car was already in the driveway, which didn't surprise me. What did surprise me was seeing Willow's grandmother's van, too.

Willow must have read my mind because she yelled over the engine, "Granny Annie was going to drop off some homemade cinnamon rolls to your mom this afternoon. Bet that's why she's here."

We parked the lawnmower in the shed then walked around to the back yard where we usually held the training sessions. I opened the gate and held it for Willow to go through, then I closed it behind me. I heard Granny Annie telling a story in her animated voice, but I didn't see her until we rounded the corner of the house.

She stood on the deck with everyone else, her hands and arms waving as she spoke.

I stumbled to a stop and grabbed Willow's hand when I glanced toward Erik's sandbox. Standing with one foot up on the edge was Brock. And by the smug smirk on his face, I guessed there was a good chance that my private time with Willow in the field wasn't as private as I had thought.

Brock lifted his fingers to his lips and twisted them like he was turning a key and tossing it away. There was no way I was letting him intimidate Willow anymore. I dropped her hand.

"Go ahead and join them up on the deck. I'm gonna go over and say hello to your brother."

Willow whirled toward me. "He just wants to make trouble. That's the only reason he's here."

"I can handle Brock," I assured her. "Go on. I'll be right over."

I watched her walk toward the deck. She looked over her shoulder at me a couple of times, a pleading look on her face. But I'd had it with Brock and his bullying.

"Hey, Brock. I'm surprised to see you here," I said as I approached.

"Thought I'd be *neighborly*, as my grandmother says." The word neighborly came out on a sneer, emphasizing how he really felt.

"Why'd you really come up? If it's to harass Willow, then I'm telling you to leave her alone." I hoped Brock couldn't see my heart battering the inside of my chest.

He shifted and hooked his thumbs in the pockets of his jeans shorts. He plastered a fake smile on his face. "I came to tell you something, too," he said. "You know that phone number the old lady gave you?"

I lifted my chin. "What about it?"

"Don't call it. There's no room in our league for you."

"I guess that's for the league to decide, isn't it? Not you or anyone is going to stop me from getting on a team."

He dropped his attention to the ground and shuffled one foot, digging his heel into the loose dirt by the sandbox. "I'd hate to have you do anything my sister would regret."

I worked his words around in my head, sure that I hadn't heard him right. "Have *me* do anything your sister would regret? You've lost me. Whether or not I get on a team has nothing to do with Willow."

He glared at me. "That's what you think." He kicked a pile of dirt against my leg and a cloud of dust swirled around our knees. "Lose the phone number."

He stalked past me. I watched his retreating back as he went to join the others on the deck. An imaginary magnetic force pulled my hand in my pocket to feel the slip of paper with the coach's number. I held it between my fingers and turned to look at Willow.

Suddenly the idea of calling the number felt like a risk.

CHAPTER EIGHT

I stepped up next to the dugout at the high school baseball field and instantly felt at home. Granny Annie obviously had good connections in Keuka Shores if all it took was one phone call to get me on a baseball team, especially since the summer season had started more than a week before.

A tall man in jean shorts, a Cardinals t-shirt and Dodgers baseball cap knelt next to several equipment bags. He hadn't noticed me yet, but I turned around and waved to Mom to let her know it was okay to leave. Erik's face was pressed up to the rear passenger window, and Scout sat next to him, her nose against it, too. Mom waved back, pulled away from the curb and disappeared down the tree-lined street.

I rolled my shoulders to loosen my muscles and calm my nerves then approached the man. "Excuse me. Are you Coach Gordon?"

He looked up, squinting one eye against the morning sun. "Yes. You must be Dylan."

"Yes, sir."

Coach Gordon dropped a bat he'd been inspecting and stood. And I thought he'd never stop. I'd never seen such a tall baseball coach. I was almost six feet tall, or at least I liked to believe I was even though I was really an inch or two shy of it, and this guy towered over me like he was a tree that had just grown in that spot. He had to have been at least six and a half feet tall, if not more.

Although he had a kind face, all I could think was that no one would dare to mess with him. Granny Annie had told me he was a state trooper. I could imagine him pulling someone over for speeding and when he walked up to the car the driver would cower and say, "I'll take two tickets please, officer," even if they weren't guilty. Since my dad was also a cop, I figured at least the coach and I were starting out with something in common.

"Good to meet you, Dylan." Coach Gordon took my hand and pumped my arm in the biggest welcome I'd ever received anywhere. "Thanks for getting here early. This will give us time to warm you up so I can see what you've got to offer before the other guys get here."

I punched my fist into the soft pocket of my glove. "Sounds great."

"Why don't we warm you up." He bent and rummaged through the big black canvas bag in produced a glove for him and a baseball. "Go on out."

I jogged out onto the field. I didn't want to tire out my arm, so I made sure to start out with softer throws. After a couple dozen, I was ready to show him what I had.

I raised my glove in the air. "I'm good. Can I take the mound and pitch a few?"

He shrugged as we started toward each other. "We already have two pitchers," he said, "and

Zach Rogers is a crackerjack who's been my main pitcher for three years now."

A twinge of disappointment hit me in the pit of my stomach, but I tamped it down. If Zach Rogers was better than me, I could live with playing a different position. But Coach Gordon wouldn't know unless he saw me pitch, so I had to at least give it a shot.

"I was the pitcher on our All Star team back in the city. Maybe I have something he doesn't."

Coach lifted his eyebrows, glanced at my glove then looked at his watch. "Well, we have time." He pushed the ball back into my glove. "S'pose I should at least give you a chance."

In order to quell the urge to fist-pump, I pivoted and jogged to the pitcher's mound. This might be my only opportunity, I couldn't mess it up. Coach Gordon was already crouched behind home plate when I turned around.

I positioned myself on the rubber mat and gripped the ball inside the glove. In order to center myself, I took a deep breath
and pulled myself up straight. Once my shoulder muscles loosened, I wound up and let the ball rip toward Coach's glove. It found its mark with a loud, leathery smack.

He bounced up and shook his gloved hand. "Well, you've got speed and power there, Dylan."

"Thanks." I fought the huge smile that yanked at my cheeks. I had to play it cool. Good pitchers never showed emotion – at least that's what Dad taught me.

"Hold up a minute." He went to the equipment bags and pulled out a catcher's mitt. "Maybe this will save my hand."

He threw the ball back to me and squatted again behind home plate. "Okay, let me see your curve ball."

I gave it my best, and it was obvious Coach was impressed.

He lifted the bill of his cap a bit as he asked, "Were you professionally trained?"

This time I did smile. "No, sir. My father started playing ball with me when I was old enough to hold a glove. He pitched in the minors one season before he decided to become a cop, so he taught me a lot. Maybe I inherited some skill."

"There's no maybe about it," Coach said, holding up his glove. "Put a few more in here."

Ten minutes later the other guys started showing up. They leaned against the chain link fence and watched me. Out of the corner of my eye, I noticed them talking after each pitch and every now and then there were deep laughs. I hoped that was a good thing. Coming onto the team a week late could be tough, but if they thought I added to the chances of winning, I figured I'd be able to ease in.

After several pitches, Coach Gordon looked over his shoulder. By now there were close to a dozen guys. "Why don't you clowns use your time wisely and come over here and swing the bat for Dylan? Porter, Brooks, Wickham and Martin, go out there and field the balls."

The four guys Coach had called out meandered toward the field. Those remaining by the fence shoved at each other until finally one of the biggest guys came out of the group and walked to the bat bag where he pulled out a black and gold aluminum bat. By the way he swaggered to home plate, it was obvious he thought he was pretty tough. He kicked at the soft dirt with his cleats then stretched the bat toward the far corner of the house-shaped plate. When he finally turned his head to look at me, the challenge in his eyes was unmistakable: these guys weren't giving me anything. I'd have to prove myself.

I waited for the coach to move back in the box, then eyed his glove, and fired. The ball sailed over home plate and through the strike zone into Coach Gordon's glove. The batter turned to look at him.

"St-ee-rike!" Coach yelled.

He threw the ball back, and I waited while the batter repositioned his stance. Two more pitches and two more strikes, and Coach yelled, "Next."

The kid grumbled as he stomped away, thrusting the bat into the next player's hand. My confidence soared with each player who stepped up as more strikes than balls flew across the plate. A couple of the guys managed hits to the infield, but most struck out. While I waited for another batter to step to the plate, two more players rode up on bikes – bikes I recognized.

Despite the exertion from the last few minutes, my body turned ice cold. Did I really get placed on the same team as Brock? Had he known that and that was why he'd told me to not call the number on the slip of paper Granny Annie had given me?

"Hey, Zach," one of the boys yelled to the kid with Brock, "you've got competition."

Damn! This was double bad. Not only had I ended up on Brock's team, but the crackerjack pitcher was his friend?

There was a little chatter as the two boys approached the group, then someone said, "Holy crap! What happened to you two? What's all over your face and arms?"

Brock moved up into the kid's face. "Nothing, so shut up, jerk!"

"Hey!" Coach yelled. "Knock it off. We need another batter here." He turned toward me. "How you holdin' up?"

I lifted my hand to wave off any concern. "I'm good."

"Anderson, grab a bat and get over here," Coach ordered.

Brock stepped away from the group and picked up a bat on his way by. There was no mistaking the bright red raised rash

on his face and all over both arms. Inside my voice hollered, *Payback's tough, isn't it, Brock?* But on the outside I kept a steady gaze on him and didn't say a word.

He stepped up to the plate and hit the end of the bat against both cleats. Then he used the toe of one cleat to dig a little hole in the dirt before finally raising the bat over his shoulder and turning his ugly glare on me. If he connected with the pitch and it came back at me, it would probably kill me. And I wondered if that's exactly what he hoped.

At first he hit every pitch that went over the plate, although they went foul. By the tenth pitch, he swung and missed for the first time. I was sure he growled.

Coach threw the ball back to me, but Brock didn't move from home plate.

"That's three strikes," I yelled. "You're out."

"Doesn't work that way when I'm up to bat," Brock said. "I get extra pitches."

I glanced at Coach, waiting for him to intervene.

"He's connected with more of them than anyone else, so give him a few more. Let's see if he can hit it *into* the field now."

Brock looked back at Coach like he was going to mouth off but seemed to think better of it. He shifted his body in the batter's box just as I threw the next pitch. Just like in the movies, everything slipped into slow motion. The ball flew a little low over the plate, but it was in just the right position for him to come up underneath it. A loud metal thud rang out as
the bat connected with the ball. I followed the trajectory as the ball sailed way over my head and deep into the outfield before crashing with a clang against the chain link fence.

The other guys near the dugout cheered and whistled. I turned back to look at Brock. Sporting a mean, smug expression, he held the bat in his hand, extended it to arm's length and pointed it at me.

I wasn't intimidated. A baseball field was my turf, too – my comfort zone – and this was one place I knew I had a chance of putting Brock Anderson in his place.

Coach stood and turned toward the rest of the team. "Okay, everybody bring it in."

I stepped off the mound just as something caught my attention next to the dugout to my left. I pulled my cap lower over my eyes to shield more of the sun so I could see clearly. Now I couldn't help but smile. Willow stood in the dugout's shadow giving me a thumbs up. I touched the brim of my hat just like I'd seen lots of professional players do and gave a slight nod. She was wearing a cowboy hat with her hair tucked up underneath, which made her look cute. She touched the brim of her hat in return, then turned and walked away. I had no idea how long she'd been watching, but I hoped she'd seen me strike out several of the guys. After practice I'd stop by and thank her for her part in getting me on a team. At the same time I could make sure Brock wasn't following through on his threat to make her pay for my place on the team. She looked good from here, though.

The guys had made a wide circle around Coach Gordon at home plate, and I stepped next to a kid they'd called Corky. Coach introduced me and then had each of them introduce themselves to me. Most of them were cool. When the introduction line reached Brock, he planted his feet and crossed his arms on his chest so his muscles bulged. I could tell everyone was trying not to look at the rash on his face and arms, but I stared right at him. He knew I'd thrown the bikes in the bushes, and I had no problem owning it.

Brock's left eye, a bit puffy from the swelling of the rash, twitched. "He knows me."

Coach Gordon rubbed his massive hands together like he was washing them. "Well, then, that's great. Take the field. Usual positions."

The guys all moved like they couldn't get out of the circle fast enough. Zach Rogers, the "cracker jack pitcher", smacked his glove against Brock's shoulder then turned to run toward the pitcher's mound. Brock walked to the equipment bags.

"Rogers," Coach called, "come 'ere."

Zach stopped in the grassy area and looked over his shoulder with a puzzled expression. "Me?"

"Yeah, I want Westcott to take the mound again."

Zach's mouth opened like he was going to say something, then his shoulders dropped and he came back toward us. I didn't move.

"But, Coach. That's my position," Zach protested.

Coach nudged me. "Get out there, Westcott."

One side of me almost argued with Coach, but the side of me that loves baseball squashed the argument. This was Coach's decision, not mine, and I was here to do what he told me to do. Despite that, I got no pleasure out of trotting onto the field past Zach. My gut knew what he was feeling. I avoided looking at him and instead concentrated on the sliver of white mound. I swept a glance around the field at the other players who all stared at me. I probably wouldn't make any friends today.

I stepped onto the mound and looked toward home plate. I hadn't had time to give any thought to what position Brock played, and considering the way my luck had gone recently, I should have known what I'd see.

Brock was snapping on the last piece of catcher's gear. The one relationship on the field that was most important was that of pitcher and catcher. Fate was not on my side. I pictured Brock squatting behind the plate and giving me his first signal for a pitch. And that signal only used the middle finger.

Considering our short history, when he did get into position, I wasn't the least bit surprised when that's exactly what he did. It seemed to be the only language he knew.

It took most of the practice, but eventually the team got into a rhythm and it was obvious they had played together for a while and were really good. There was still almost half an hour left when our SUV rolled into the parking lot and came to a stop in the shade of a big tree. I stood at home plate with the bat poised for another pitch from Zach, but now I didn't look in his direction. Why was Mom back so early? I silently prayed that she and Erik wouldn't get out and come to sit on the metal bleachers on the other side of the fence. Who knew if Erik would stay off the field or have a meltdown because he was told he couldn't touch the equipment or play? These guys needed time to get to know me before I had to explain about Erik.

"Yo, dufus!"

I snapped my attention back to Zach. "Uh, yeah, sorry." I tried to focus on the next pitch, but I couldn't help but listen for a car door opening. The ball flew over the plate, and I swung but missed.

"St-ee-rike!" Coach called. "Nice pitch, Rogers."

That got my attention. I'd had a great practice and felt pretty confident that Coach Gordon was seeing me as a real contender for the pitching position, but if I let Zach strike me out, I'd lose some of the imaginary points I was keeping in my head. I took two practice swings and readied myself for the next pitch. Just before it came over the plate I swung, sending it straight over the second baseman's head. It was only batting practice, so I didn't have to run, but if I'd had to, I probably would have easily made it to second base, if not third. I was on a roll.

I glanced back toward the SUV. Mom didn't seem to be making a move to get out of the vehicle, so I relaxed as I took the last few swings for my time up at bat. Deep down I didn't want it to matter if my teammates saw Erik and realized he was different, but the truth was, it did matter to me. I didn't want to be judged by my little brother. And, this I could say for certain: I didn't want them to judge him, either, and I knew from experience that it would happen.

It was a relief when Coach Gordon finally called us in to the dugout. I strategically took a seat next to Corky on the opposite end of the bench from Brock and Zach.

"Great practice today, team," Coach said. "We had a lot of good stuff happenin' out there on the field, and with the battin', too." He looked at the clipboard in his hand. "Only two more practices and we have our first game next week against the Tigers. They have a lot of their players returning, so we know it's going to be tough, but maybe this is our year to finally take the championship trophy back." He nodded toward me. "And, they're not going to be expecting our new secret weapon on the pitcher's mound."

Every head in the dugout snapped in my direction. Heat shot through my body. I was psyched by the compliment, but I didn't want everyone staring at me. And they were. I looked down at my cleats where dust covered the toe area of the black material. I was dying to look up to see how Brock and Zach were taking the news that I might replace Zach as the starting pitcher, but I didn't.

Brock's deep voice broke the silence. "Coach, he hasn't been here for all the practices. It's not fair to bench Zach after one practice."

"You wanna win this season, Anderson?"

"We win with Zach on the mound," Brock challenged.

I looked up. Coach tucked the clipboard against his side, jutted out his chin and stared at Brock. "Yes, we do, but with two great pitchers, we just might win *more* this year. And, keep in mind, the reason *I* make these decisions is because *I'm* the coach, and I've been around the bend a time or two, Anderson. You start questioning me and we may find another starting catcher, too." The tension hung in the air as the two stared at each other. "Have anything else to say?"

To my surprise, Brock backed down. "No."

"Good decision." Coach turned his attention back to the rest of us. "Next practice will be Wednesday at 6:30." He held his hand out in front of him. "Okay, everyone into the huddle."

We stepped up, each of us reaching in to stack our gloved hand on top of the last until we were squeezed together and barely able to move. "Every one of you is a valuable asset to this team. And there's no 'I' in the word team. Don't forget that. Okay, on three 'Let's go, Renegades'."

Coach counted up, and when he hit three, our fifteen voices melded for the cheer. Then like we were a bunch of magnets repelling each other, the huddle disintegrated. Most of the guys wandered away from the field with a buddy, but three of the guys - Randy, Tyler and Connor - hung back.

Tyler held up his hand for a fist bump. "Impressive, dude. Glad you're on our team."

I met his fist with mine and smiled. "Thanks. Wish I'd known about this league when we first moved here so I didn't have to come in after you guys had started."

Randy and Connor followed suit with the fist bumps. "Hey, it's cool," Connor said. "Maybe you can get pizza with us before practice on Wednesday."

"Sounds good," I said.

"Five o'clock at The Nest on Main Street. You know where it is?" Tyler asked.

"Yup. Main Street's not too big." That was an understatement.

The boys stepped out of the dugout. "Okay," Connor said, "see ya Wednesday."

I raised my hand. "Yeah, see ya."

Coach smacked me on the back. "They're good kids. They'd make good friends for you. Welcome to the Renegades, Westcott."

"Thanks, Coach."

My insides had to be glowing. I had a new team. It looked like I might have a couple of friends. And there was a girl I liked. For the first time in over three weeks I felt like I belonged. I tucked my glove under my arm and rounded the corner of the dugout to leave. I'd only taken a few steps when I was stopped in my tracks. I couldn't believe what I was seeing.

"Dad?"

He was leaning on the gate, looking like he always waited for me there. I hadn't seen him since we'd moved. I'm sure my smile had to have covered my whole face. "When did you get here? How long are you staying?"

He laughed and swung the gate open so I could get through. "Whoa, buddy. One question at a time." He threw his arm across my shoulder and squeezed me against his side. "I got in a little over an hour ago, and I'm only here for a couple of days."

My excitement was dampened a little. "Did Mom know you were coming?"

He grinned. "Nope. I surprised her, too. I brought up a load of stuff from the apartment so when I come up for good at the end of the summer there's less to move."

I hated to think of another month and a half without Dad around. Our family had never been separated like this before. My thoughts flicked to Willow. I didn't have anything to complain about.

At least I knew our family's situation was temporary. Although she'd never come out and said it, I got the feeling she had no idea when, or if, she'd see the rest of her family again.

"Well, it's great to have you here, Dad, even if it's only for the weekend."

Dad steered me toward our SUV. "It's good to be here. Let's go. Mom and Erik are waiting for us at home. We're grilling bacon cheeseburgers. How does that sound?"

"Awesome!" My mouth watered. Because we had lived on the sixth floor of an apartment building in New York City, grilling wasn't an option. One of the first things Dad bought when he moved us to the new house was a big gas grill, and this was only the second time we'd used it.

We crossed the driveway to the spot where he'd parked.

"Did Mom tell you I got my stitches out last night?" I turned my head so he could see where they'd been.

"Yeah, she told me. Still pretty bruised, I see."

I shrugged. "Yeah, that will go away. At least now I can go swimming."

We reached the parking lot and the car made high-pitched beeps as Dad unlocked the doors. Even though the car didn't need to be locked in such a small town, the habit was hard to break.

"So did you meet Scout already?"

"I sure did." He went around the back of the vehicle while I slid into the passenger side. When he opened the door I continued.

"She's a smart dog. And wait until you meet Willow."

He got in and put the key in the ignition. "Is that another dog?"

I burst out laughing. I could see why he misunderstood. "She's definitely not a dog. Willow's the girl who lives on the farm down the road. We've been hanging out."

"I guess your mom did mention that on the phone. Just didn't know her name." He backed the SUV out of the parking space and headed toward Main Street.

"Some of the guys on the team just invited me to meet them for pizza on Wednesday." I craned my neck as we passed a row of attached old brick buildings that housed a small grocery
store, the post office, an antique store, a hardware store and The Nest, the restaurant they had mentioned. A sign with a blue egg in a nest hung above the door. "There it is."

It didn't look fancy, but I figured in a small town the people would be happy to have any restaurant. I looked above the businesses and guessed there were apartments on the upper floors since the buildings were mostly three stories high; tall buildings for here. They were nothing compared to what I'd grown up around. Across the street from the buildings was a rectangular park with a gazebo and massive trees that shaded every inch of it. I turned back toward Dad. "Not like Manhattan here, is it?"

"Nope, buddy, it's not, but I'm looking forward to the change."

For the first time in my life, I noticed Dad's city accent. He'd also grown up in Brooklyn, and he and Mom met when she spent a week at a Connecticut beach with one of her college roommates and Dad was best friends with her roommate's boyfriend. My upstate cousins told me I had an accent, too, but it wasn't as strong as Dad's. Until today, I'd never heard it.

"Maybe I'll like it here better when school starts. I miss my friends." We were already driving out of town since it took about two minutes to get from one end of Main Street to the other end on the outskirts.

Dad glanced at me. "I would expect you'd miss your friends. But the more you get involved in here, the faster you'll settle in."

"Do you think we're really here for good?" Somewhere deep inside I held out hope that my parents would realize this was a really bad decision and we shouldn't permanently move after all.

Dad nodded. "Done deal. Our apartment has already been leased to someone else starting in September." He reached across to my seat and put his hand on my shoulder. "We know it's toughest on you, Dylan, but we almost lost Erik last winter." He squeezed my shoulder as his voice trailed off, and at the end, I thought I heard pain. Neither of us needed the reminder, and he knew it.

"So, how about those Yankees?" Dad changed the subject so fast that I didn't even have a chance to feel sorry for myself that this move was permanent. "Uncle Rick had tickets for last week's home game, so I got to go," he said.

"The one against the Red Sox?"

"Yep." He smiled and drummed his fingers on the steering wheel. "Yankee Stadium was rockin'."

"I saw it. The Yankees crushed 'em." My body sang with the familiarity of this scenario. I loved it when Dad and I talked baseball. I pushed the button to roll down the window and laid my arm along the opening. The warm breeze pushed my baseball cap against the headrest. I grabbed it before it got sucked out the window and shoved it under my leg. My Monday couldn't get any better.

We were deep into the statistics of the Yankees' season when we pulled into our driveway. I stopped talking when I saw a black and white horse tied to a small tree near our shed. It was munching the grass near the base of the trunk and Mom was squatting and looking at one of its front legs.

"Whose horse is that?" Dad asked. He stopped the SUV in front of the garage.

I reached for the door handle before he'd cut the engine. "I've never seen it before. Do you think Mom brought it home?"

He chuckled as he got out of the car. "I doubt your mother brought a horse home."

I was careful to not slam the door because I didn't want to scare it. Dad made a big arc around it as we approached. The horse lifted its head to check us out. Blades of grass bounced against its lips as it chewed. Mom ran her hands along the horse's front leg near, what I assumed was, its knee.

"Where'd the horse come from?" I asked.

Mom straightened and patted the animal's neck. "Willow rode him over. He has an abrasion on his leg, so I told her I'd take care of it while she plays with Erik and Scout. We were doing some hide and seek exercises when she came over."

"Is it her horse?"

Mom tipped her head like that was a surprising question. "You know, I didn't ask. I just assumed."

"She didn't show me a horse the other day," I said, "and I thought I saw all of her animals."

I took a step closer to look at some scars on the horse's backside. "Is that a brand or something?" I asked. I was tempted to run my hand along the raised spots to see if they made a pattern or someone's initials like the brands on horses in the old western movies, but I didn't know if that would make a horse kick.

"No, it's not a brand," Mom said. She did step up next to the horse and she ran her hand across the bumps. "Willow said those scars were on the horse from its previous owner." She leaned in closer and lifted the horse's hair to examine some of the spots. "It looks like he's been poked with something sharp or he got into something with a bunch of nails, maybe. The wounds look mostly healed."

I turned toward the back yard to see where she and Erik were. "Are they out back?"

"Yes."

Dad walked over to Mom and wrapped his arms around her before planting a kiss on her forehead. "I missed you," he said.

"I missed you, too." Mom stretched on her toes and kissed him on the lips. Really? He'd probably only been gone half an hour. I decided it was the perfect time for me to find Willow, Erik and Scout.

"I'll see you later," I said, but I honestly didn't think they even heard me. They were still hugging when I opened the gate to go into the fenced-in back yard. I found Willow, Erik and Scout by the wooden swingset that had been left by the previous owner. Erik was trying to swing and Willow was encouraging him to kick harder.

Although Erik and the swing kept getting in the way of my view of Willow, I could tell something was different about her appearance. She wore the same cowboy hat she'd been wearing at the ball field and it looked like her hair was still tucked up inside because it wasn't hanging down her back, not even in the long, shiny braid she sometimes wore. Scout lay just a few feet away in the shade of a bush, but her attention was glued to Erik.

"Hey," I said as I approached.

"Higher!" Erik begged. Willow gave him a strong push to help him swing higher. He squealed and scissor-kicked his legs.

"Hi," she responded, and then her attention was on Erik again. "If you want to pump and go higher, you need to keep your legs together and move them together," she said. "Here. Watch me and do what I do." She sat in the swing next to him and pushed off. The dark bruises on her arms and legs caught my attention again. "Just like this, Erik," she instructed.

Within seconds her legs and body moved rhythmically as she pushed her swing higher. At one point the hat started to fly off and she hooked her elbow around the chain and threw her hand up to trap the hat on her head. Erik watched, then, because of her coaching, started to catch on and he was going higher on his own.

"See, you can do it!" Her smile was wide and her eyes danced with delight. She let go of the hat and pushed higher on her swing. This time the breeze from it knocked her hat onto the ground and it tumbled toward me.

"I've got that," I said. I snatched it and walked closer to the swings.

A jolt buzzed through me when I looked up. Her long hair hadn't been tucked up under the hat after all. It was chopped short and very unevenly. I didn't want to offend her if she'd purposely had it styled that way, but it was by far the worst haircut I'd ever seen.

"I didn't know you were getting a haircut," I said. I set the hat at the top of the metal slide.

"Neither did I," she responded. Her toes kicked out straight into the air.

"I'm not following you," I said. "You didn't know you were getting a haircut?" I stepped more behind her to get a better look. I'd never say it out loud, because she or her grandmother probably paid good money for it, but it was a hack job. "Whose idea was it?" I asked.

"Brock's."

His name hung in the air for a few moments because I sure didn't know what to say.

"He cut it off when I was sleeping. It'll grow back."

"What? That's crazy!" I couldn't hide my incredulousness. "Didn't you wake up when he was doing it?"

She scowled. "Of course I did."

"Then why didn't you stop him?""He was holding scissors." If she had said *duh*! at the end of that comment it would have matched her expression.

"Why didn't you yell for your grandmother?"

Willow didn't even look back at me but continued as if this were a normal conversation. "He was holding scissors," she repeated.

Anger burned in my chest.

"Why'd he do something like that?"

"To get back at me."

Her matter-of-factness annoyed me. She'd had gorgeous, silky hair that hung to the middle of her back. Now it was a ratty mess. "What did you do? Why was he getting back at you?"

"He found out last night that I had asked Granny Annie to help get you on a baseball team and that you ended up on his team." She looked toward Erik who was again struggling to keep his swing going. Despite my shock, I had enough awareness to step around her to Erik and give his swing a little push. He laughed and his body shuddered once as he went higher.

"I don't get it. That was worth chopping your hair off?"

She dropped one foot to the ground and dragged it to slow herself. "I'm sure the whole poison ivy thing didn't help either. End of story."

"But *I* threw the bikes in the bushes. You didn't. So why didn't he come after me?"

"He did. He knew you'd be mad if something happened to me."

"But he hacked your hair off." My blood pounded in my ears. At that moment I hated Brock.

"That's how my brother thinks. After he cut my hair he said, 'Bet that jerk from the city won't want to look at you now.' That's when I knew this time it wasn't really about me." Whether she realized what she was doing or not, she reached up and touched her hair in the back.

It didn't matter to me that her hair looked horrible. She was beautiful, regardless. What did matter was that apparently Brock bullied his way through everything and Willow was taking a hit for me.

"I'll quit the team. It doesn't matter that much to me." That was a lie, but if it would help Willow, I'd do it.

"No! You're not quitting the team. You love baseball. You should play."

I couldn't decide if she was being unselfish or a martyr. "Not if Brock is going to take it out on you. What'll he do if I end up taking the lead pitching spot over his buddy, Zach?"

"It's done. Over. What more could he do? Shave my head? I doubt he'd do that."

"He shouldn't be touching you. Why doesn't your grandmother do something?"

"All brothers and sisters do stuff like this to each other. She says he'll grow out of it."

"What? He's almost fifteen. He should have grown out of it a long time ago." Now my hands were shaking so I shoved them in my pocket to hide it. "Why don't *you* do something about it?"

She stopped the swing completely, got out of it and stepped toward me. "I try, okay." Her voice was quiet and even. "I annoy him. This is what happens. So, I avoid being anywhere near Brock as much as possible, but I can't avoid him 24/7. We do live in the same house. "

The tension was so great in my body that it felt like little electrical currents were shooting to my extremities. Willow wasn't playing the victim. She actually believed that it was her fault he was bullying her.

"Let me help you." I tried to keep the same, calm tone that she was using, but it took all of my willpower.

"What are you going to do?"

"I'll tell my parents. They'll know what to do."

Willow grasped my arms and moved close to me. "No. I trusted you, Dylan. I wouldn't have told you the truth if I thought you were going to tell somebody."

Scout must have sensed a problem because she got up from under the bush and came to stand next to us. Even though I was looking at Willow, I could tell Scout was looking at me.

"But you don't deserve what he's doing to you," I said. "Look at your arms. Your legs. You have bruises everywhere."

"They'll go away." Her hands slid down to my hands and she held them tight. "Promise me you won't say anything to anyone. I don't want the social workers to come back."

I was curious about why they'd been there before, but it was none of my business. "Maybe I don't need to say anything. Maybe my mom has noticed the bruises, too."

Willow pulled her hands from mine and stepped back. "She did. And I told her I'm a tomboy so I do a lot of rough things."

I stared into Willow's eyes. "I'll tell her you're lying."

Willow held my stare and sucked in her lower lip, then said quietly, "And if you do, then you'll never see me again, Dylan. It will be the end of our friendship, because I'll know I can't trust you, either."

I took a step back to give some distance between us and those words. I couldn't believe the threat. Our friendship had barely begun, but I was already falling for her. Hard. I didn't want to lose the only friend I had made here.

I didn't want to lose *her*.

I pushed my fingers into my hair and held them there, shaking my head. I was boxed in, wishing that I didn't care.

Next to us, Erik continued to pump his legs and now was humming a monotonous tone, oblivious to the fact that Willow was ripping my guts out. Scout sat, but her attention was still riveted on me.

I pulled my hands from my hair and laid a palm

against Willow's cheek. She was warm. And soft. All I wanted to do was protect her.

She moved her hand to cover mine. "Promise me, Dylan," she pleaded.

I didn't want to make the promise, but I didn't want to lose her, either. I reached out and pulled her to me, holding her head against my shoulder. I ran my hand up along the back of her neck, through her thick, unevenly chopped hair, picturing Brock taking out his anger about me on her. Anger boiled inside me.

In that moment, I realized what I had to do. I was sick of bullies. It was time for Brock to meet his match.

CHAPTER NINE

Most of the booths were filled at The Nest when I walked in. It took half a minute for my eyes to adjust, but when they did, I saw Tyler holding his hand up from a booth in the back. I recognized Paul, our second baseman, sitting with his parents and I assumed a younger sister at another booth I passed.

"Hey," I said to him. "How's it goin'?"

Paul's mouth was full of cheeseburger, but he lifted his chin and managed a muddled greeting. "Hi." His parents looked at me curiously and, as soon as I was by them, I heard him mumble who I was.

I straightened my shoulders as I passed the last three booths. I wasn't a "nobody" in the town anymore. It was a step in the right direction for the summer getting better. When I got to the booth where Tyler sat, I saw Randy and Connor sitting facing him.

"What's up, man?" Tyler asked as I slid onto the green plastic seat next to him.

"Not much." I nodded at the other two guys. "Hey. Sorry if I'm late."

"You're not late," Connor said. "We all rode together. My dad had to drop us off early."

Randy pointed toward a blackboard menu on the wall. "There're all the choices if you want something different, but we always get a large cheese pizza."

"Works for me," I said. This wasn't the time to be different.

A waitress, who looked college aged, walked by balancing a tray of dirty dishes on her shoulder.

"Hey, Deanna?" Tyler called.

She stopped just past our booth and took a step back. "Yeah."

"Can we order a large cheese pizza and a pitcher of cola? We have baseball practice in an hour, so we're kind of in a hurry."

"Sure thing, hot stuff," she responded, winking at him before she hurried through a swinging door into the kitchen. I couldn't figure out how she kept the tray from crashing to the floor.

I turned to Tyler. "Hot stuff?"

He smiled and shrugged. "She's my brother's girlfriend. What can I say? She calls it as she sees it."

"Obviously she needs to go to the eye doctor," Randy joked.

We laughed together. Man, did that feel good.

Tyler jabbed me in the side with his elbow. "Somebody who *is* hot is Willow. Are you two going out?"

In my peripheral vision I saw Randy and Connor lean forward like a couple of girls ready for the gossip.

"No. We're just friends."

"Dude," Connor said. "Are you nuts? She's Brock's sister."

I looked across the table at him. "Yeah. So?"

"And, Zach Rogers wants to ask her out."

I shifted on the seat and the plastic squeaked. "Not my problem."

Randy chimed in. "Brock's already pissed that Coach had you pitch instead of Zach, even if you are better than him."

"Yeah, so?"

Deanna came with the pitcher of cola and four glasses with ice, interrupting our conversation.

"Here you go." She set the glasses in front of us then left.

Tyler picked up the pitcher and poured our drinks.

Randy looked around the side of the booth like he was concerned about who could hear. "Dude, we're just tellin' ya. Pick one or the other."

I took a straw and tapped it on the table to remove the paper. "Pick one or the other of what?"

"Either Willow or the pitching spot."

I dropped the straw into the glass and leaned back in the booth to stare at him. "No. I'm not picking one or the other. If Coach thinks I'm good enough to pitch, then I'm pitching. And I like Willow, and if I want to ask her out, I will. This isn't about Brock."

Tyler picked up his glass and swirled the contents. "To Brock it is."

Randy moved his glass in a circle on the table, staring at the wet pattern it created. Connor stared at the tabletop as if it were the most interesting thing he'd ever seen. These guys actually looked nervous.

"What's going on?" I asked.

"Just watchin' your back, man," Tyler said.

"What's Brock's deal? Why is everybody afraid of him?" I sounded brave, but my mind flashed to when we met. The area above my eye where the stitches had just been removed was still bruised.

"He's been to juvee," Connor said, his voice barely above a whisper.

I took a sip of the soda. "Big deal. I know lots of kids who have been in and out of juvenile detention."

Connor lowered his voice. "That's the city, Dylan. Maybe there it's not a big deal, but it's different here."

Okay, I got that. I'd come from a different world. "So, what was he in for?"

They looked at each other, then all three shrugged like a scene out of a Three Stooges movie.

"He's always had anger issues," Randy explained. "His father is an army guy. Did you know that?"

"I heard something about it." I tapped my straw against the bottom of the plastic glass while looking at all three of my new friends. "What does that have to do with anything?"

Tyler took over the storytelling. "When we were in sixth grade, his dad came home on leave after being overseas and Brock was happy. But when his dad left again, Brock went nuts. He took a baseball bat downtown and smashed out the windows of any car parked along Main Street."

I pictured Brock swinging the bat at the peacock. If he'd connected with it that day, he could have beat it to smithereens, especially if he was able to smash out car windows.

Randy continued, "He smashed store windows, too. Nobody knows why he went psycho that time. His dad had come home and left before. Anyway, after that, they sent him to some place in Pennsylvania."

It was like tag team storytelling, because then Tyler added, "When he came back, he was different. He was kind of normal again, but when something doesn't go his way, watch out. It's almost like he learned how to be sneaky there. We know he's done things, but we can never prove it."

"Yeah, like when the boys' locker room showers were flooded," Randy said. All three of them nodded. "Drives the teachers crazy."

At that moment, Deanna showed up with the pizza on one of those metal pedestal-type servers. "Here you go, guys." She set it on the table between us then handed us each a plate, silverware and a stack of napkins. Tomato and cheese steam swirled above the pizza. "Can I get you anything else?"

We all shook our heads, and I guessed their mouths were watering like mine. I swallowed the saliva that surrounded my tongue, and my stomach growled at the same time. The story about Brock hadn't taken away my appetite.

Randy reached for a slice of pizza and slid it onto his plate.

"I'm tellin' ya, Dylan, we need you as pitcher. Forget about her. Willow's not worth it."

Connor and Tyler reached for pizza as well, the warning about Brock suddenly less important than food.

I stared at them and decided to silently disagree. There were things I now knew about Willow and Brock that they probably never would. I'd give up baseball before I'd give up on her.

But I had no intention of giving up either. I was ready to take on Brock.

"Don't make any sound or move," I instructed Erik as we lay on our stomachs under the thick bushes at the edge of the field behind our house. I tried to concentrate on this search and find lesson with Scout and the instructions Charlotte had given us, but my mind kept wandering to the conversation with the guys at the restaurant the night before. They considered their message a warning. I saw it as a challenge.

"Status," Charlotte said over the two-way radio.

She, Mom and Jamie were supposedly distracting Scout in the house while we found a good hiding spot outside in the wooded area.

I pressed the button on my two-way radio to respond. "We're set here." The radios made me feel like we were playing army or cops and robbers or something.

I pictured Mom holding one of Erik's favorite t-shirts in front of Scout so the dog could focus on his scent. This was the third day of what I called "hide and seek" training, and Scout's performance was impressive.

Charlotte's voice crackled over the two-way radio. "Give us a couple of minutes. We want to try and disorient her so she has to work for this. Are you two okay?"

"Yeah, I think we're good," I responded. However, I couldn't decide if encouraging Erik to hide was a good or bad thing. He was already an expert, but there was no other way to train Scout to search for and find him.

"And you do have the can of Cheez Whiz with you?" Charlotte added.

Since I felt like an army guy right now, I decided to answer like one. "Roger that."

Erik used his elbows to crawl into the open. "Where'th Thcout?"

Man, this kid was fast. I snagged the end of his t-shirt and pulled him back under the bush, careful not to touch his skin. "Mom's going to let her go in just a minute so she can find us."

"Are we ready to whiz?"

Laughter exploded inside me, but I managed to contain it to a loud snort. If I'd been drinking something, there would have been an explosion out my nose and mouth.

"We're not whizzing, Erik. That's something totally different. We're giving Scout Cheez Whiz if she finds us." I pulled the can from my back pocket. "Right here." Suddenly I had an idea. "Hey, Oops, maybe this time you can have the Cheez Whiz in *your* hand. Whaddya think?"

His eyes widened and he shoved his palms under his body. No words were necessary. The Cheez Whiz was going in my hand - again. That was okay. I actually enjoyed these times when Erik seemed like every other six year old in the world, and I was sure most of them would have reacted the same way. I wished he was like that all the time.

I'd barely had time to contemplate how different our lives would be right now if that were the case when my cell phone vibrated in my pocket. I rolled my hip off the ground to reach it. I hoped it was Willow. Because the minutes on her cell phone were so limited, I always waited for her to call me, and I'd been waiting a couple of days again. Although I'd done things to distract myself, I caught myself looking down toward her farm or glancing at my phone more often than I wanted to admit. She was definitely under my skin.

I pressed the send button and propped up on my elbows. "Hey! It's about time," I said just above a whisper.

"Hi, O'Dylan. What's up?"

Sweat popped out on my palms. I kept my voice quiet in case Scout was on her way. We had a great hiding spot today, so it would be more challenging for her to find us. I didn't want to take the chance of her hearing my voice, so I continued to whisper.

"Not much. I've been wondering what's up with you. Haven't seen or heard from you in a couple of days."

"What's wrong with your voice?" she asked. "You sound weird."

"We're in the middle of a hide and seek training session with Scout. Erik and I are hiding under a bush."

"Aww, I miss Scout. I hope I can come over for some more training sessions."

"That would be cool." Just as I'd suspected the first time we met Scout, the dog kept drawing Willow back to our house.

"And Erik, too." She sighed. "He is the coolest little kid."

I glanced at Erik then away again so he couldn't hear me. "Wait, are you talking about my little brother?"

"Yeah. He's awesome. You never have to guess what he's thinking because he's so honest."

I stifled a snort. "Like the time he told my friend's pregnant mother that she was getting fat?"

Willow burst out laughing. "Well, okay, maybe it's not always a good thing, but it's better than dealing with my brother. At least you can trust Erik. I bet if Erik took something of yours and you asked if he took it, he'd run and get it and hand it to you."

"Yeah, you're right. He's always honest."

"When Brock takes something of mine, even if I know for a fact that he took it, he lies to my grandmother and me and then destroys it just to make sure he's not caught."

"He's done that?"

"Yep. Many times."

We were both quiet for a minute. I tried to comprehend living like that.

Finally I said, "You win. I'll take my brother over yours."

"Yeah, I thought maybe you'd see it that way." I could tell she was smiling by the sound of her voice.

The two-way radio squealed before I heard Charlotte. "One more minute then we're letting her loose."

Erik turned and looked at the radio. I started to answer, then changed my mind and held it out toward him. "Hey, Erik, do you want to tell Charlotte 'okay'?"

His eyes lit up, and he moved his face close to the speaker. I pressed the button, but he only stared at the radio. "Tell her okay," I whispered.

"Okay," he whispered. I wasn't surprised that he'd whispered just like me.

"No, say 'okay' louder so Charlotte can hear you."

"Okay," he said. The smile that followed was so bright it could put the sun to shame. Maybe Willow was right. Maybe Erik wasn't so bad.

Willow must have heard our exchange with Charlotte. "Want me to call back?" she asked.

"No, but I can only talk for another minute." I decided to get back to my original question. "Why haven't you been around?" I needed to know if she was avoiding me because we'd kind of had a fight or if she was embarrassed by what Brock had done to her.

"It's only been a couple of days."

"Three."

I realized I probably sounded like a girl by admitting that I'd been counting the days. "Is it bad that I like being with you?" There. My feelings were out in the open.

"No, but your dad was here. Your family needed to spend time together. Did he go back to the city yet?"

"Yeah, two nights ago." It had been hard to watch him pull out of the driveway and out of sight down the road. Mom had cried, which made me want to, but I held it together. Soon Dad and Trent would be here. Then our family would almost be back to one piece. "He's sending a moving truck with most of the rest of our stuff. It's coming sometime this week."

"Guess that means you're here to stay, huh?"

"I guess."

"You could sound a little happier about it, O'Dylan. I mean, *I'm* here. Doesn't that count for something?"

I rolled away from Erik to make it feel like this was a more private conversation and stared off into the woods. "Yeah. You're the one good thing that's happened since I moved here, Willow."

"What about getting on the baseball team?"

I laughed. "That's pretty cool, too, but it would have been nice to not end up on Brock's team."

Willow sighed and it was loud on my end of the phone. "Yeah, sorry 'bout that. Granny Annie thought it would be a good way for you and Brock to become friends since you're new here. I messed up again."

"What?" I was louder than I meant to be, and Erik hit me. I twisted to look at him.

"Quiet," he scolded in a whisper, holding his finger up to his lips. Another rare moment of normalcy.

I cupped my hand over my mouth and the bottom of the phone and whispered again. "Everything isn't your fault." I didn't like the pattern I was starting to notice. Willow had told me it was her fault Brock picked on her because she annoyed him. Now she was taking responsibility for a decision her grandmother made. "No. Your grandma thought she was doing something nice for me. She can't help it if she's clueless." I didn't like the way that sounded as soon as it was out of my mouth, but there it hung.

Willow didn't respond. I had to learn to keep my opinions to myself or I'd never see Willow again. "I'm sorry," I said. "I didn't mean to disrespect your grandmother." I almost added *again* as I recalled my rant three days earlier about her grandmother not intervening with Brock's bullying.

The two-way radio squeaked, then Charlotte's voice came over. "We're releasing Scout."

"Okay," I whispered over the radio as if I were still talking on the phone. "We're ready," I added in a more normal voice.

"Hey, gotta go," I whispered into the phone. "Maybe we can get together later."

"That's why I'm calling," Willow said. "The County Fair opens today. Do you want to meet me there?"

"Sure," I answered, not even knowing where it was or if I had a way to get there. "Where do you want to meet and when?"

"Four o'clock in the 4-H horse barn."

"How will I find it?"

"It's not a big fair. Come in the main gate and go to your left. You'll see the barns."

"Okay. County Fair. Horse barn. Four o'clock. Got it." My brain whirled and I smiled. This sounded like a date.

"Call me on my cell if for some reason you can't be there, okay? I'm at my friend's house, so I won't be home."

"I'll be there." Nothing would keep me from this chance with Willow.

"Okay, see ya. Have fun with the hide and seek training," she said.

"Four o'clock," I repeated. "See ya." I hit the end button. A real date with Willow. I looked at the time. I only had to wait three hours.

The timing of the end of the call was perfect. Through the leaves of the bush I saw Scout sniffing near a tree where Erik and I had first stopped to hide, but then I'd changed my mind and decided to go for the bush.

I flattened my chest against the ground and leaned toward Erik's ear to whisper. "Don't move. Scout's nearby." I rested my chin on my hands just as Erik was doing and watched the dog make her way toward us, her nose to the ground. She zigzagged, making me wonder if Erik had walked like that when we came out here. The closer she got, the straighter her path got. She sniffed loud and fast. Even with her head down, her eyes were alert, looking in a wide arc without moving her head.

The dog was less than twenty feet from us. I held my breath. I didn't want to give her any clues to our location. When she was within ten feet, she stopped. Her head shot up, her ears raised and her nose wriggled in the air. A few seconds later she crawled under the bush. When she got to Erik, she pushed her nose against his shoulder then stretched next to him, pressing her body into him. He threw his arm around her and hugged her, his fingers lost in her golden fur.

I keyed the button on the radio. "Score another one for Scout!"

In the distance I heard my mom's loud, "Woo hoo!"

Charlotte's voice came through the speaker. "Come on back. We're done for today."

The Cheez Whiz can sat just inches from us. At first I considered not even using any. Scout seemed happy that she'd found Erik without it. Why bother to get my hand all goopy and slobbery? Then, like she'd read my mind, she lifted her head and tipped it. Her lower jaw dropped open and her tongue jockeyed back and forth across her teeth as she panted. To me, it looked like a smile. Her eyebrows kept lifting like she was saying, *Well, where's my reward?*

Despite the drops of saliva dripping off the end of her tongue, there was no resisting her. I lifted the can and pressed the plastic tip until a tiny orange mountain sat in my palm. I extended it to her.

"Good girl, Scout."

She licked gently, her coarse tongue tickling my skin as she worked at getting every drop. I never imagined a dog could make such a difference in our lives, and my admiration for her grew daily. When she finished, I wiped my hands on my jean shorts to get at least some of her spit off me.

"Let's go back, Oops." Still on my stomach, I backed myself out from under the bushes. The broken pieces of sticks on the ground dug into my legs. Getting under the bush had definitely been less painful.

Erik worked his way out like a worm. Although the sticks were jabbing at his skin, too, he didn't protest at all as if he didn't even feel them. When we were both out, I quickly brushed off as much of the debris and dirt from his legs as I could so he wouldn't freak. He didn't even notice. His focus was on Scout, who had crawled out with him.

"Thcout ith a good dog," he said. Since she'd moved in with us, Erik used that phrase several times a day. He knelt and wrapped his arms tight around her neck. To me it looked too tight, but she stood like a statue and took it.

"Let's go back to the house. Tell her to heel, Erik."

He let go of her and started to walk, but he didn't have to say a word. Scout walked next to him at his pace. A few times he sped up, apparently testing her. Halfway across the field he laid his hand on her shoulder and they walked the rest of the way like that.

Mom, Charlotte and Jamie waited for us at the picnic table. As we approached, they started clapping. Scout's tail wagged like she knew the applause was for her.

"We weren't making a noise, and she found us no problem," I called as we approached.

Erik and Scout stopped in front of the picnic table. Scout sat with her shoulder pressed against Erik's thigh.

Charlotte nodded and looked at Mom, whose smile couldn't have been any bigger. "Julie, your family and Scout are going to pass this training with flying colors. I'd say we've made a perfect match."

In my mind I pictured Willow, and couldn't help but wonder if actually two perfect matches had been made since we moved here.

After lunch I was in my bedroom in the middle of checking my favorite baseball stats website on my computer when Erik's panicked voice shattered the silence.

"No! No! No!" His footsteps fell hard as he clomped up the stairs and ran to his room. I could hear drawers and doors slamming as he yelled repeatedly, "Where ith it? Where ith it? Where ith it?"

"Erik," Mom called from downstairs. "Is it there?"

As much as I wanted to stay uninvolved, curiosity got the best of me. I stepped into the hallway just as Mom reached the top stair. "What's he looking for?"

"His treasure tin. Charlotte gave him a special dog tag she had made with Scout's and his name on it, and he wants to put it in his tin."

"Nope, I haven't seen —" I stopped mid-sentence. "Oh, no! I might have an idea where it is, but I hope I'm wrong."

I hurried down the hall to Erik's room where he was pulling everything out of his dresser drawers. Piles of clothes were strewn all over, reminding me of my messy room. Even the earless stuffed cat had been flung. Scout stood just behind him, a red t-shirt flung across her back. She nuzzled his side with her nose, but he kept yanking out clothes.

"Erik, stop," I said. He didn't stop. He was focused on searching every corner of every drawer. "Erik, did you bring your treasure tin back from the pond the other day? Remember you took it with you?"

His head snapped up and he looked wide-eyed. "Dock."

"Did you leave it on the dock?" I asked.

He nodded. "Under the dock."

Mom stepped into the room. "Are you sure, Erik?" He stared at her.

"I remember him carrying it when we met Willow at the end of her driveway because he was looking for treasures along the side of the road," I said. "I don't remember seeing it at the pond."

Erik jumped up and down. "Yeth! Yeth! Yeth!"

"Yes, it's at the pond?" I asked again.

"Yeth! Yeth! Yeth!" His cheeks were getting red, and I wasn't sure if it was excitement or if he was headed for a meltdown.

I pulled my phone out of my pocket. Two o'clock. I could get to the pond and back in less than half an hour if I rode my bike. That would still give me an hour and a half before I had to be at the fairgrounds. I hadn't asked Mom yet, but the timing of this actually couldn't have been more perfect. If I found the tin and saved the day, how could she refuse my request to meet up with Willow?

"I'll go out and see if I can find it," I said.

Erik darted for the door ahead of me. "Me, too! Me, too! Me, too!"

"No, I'm going to take my bike, Erik. That way you'll get your treasure tin even faster."

Mom stepped in and guided him back into the room. "You and I will stay here and take care of these clothes you took out of your dresser. Dylan will be right back." She took the t-shirt off Scout's back and proceeded to fold it and put it back in an open drawer.

Erik looked between us like he was trying to decide whether this was a good plan or not. While he considered it, I hurried out the door. "Be right back."

I stopped at the bottom of the stairs to slip into my sneakers, then I was out the door and into the garage to get my bike before Erik could protest. I had to make this fast. I snapped on my helmet, a left over habit from city bike riding. When I got my license, bike riding would be history.

The clouds kept the temperature more bearable as I raced down the road. Someday I'd probably learn other routes to get to the pond, but for today I had only one choice – to take the path past Willow's house. Since she'd mentioned being at a friend's, I wasn't going to look toward the house, but I couldn't resist when I heard some sort of loud, repetitive thud coming from that direction. I wished I had resisted. Brock was
 swinging an ax against the trunk of a tree along the driveway. While he didn't offer his typical friendly gesture this time, he did stop swinging the ax to stare at me as I passed. I turned my attention back to the road. At least now I knew where he was.

Not far down the road, I jumped the ditch with my bike and pedaled along the weedy path. Unlike the cement sidewalks I was used to riding on, the path was rutted and caused my bike to twist and bounce, making it hard to control. I pushed forward, praying Erik's tin really was under the dock. Back at the house, in my quest to be a hero and secure my chance to go to the fair, I hadn't considered that maybe he was wrong about leaving it there.

I followed the winding path into the woods, thankful I could avoid going up the hill toward the ravine. Maybe Willow found that part of the woods fascinating, but to me, it was the setting for a horror movie. I didn't care if I never saw it again.

The only spot that gave my memory trouble was where the path split. I was pretty sure we'd gone to the left, so that was the way I went. Because I was focused on the trail, I didn't notice a deer until it crossed in front of me. I jerked my handlebars to the right and nearly collided with a tree. The deer bounded up the trail ahead of me then veered into a denser part of the woods. I could no longer see it, but I could hear the snapping of twigs and rustling of leaves that grew fainter as the deer went deeper into the forest.

A minute later I came into the clearing at the pond. The sun poked through the clouds in a narrow beam that lit up the end of the dock. I almost laughed at the coincidence. It wasn't a rainbow, but it would be pretty ironic if Erik's treasure tin was under the dock in that exact spot.

I skidded to a halt when I saw a figure sitting at the end of the dock with a fishing pole hanging out over the water. If I hadn't seen Brock at his house ten minutes earlier, I would have believed it was his wide back I was looking at. But, it wasn't possible. Was it?

Laying my bike in the grass, I approached cautiously. Normally I would have been relieved to not be in the woods alone, but for some reason this creeped me out.

"Hey," I called.

The guy at the end of the dock slowly turned toward me, and my heart hurtled into my throat. How could Brock be in two places at once? My first thought was to get on the bike and head back out, but the image of Willow's chopped hair and bruised arms and legs pushed that thought out of my head. I was tired of Brock being in control.

"Saw you go by the house," Brock said. "Thought you might want to get in a little fishing with me."

"I don't fish."

He shrugged. "Too bad. My friends like to fish with me."

I resisted the urge to tell him he wasn't my friend, and opted to ignore the comment instead.

"How did you get out here so fast? You were hacking at a tree when I went by."

He set his pole down on the dock and stood. "Nobody knows these woods better than I do. There's a shortcut."

"And you just *had* to go fishing now?"

He walked up the wooden dock toward shore. The dock swayed with each step. The red splotches of poison ivy on his face made him look even meaner. "Told you," he said. "Thought maybe you'd like to try fishing. My grandma thinks we should be friends."

I made a big show of looking toward the ground and all around me. "Oh, wait, did I miss that?"

"Miss what?"

When I looked back up, I almost laughed to see him staring at the ground. "Did Hell freeze over?"

"You're a barrel of laughs, Westcott." He stopped a few yards from the end of the dock and spread his feet in a wide stance. His posture had challenge written all over it.

I squared up as well. "Look, I came to get something that my brother left here. I'll get that and leave you to fish in peace."

"Maybe it's in the bush with the poison ivy."

I glanced toward the bushes. How would he know about Erik's tin? Then I realized he was bluffing.

I looked him straight in the eye. "I didn't come here to start trouble."

"I think trouble's your middle name." He took a few steps closer. "If you quit the baseball team, things might go better for you."

I didn't flinch. Just how far did I want to take this? "Things are going just fine for me. Thanks for your concern, though. I'm sticking with the team. It's not my fault if I'm a better pitcher than your side kick."

His swollen eye twitched. "No one messes with my friends."

His threat wasn't lost on me. But instead of scaring me, anger heated my gut. "No one messes with my friends, either, and your sister is my friend."

"She's a bitch, and she deserves everything she gets," Brock spat.

The anger in my gut exploded, blinding me with fury. Unable to see clearly, I lunged in Brock's direction, my hands aiming for his throat.

My sudden movement surprised him, and he lost his balance as he stumbled backward. His arms flailed and he was unable to catch himself before his back slammed against the wooden slats. The loud crack of one of them splintering echoed off the pond's surface. He was fast and took advantage of the swaying dock that was causing me to be unsteady. In one swift sideways kick, he wiped my feet out from underneath me, sending me sailing backwards into the water.

I threw my arms behind me to brace for the impact. When I hit, my body sank a couple of feet, then hit bottom because we were so close to shore. I struggled to get my feet under me and get up out of the water, but I had barely gotten my head above the surface when Brock rolled off the edge and on top of me. I pushed against him, trying to get distance between us, but he had landed face down on me and was able to get to his feet faster.

His teeth were bared and he growled as he grabbed my arms at my biceps. I managed a big gulp of air before he thrust me back, forcing my head under water. My mind buzzed with adrenaline. Was he so crazy that he'd actually hold me under water until I drowned? How long would it be before someone found me way out here?

Too late, was the immediate answer in my mind. I concentrated on my legs and the position of his body. Body awareness. I'd learned it in Taekwondo. It was time to use something else I'd learned in that class, too.

My red belt training kicked into gear. I focused all of my effort on propelling my right leg and foot up. Fortunately the pond wasn't deep here, and after the initial drag of the water, I managed the momentum I needed.

My foot burst out of the water and landed squarely in Brock's crotch.

He howled and flopped back in the water.

I thrashed around until I got my feet under me and stood up. With water pouring off my t-shirt and shorts, I labored to catch my breath as I stared at him writhing like a beached whale with water lapping around his shoulders. His eyes were squeezed shut and his hands cupped the target I'd perfectly hit. He groaned, unable to make an intelligible sound. He was just far enough from shore that, in his struggles, his head dropped below the surface of the water until he managed to thrust himself up to gasp for air.

I made a wide arc around him so I could get to shore. He struggled for a minute, but worried that he'd tire and not have the strength to keep his head out of the water, I stepped back in and grabbed his shirt collar, pulling him closer to shore. Most of his body was still in the water, but his head was propped on the muddy bank.

Confident that at least he wouldn't drown, I lumbered to my bike, the adrenaline rush over and my arms and legs shaking from the exertion. I started to lift the bike off the ground then remembered Erik's tin. If it wasn't under the dock where he'd hidden it from Willow and me a few days earlier, then I wasn't taking the time to look for it. Brock would be down for just so long, and I didn't think there was even a word in the English language that would describe the depth of his wrath.

I jogged back to the dock and bent to look underneath. At first I didn't see it, but when I got down on my knees and looked, I saw green metal wedged into the farthest angle between a piece of the flat, rusted metal dock frame and the dirt at the shoreline. I scanned the area for the huge spider that had been hanging over Erik's head when he was under there. I didn't see it, so I reached back and I worked at the tin until it finally came free. The contents rattled. I'd only seen a few of the treasures in Erik's tin box, but at the moment, I seriously doubted any of them were worth the hornet's nest I'd just stirred up.

I returned to my bike and got on, clutching the box against my stomach while I struggled to pedal and hold just one side of the handlebars. I didn't bother to look back at Brock. He'd caught his breath, and I could hear the curse words spewing from his mouth. I figured in the long run this scenario could end one of two ways. Either I'd managed to teach Brock a lesson, or –

I didn't want to think about the *or*. There were too many possibilities, and all of them looked ugly in my mind. At this point, all I wanted was to get home, get changed and go to the fair.

My clothes had quit dripping by the time I wheeled into our driveway. Erik burst out of the side door and raced toward me.

"You have my treathure boxth."

I hadn't even put my foot on the ground before he yanked it from my hand. Mom came out of the house, drying her hands on a dish towel.

"Oh, good," she said. "You found it."

I dropped my feet to the ground and climbed off the bike. My heart pounded from riding so hard, and it was a struggle to breathe. "Yeah, it was under the dock." I bent over to take a deep breath before I started to wheel the bike toward the garage.

"How'd you get so wet?" Mom asked.

Was there any point in telling her the truth? I found Erik's treasure tin. That's really all that mattered. "It's stupid, really. I tripped on the side of the dock and fell into the water. Kind of clumsy, I guess."

She eyed me suspiciously. "I guess," she said slowly. "Thanks for being such a great big brother and finding that for him. You know what it means to him."

"Yeah. I do."

I was almost in the garage when Mom yelled, "You'll need to hurry and get changed. I just got a call from Cal, your dad's co-worker who's coming with the moving van. He made good time coming up from the city and they'll be here in about half an hour. He needs to head back tonight rather than tomorrow, so we're going to have to unload the truck as soon as he gets here."

I dropped the bike against the side of the garage and whirled toward Mom. "I can't. I'm going to the fair tonight."

"Sorry, Dylan. You'll have to go another night. It will be there through the weekend."

"But, Willow is going tonight."

She shrugged. "I'm sorry. This has to be done tonight. Just call her and explain. I'm sure she'll understand. She probably goes to the fair more than one night, like most of the kids."

She turned and walked up the steps and into the house. I couldn't believe this was happening. I could only hope Willow would understand.

I reached into my pocket for my phone. Before my fingers even touched it, disbelief stabbed my chest. I pulled the phone out and stared at the moisture covering it. The face was completely dark. I pressed the button to see if it would turn on, but nothing happened. The phone was dead.

Whether it was from the pond water I'd sucked in or the sickness I felt at standing her up, my stomach twisted. I had no way of calling Willow to explain what happened because the only place I had her number was in my contact list.

On my dead phone.

CHAPTER TEN

By the time we had the moving truck unloaded, the sun had dipped behind the distant hills and only a faint spattering of orange and pink reflected off the clouds. Every muscle in my body ached from carrying boxes and furniture. Mom hadn't just wanted the truck unloaded; she wanted everything put into the room where it belonged, which meant multiple trips up and down the stairs to the bedrooms and basement.

I hadn't cared where the stuff went. Every trip out to the truck, I'd looked down the road toward Willow's, wondering if she'd ever speak to me again and how long it had taken Brock to recover and make his way back home. But I didn't have much time to think. Except for a twenty minute break for pizza and salad, we worked for six hours straight. My dad's friends left as soon as we'd taken the last coffee table into the den, deciding they would stop halfway back to the city to spend the night.

We stood in the driveway and watched the taillights of the big, empty box truck as it rumbled down the road. Once it was out of sight, we went back into the house. Erik had fallen asleep on the couch in the living room more than an hour earlier. Mom flopped onto the big recliner next to the couch.

"Thanks for your help, Dylan. We couldn't have done all this without you."

"You're welcome," I grumbled, although I really didn't mean it, and I'm sure Mom knew it. Six hours of worry and frustration over what Willow was thinking had made me more tired than the physical work of emptying the truck. "I'm beat. I'm going to bed."

"Me, too, once Erik wakes up." Mom yawned then curled up in the chair. "Grandma said she'd watch Erik tomorrow to give you a break. I don't go into the clinic until after lunch, anyway."

Finally some good news. "Great. I want to go first thing in the morning to let Willow know why I didn't show up tonight."

"I'm sure she'll understand. I'll see you in the morning." She blew me a kiss. "Love you." Fortunately Mom loved me enough to never do that in front of my friends, but it was typical when it was just us.

"Good night." Instead of going straight to my room, I headed to the kitchen to see if the rice in the bag had worked magic on my waterlogged phone. The plastic bag sat on the counter near the refrigerator. The phone was buried in the white pile, so I picked up the bag and shook it until the top part of my phone showed. I don't know what I thought I'd see, but I didn't see a difference, and I knew I'd have to wait until tomorrow night before I dared to turn it on again. Knowing that there was a possibility of bringing it back to life lifted my mood a little.

Once upstairs, I left my light off while I went to look out my window toward Willow's house. Now it was dark enough that the stars had started popping out across the sky, and I could see the dots of light in the windows at the farmhouse. Although the house was too far away for details, I imagined Willow settling in for the night. Or was she still at the fair? Ugh! Why did that have to pop into my head? I yanked down the shade. This would be the longest night of my life.

There was nothing I could do until morning. I'd try to make this situation with Willow right then – that is, if Willow would still talk to me. Trista, my last girlfriend, definitely wouldn't have given me the time of day if this had happened with her. I hoped Willow was different.

As exhausted as I was, when I finally got into bed, I tossed and turned. I kept my eyes closed and gave in to where my mind wanted to go, even though the images left an ache in my gut. I imagined Willow at the fair. Since I had no idea what the fair would be like, I pictured Coney Island in Brooklyn. Every
summer our family went to the amusement park at least once, and it was there that my cousin, Tommy, and I got stuck at the top of the Cyclone rollercoaster. Despite the warmth in my room, I shuddered. That was the day I was sure I would die - the day a major fear of heights became a part of who I am. I forced myself to wipe that image out, and I shifted my thoughts back to Willow.

I pictured her walking around and what she would do there. She probably liked cotton candy. Yeah, pink cotton candy, so she'd be carrying around a big, fat, pink bag of it. And I could see her standing in front of the game where the players shot water guns into the mouths of clowns to see whose balloon popped first. Or maybe it was *me* shooting and winning so she could pick out the biggest teddy bear on the prize rack. She'd carry it around the whole fair and then take it home and keep it on her bed so it would remind her of me. Maybe she'd even hug it, *pretending* it was me.

I felt my mouth curve into a smile. We could take the bear on the carousel, and as we rode around, everyone would see that we were together and that I had won the bear for her. My imagination was getting carried away with the image when my eyes flew open and my heart jumped. Rides! I didn't even know if she liked rides. What if she liked the Ferris wheel or roller coaster? Knowing my luck, she probably liked every high ride ever invented.

No. Knowing my luck, she wouldn't even want to be friends after I had stood her up tonight.

I flipped onto my side and yanked the sheet over my shoulder. I had to quit thinking; had to get to sleep so I could get over there early in the morning. A hundred thoughts raced through my mind as I started to drift off, and then the scene at the pond earlier popped in. Brock's face, twisted from the pain after I kicked him, was the one that jumped out at me. I hoped it would teach him to leave me alone.

My muscles tensed again as a realization hit me. If Brock had chopped off Willow's hair to get back at me for throwing his bike into the bushes, would he go after her again because of what I'd done at the pond? A sick feeling slithered in my stomach. I rolled onto my back to try and make it stop. Instead of teaching Brock a lesson, had I made Willow's life with him worse?

Once again my pillow took the brunt of my frustration. Morning couldn't come soon enough.

I woke to an unfamiliar sound – Erik giggling. There was light seeping around the edges of the window shades, so I knew I wasn't dreaming. I rolled toward my clock. It was already almost 8:00. Since Willow had told me that she feeds her animals early, I figured she'd be up. I grabbed clean clothes and ran for the shower, nearly colliding with Erik and Scout in the hall. Scout sat facing Erik, and Erik was balancing a plastic cowboy figure on Scout's muzzle halfway between her eyes and nose. Even though the figure would fall to the floor, Scout sat like a statue, waiting for Erik to place the toy on her again.

"Look at Thcout," Erik said as I passed.

"Yeah, cool," I said, then hurried into the bathroom. It was amazing how Erik and Scout had bonded. Even his meltdowns seemed less frequent. I wondered why we hadn't gotten her, or another assistance dog, before this. Then it hit me. Probably because our building in the city was a no pets building so it would have been a big fight to convince anyone that a dog really could change a little kid's life. We had proof, now.

Ten minutes later I was out of the shower. Scout and Erik were no longer in the hall, so I guessed they'd gone down for breakfast. I tossed my dirty clothes through my open bedroom door and onto the floor before hurrying downstairs. Mom was humming in the kitchen as she moved from the stove to the refrigerator and to the counter.

"Want pancakes?" she asked.

"No time," I said, grabbing an apple from the basket on the island. "I have to get down to Willow's." I glanced at the bag of rice with my phone in it. A few more hours and I'd be able to see if it had survived the pond dunk.

"I have some already made and keeping warm in the oven."

"Okay, I'll take one." I pushed the apple into my pocket.

Mom removed a cookie sheet from the oven and pulled back the aluminum foil that was keeping the pancakes warm. I picked up two.

"Dylan," she scolded. "Don't use your fingers."

But she was too late. I grabbed the jug of maple syrup from the counter, drizzled syrup on my pancakes, rolled them into one and headed to the door. "Thanks, Mom. You're the best." I reached for the handle to the back door at the same time as I lifted the pancake roll above my head and let the syrup drip onto my tongue.

"Really, Dylan?" I could hear in her voice that she was trying to be disgusted, but she sounded amused.

"See ya later." The door was almost shut behind me when I heard Erik.

"Where'th Dylan going? I want to go, too."

I never heard Mom's response. The door slammed behind me as I jumped from the top step to the ground. I glanced toward the shed and considered taking my bike. Nope. Flat tires were nothing compared to what Brock would probably do to it now. I opted to run instead.

A cheetah couldn't have caught me as I raced down the road before Erik had a chance to convince Mom he had to go with me. One of the things I liked about our road was that it was tree-lined, making it look picturesque. When I was a safe distance from the house, I slowed to a walk so I could finish my pancake roll. I hadn't realized I was squeezing it until I lifted it for a bite. It was no longer a neat roll, and my fingers were imprinted on it. I tore it in two and shoved one half in my mouth, trying to chew and catch my breath at the same time. Although it looked ugly, it tasted good sliding down my throat. Except for my sticky thumb and pointer finger, all evidence of my breakfast was gone by the time I got to Willow's driveway.

Now it was instinct to look up toward the window where I'd seen Brock before. He wasn't there. I scanned the area around the house in case he was lurking in the bushes or behind a building. I didn't think he'd be stupid enough to do something to me where his grandmother could see, but considering the way he was able to bully Willow and get away with it, I couldn't count on Granny Annie to stick up for me.

As soon as I knocked on the door, Napoleon's deep bark broke the silence of the morning.

"Come on in," Granny Annie called.

I wondered if she even knew who was knocking. Did she invite anyone who knocked into her house without checking first? I opened the screen door then turned the handle on the inside wooden door slowly, opening it just enough so I could speak through the crack. It felt wrong to just walk into the house.

"Hi, it's me, Dylan Westcott."

"We're in the kitchen. Come in. Come in."

I'd never been past the porch, so I had no idea where the kitchen was. I opened the door a little more and took one step closer so I could poke my head inside. It felt like I was walking into the lion's den. Napoleon continued to bark but never came where I could see him. Were Willow and Brock in the kitchen, too?

Inside it smelled like coffee, bacon and homemade bread, reminding me of my grandparents' house. My grandmother baked bread twice a week, and always first thing in the morning. I loved waking up to the smell when we'd come up for weekend visits.

"Napoleon, eat your breakfast." Granny Annie's voice came from my right, and I looked that way but didn't see her.

The living room took up the whole front half of the house. There was a long, black leather couch that went along one wall, continued with a curved piece in the middle and then there was another long piece along the adjoining wall. Small blankets with unusual designs were folded across the backs. A couple of matching recliners sat on either side of the big window that faced our house. I didn't know what I expected, but it sure wasn't something normal like this. I looked behind the door to make sure no one was waiting to ambush me.

"Are you coming in or not?" Granny Annie's voice came from somewhere beyond the living room. She peered around a doorway at the far end of the room. "Napoleon and I were just sitting down to have breakfast. Are you hungry?" She disappeared as quickly as she had appeared.

"I already ate. Thanks," I said not too loud. If Brock was home but not in the kitchen, I had no interest in alerting him to my presence. Even though I felt like I'd evened the score with him at the pond, there was no reason to tempt fate.

Keeping an eye on the stairway to the second floor, I walked into the living room. The walls were covered with dozens of large framed photos, mostly of Willow's grandmother in exotic and unusual settings. I didn't take time to study them closely, but scanning the walls I could see that in most pictures she was surrounded by people who were clearly not from the United States, and she was obviously in different countries. Even her clothing style matched that of those with her. What looked like unusual souvenirs took up more wall and shelf space.

"Don't get sloppy," Granny Annie was saying in the kitchen.

I stepped up to the doorway and stopped. She sat at a round table with a plate of eggs, bacon and toast in front of her, and Napoleon sat on a chair next to her, a small blue bib tied around his neck.

The dachshund's attention was fixed on Granny Annie as she held a spoonful of egg out for him to eat. His tongue flicked out first, like he was testing the food, then he opened his mouth and took a small bite. A bit of the egg fell onto the table, and he retrieved that before eating the rest off the spoon.

"That's a good boy," Granny Annie said, patting his head as he licked both sides of the spoon. "You want a piece of bacon, now?" She picked up a piece of the meat from her plate and held it out for Napoleon. Half of it broke off in his mouth when he bit it, and he crunched contentedly while Granny Annie ate the remaining half.

My throat tightened in response to the bile that lurched toward it. All I could picture was where the dog had probably had his nose and tongue last – like any dog.

Granny Annie chewed and smiled at me. After swallowing, she said, "Breakfast is Napoleon's favorite meal of the day. I'm sure you think this looks odd, but my opinion is, if you're
going to have an animal, you should treat it like it's a member of your family." She nodded toward the other side of the table. "Pull up a chair, Dylan."

Napoleon whined, so she gave him a piece of toast.

I sat and hooked my thumbs on my pockets because I didn't know what else to do with my hands. "Does he always eat breakfast like this?" I asked.

"Oh, no, no," she said. "Sometimes we just have a bowl of cereal."

I know my eyes widened as I pictured one bowl and two spoons. A spoonful of Cheerios for Granny Annie then a spoonful for Napoleon. Or did he get his own bowl and he just buried his nose in the milk and cereal? The scene in my imagination made me want to laugh and gag at the same time.

It was hard to sit still in the chair. I glanced around the kitchen, which was pretty ordinary. The stove and refrigerator seemed kind of new. On top of the stove sat four loaves of bread on wire racks. No wonder it smelled so good in the house.

I wanted to be polite, so I said, "My grandmother bakes bread, too."

"I do it because I think the aroma has a calming effect." She winked. "And the bread tastes pretty good, too."

Obviously it hadn't worked on Brock.

I looked at the refrigerator which was covered with pictures, magnets and recipes. One picture stood out because it was
bigger than the rest. It showed a young man and woman with a much younger Willow and Brock in front of the woman. If I'd known Granny Annie better, I would have asked questions about the picture, but it didn't seem appropriate now. I struggled to think of something else to say.

Fortunately, Granny Annie took the lead. "How are all of you settling in? I saw a moving truck at your house yesterday."

"We're doing okay. A couple of my dad's friends brought up a bunch of our stuff from the city, so now all we need is Dad and my brother, Trent, to move here in a little more than a month with a few more things and it's all done," I answered.

"When you go home today, I want you to take some of that bread with you, okay?"

"Sure. Thank you."

She took a sip from her coffee mug. "I should stop up and see if we can help in some way." I would like it if her "we" included Willow, but as far as I was concerned, the farther Brock was from our house, the better.

Napoleon stared at the last few pieces of bacon on the paper plate on the table. Drool dripped onto his bib and the chair seat. When Granny Annie noticed, she took a napkin from a pile and wiped the dog's mouth. "Silly boy. We need to save some bacon for the kids."

"Is Willow here?" Willow's grandmother was nice, but I hadn't planned on joining her and her dog for breakfast.

"She's up in her room getting dressed. I'm sure she'll be down in a minute because she has to feed her animals. She got home late, so she slept later this morning."

I didn't really need the reminder about Willow's night at the fair, but there it was. If she got home late, she must have had a good time without me. That reality didn't settle well in my stomach. Maybe she hadn't even cared that I hadn't shown up.

Granny Annie grabbed her cup, rose from the table and poured herself more from the coffee maker on the counter. "Sure you don't want a cup of coffee or orange juice or something?"

"No, thanks." I pushed the chair away from the table and stood, relieved to know Willow hadn't spent the night at a friend's. I also didn't need to experience Napoleon's whole breakfast ritual. "I think I'll wait for Willow out on the porch so I don't miss her when she goes to the barn, if that's okay?"

"Of course," she said.

At the same time I heard whistling coming from the other room and then the front door slammed.

I started out of the kitchen. "I'm going to see if that was Willow. I'll see you later." I hoped it wasn't Brock.

Napoleon barked and Granny Annie laughed. "You're so polite, Napoleon. That's his way of saying goodbye."

"Bye," I called, feeling stupid for responding to a dog. I hurried through the living room. As I passed the front window I
 saw Willow walking toward the barn. Her cowboy boots kicked up dust from the driveway. I purposely let the screen door slam behind me so Willow would know I was there.

It worked as I'd hoped. She glanced over her shoulder then stopped in the big oak tree's shadow along the driveway when she saw me jogging toward her.

My throat tightened, and I knew it wasn't from the short run. "Hey!"

She put her hands on her hips and tipped her head. She didn't wait for me to reach her before she let me have it.

"Wrong barn, O'Dylan. You were supposed to meet me at the barn at the fair." She pulled her phone out of her pocket and glanced at it. "Oh, yeah, and you're about sixteen hours late." She scowled. "Thanks for the call."

I stopped in front of her, willing my voice not to squeak from tension. "I can explain."

"So can I. What else should I expect? You're not dependable. You're a guy."

"No, you're wrong."

She arched an eyebrow, but I hurried on before she could say more.

"I mean, yeah, I'm a guy, but it's not what you think." I started talking faster so I could get it all in before she could interrupt. "I planned to meet you at the fair. Everything was all set until my mom sent me back out to the pond because Erik left something under the dock. When I got there Brock was waiting. He saw me go out into the woods and he took some shortcut. I know he went out to start something with me, and I was fine until he called you a name, and —"

"What name?"

My stomach clenched just remembering what he'd said. "Doesn't matter." I hurried on with my explanation. "But I went after him, and we ended up in the water. Then I got home and found out my dad had sent some of his friends with a moving truck full of our stuff, so I had to help empty that. I wanted to call you, but that's when I realized my phone had been in my pocket when I fell in the water, and that was the only place I had your number, so there was no way to call you."

I took a breath. "And, I probably really pissed off Brock, too."

"So, what's new?" she responded. She turned and started walking toward the barn again.

I caught up to her just as she started to slide open the door. As if someone had pushed a button, the barn inhabitants started making their animal noises.

"Well, this time I got him where it really hurts – literally."

"What do you mean?" She had one of the big, wooden doors pushed open about six feet. Her peacock strutted out of the dimly lit interior right to Willow.

"When he put my head under water, I kicked him in the —" I wasn't sure how I should word it to a girl. I knew what I'd say if I was talking to another guy.

She burst out laughing and threw her hands over her mouth. "Seriously? Are you crazy?"

I laughed at her choice of words. "Well, I'm still alive."

"I wish I'd been there."

She reached into her pocket and took something out. "Here you go, Einstein." He took it from her hand then bobbed his head almost like he was saying thank you.

"What was that?"

"Cat food." She gave him more. The blue antenna things on top of his head bobbed.

"He likes cat food?"

"He likes cheese better."

"What!" I couldn't imagine a bird eating cheese.

She started to push the door open wider, so I stepped up and shoved the other one open a few feet, too.

"So, are you going to forgive me?" I asked

"Forgive you for what?" She started into the barn with Einstein strutting next to her.

"For standing you up." I followed, not sure that I wanted to vie with a peacock for a spot next to her.

She shrugged. "Family comes first. Your mom knew she could count on you. I can't fault you for being there when she needed you."

I caught up to her, my mind formulating my comeback that wasn't even needed.

"Yeah, you're right."

Two black and white calves to our left stood up on the bottom boards of their pens and stretched their noses in the air as they blatted at Willow. I stopped to look at them as Willow proceeded to the right toward the smaller animal pens. She flipped on a switch that lit up the barn's interior.

When I held my hands in front of each of the calves' noses, their slimy, rough tongues stretched out and licked my palms. Scout had gotten me past the whole animal tongue thing.

"Do these calves have names?" I asked.

"Brock!" she screamed.

I whirled around, expecting Brock to be standing in the barn, but instead Willow was yanking open the door to an owl's cage and reaching in. By the time I got to her side of the barn, she was bent way into the cage past the owl perched high up on a stick. She wrapped her hands around reddish-brown fur. I realized right away that it was one of the little rabbits.

"What's the rabbit doing in there?"

Willow ignored me and instead murmured to the rabbit cowering in the corner. "You're okay, Cinnamon. Don't move." Although she spoke in a calm voice, her hands shook. The grey and tan owl swiveled its head from Willow to me and back to her again. The heart outline on its face added to the intense expression in its dark eyes. Willow slowly pulled the rabbit forward past the owl, keeping her attention on the bird every second.

"Dylan," she whispered, "when I get Cinnamon out of here, slide the cage door closed fast. Got it?"

"Yeah." I stepped beside her and put my hands in position. "Okay."

While she pulled the rabbit toward the door she shifted her body so her back was toward me. The rabbit kicked out one leg and at the same time the owl flapped its wings. In one swift movement Willow whipped the rabbit through the opening and hugged it tight to her chest and I slammed the door closed.

The owl opened its beak and flapped its wings again, annoyed by our sudden movements and the loud bang of wood hitting wood.

Willow held the bunny up and checked it over. "Are you okay, baby?"

"How did it get in there?" I was pretty sure I knew, but I wanted to hear her admit it.

"We can both figure that out," Willow said. Apparently satisfied that the rabbit wasn't injured, she tucked it against her chest.

I'd known bullies in my life, but Brock was beyond mean. "Would an owl hurt a rabbit?"

"Yeah. It usually eats mice and rats and things like that, but since Cinnamon is so small, it might have eaten him, too."

I pictured the ball of fur being ripped to shreds by the owl. I could only imagine the carnage. "Why didn't he?"

"He was probably full from the mice I gave him last night." She lifted Cinnamon and pressed her cheek against the top of his head. "Otherwise —"

She didn't finish the thought, and she didn't need to. I reached out to pet Cinnamon's fur - partly because I hated to think what could have happened and partly because it meant I would touch Willow's fingers, too. She didn't seem to mind, but I hoped she noticed. Her fingers were as soft as the rabbit's fur.

"I'm glad Cinnamon is okay," I said.

"Yeah, we got lucky this time."

I felt an imaginary punch in the gut. My mind snapped with images of all of the mean things Brock had done in the last couple of weeks - from going after Einstein in our tree to the physical abuse of Willow to his actions on the ball field and at the pond, and now this.

I stopped and held my hand on hers, ignoring the rabbit. "I'm sorry. This is my fault for kicking him," I said.

"Yeah, probably. But Brock looks for excuses, O'Dylan. Don't think you're special."

"Has he always been this mean?"

Willow walked to the rabbit cages and gently set Cinnamon in one. The rabbit hopped to its bowl of food and started munching like he hadn't almost been dinner himself. She took a long time to answer.

"I guess it's been worse in the last year. Since our dad's been gone."

"Where is he?" I watched her carefully for a reaction, hoping I hadn't asked something that would cause her pain.

"He's doing another tour of duty in the Middle East, I think. But he moved to another state, too."

"He's in the army?"

She nodded. "Yeah.." She took the water bottle from inside the cage and immersed it in a bucket of water to refill it.

"Man, and I worry about my dad being a policeman."

She shrugged. "Big cities can be pretty dangerous. Maybe my dad is safer." She hooked the water bottle back onto the wire cage and snapped the door shut.

"Why does that make Brock mean? Is he better when your dad is home?"

"That's the problem. He hasn't really been home in a couple of years. Just a couple of hours here and there. He has a new family with someone he met in the army."

I was beginning to think that our family, even with Erik's autism, was much luckier than Willow's. "Wow, that's tough."

"Eh, that's life." Willow moved to the cage with the big colorful woodpecker.

She removed the lid to a small metal container, scooped some kind of bird seed out and put that in the dish in the cage. The bird didn't move. It stayed in the back corner on the stick perch.

I figured I'd gone this far, I might as well completely satisfy my curiosity. "Where's your mom?"

Her expression darkened and she turned to walk toward the other cages. "Dead."

Staring at her back, I gulped. Was there something I should say? "Sorry," was the best I could do.

She shrugged, but it didn't appear she wanted to say anything more about it. She continued to fill food and water bowls at each cage like she hadn't just dropped that bombshell.

"I'm going to ride Lightning later," she said. "Want to come?"

"Is that the horse you brought to our house?"

"Yeah."

I was surprised she'd invite me to do anything else. "You're not mad about the fair?"

She looked over her shoulder. "You must be telling the truth. No one would make up a story about kicking Brock in the balls if it wasn't true."

My jaw dropped so low a football could have fit in my mouth. This girl was totally different than any I'd hung with in the city.

"Close your mouth, O'Dylan, or you're going to catch flies." She grinned and moved to the next cage.

And gasped.

CHAPTER ELEVEN

"Oh, no! Shadow!" Willow threw open the cage door and reached into the baby raccoon's cage. The animal made a hissing sound and tried to jerk away from her.

Her loud voice and sudden movement startled the woodpecker, which hopped from the perch and flapped its wings. The baby rabbits cowered in their cages as if frozen.

I stepped closer and could see that one of the raccoon's front legs was stuck in a small hole in the side of the wire cage. Blood covered his fur from the end of his paw all the way up to his front leg as far as I could see.

"What happened?"

"It looks like he tried to reach for that egg next to the cage on the table and got caught on the wire."

Bits of fur stuck to sharp pieces of wire. "That's a weird place for an egg, isn't it?" I asked.

"Yup." She tried to bend the wire with her fingers, but wasn't having any luck.

"Here, let me do that." I stepped around her and reached for the wire. Shadow snapped in my direction like he was going to bite. I yanked my fingers back. "Whoa!"

"I'll hold his head," Willow offered. When she reached toward him, he hissed again. "Shadow, it's okay," she said. She made another attempt to touch him, but he squirmed then flipped upside down against her arm. His caught leg twisted, and he let out a short, piercing screech.

"Get back!" I ordered.

Willow yanked her arms from the cage. Blood was smeared on her, too.

"Did he bite you?" I took her hand and turned it over to see both sides.

"No. The blood is his. But he's still caught, and I can't see where he's hurt." This was only the second time I'd seen Willow lose her cool. The first being when I confronted her in our yard about Brock bullying her. "I have to get him out."

I grabbed her arm just before she reached back in. "This is a *really* bad idea."

She glared at me. "We can't just leave him. He's scared. That's why he's acting like that."

"He's a wild animal," I countered. "*That's* why he's acting like that."

"We're wasting time arguing," she said. "He's hurt. He needs help."

"I'm calling my mom," I said. I reached into my pocket then realized my phone was at home on the counter in the bag of rice.
"Where's your phone?"

Willow looked annoyed. "We don't need your mom."

"Shadow does. He's hurt. She knows how to help."

She pressed her lips together and glared at me.

"Willow, Shadow is scared. Let me call my mom."

She sighed and plunged her hand into her pocket, producing her cell phone. I punched in my mother's number then watched Willow while it rang. I couldn't tell if she was annoyed, scared or maybe both.

Mom answered after the third ring.

"Hey, Mom, it's me. Can you come down to Willow's? Her raccoon's leg is caught in the cage. It's bleeding. A lot."

"Her raccoon?"

"Yeah, she found it along the side of the road. Its paw is stuck in the side of the cage. I'm afraid he's going to bite us if we try to get it loose."

"Don't touch him," she warned. "I'll be right there."

Mom's warning sent my heart racing. "Willow already touched him. She has blood on her."

"Was she bitten?"

"No, it's blood from the raccoon. Is she going to be okay?" I knew Mom was concerned about rabies, and so was I.

"Tell her to wash it for five minutes with warm, soapy water. That way she'll be able to see if she has any marks on her. If it's the raccoon's blood and she wasn't scratched or bitten, she should be okay."

I turned to Willow and relayed Mom's directions.

"Shadow's not sick."

Mom must have heard her because she said, "Tell Willow even if he's not sick, she needs to go and do that now. This will have to be reported."

"Here, you tell her." I handed Willow the phone.

"Hi, it's Willow."

She listened for a couple of minutes, occasionally responding with "yeah" or "okay". Finally she handed the phone back to me.

"Okay, I'm going in to clean up. I'll be back in a few minutes." She jogged from the barn, but she didn't look as worried as I felt.

"Thanks, Mom," I said. "We're in the barn."

"Okay. Let me get Erik and we'll be down."

"Thanks."

The phone went quiet.

I backed away from the cage, praying the raccoon wasn't sick. While I waited, I wandered around the barn and looked at all of her animals again. I wasn't convinced that she could possibly know enough to care for and handle some of these wild animals – even with all of the information she could get from the Internet. Mom worked with a training program for wildlife rehabilitators and not everyone ended up qualified to do the work. Willow loved animals, but it didn't make her an expert. I knew that. My interest in her blinded me to what I really should have done after I saw the animals for the first time. I should have told my mother.

While I was mentally kicking myself, Willow returned. Her arms were dark pink from where she had scrubbed.

"Any bites or scratches?" I asked as soon as she came through the barn door.

"Nothing. I knew it was just Shadow's blood."

She hurried back to Shadow's cage and I followed. The baby raccoon had settled down, and although he was breathing heavily, he was at least calm. We stood silently staring at him like something was going to change. Once in a while I looked at Willow out of the corner of my eye. She chewed on her lower lip and occasionally nibbled on the end of her thumbnail.

I hated seeing her so worried, so I stepped closer and put my arm over her shoulder. When she didn't resist, I pulled her in tight against my side. She was warm and soft. I'd stand like this all day if I could.

"He'll be okay," I said.

I had confidence in Mom's veterinary skills, but I also knew sometimes animals' injuries were more than could be fixed. I hoped for Willow's sake this wouldn't be the case with Shadow.

"This is Brock's fault," she muttered. "I'm sure he put that egg there to tease Shadow."

"Maybe one of your chickens laid it there."

She shook her head. "A chicken isn't going to go near a raccoon." She glanced around. "Besides, none of my chickens are loose."

Annoyance jabbed my stomach. "Brock's out of control." I'd known a lot of crazy people in my life, but Brock was leaping to the top spot.

The crunch of car tires out on the driveway caught my attention. "I think Mom's here."

With another squeeze of Willow's shoulder, I said, "Be right back."

I ran out to show Mom where we were. The sun lit a straight line through the open door and into the barn, almost like a path. She was just opening the driver's door as Erik was opening the passenger one behind her. Scout followed Erik out and bounded to the ground. He scooped up her leash.

"Good dog," he said when Scout sidled up next to him.

Mom went to the trunk and took out a large dark blue duffle bag. "How badly is the raccoon hurt?" she called as I approached.

"We don't know, but there's a lot of bl – red stuff." I feared the mention of blood would panic Erik.

She slammed the trunk closed and came around the car. "Stay here, Erik," she said as she hurried past him.

I started to walk fast along with her. "Willow thinks maybe Brock purposely put a chicken egg outside the cage to tease the raccoon. His front leg got stuck in the wire."

She didn't stop walking but she glanced at me. "You need to stay out here with Erik, please."

I hadn't even considered I wouldn't go back in to be with Willow. "But you might need my help."

"I'll send for you if necessary. Just stay with Erik," she ordered. She was all business as she passed me and entered the barn.

While I stared at her retreating back, Napoleon barked in the house. I turned quickly, concerned that Erik had already wandered off. Although the sound of the dog's bark was muffled, it had caught Erik and Scout's attention. They both stared in that direction.

The porch door opened and Granny Annie came out, with Napoleon attempting to follow. She picked him up and held him football-style under her arm.

"What's going on?" she called.

"Willow's raccoon is hurt. My mom's a vet. She came to help."

Granny Annie pushed Napoleon back inside the house then came down the porch stairs. She ignored the dog's deep protests. "Is it sick?"

"No. His front leg is caught in the cage, and we can't get it out. He's bleeding."

I was impressed when she jogged across the driveway.

"I was in the backroom making soap when I heard Willow run in and out of the house and heard the car come in the driveway." She stopped in front of Erik. "So, who's this guy?" She reached toward him like she was going to pat his head, but he ducked out of her reach.

That was his typical reaction, but there was no way for her to know it wasn't anything about her.

"Sorry about that. This is my brother, Erik." I shrugged. "He doesn't like to be touched."

"Hello, Erik," she said.

He didn't look up or respond. Also typical.

She knelt and held her hand out to Scout. "And who's your friend?"

I held my breath. Erik's responses to people approaching him were not always appropriate. That was an understatement. Sometimes he was embarrassingly rude. He put his arm around Scout's neck and held her so she couldn't go near Granny Annie. "Thith ith *my* good dog." He emphasized the word "my", making it clear that he wasn't interested in sharing her attention with anyone.

Granny Annie withdrew her hand, but she remained kneeling. "You know, Erik, she *looks* like a good dog. You're a lucky boy." Her kindness toward Erik and apparent understanding even helped me relax. "Does your good dog have a name?"

"Thcout," Erik mumbled. At the same time he reached toward his pocket. I knew what he was doing. He took out the ear from the stuffed orange cat, turned his back to Granny Annie and began rubbing the ear against his face.

To her credit, she didn't act like his behavior was unusual. "It was nice to meet you and your good dog," she said to Erik. "I'm going to go in the barn and see if I can help." She walked through the wide door and out of sight.

I hated that I had to stay outside and couldn't be with Willow. I leaned against the hood of the car and stared at the barn. Other than the occasional calf blat, none of the animals made noises. To keep myself occupied, I grabbed Mom's phone from the front seat and sent a couple of text messages about the baseball team to my buddies back home. I knew she had their numbers in her phone because in the past if she couldn't get me to answer a text when we were together, she'd contact them. Too had she hadn't asked for Willow's, because if she had, last night's lack of communication never would have happened.

A few minutes later, Mom and Willow came out carrying Shadow's bulky cage between them. I hurried in their direction. Shadow's leg was free.

"Let me carry one side," I offered.

"You don't have gloves," Mom pointed out. I glanced at
Willow who now wore a big pair of gloves, like Mom's, that reached way up her arm. Granny Annie followed with Mom's blue duffel bag. She hurried past them and set the duffel bag next to our car, then she went into the house.

"Where are you taking him?"

"Ann is taking it to Safe Haven Wildlife Rehabilitators," Mom said. "They're experts on raccoons. I'm not."

I wondered if what Mom had just said registered with Willow. Even Mom, who was a vet, said she didn't have the knowledge to handle the raccoon.

"Is he going to be okay?" I asked.

"I think so. At least he doesn't appear to be sick." She was a little out of breath from carrying the cage. The raccoon was moving around inside, making it harder for them to keep it steady.

I glanced at Willow but couldn't read her expression. She didn't look happy, though.

Granny Annie came back out of the house with her purse and keys for her mini van. She hurried around to the back and opened the hatch.

"Let's put the cage here."

Mom and Willow slid the cage in then closed the door. Mom pulled off her gloves and took the ones Willow had been wearing as she came toward me. "I'm going to go with Ann and Willow. I'll need you to watch Erik. If you don't mind walking home, I'll get the car later."

"If I do mind walking home, can I take the car?"

Mom cocked her head and grinned. "In your dreams."

"Yeah, pretty much," I replied.

She lightly punched me in the shoulder. "You're a good kid, Dylan."

"Thanks." I held her cell phone up. "I borrowed your phone to text the guys back home while I was waiting. Here."

"No, hold onto it," she said. "You can call my pager if there's a problem."

I put her phone in my pocket. It wasn't the morning I'd planned with Willow, but if Willow wasn't going to be home, it didn't matter anyway.

Mom and Granny Annie got into the front seats of the van, and Willow started to get in through the sliding door then stopped and came back.

"Want to go for a ride on Lightning when I get home, O'Dylan? I'll need the distraction."

I shoved my hands in my pockets. I wasn't so sure about being on the horse, but I imagined I would have to wrap my arms around her to hold on. That part sounded good. "Yeah, I guess."

She lifted her chin and narrowed her eyes. "Love the enthusiasm."

I didn't know if I should admit I'd never ridden a horse before or not. I opted for not – at least for now. I forced a smile. "It's a plan."

"Okay, see ya later." Willow climbed into the van and Granny Annie pulled out of the driveway. I could see through the back window that Willow was turned around in the seat checking on Shadow, so I didn't bother to wave.

I turned to Erik. "Come on, Oops. Let's go home."

He didn't move and was again rubbing the cat ear against his cheek, which didn't make sense. He only did that if something made him nervous. Other than a few clouds, it was a clear day with no threat of a thunderstorm, so I knew that wasn't it. "What's up?" I asked.

"Lightning." He rubbed the fabric faster against his cheek. Apparently sensing Erik's worry, Scout pressed closer to his leg.

"What?" I pointed up. "There's no li—" I put my hand down. "Lightning. That's the name of Willow's horse, Erik. There's no storm. It's okay."

He looked up at the sky and studied it for a minute. I knew he believed me when his hand and the cat ear came away from his face and he shoved the ear back in his pocket.

"Let's go home."

Without hesitation he started down the driveway. It amazed me how his emotions seemed to have on and off switches. Scout walked so close to him that I worried that Erik might trip over her. We were almost to the road when Brock yelled from behind.

"Hope you don't think you won, Westcott."

His voice jolted my nerves. I straightened my shoulders and turned slowly to face him. He stood at the bottom of the porch stairs, his eyes narrowed and his jaw jutted out.

I purposely made sure the pitch of my voice was low. "Didn't know there was a competition."

"You declared war."

I glanced at Erik, not really wanting him to witness this exchange. I scratched my head. "Uh, no, I defended myself. Nothing more."

Brock walked toward us, but I stood my ground. I looked at Erik out of the corner of my eye because I didn't want to turn my head away from Brock.

I tried to sound natural and calm even though inside my stomach had clenched so tight it hurt. "Erik, you and Scout hop across the ditch and walk up the field toward home. I'll be right behind you."

Erik glanced toward Brock, whom I could see was still walking toward us. By the way Erik's eyes darted between looking at me and looking at Brock, I knew Erik wasn't going to go without an argument.

Brock stopped about ten feet from us. "Does that stupid dog bite?"

Erik's hand plunged into his pocket with the cat ear and he started mumbling the same thing repeatedly. "Thcout ith my good dog. Thcout ith my good dog." The cat ear came out and he rubbed it against his face. "Thcout ith my good dog."

"Yes, you're right, Erik, so take your good dog and start walking home," I repeated.

Brock caught on quickly to one of Erik's triggers. "Take your stupid dog home."

Erik's voice rose. "Thcout ith my good dog. Thcout ith my good dog."

"It's a stupid ugly dog," Brock sneered.

I whirled toward Brock. "Knock it off. This is between you and me. It has nothing to do with him." Behind me the pitch of Erik's voice rose as he repeated himself.

"I'll say whatever I want. You're on my property. And I say that's a stupid, ugly, dirty dog."

"No! No! No!" Erik screamed, and at the same time he balled his hand into a fist and pounded it against his head. "Thcout ith my good dog. Thcout ith my good dog."

Although I didn't want to turn my back on Brock, I couldn't leave Erik to bang his head with his fist. I ran to him, grabbed hold of his wrists and forced them down to his sides. I knew it wasn't the best approach, but I wanted to keep him safe. He thrashed against me, kicking at my legs and screaming. Scout attempted to move closer to Erik, but I was afraid he would kick her. I stepped sideways to move him away from her and lost my footing on the edge of the ditch. When I felt myself going backwards, I let go of Erik so he wouldn't fall, too. My arms swung like windmills and I caught my balance just in time.

Erik dropped to the ground on the side of the ditch and continued to kick and bang his head with his hand. Scout moved in on top of him, nearly covering his body with hers. When Erik tried to push her away, she ducked under his hands and pressed her head against his shoulder and neck. She didn't give up, and after a minute his body relaxed and instead of flopping around, he wrapped his arms around his dog and held onto her. The cat ear dangled from his fingers. I could barely make out Erik saying, "Thcout ith my good dog."

My heart banged against my chest. Even though I lived with it, every time he had a meltdown I worried that he would hurt himself. I'd never seen him calm this quickly before.

Brock had taken a few steps back. "What the hell was that about?"

I turned and glared at him. "You knew exactly what you were doing when you teased him about the dog. Do you feel like a bigger man now?"

"That kid has issues."

It took every ounce of self-control that I'd learned in martial arts to not move a muscle and go after him. "Go look in a mirror. So do you." As soon as the comment was out of my mouth, I regretted it. Even though I had restrained myself physically, I realized that I had taken myself down to Brock's level.

By the look on his face, I believed at any moment fire would shoot from his nose and mouth. "Big mistake," he hissed. The words were so drawn out that anyone else could have spoken two sentences in the amount of time he used for the two words. He pivoted and marched back toward the house.

I didn't respond. I knew he was right.

A little over an hour later Erik and I were in the fenced-in back yard when I heard the car tires on the gravel driveway. He was playing hide and seek with Scout while I sat at the picnic table searching the Internet for how to ride a horse. Even after watching several short videos, I wasn't sure I'd learned enough to hop on a horse and ride. My image of clinging to Willow was looking more realistic with each viewing.

I got up and wandered to the gate. Mom was talking to someone on her phone when she stepped out of the car. "Tracy's going to stop over tomorrow and pick up the animals that need to go to Safe Haven. Some may even be ready for immediate release." She closed the car door and waved to me while she listened to the person on the other end of the phone. "I know. They all think if they love animals then they're experts," she finally said. She walked toward me as she listened for another minute then said, "I think she understands now. Look, I'm home and I have to get ready to head to the clinic. Give me a call if there's anything I can do to assist." She nodded. "Okay. Bye." She pressed end on her phone.

She looked past me into the yard. "Where's Erik?"

I spun around. "He was just here. There's no way he could have gotten out of here without me knowing." Just as I was ready to sprint across the yard, Erik and Scout crawled out from under a bush by the deck. I took a deep breath and let it out. Would I ever get used to having to be on guard every minute? I turned back to Mom.

"How's Willow's raccoon?"

She leaned against the gate. "The raccoon will be fine. Why didn't you tell me she was keeping wild animals in her barn?"

I shrugged. "I don't know. I guess I didn't think it mattered."

"It does matter, Dylan. What she's doing is illegal."

That sounded crazy. "Helping hurt animals is illegal?"

"It is if you're not a trained and certified wildlife rehabilitator."

My scalp prickled as I came to Willow's defense. "Was she supposed to leave the raccoons by the side of the road to die?"

Mom put her hand on my arm. "Relax, Dylan. She didn't know. She loves animals and thought she was doing the right thing. Like many people who want to do the right thing, she thought that just reading things from the Internet made her an expert on how to take care of them. They mean well."

I opened the gate to let Erik and Scout out of the yard, then I followed them and Mom to the side of the house. "Will she be arrested?"

Mom shook her head as we climbed the porch stairs. "Of course not, although she could have been fined. Actually, Ann would have been fined." She opened the door and Erik scooted in ahead of her with Scout close on his heels. "Tracy from Safe Haven is going over tomorrow to pick up the animals Willow can't keep."

"Willow must be bummed." I knew how much she cared about the animals, and I couldn't imagine how she felt.

"I think she understands, Dylan. She's a smart girl." Mom took a pitcher of lemonade from the refrigerator and proceeded to pour herself a glass. "Want some?"

"No, thanks."

"I'm going to get ready for work. Grandma should be here soon. What are you going to do this afternoon?"

"Willow offered to take me for a ride on her horse."

"Have you ever ridden a horse?"

I sat down at the kitchen table. "Nope. While I was waiting I searched for videos on the Internet that showed me how to ride."

Mom sipped her lemonade then set the glass on the counter. "Case in point. You kids think you can learn everything from the Internet. Did it help?"

I laughed. "It reminded me that horses can be pretty tall and easy to fall off from."

She wiped the sweat off the side of her glass. "Take your bike helmet with you in case Willow doesn't have two riding helmets."

"A helmet to ride a horse? Mom, I'm almost fifteen."

Mom held up her hand with her fingers extended then pulled her fingers down one at a time as she made each point. "You could fall. You could get kicked. You could fall and your head could get stepped on. You could hit a low branch on a tree. Those are the things people don't think about. So wear your helmet."

I got up from the chair. "Okay. Good to know." I opened the refrigerator door and peered in. "I'm hungry. What's for lunch?"

"You're always hungry. And, as you said, you're almost fifteen. I think you can make your own lunch." With the door still open I looked back at her, ready to protest when she added, "And Erik's."

I turned back to the refrigerator and pulled open the drawer with the bread in it. "Like I said, Erik and I love peanut butter and jelly."

Mom chuckled and left the room. I closed the drawer without taking out the bread. Maybe I'd wait for Grandma to arrive and take pity on us. Instead I picked up the bag of rice with my phone in it and decided to take a chance and see if it would turn on.

As soon as I pressed the button, the screen filled with the welcome logo then I got the tone telling me I had a voice mail. I looked and saw that actually there were four of them – all from Willow. Three of them were from the time she would have been at the fair. The last one had been left less than ten minutes before.

The message said she'd be up with Lightning at 1:00. I glanced at the clock on the stove. Fifteen minutes. I dropped the phone on the counter and yanked open the refrigerator door again. I grabbed the bread from the drawer and the grape jelly from the top shelf and used my elbow to slam the refrigerator closed.

"Erik, come and get lunch." I wasn't sure if he could hear me. I took a knife from the silverware drawer, the peanut butter from the pantry cupboard on the other side of the refrigerator and slapped together three sandwiches – one for Erik and two for me.

"Erik," I called again while taking the milk out of the refrigerator. "Sandwiches are ready."

A tennis ball flew through the open doorway between the kitchen and hallway and bounced off the cupboard. Scout raced through the door after it, skidding on the ceramic tile when she rounded the corner by the island. Erik was right behind her.

"Get up on the stool and have some lunch." I put his sandwich on a napkin and poured him a glass of milk while he climbed up onto the high seat at the island.

I took huge bites of my sandwich as I moved around the room trying to take care of everything I used while I ate. I turned in time to see Erik push the napkin and sandwich away from him.

"What's wrong with the sandwich?" I asked.

He folded his arms on the island then put his forehead down on his wrists. "I'm allergic to crutht."

I took the sandwich and grabbed another knife. I knew he didn't like crusts, but I was too distracted to pay attention to that detail.

"You're not allergic to crusts." I cut the crust off then put the sandwich back in front of him. "There."

He stared at it like it was covered with bugs.

"Now what?" I glanced at the clock. I still needed to change into jeans and shoes before Willow got here.

"The crutht touched the bread."

I checked my irritation. "No, I made sure I cut far enough in so the crust didn't touch the part of the bread that you're going to eat. It's safe."

I shoved almost half the sandwich in my mouth as I dropped the second knife into the sink. Just then Mom walked back into the kitchen.

I swallowed the big sticky lump of bread before asking, "What time will Grandma be here?"

"She just pulled in the driveway. Erik, eat your sandwich."

"I'm allergic," he repeated, and put his head down again.

I gulped down half a glass of milk. "I need to go change before Willow gets here. Can you or Grandma take care of this?"

"Yes." Mom winked at me then leaned in next to Erik. "I'll sanitize the sandwich. It only takes thirty seconds in the refrigerator." She picked up the napkin and sandwich and put it in the refrigerator. Erik turned his head just enough so one eye was peeking at her. "Thirty, twenty-nine, twenty-eight," she counted down. I could hear

Erik doing it quietly with her even though he pressed his mouth against his arm.

I hurried from the room in the middle of the sanitization. It might take me all summer, but I'd probably learn all of these tricks that Mom had for dealing with Erik. I ran upstairs and pulled a pair of jeans from under my bed and put them on. Next I took socks from the dresser and headed downstairs. I had an old pair of Nikes in the shoe bin in the mudroom. Those would be good for riding a horse since I didn't have cowboy boots.

I decided to start down the road to see if I'd meet Willow part way. Grandma and I passed on the porch steps.

"Thanks for watching Erik. I'm going to ride Willow's horse. See ya later."

"Have fun," I heard her say as I jogged to the garage to get my helmet. It seemed lame to wear a helmet to ride a horse, but I knew Mom would be watching. After I got it, I waved toward the house in case she was watching then headed down the road. I was about halfway when Willow and the black and white horse came through a bunch of trees and into the long field between her house and ours.

She waved and yelled. "Hey!" The horse jumped from a walk to something a lot faster. Willow didn't even bounce on the horse's back; instead the two of them moved together like they were one flowing mass. I hoped the horse wouldn't run like that when I was on because I would probably bounce off its back. When they got closer, Willow slowed the horse to something a bit bouncier, but she still looked comfortable. I was amazed to see she was riding the way the Indians rode their horses in the cowboy movies. There was no saddle, but she was wearing a dark blue helmet that completely covered her chopped off hair. When she was in front of me, she stopped. The horse pranced in a circle and snorted like it wanted to run.

"Hey, you look good up there," I said, "but you forgot the saddle."

"Don't have one. Don't need one. I see you brought a helmet."

I glanced down at the helmet that dangled from my fingertips. "Yeah. Mom insisted."

Willow tipped her head. "Someone I know didn't wear a helmet on a trail ride and the horse spooked and she fell. The horse stepped on her head."

"Really? Did she die?" I was rethinking getting on the horse, even if riding did mean I'd have my arms wrapped around Willow.

"No, but she was in the hospital for a long time and still has trouble seeing right. Just put your helmet on and get up here."

While I snapped the helmet strap, I looked at the horse's back which was level with my shoulders. "How?"

"Yeah, sorry. I had planned to pick you up at your house so you'd have something to get up on, but that's not an option now." Willow leaned way forward over the horse's neck. "Jump up on your belly onto Lightning's back and then I'll pull while you swing your leg up and over. It's easy. That's how I always get on."

I glanced around but there was nothing I could step up onto, so I had no choice.

"Okay, here goes." I took a few steps back, did a short run and jumped. I hit Lightning's back with my stomach then proceeded to slide right off the other side and onto the ground. Willow burst out laughing while I lay on the ground looking up at the horse's black and white belly. I rolled away before I was stepped on.

I stood and brushed off the dirt and grass from my pants and t-shirt. "That worked well," I mumbled. "Maybe I'll just walk."

"Try again," Willow directed.

I approached the horse's right side.

"No, mount from the left side," she said.

I went around the horse and looked at its back again. "Really, I think I'll walk next to you."

She extended her hand and wiggled her fingers toward me as if to say 'come here'. "Nah, you can do it. It'll be fun. Come on. Try again."

Although I was really klutzy doing it, at least I made it onto the horse's back on the second attempt. And I was glad I had. I slid right in behind Willow, let my chest press against her back and wrapped my arms around her middle. My arms fit perfectly. This was a better idea than I thought. I was so close that I could tell she had just taken a shower because, even with a helmet on, the fresh, clean smell of her hair made filled my senses.

"Ready?" she asked.

I tightened my arms around her even more. "As ready as I'll ever be."

Her legs squeezed against the horse's sides and she made a clicking sound. The horse stepped out immediately. Its gait was smooth so, as long as I held tight to Willow, I didn't feel like I was going to fall off.

"I've never ridden a horse before," I said. I wanted to add, *So this is fast enough*, but I didn't want to sound like a wimp.

"I figured," she responded.

"So, where are we going?"

"We'll ride the trail in the woods and maybe go over to the pond. It'll be cooler riding there."

I had mixed feelings about the destination. My memory there with Willow was awesome. The memory with Brock was a different story. The sun was hot against my back, but as soon as we entered the woods there was an instant cooling. This was a different path than the usual one near her house. It was fairly wide like people rode ATVs or something on it. Occasionally a low branch brushed against our helmets, but for the most part it was wide open except for the umbrella of trees over us.

While we rode, Willow chatted about the good time I missed at the fair. Any other girl I knew would have still been mad because I stood her up, even though I couldn't help it, and they wouldn't have talked about it. I guess there was a lot for me to learn about her. Suddenly I realized she'd mentioned playing games and seeing shows in the grandstand, but she'd omitted one important aspect.

"You didn't say anything about the rides," I said.

"What about them? Duck." She tipped her head to the left, so I followed suit as the soft bristles of a pine branch slapped against my cheek.

"What rides did you go on?" I asked.

We straightened. "I hate most rides," she said. "My friends all go on them, but I just watch."

"That's awesome," I blurted out.

She tried to turn her head to look at me, but our helmets clunked together. "Why is that awesome?"

"Because I don't like most rides, either."

She moved the hand that wasn't holding the reins and pressed it against my clasped ones on her stomach. "Then I guess we're a good match, aren't we O'Dylan?"

"Yep." My throat was so tight I didn't dare say anything more for fear that my voice would squeak. I tightened my arms around her even more. If we hadn't been on the horse, I would have kissed her.

Willow asked me questions about the city and my friends. I told her about my school, my friends, my sports teams, Central Park and how to navigate the subway system.

"I want to go there some day," she said, "but I'd be scared about getting mugged. That happens a lot, doesn't it?"

"That's what everyone thinks, but you'd be surprised how safe you actually are there."

"That's cool. I want to see Broadway shows, the Statue of Liberty and Ellis Island. And I want to go to the top of the Empire State Building and take a horse-drawn carriage ride through Central Park. Have you seen all of those places?"

"Lots of times," I said, trying not to sound like I was bragging. "And all of my baseball games were at the field in Central Park. Maybe someday you can go down for a visit with me and my family and I can show you everything."

"I'd like that," Willow said. And then she was quiet. I figured maybe she was imagining herself in the city.

Lightning stepped on a dead branch and it snapped, flinging pieces all around us. Willow absently reached out and patted his neck.

Even though I was more comfortable on the horse now, knowing that he was so gentle, I still held tight to Willow because it felt good. And she didn't seem to mind.

I looked around at the woods. Squirrels darted from tree to tree, rattling the dead

leaves, but other than that, we didn't see any other wildlife. When I lived in the city I used to imagine that the woods near my grandparents' house were full of wolves, coyotes, snakes and rabbits. These woods sure didn't rise to my imagination.

After a few minutes we came to the path that I recognized led to the pond.

"Hang on, O'Dylan," she said, "we're going to trot." She gave Lightning a little kick and made a clicking noise. He sped up into a rougher gait. I bounced around behind Willow, slipping and sliding from side to side. She was like an anchor, and as long as I held onto her, I didn't fall off. After a minute we came into the grassy clearing by the pond. She slowed Lightning to a walk and stopped next to a small tree by the pond's edge.

"Slide off," she said.

It was awkward, but I pushed myself away from her and managed to get my right leg over the horse's back. Willow was solid on his back, and even though I was pulling on her as I tried to stay steady, she balanced in place. Once I was on the ground, she slid off and landed on her feet next to me. She took the reins and tied Lightning to a tree.

"So," she said, taking my hand and leading me toward the dock, "we return to the scene of the crime."

"The crime?"

"Isn't this where you taught Brock a lesson?"

I smiled. "Yeah."

Still holding my hand, she turned toward me. "Then teach me."

"A lesson?" I asked.

"No, teach me how to do what you did."

I rubbed the back of her hands with my thumbs. "That's not a good idea."

"You're the one who yelled at me in your yard because I don't defend myself against Brock. Now you can do something about it. How did you know what to do?"

"I took Taekwondo for six years."

"Okay, then you're an expert, right?"

"Wrong. I'm far from an expert."

"Brock's bigger than me," she continued. "I want to know how to defend myself. So, let's pretend some situations that I've been in and you can teach me what to do to protect myself."

I stared at her. I wasn't sure it was a good idea to give her just a little knowledge when I'd learned it all over several years.

She squeezed my hands, lifted up on her toes and stared into my eyes. "Please." It was almost a beg.

How could I refuse?

"Okay, I'll teach you a couple of moves because all of those bruises piss me off." I dropped her hands and stepped back. "What's one situation you'd like help with?"

"When he comes up from behind and kicks my legs."

Just hearing her verbalize the specifics of the bullying made my muscles tense. That erased my reservations. It was definitely time for her to know how to defend herself.

We spent the next hour perfecting the moves. She was a fast learner and stronger than I expected. Despite that, I was surprised when one time she mixed a couple of moves together and flipped *me* onto the ground. I hit with a thud, but she had controlled it enough so it only knocked the air out of my lungs a bit.

In a quick move she pinned my arms to the ground over my head and locked one foot against my leg so I couldn't move without risking hurting something. And she held me there.

"You're a good teacher."

I couldn't catch my breath, so I made a grunting noise.

She lowered her face closer to mine. "Are you having trouble breathing, O'Dylan?" she whispered through her own ragged breaths.

I nodded.

Willow leaned in so close to me that I could see the specks of dirt on her cheeks and forehead from earlier moves we'd practiced. Her lips hovered above mine. Her breaths became mine and my mouth went dry. Finally the air returned to my lungs, but it came in gasps.

I forced myself to suck in enough air to talk. "I kn-know wh-what would s-save my life."

She smiled and her eyes sparkled. "So do I."

No lips had ever tasted sweeter.

CHAPTER TWELVE

Willow leaned away from me and smiled, her arms and leg still pinning me to the ground. "And there's a lesson for you, O'Dylan."

My heart pounded. "Wow! I like your kind of lessons better than mine." I wondered where she'd learned to kiss like that, but I didn't really want to know, either.

Lightning pawed the ground next to the tree, distracting Willow. "I know you're sick of being tied to that tree." She kissed me once more then moved away. As she got up from the ground, I noticed her jeans had dirt and grass stains on them. That would be bad if someone saw them. At the same time, she leaned over and started brushing the grass off her knees as if she had read my mind.

"Sorry about your pants getting dirty." I rolled over to get up. "Think anyone will buy the excuse that we fell off Lightning?"

She raised her eyebrows. "Who do you think is going to ask?"

I straightened and shrugged. "I dunno." My grandmother's face flashed through my mind.

"You worry too much about what other people think."

"Probably. I guess growing up with Erik and having him and our family judged all the time has made me more aware of what other people think."

While I swiped at my jeans, she untied Lightning. After snapping her helmet on, she took mine from another branch where we'd hung it and tossed it to me.

"Come 'ere, Lightning," she said as she led the horse to the edge of the pond. "You need a drink." I was surprised when he stepped in up to his front knees and slurped the water. His whole neck moved as the gulps of water traveled up it.

I slipped my helmet on but left the straps unsnapped. "What if he goes all the way in?"

Willow shrugged. "He'll get wet."

"No kidding." I started toward the dock. "Can he swim?"

"I've never had him in water that deep, so I don't know. If he's like the ponies of Chincoteague, then I'm sure he can."

"What are the ponies of Chincoteague?"

She shifted the reins in her hand and swung them in a small circle in front of her. They made a whirring sound in the hot air. "Google it, O'Dylan. Everyone should know about them."

Lightning finished drinking and backed away from the edge. Willow easily jumped onto the horse's back, walked him a few feet into the water then turned him toward me.

"We'll make it easier on you this time. Come up on the dock to get on." She maneuvered him so he was just a few inches from the wooden edge.

This time I slid on behind Willow without a problem. She nudged Lightning with her heel, and he splashed his way out of the water and toward the path through the woods. We rode for a few minutes without talking. Somewhere nearby a tractor engine sputtered, and I wondered what the farmer was doing that would be hard for a tractor. Willow started to hum a tune I didn't recognize, and even her humming was pretty.

"Why don't you sing me a song?" I suggested.

"Lame."

"What do you mean lame? You have a great voice."

"I don't want us to come out of the woods looking like we're reenacting a scene from some cheesy love story movie."

I laughed. "That definitely puts a weird twist on the idea. I guess singing to your animals in the barn doesn't seem like a scene from Dr. Doolittle, then?"

She jabbed me in the rib with her elbow. "That's different. My animals never complain, even when I'm off-key or forget the words." She went back to humming but stopped suddenly. "I hope Shadow is going to be okay."

"My mom said he would be."

This seemed like an opportunity to bring up something I'd been thinking about since Mom had returned from the animal sanctuary.

"Did Mom say anything to you about it being against the law to keep wild animals?"

"Yeah, but I already kind of knew it."

"Is that why you didn't want me to call her?"

"I guess." She paused, and I didn't say anything because I thought maybe she was thinking about it. "I had a fawn once whose mother got hit and killed by a car. He was hit, too, but not hurt as bad. I brought him home and kept him in my barn and took care of him. Then, one day, some people showed up and said they heard I was trying to rehabilitate a deer and that only professionals were allowed to do that. And they took him and gave me a lecture."

"Did they tell you it was against the law?"

"Well, they didn't come right out and say those words."

I considered this and realized she wasn't being completely honest. The possibility bothered me. Sometimes my friends picked on me because I was such a rule follower, but I'd grown up with a dad who was a cop. I listened to his stories about the people who he said 'didn't think the laws and rules applied to them' and where they ended up. I guess I had an inside perspective that my friends didn't get. I wasn't a goody two shoes, either. I'd served a couple of detentions in school, and I'd been grounded plenty of times. But I'd never done anything on purpose that was breaking a law, so I didn't always get it when other people didn't think like me.

"If you knew it was illegal, why did you keep all of these new animals, like the raccoon?"

Her back stiffened. "Really? I don't need a lecture from you, too. Drop it."

I tensed at the anger in her voice. "I'm sorry. I wasn't – I didn't want — "

Willow interrupted me. "I'm going to lose all of my animals. They're being confiscated. Nobody loves them as much as I do." She sounded more sad than mad now. "They know they can depend on me. Everybody wants to know they have someone who loves them so much that they'll do anything for them and always be there."

Her wording caught my attention. "Every*body*? Willow, they're animals, not people."

"Okay, every *thing*. Is that better?"

I clamped my mouth shut because I could tell she was getting angry. I thought about her parents not being around and wondered if there was any connection between that and doing whatever she could for the animals even though she knew it was illegal. Maybe she wanted to give them what she didn't have. Because of that, I squeezed her even tighter.

We rode in silence for a while. I figured I'd let her decide when we'd talk again, and finally when we were crossing the field toward my house, she did.

"Brock was grumbling to Granny Annie last night about you being the first string pitcher on the team. That's pretty cool."

"What's cool? The fact that I'm pitching or that he's grumbling?"

She laughed. "Maybe both. Brock and his friends are used to everything going their way. You come along and all of a sudden they aren't as hot as they think."

"They're all really good baseball players."

She reached back and laid her hand on my leg just above my knee. "Yeah, but you're great."

I looked at her hand and smiled. Life didn't get any better than this. "Thanks."

"Yeah, I like that my boyfriend is a star."

The only word I heard was 'boyfriend'. The sun was beating down on us, so I wasn't sure if that's what was making me sweat or if it was what she said.

"I'm your boyfriend?"

She took her hand off my leg. "Don't you want to be?"

"Well, yeah."

She put her hand back on my leg. "Then what are you waiting for? Ask me out."

I dropped one of my hands from her waist and laid it on top of her hand on my leg. "I don't think I have to. It sounds like you just asked me out."

"Don't you know how to be romantic, O'Dylan?"

Now she was sounding like every other girl I'd ever gone out with.

"Um —"

She slipped her hand from under mine and off my leg again. A yoyo didn't move that fast. I was losing count of how often she was taking it away. "Never mind," she said. "I'll wait for you to think of a romantic way to ask me out, and then it will be official."

That conversation happened so fast that I wished I could rewind and start over. Maybe then I'd say all the right things. If I even knew what the right things would be. I glanced down where our hands had just been. I swore I could still feel the heat from her palm there. Just as I reached around her waist to take her hand and put it back on my leg, we came to the edge of a ditch at the side of the road.

Without warning she said, "Hang on!"

Willow squeezed her legs and coaxed Lightning to jump. His muscles tightened under us as he leaped from one side to the other. Despite my quick reflexes, my arms didn't go around Willow fast enough, so I flopped against her back when we landed, making my helmet hit hers. My backside slid toward Lightning's side, but Willow threw her elbow back just in time to stop me from falling. While I attempted to steady myself, Willow turned Lightning up the road toward our house and slowed him to a walk again.

"Thanks for the save," I said, "but you could have given me more warning."

She laughed and waved her hand in the air like she was trying to get a butterfly off it. "Spontaneity, O'Dylan. My grandmother says it's the only way to live."

"Yeah, if you live *through* it."

Willow patted my leg. "I'm tellin' ya. Stick with me, and your life will be full of spontaneity."

"That's not my strong suit," I responded. "I'm kind of like Erik in that way. Maybe I'm that way *because of* Erik, but I like things to be predictable."

"Lucky you that predictability has been a part of your life."

Was the envy that I detected?

Before I could pursue it, she made a kissing sound and gave Lightning a little kick. From the nice, gentle walk he jumped into a run, and again she was laughing.

I pressed my helmet against hers and said toward her ear, "You know that warning thing I mentioned earlier?"

"Yeah."

"That was a perfect opportunity and you blew it."

After the rough start, we moved smoothly with the horse's strides. It wasn't quite like the smooth up and down of a carousel, but it was actually closer than I expected. A warm breeze swirled around us, and even with the bit of concern tugging at my conscience about Willow's dishonesty regarding the animals, all seemed right with my world.

I could see that one of Willow's hands was tangled in Lightning's black mane, but the one

holding the reins pressed against my hands
clutching her middle.

"Like I said, O'Dylan, hang on! Life should be
full of surprises."

"You were a surprise," I said. "I never
expected to meet you, but I'm glad I did."

"Hey," she said, "I think you might be
catching onto that romantic thing after all."

I wanted to respond to her comment, but I had
nothing. Obviously I was barely catching on to the
romantic thing.

We came to the end of my driveway, so she
slowed Lightning to a walk as we turned into it.
The clip clop of his hooves was only half the
speed of the beating of my heart. Each time with
Willow had gotten better than the last, and I
wasn't ready for this to end.

"Wanna come in and get something to drink?"

"Sure." She stopped Lightning under the same
tree where I'd seen the horse for the first time with
Mom. "I'll tie Lightning here."

I slid off the horse's back, a little less awkward
than the first time, and Willow slipped off right
after me.

"Let me impress you," I said, and reached for
the reins. "Dad was a Boy Scout and taught me all
kinds of knots." I looped the reins around a lower
branch and tied them. "This is a bowline knot. He
told me that it never slips. There's no way the
horse can get loose from this."

"Cool. Maybe you can teach me that
sometime," she said. "Is Erik here?"

I glanced at the house then back at her. "Yeah.
My grandmother's watching him. Why?"

"I like him. We had fun on the swings the other
day. Come on." She took my hand and pulled me
toward the side porch like it was her house and she

was inviting me in. Her soft palm molded perfectly around my fingers. I stumbled to get into step with her.

My friends back home had always been nice to Erik, but none of them ever did more than say hi to him. I'd never had a friend look forward to seeing him.

The kitchen was empty, but I could hear the music and voices from characters in the *Cars* movie on the television in the living room. Erik could watch it ten times in a row and never get tired of it. Most times I'd see his mouth moving like he was saying the characters' lines. I knew Grandma was probably reading or knitting because those were two of her favorite activities.

"Who's there?" Grandma called.

"Willow and me – I – me - I." I tried to correct my grammar before Grandma did, but I confused myself. Fortunately she let it go. That was the rough part about having a grandmother who was an English teacher.

Scout trotted into the kitchen, her tail wagging and her nose in the air. I figured we probably smelled like horse, and it looked like she was happy with that. Willow kneeled in front of her and gave her a hug.

"You're such a good girl."

Scout laid her head on Willow's shoulder, and I swore the dog smiled.

I reached into the cupboard over the dishwasher and took down two tall glasses and set them on the island. "Let me see what we have to drink."

I opened the refrigerator and peered in. "Let's see. Lemonade, iced tea, orange juice, water and milk."

Willow gave Scout a kiss on top of her furry head then slid onto a stool at the island. "I'll have whatever you're having."

That sounded like such an adult thing to say that it caught me off guard. I looked over my shoulder. "Orange juice?"

"Sure."

After pouring us both a glass, I sat next to her. She sipped hers while I guzzled mine. It was easier to drink than talk since I didn't know what to talk about.

Scout padded out of the room. A moment later I heard Erik say, "Thcout ith my good dog."

That caught Willow's attention and she craned her neck like she wanted to see around the wall. "That's so cute," she whispered. "I love his little lisp because of his missing teeth. And, I'm picturing Erik hugging Scout right now. Do you think that's what he's doing?"

"I dunno."

She slid off the stool and moved to the kitchen doorway. "Can we peek in and see?"

"If you want." I got off my stool. "Usually when he's watching this movie he has all of his Matchbox cars lined up in front of the TV like they're watching, too."

We walked quietly through the dining room and stopped at the entrance to the living room.

Willow looked in, then turned and flattened herself against the wall. She threw her hand over her mouth and looked at me with her eyes wide. Her cheeks lifted above her hand so I could tell she was hiding a huge smile.

"That - is - adorable!" she whispered again.

I glanced in. Scout was lying next to Erik, and Erik had lined up his cars and trucks along Scout's back. A sports car was balanced on the top of her head. Her eyes and eyebrows moved, but not another muscle in her body did. Willow was right. It was a cute scene.

"It must be so much fun to have a little brother like Erik."

"Sometimes." Fun wasn't the word I would have chosen, but her response made me think of more of the positive memories than the negatives. I had to admit that sometimes Erik would giggle uncontrollably, and it would make everyone else in the room laugh, too. And he was a really good artist. He'd put details in his drawings that most six year olds wouldn't even notice.

We watched him run his cars and trucks all over Scout's body for a few minutes. Sometimes he'd pick them up and act like they were characters in the movie. At the moment, it was easy to forget he had autism.

My attention shifted to the dining room window when I saw something move outside. I had a perfect view of Lightning by the tree. He was rubbing his head against the bark and looking bored.

"Maybe we should go and finish our juice so we can get out to Lightning. We can take him to eat grass in the side yard."

"Good idea," Willow said.

She followed me back to the kitchen and we stood side by side at the island, our arms occasionally touching.

"So, are you pitching in tomorrow night's game?" Willow asked.

"I'm supposed to, unless Coach changes his mind."

Willow swallowed her mouthful of juice. "My friends, Cassie and Janelle, are coming with me to watch. I told them about you."

"Cool. I'll have my own fan club." I wrapped my hands around the glass and let the coolness seep into my sweaty palms. "Maybe afterwards we can go to The Nest to get some ice cream or something. I'll buy."

Willow tipped her head toward me. "Aww. That's the second romantic thing you've done today, O'Dylan. That's a great idea."

I smiled and leaned toward her until my shoulder bumped against hers. "So I'm batting a thousand?"

"Don't flatter yourself, O'Dylan. It takes a lot more than —"

The screeching of tires and the blaring of a horn interrupted her sentence. We bolted from the kitchen and ran for the side door. As soon as I was out on the steps I looked toward the road. A big, silver pickup truck was stopped at the end of our driveway. A middle-aged guy dressed in a worn t-shirt, jeans and a baseball cap came around the front of the truck. By the set of his shoulders, it was obvious he was angry. Willow cleared the steps behind me.

"That horse yours?" the man yelled.

I turned toward the tree where I had tied Lightning. He wasn't there.

"No, he's my friend's," I said.

Willow ran to the tree and held up the reins. "Oh, no! He rubbed his bridle off."

The man pointed down the road toward Willow's. "I damn near hit the thing when it ran outta your driveway. You better hope another car doesn't come along 'cause he's runnin' down the middle of the road."

Almost on cue, a car horn blew somewhere beyond where we could see.

Willow untied the bridle and raced past me toward the man. "Can you give me a ride so I can catch up to him?"

He glanced at his watch. "Get in. I can drop you off. I'm goin' that direction anyway."

I jogged toward them. "Hey, Willow, you know him?"

She yanked open the truck door and climbed in. "It's the country. Everybody knows everybody."

The man lifted his John Deere cap toward me as he hurried back to the driver's side of the truck. "Tom Wolcott. Nice to meet ya."

Once in the truck, he gunned it and the tires spun for a second. I stood at the side of the road, feeling helpless and praying I didn't hear a loud crash somewhere down the road.

I couldn't just stand there. I had to help in some way. I ran to the house and yelled through the screened porch door. "Grandma, I'll be back," I called. "Willow's horse got away. I'm going to go help catch it."

I ran to the shed to get my bike before she could argue – if she even would. I didn't want to take the time to grab my helmet, so I jumped on the bike and raced down the road. Granny Annie was just pulling out of her driveway in her van, so she stopped and leaned out her window.

"What's the hurry, Dylan?"

I skidded to a stop next to her. "Willow's horse got loose and it's running down the road."

Her eyebrows snapped up like little mountains above her eyes. "Willow doesn't own a horse."

I looked at her in confusion. "Yeah, Lightning. She took me for a ride through the woods, then when she took me home she tied him to a tree but he got loose."

Granny Annie slapped her palm against her forehead. "Oh, Lordy! When is that girl going to learn she can't save the world?"

"I'm sorry. I don't understand."

"Lightning isn't Willow's horse. He belongs to Mr. Pierce, the old hermit the next road over. That's not even what the old man calls him. Willow named him that."

Confusion muddled all of my thoughts and I tried to make sense of them. "But he lets her ride Lightning when she wants to?"

She shook her head. "No. In fact, there was quite a ruckus last summer about her taking him without permission."

"Willow stole the horse?"

I was beginning to wonder if I really knew Willow after all. First it was the animals she was keeping illegally, even though she knew it was against the law, and now, I found out she took someone else's horse and pretended it was hers.

"Stole might be a strong word. She thinks what she's doing is right."

The heat pulsing through my body had nothing to do with the sun. My thoughts tumbled like a kaleidoscope. I looked down the road in the direction the man had taken Willow. Could I even trust her anymore?

Granny Annie pulled her arm back into the car. "I'd help, but I have an appointment, and I can't be late."

I grabbed onto the door. "Wait! You're not worried that something bad could happen?"

"Dylan, so many bad things have happened with those kids that a runaway horse is nothing. She's almost fifteen. Part of life is learning from your mistakes. Maybe if I hadn't stepped in to try and make things right every time her mother made a mistake, then maybe she'd have learned to take responsibility for herself and she'd be here taking care of her kids instead of leaving it to me."

She reached down and pressed a button on the car's console. The air conditioner blasted on. I thought she was done, and I was speechless, but when she looked back at me her eyes were wet.

"Don't get me wrong. I love my grandbabies, but my whole life changed, too, when they ended up with me." She pursed her lips, drawing in her cheeks, and stared at the middle of the steering wheel. "I had my own life. I used to travel all over the world. And I can't do that now because someone has to be here for them. I'll be able to travel again someday, but for now, I'm all they have." A tear rolled from her eyelid and made a crooked line down her cheek. "I make sure they have everything they need, but I only have so much I can give of myself." She smoothed her fingers across her cheek to wipe away the tears. "I'm glad she has you, now, Dylan. I have to go." She rolled up the window and drove away in the opposite direction of Willow.

I stared at the back of her van until it was out of sight. I'd never known such a complicated family, and I had a new appreciation for mine, even with our flaws. I sat back on the seat of my bike and stared at the silver knob that connected the handlebars. Less than an hour ago everything seemed perfect.

Out of the corner of my eye I caught movement down the road. Lightning came up the little hill with Willow on his back. One part of me was relieved that he hadn't been hit. I couldn't really describe the other emotion I was feeling, but it was close to betrayal.

I put my foot on the bike pedal and pushed off, deciding to go home. Willow had her horse back. No, Willow had someone else's horse back.

She had lied to me.

I didn't pedal fast, and before I knew it, I heard the fast beats of Lightning's hooves coming closer. The blood at my temples thrummed.

"Dylan, wait!" Willow called.

I put on the brakes and sat on my bike but didn't turn toward her.

She brought Lightning up next to me. "Where are you going?"

"Home."

"Do you want to hang out more after I put Lightning away?" As if his name cued him, Lightning stomped a foot on the ground.

I looked up at Willow. Through a break in the dark clouds, the sun circled her head like a halo, but I was seeing her as anything but angelic. Her grandmother was right. Willow needed to take responsibility for what she was doing, and if everyone just kept covering for her, she'd keep on making bad decisions.

"No, I don't want to hang out. You lied to me."

"About what?" Lightning moved around, and she patted his muscular neck to quiet him. "Easy, boy," she said to him.

"Lightning's not your horse, Willow."

"I never said he was."

I glared at her. "You never said he wasn't, either. In fact, I had an interesting conversation with your grandmother." I paused to see her reaction, but there was none. "You *stole* Lightning."

"No, I take care of Lightning because his owner doesn't."

"He's not yours to take care of."

She slid off the horse's back and grabbed the front of my handlebars as if she needed to hold onto something. Her expression darkened at the same time that a cloud covered the sun.

"If it weren't for me, this horse would be rotting in a field. I asked Mr. Pierce to let me buy him, but he's cranky and selfish and doesn't want anyone else to be happy. And he doesn't care about Lightning. He was skin and bones the first time I saw him two winters ago. I saved his life. I'm the one who takes Lightning to the Mennonite farmer to have his hooves trimmed. I'm the one who makes sure when it's zero degrees out that there's extra hay and water in the field for him."

I tried to picture everything she was saying. The Mennonites were the people who lived in the area and drove horses and buggies and wore kind of old-fashioned clothes, so I figured they'd know how to take care of horses' feet. That part made sense. But I didn't know Mr. Pierce, and I didn't know how much of this was true or how much of it Willow wanted to be true to justify stealing someone else's horse. I shook my head, but before I could say anything, Willow continued.

"Someone has to care. Don't you see that Dylan? We all want to know someone cares for us. We all want to be saved. Animals are no different."

I stared at her for a second. This was the second time today she'd made a comment about wanting someone to care. And it made even more sense after my brief conversation with her grandmother. I understood Willow's point, but this was all more than my brain, and heart, could handle for one day. Her grandmother was glad I was here for her, but I wasn't sure I could be.

"I've gotta go." I turned the handlebars to loosen her grip, and she dropped her hands. "See ya," I said.

When I was a few feet away, she called to my back. "I'm not perfect, Dylan."

I raised my hand without turning around. I wasn't looking for perfect, but right now I was scared about how confused I felt.

I hadn't gone far when she added, "I don't care if you run away from me, too. I'm used to that."

Guilt slammed into my chest. Her words hit home. I did care. In fact, I was afraid I cared too much. If Granny Annie was right, I had fallen for the girl who wanted to save the world. And because I was so homesick for Manhattan, I wanted someone who would save me from a horrible summer.

But I was no longer sure Willow was the one to save me. I needed someone I could trust.

And so did Willow.

CHAPTER THIRTEEN

"Safe!"

Cheers erupted from the fans in the small bleachers and from my team on the bench. From the ground, I looked up at the umpire who stepped back from the play.

I rolled away from home plate and jumped up, trying to catch my breath. The catcher flipped his mask off his face and it sat on top of his head. He stood behind the umpire, scowling, with the useless ball clutched in his glove. Three of my teammates had crossed home plate before me, and I'd turned on all my speed and skimmed across just seconds before the ball smacked into the leather pocket of the catcher's glove. My first grand slam for the team, and at the crucial point: last ups and down by two.

"That's the game," the scorekeeper announced from the table behind the fence. "Renegades win 7-5."

My teammates, most of them, anyway, charged from the dugout to line up, ready to high five me as I jogged past them. My lungs still burned, but I was so pumped that it made it easy to ignore the pain. Brock and Zach moved toward the line, too, but they weren't breaking any land speed records.

They were only doing it because they knew Coach would bench them if they didn't. When I got to them, Brock held his hand up like he was going to slap mine, but at the last minute pulled it out of reach. His sneer said it all. I moved along to Zach, who looked away and held his hand up, forcing me to make the move. I hit his pitching hand – the one that hadn't seen any action this game. Guilt tugged at my conscience, but I squelched it. Coach had made the line-up decision, not me.

The team surrounded me, and I was forced toward the dugout. At first I moved along with them, but in the end my curiosity won. I froze in place and let the guys push past me as I sucked in air to catch my breath. Before I joined the line that was forming to shake hands with our opponents, I had to look toward the bleachers.

Grandma and Grandpa were easy to spot, sandwiched between other grandparents on the lowest bench. Grandpa sat with a huge smile, and lifted his baseball cap when he saw me look his way. Grandma stood in front of the bench, yelling my name and clapping her hands so hard I thought her bones would break. Mom stood next to the stands cheering, too, but her attention was divided between me on the field and Erik and Scout on the grassy area behind her. Erik was engrossed with kicking a soccer ball, lost in his own world and completely unaware that his older brother had just had a spectacular, game-winning hit.

That didn't matter to me, though. As much as I hated to admit it, what did matter was if Willow had seen me hit it. I scanned the entire bleacher area and beyond. I didn't see her. Convinced that maybe sweat was messing with my vision, I swiped my batting glove across my eyes to clear them. But, when I looked again, there was still no sign of her. I would have been satisfied to see her back as she walked away.

And at that thought, I gave myself a mental kick, annoyed by my disappointment. After all, this was what I wanted. I needed distance and time.

For a moment the image in my mind of the long lashes surrounding her brown eyes and her soft, pink lips blocked out the rest of my world. The muscles in my arms even felt heavy as if I'd just held her.

I returned to my teammates. We snaked along the line of approaching players from the other team, sharing our less than hearty, "Good game" comments. I'm sure I wasn't a favorite among them at the moment, but each guy did hit my batting glove.

When we reached the end of their team line, we circled toward our bench. As much as I wanted to keep looking for Willow among the fans, I knew it was best to go back and celebrate with my team.

And I suddenly realized there were two things to celebrate: tonight's win, and the fact that I'd learned the truth about who Willow Anderson really was before I was in too deep.

So then why, even after a week, did my stomach twist when I thought of her?

"Hey, slugger!" Coach yelled. "Don't stand there basking in your glory. Get over here with the rest of the team."

I hadn't realized I'd stopped walking.

"Just catching my breath, Coach." I leaned over for a second to make it look good then joined them.

Corky, one of the guys who didn't play much but was definitely all for what was best for the team, punched my arm. "Dude, that was fantastic."

I smiled, but I really didn't like the attention. "Thanks, man. The guy's pitch helped."

Tyler and Randy edged their way to me. We'd hung out a couple of times after practices and games in the last week, and while I was happy to have new friends, it wasn't like hanging out with Willow.

Tyler whistled low. "That was sweet, man. Wish I could do that."

"Me, too," Randy said. "Best I ever got was a double."

I shrugged. "Thanks. It was just the right —"

"Guys, get over here," Coach yelled. "I want to get cleaned up here before those clouds break loose."

I looked up. It had been cloudy when the game started, but at some point low, dark gray clouds had rolled in.

The pep talk and critique from Coach lasted about five minutes. He was almost done when a rumble of thunder shook the ground and made us all jump. Every one of my teammates looked toward the sky. I snapped around to look in the direction where Mom and Erik had been.

As I feared, Erik was sprinting across the grass toward the parking lot, his hands covering his ears. Mom wasn't far behind, but he was fast and she was wearing sandals, so it slowed her down. Scout was running at the end of her leash
pulling Mom forward.

"Erik," Mom yelled. "Stop! Wait for me."

I glanced toward the parking lot where cars were pulling out of spaces. I assumed Erik was trying to get to our car, but that meant running across the driveway. I broke into a full blown run, dodging small groups of people who were making their way toward the parking lot.

There was no one else close to him. The other parents and grandparents stopped and froze in place when they realized what was happening. One dad tried to cut him off, but Erik careened around him, headed straight for disaster. Another roll of thunder added to the chaos.

I couldn't believe this was happening again. In my head the scene from back in Manhattan when he'd been hit by the taxi flashed like a neon sign that only I could see. I dug my cleats harder into the grass, but I wasn't fast enough. And neither was Mom. She stumbled and fell, dropping Scout's leash when she hit the ground. Now free, Scout raced toward the parking lot as well.

The next few seconds became a blur. While I ran, I watched Erik dart between a car and a truck parked near the sidewalk, straight into the path of a silver pickup that had just pulled out. I prepared myself for the sound of the inevitable horrible thud because I couldn't see what was happening beyond the cars.

And then I heard it. The squeal of brakes. The near simultaneous thud. Gasping and yelling people.

I dashed between the same two cars Erik had gone between and skidded to a stop. He stood at the edge of the driveway with his hands flapping, the stuffed cat ear in one hand.

He was breathless, but I could make out what he was muttering. "My good dog. My good dog. My good dog."

My heart slammed against my chest when I looked toward the truck. Scout lay next to the front tire. There was no blood, and I could see Scout's eyes were open and she was breathing, but she didn't move. The driver, a man I recognized as a parent who had been to all of our games, came running around the hood.

"They came out of nowhere," he said. He pushed his shaking hands into his hair and held them there. He looked at me. "Is the boy okay?"

I nodded. "Yeah. I think so." I scooped up Erik, knowing that in the zone he was in at the moment, he wouldn't even realize I'd done it. Just as I turned him away from the scene, Mom ran up to us.

"Oh my god, is he all right?"

She started to reach for Erik, but then she saw Scout, and I could see she was torn between her responsibilities as a mother and those of a veterinarian.

"I've got Erik, Mom," I said, moving us farther away. "He's not hurt. But you've gotta help Scout."

"Did Erik get hit?"

"No."

She looked back and forth between Erik and Scout.

"Mom, he's okay," I repeated. "Take care of Scout." I'd never talked to my mother that way because she never would have allowed it, but at the moment, I was in charge. Panic clutched at my chest, but I fought it for Erik's sake. She couldn't let Scout die.

Grandma and Grandpa reached us at the same time. Grandma wrapped her arms around me and Erik, but I wasn't

letting my little brother go. Not even to Grandma. Grandpa moved past us, and I knew he was going to help Mom since he was a retired veterinarian.

I couldn't look behind me, but I saw Grandma look. On one level I wanted to know what was going on, but on another level I wanted to pretend this wasn't happening.

A bolt of lightning streaked across the sky in the distance, followed by more thunder. Erik's body tensed and he slammed his hands against his ears. His eyes were squeezed shut so tight that there were wrinkles from his cheeks to his forehead. I had no idea how long he would let me hold him if this storm got worse.

Behind us in the parking lot, people were finally starting to talk. I could hear them and wanted to shout at them to stop talking about it, but it wouldn't have made a difference. Anyone here would be affected.

"What happened?" a man asked.

"That dog ran out and stopped the little boy from running in front of the truck," a woman responded.

"I think the dog got between the truck and the kid on purpose," the truck driver added.

I couldn't listen to the conversations so I moved farther away and onto the grass. My chest was getting tighter every second. Erik started kicking his legs, trying to get down.

"Thcout! Thcout! Thcout!" he screamed.

"Mom's taking care of Scout," I said. I grasped his calves and pulled them tight against my hip. I didn't want to let him go.

I couldn't let him go.

Drops of rain hit my bare skin below my uniform sleeves. First it was just a splash here and there, then it was like the skies opened up and the rain poured down. So many people, including several of my teammates, gathered on either side of us, trying to see what was happening. People whispered and pointed, sometimes toward the truck and Scout and sometimes at Erik and me.

Even though I knew they were just curious about what had happened, I couldn't stand to have them staring at us.

"Grandma, can we take Erik to your car?" I asked. "Ours is probably locked." Locking it was a habit from the city. Even five miles out in the country, our car doors were always locked.

"Good idea," she answered, and she led us toward her beige Chevy, far away from the action. It was awkward, but I managed to slide onto the backseat even with Erik squirming in my arms. Grandma got into the driver's seat then angled toward us.

"That was so close," she whispered.

I nodded. I didn't even want to think about how close it was.

"You're a wonderful brother, Dylan. You knew just what to do."

I stared at her. At the time I hadn't thought about what I was going to do. I had just done it. I'd never even thought about whether it was right or wrong.

"I was scared," I admitted. My knees were still shaking.

"You were brave and mature," Grandma corrected. "Protecting Erik was the only thing on your mind."

"Scout protected Erik," I said. I pictured her lying motionless. "I heard the truck driver say she ran between Erik and the truck. What if she die—"

Grandma put her finger up to her lips to silence me before I said the word. "Your mother and Grandpa will do everything they can."

I pressed my cheek against Erik's head. He had actually settled against my chest, but as soon as I loosened my grip, he crawled away from me and onto the far side of the seat where he rocked. It didn't surprise me. What *had* surprised me was that he'd allowed me to hold him that long at all. I also wasn't surprised when the cat's ear came out of his pocket and he rubbed it against his cheek. Relief spread over me.

"Oh, good," I said to Grandma. "He's acting normal."

My choice of words made both of us look up and stare at each other. I'd never used the word "normal" to describe Erik before, but I suddenly realized, Erik did have a "normal", and it didn't have to be the same as everyone else's. It just had to be normal for him.

A knock on the car window startled me. I turned to see Grandpa, and he was talking. I opened the door so I could hear.

"...be fine," he said.

"What? I couldn't hear you through the window." The rain rolled off the bill of his hat and dribbled down onto the inside handle of the car.

"Scout's going to be fine."

I turned in the seat to face him. "How is that possible? She wasn't moving."

"Someone who witnessed it said she ran around in front of Erik and stopped him, but she got nicked and it threw her into the hubcap of the wheel. It appears that it only stunned her."

I didn't care that I was a guy and guys aren't supposed to cry. I was so relieved that I could feel hot tears pushing against my eyelids.

"Thank the Lord," Grandma said.

"Your mom's going to take her to the clinic to get a few x-rays and maybe treat her for shock, but we both think she'll be fine."

I glanced at Erik. I had thought he was lost in his own little world, but he was staring at Grandpa with wide eyes. Instead of rubbing the ear against his cheek, now he just pressed it there.

"Thcout'th my good dog," he said.

Grandpa chuckled. "That's an understatement, young man, but you're right. Scout *is* your good dog."

I slumped back against the seat. Despite the rain pouring outside, there was a sun shining inside me. I pictured my older brother. 'Take that, Trent.' I thought. 'I'm not the loser you think I am.'

Without anyone telling me what to do, I had taken care of Erik during a crisis. And I'd done it well. It was step one in reaching my goal for the summer. And that goal included keeping him safe from any other crises.

Because of the storm, Grandma waited with Erik and me at our house. Erik went right to the table in the den where he'd left out a big wooden puzzle of the world. He climbed up on a chair and sat on his knees.

"Where'th Thcout?" he asked for at least the tenth time since we'd left the park. He didn't look up as he grabbed a piece from his puzzle.

"Mom took her for a ride to the clinic," I said. As usual, he didn't acknowledge that he'd heard me, and he didn't ask for details.

Within seconds, he was humming random notes and totally focused on his puzzle as if nothing traumatic had happened less than a half hour before.

"I'm going to start something for dinner," Grandma said. "Can you stay with Erik?"

"Yeah." I took out my cell phone and tossed it on the table then sat in a chair at the other end. I watched Erik as he picked up a puzzle piece, turned it around in his hand, said what country it was without looking at the back, and then put it in the correct spot on the base. Despite my years of taking geography classes, I was embarrassed to admit there was no way I could name even half of the countries of the world, let alone place them in the correct location on a board.

As soon as Grandma left the room, our house phone rang and she picked it up in the kitchen. I heard her say hello to my dad and then proceed to explain in detail what had happened. I was glad she was doing that. My voice would probably get shaky if I had to retell the story. I picked up my phone and pulled up the Internet on it. I needed a distraction to help my nerves settle.

When I heard Grandma hang up I yelled, "How did Dad know what happened?"

Pots and pans rattled in the kitchen. "Your mom called him on the way to the clinic. He let Trent know. He's going to try and track down Christina."

No sooner had she told me that than the phone rang again. I heard her say hello to Christina while she continued to get out utensils, open cupboard doors and drawers. I never realized how many noises were associated with making a meal until I tried to listen to what she was saying and couldn't hear over top of the banging. Trent called her right after that, and as I listened to her reassure each of them, all I could think was I couldn't wait for all of us to be together again. I didn't know if Christina would ever move back home, but even Trent, as annoying as he often was, would be nice to have around. At least at times like this.

There were a few minutes of quiet before the phone rang again. I jumped up from the chair hoping it was Mom calling with an update. Grandma talked for a moment then called to me.

"Dylan, it's your dad. Can you pick up the phone?"

I grabbed the cordless phone off the credenza and pressed the on button. "Hey, Dad."

"Hi, slugger. You're just the guy I wanted to talk to."

"Really? I don't know any more than what Grandma told you," I said. I returned to the chair at the table and watched Erik meticulously pick up pieces that abutted each other on the board and put them in place.

"I'm calling for a different reason," he said. "Grandma and
your mom both told me that you really stepped up to the plate for Erik today."

I thought it was funny that he was using baseball references but not talking about the game. "Scout is the one who saved him. I didn't do anything."

"Grandma said you removed him from the situation and kept him from bolting again. You made the right decision about what needed to be done. And I'm proud of you for it." His voice was even deeper than usual. Was he choked up?

I sat up straighter in the chair. Although I was sure it was never on purpose, I'd never felt like I matched up to Trent in Dad's eyes. Trent had always been the star at everything he did: soccer, basketball, baseball and even dealing with Erik.

"Uh, thanks." My tongue was tied. I was talking with my dad, and I didn't know what else to say. That was crazy.

There was an awkward silence, at least awkward for me, until Dad cleared his throat and said, "How did your game go tonight?"

I thought about it for a few seconds, trying to decide what to say. Finally I settled for, "We won."

"That's great," Dad said. "How did you do?"

"I had a good game."

I picked up one of Erik's puzzle pieces and looked at it without really seeing it. My brain was overstuffed, and my homerun was insignificant. The real grand slam of the night was the fact that Scout had protected Erik, just as she was trained to do and, if Grandpa was right, Scout would be okay, too.

"Good." He paused then said, "Well, look, I have to get back to work. I'm glad we dodged a bullet tonight."

I hated when he used that term, because he literally dodged a bullet once. It had happened before I was born when he was sent to an attempted robbery, but it reinforced the daily danger he faced.

"Yeah, we did. 'night, Dad."

"Good night, Dylan. You keep up the good work."

"Okay." I hesitated, then hastily said, "Dad?"

I'd spent the last few years wanting Dad to treat me like a

grown up. And now that he was, something inside me wanted to be a little kid again so he'd wrap me in his strong, protective arms.

"Yeah."

"I miss you." I had no idea growing up would get so complicated.

I heard a heavy sigh on his end. "I know. I miss you, too, bud. Hang in there."

The phone clicked on his end without him
saying goodbye. I stared at the handset, a wave of
loneliness swooping over me. I missed him. I
missed my friends.

And as much as I didn't want to admit it, I
really missed Willow.

Erik and I had been so distracted that we'd
forgotten about the storm, but when a bolt of
lightning lit up the sky we both looked toward the
window. The boom of thunder followed a few
seconds later, and Erik leaped from the chair and
ran from the room. I ran after him to see where he
was going. He was so focused on getting away
from the storm that he wasn't even aware of me.

He dashed through the living room and opened
the door to the closet in the foyer then slammed it
shut again. He ran back to the living room and
dropped to his knees on the far side of the couch.
It moved a bit away from the wall and he
squirmed his way behind it. It reminded me of my
friend's dog that squeezed behind the couch when
someone would take out the vacuum cleaner.

If Scout were here, she would have crawled in
there with him and laid as close to him as she
could to calm him. Without her here, I had to
come up with a different plan. I didn't want Erik
staying behind the couch all night.

Then an idea struck me. Since I knew Erik
probably wouldn't move from behind the couch, I
ran back into the den to the entertainment center. I
snagged the noise-cancelling headphones and went
back to the couch.

"Erik, I have something for you that will make
the thunder go away."

He didn't respond.

"I promise it will cover the sound. Trust me."

I was shocked when he backed out of the space. He trusted me.

"Here, put these on, then we can go back and finish putting the countries together. You can teach me about them, okay?"

He reached out and took the headphones from me and slid them over his ears. The tense expression on his face loosened. The real test came when another bolt of lightning struck outside and the flash bounced off the walls. His eyes got big as he waited for the thunder. But he didn't hear it. And he knew it. He got back up and took hold of my hand.

"Come with me, Dylan. You have to learn countrieth."

I went with him and we sat at the table again. The headphones looked big and clunky on his little blonde head, but he didn't seem to mind. He picked up the cut out of a European country and snapped it into its place.

"Belgum," he said, mispronouncing the name. "The capital is Bruthelth." He tapped the piece to make sure it was in securely. "I don't like bruthel throutth. They're green."

Christina had been the one to teach him about all of the countries and capitals around the world. While he picked up Switzerland and put it into place, I thought about the times back in the city when I had showed off his memory skills to my friends. All anyone had to do was tell him something once or twice, and he never forgot it. It was a skill that would be great for him to use when he had to take tests in the future – as long as nothing ever changed in how he was asked.

I was completely lost in that train of thought when my cell phone vibrated on the table. I picked it up and saw a text from a number I didn't recognize. A misdial? I slid my thumb across the screen to pull up the message.

Meet me at cabin 2morrow at 10

I stared at the screen. I guessed it was the cabin Willow had shown me in the woods. I texted back.

Who is this?

Willow

My heart sped up, and I sat back in the chair and stared at her name. My brain told me to turn the phone off and ignore her messages; my heart wouldn't allow me to do it.

Whose phone is this? I texted back.

Briannas Im at her house I want to c u

Why?

have to talk

I thought about it for a minute. Given what I'd learned about her, I probably couldn't trust anything she had to say. It was best if I kept my distance. My fingers flew over the keypad.

Can't. Have to watch Erik

Bring him Then she added, **_PLZ COME!_**

I could hear her voice in the written plea. I'd missed her so much that whenever I thought of her over the last few days my chest ached with loneliness. I'd never had a girl affect me that way before. I took a deep breath and let it out slowly. There was only one word to describe me right now: sucker.

ok

I held the phone for a moment then pressed send. My heart swelled, but my gut told me I'd just made a mistake.

CHAPTER FOURTEEN

I rolled over on the couch when I heard a noise coming from the area of the back door. Startled, I sat up, trying to orient myself. My brain was fuzzy from sleep, and it took a minute for my eyes to adjust with only the one small lamp on in the corner of the living room. I listened for more noise. At first all I heard was the rain pelting the windows. Fortunately, there hadn't been thunder or lightning for a while. The back door slammed and then there were muffled voices.

I glanced at the loveseat and saw that Erik, his ears still covered by the headphones, was stretched out across it and in a deep sleep. He clutched the cat ear in his outstretched hand.

"Mom?" I called.

There was no answer. I got up from the couch to see if it was Grandma. I didn't even make it to the doorway before Scout lumbered around the corner, her tail wagging. A wave of relief washed through me.

"Scout!" I kneeled and held my arms out for her to come in for a hug. "I'm so happy to see you." She stopped long enough for me to pat her on the shoulder, but she wasn't interested in me or my hug. She wiggled out of my arms and trotted to Erik on the loveseat.

He didn't wake when she climbed up and stretched out next to him, settling her golden face against the crook of his arm. Without fully waking, he shifted onto his side and threw his other arm across her so he was holding her in a loose hug. One of the puzzle pieces dangled from the fingers of that hand. Australia, maybe. Scout nuzzled her nose under that hand until
the puzzle piece tumbled to the floor and his fingers settled on her ear. She drew in a deep breath and let out a contented sigh. She was with her boy, and she was happy.

I heard footsteps behind me. I stood and turned as Mom, Grandma and Grandpa came into the room. Grandma's eyes were watery, but her smile couldn't have been wider.

"Is Scout okay?" I asked. She looked fine, but I couldn't shake the image of her lying lifeless on the pavement.

Mom nodded and smiled. "Yes, she's a lucky dog. Nothing showed up on the X-rays, and we gave her fluids as a precaution for shock. She was moving normally by the time we got to her, but her muscles are a bit bruised, so we have her on some meds to keep her comfortable."

I wasn't cold, but I shuddered. "I keep thinking about what might have happened to Erik if Scout hadn't been there."

Grandpa stepped next to me and put his arm over my shoulder. "You can't be ruled by the 'what ifs' in your life. You can't change the past, but you can learn from it. The important thing is both Erik and Scout are none the worse for the wear."

I nodded. He was right. I lowered my voice even though Erik's ears were covered. "You know, Erik can be a pain in the butt sometimes, but I don't ever want anything to happen to him."

Mom moved next to us, too. "Erik forces us to be better people and more understanding. I've already noticed a difference in your maturity since we've been here. I know this move and the added responsibility for Erik has been hard on you, Dylan, but I appreciate that you haven't complained."

I forced a smile and looked toward the floor. I thought of my episodes of anger when she and Dad broke the news about the decision to move. I'd been grumpy at every mention of it after they'd told me. Mom had to have noticed when she had asked me to start packing that I had stubbornly put it off until a couple of days before, which had only caused everyone more stress. At the time I believed I was proving a point. I was, all right. I was proving how self-centered and immature I could be.

The truth was, if I'd had a choice, I'd still be in Manhattan.

But then I wouldn't have gotten to really know my little brother, and I wouldn't have met Willow.

I thought of the text she'd sent earlier. Considering what I'd put Mom and Dad through with this move, maybe I needed to be a better person before I condemned Willow for her imperfections.

"I'm trying to do my part," I finally mumbled. It was true, and at that moment, I resolved to try even harder.

"That's all we ask," Mom replied. She tiptoed across the wood floor, knelt next to Erik and Scout and laid her hand on Scout's rump. Scout's tail thumped a couple of times against Erik's leg. Mom leaned over and kissed the top of Erik's head then pressed her cheek against Scout's ear.

For the moment, everything felt right.

"It's after ten," Grandma said. "Time for us to take these old bones home now that everyone is safe and sound. I'll see you the day after tomorrow."

Mom didn't get up, but she turned and waved. "Thanks, Mom and Dad. You're both the best."

Grandpa walked by me and clamped his hand on my shoulder. He was almost seventy but he still had the strongest grip of anyone I knew. Besides Dad.

"Great job in that game tonight," he said. "We were mighty proud of you."

The game. It seemed like it was days ago rather than hours.

"Thanks."

They went out through the kitchen and the back door slammed behind them. I turned back to Mom. "Do you want me to carry Erik up to bed?"

She shook her head. "No, I'll stay down here with him and Scout. I want to call your dad again anyway."

I sighed. "It will be nice when he's finally here for good, too."

Her eyes looked tired as she nodded. "Yes, it will."

"Well, g'night."

"Good night, Dylan. And thanks again."

I lifted my hand in acknowledgement and headed up the stairs. With the scare with Erik and Scout over, my mind shifted to Willow. I couldn't lie to myself. I couldn't wait to see her in the morning.

I started to flip on the switch for my overhead light when something caught my attention outside. I left my light off and plowed through the clothes scattered on the floor to get to my window.

There was no mistaking the long red and white light bars on top of the two cars parked in Willow's driveway. I raced from my room and pounded down the stairs.

"Mom!"

She met me in the foyer. "Dylan, why are you yelling?"

"Come 'ere." I hurried toward the living room and pointed out the window. "Look. There are cops at Willow's house."

Mom took a deep breath. "Oh, boy."

Trying to relax the knot in my stomach, I turned to her. "What are we going to do?"

"We aren't going to do anything."

"But what if something's wrong?"

"If Anne needs us, she'll call. It's their business, not ours. Hopefully it's nothing big."

The knot in my stomach tightened. Two cop cars was a big deal. What if Brock's bullying had gotten out of hand and he had really hurt Willow? Maybe he was mad because my homerun had won the game tonight and everyone was treating me like a hero so he took it out on her. Bile rolled up toward my throat.

I turned from the window and paced. "Maybe I'll ride my bike down and see."

"No," Mom said. "Go to bed. You're tired. Your emotions are on overdrive. If they need help, they'll contact us."

I wanted to argue, but that was pointless. I dragged myself up the stairs and sat on the edge of my bed, staring across the wide field. Then I thought of the text from Willow earlier. If she was

still at her friend's house, then maybe they'd
answer a text from me. I pulled my phone out of
my pocket and texted.

"Is Willow okay?"

I stared at the phone for a few minutes, praying
it would vibrate with a response. Finally, I looked
back toward the window. I sat staring for a long
time until my eyelids got heavy and my eyes
burned. My head dropped to my chin a couple of
times, but I jerked back up, not wanting to fall
asleep. Time dragged, and focusing on the red and
white lights had almost hypnotized me. I decided
to lie on my bed facing the window.

I never saw the cop cars leave.

"Dylan. Time to get up."

Mom's voice was coming out of the umpire's
mouth. He should have been saying, "Batter up." I
glanced at the bat in my hand, but as soon as I
looked down, it disintegrated. Coach yelled,
"Dylan!" and pounded his fist against the side of
the dugout, then he, too, disappeared.

What was happening?

Willow stepped around the dugout. "Dylan!"

"What?"

More banging. I popped up and looked for my
teammates. For Willow. I blinked my eyes fast
and looked around. It was then that I registered
that I was in my bed and someone was knocking
on my bedroom door.

"Dylan, are you awake?" Mom asked. "I have
to leave for work in a minute, and Erik is already
up and at it, so you need to get down here."

"Yeah, I'm awake" I answered, my voice
raspy. I flopped onto my pillow and stared at the
ceiling, trying to shake the disoriented feeling. At

some point during the night I had changed out of my uniform and gotten under the covers. I tried to shake the dream haze by orienting myself. I wasn't at the ball field. The bat and Coach hadn't just disappeared. And Willow wasn't standing next to the dugout.

I glanced toward my door, wishing I'd see her there, but at the same time thinking that would be kind of weird. Then I remembered the cop cars from last night. I twisted in my bed to look toward her house. The cops were gone, and all looked quiet. Maybe Mom was right. Maybe it was nothing big and everything was okay this morning.

My phone laid next to my pillow. I grabbed it, hoping there was a return text. There was nothing. It was 8:03. In a couple of hours I would see Willow again. The last week had been like that interminable time the week before Christmas when each day drags by like it has 48 hours in it. And now I wanted to know why the cops had been there.

There were no rain sounds, but it was still unusually dark for this time of the morning. The weather men had predicted three days of possible storms starting last night. They had hit that forecast. I thought of Erik and hoped they were wrong about the next two days, and more importantly, about today. We wouldn't be able to meet up with Willow at the cabin if it was raining.

"I'm leaving," Mom called again.

"I'm up." I threw back the sheet and rolled off the bed. Tomorrow. I'd sleep late tomorrow, because Erik would go to Grandma's.

I hadn't even hit the top of the stairs when Mom yelled, "There's leftover lasagna and garlic bread in the refrigerator to warm up for lunch. I'll be home around six. Any problems, try Grandma, and if she doesn't answer, call the clinic."

"Okay. Did you hear anything about what was happening at Anderson's last night?" I was halfway down the stairs when she came to the bottom, her teal lunch bag hanging from her hand.

"No, not a word. I'm sure everything is fine."

"I hope you're right." I realized I did feel a little less tense. "How's Scout doing today?" I asked.

"Looking good, but if she starts vomiting or acting lethargic, call me right away." Mom opened the front door. "Have anything on your plate today?"

I almost blurted out that I was going to meet Willow in the woods, but decided against revealing that. Instead, I joked, "Well, hopefully not vomit." I came the rest of the way down the stairs.

Mom wrinkled her nose and made a disgusted face. "Yuck."

I shrugged and laughed. "Hey, you brought up the vomit, not me."

"Yeah, well, leave it to you to twist that comment around. Erik's in the den playing."

I waved. "Okay, see ya."

I figured Erik was probably working on his world map puzzle again. One thing consistent with him was that once he started something, he always saw it through to the end. He always liked things to be finished.

My stomach growled. It was a relief to feel relaxed and hungry. I had no choice but to believe Mom was probably right about everything being okay at Willow's.

"First things first," I said, and patted my stomach.

I went to the kitchen and opened the cupboard with the cereal. Cheerios, Froot Loops, a bran cereal and Erik's Lucky Charms were lined up by height. It was typical of Mom to have the cupboards orderly with everything arranged by size. Obviously Erik had inherited that organized gene, not me. If I'd put the groceries away, everything would be tumbling out right now.

I stared at the boxes and decided it was a Froot Loops kind of day. After shoving the cereal box under my arm, grabbing a bowl, a spoon and the half full gallon jug of milk, I carried everything to the den to see what Erik was doing. On my way past the dining room I was surprised to see four of the high-backed wooden chairs missing from around the table. Had Mom taken them to the garage because she was going to refinish them again?

My question was answered six steps later when I turned into the den. Although the chairs weren't visible, there was no doubt they were under the non-matching floral and striped sheets that were draped to make a fort in the middle of the small room. I turned sideways to squeeze between the recliner and floor lamp and Erik's bulky creation. There was a click and the beam of a flashlight shone up through the fabric, moving back and forth like a light saber.

"Who'th there?" Erik sounded cute with his missing front teeth, but every now and then my brain still cringed remembering the meltdown when the first tooth fell out. Even though the dentist and Mom had tried to prepare him for it, when it actually happened, he was still convinced his body was falling apart.

I made my voice deeper and responded, "It is I, Luke Skywalker."

The flashlight snapped off, then the split in the sheets that created the door snapped apart and Erik popped his head out. He scrunched the cloth tight around his neck and under his chin to prevent me from seeing in.

He scowled. "You're not Luke Thkywalker."

I blinked and his scowl morphed into narrowed eyes and an untrusting expression. "You didn't tell the truth," he added.

There it was - the side of him that hadn't yet learned that pretending was supposed to be fun. With Erik, everything was straightforward. There was no gray, only black and white.

"I know I'm not Luke Skywalker," I said. "I'm pretending. Pretending isn't lying. Pretending is —" I stumbled for a definition that would make sense to him. "Pretending is like playing a game, and you make believe you're someone else."

He stared at me like he still didn't believe I was telling the truth. Everything was literal in his world. I pulled in a deep breath and held it, forcing myself to be patient, and like a miracle, I thought of a way to explain it on his terms.

"It's like when you swing from the swing set and make monkey noises. I know you're not really a monkey, but you're pretending you are. You aren't lying. You're playing make believe. That's what little kids do."

"Oh," he said, and flung open the sheet doors. "You're a kid. Wanna come in my fort?"

Just like that I was granted entrance to his world, another score for me in the game of learning how to deal with Erik on my own. I looked at the makings of my breakfast in my hands. "Can I have breakfast in there with you?"

"I ate my breakfatht. Thcout ate her breakfatht." He crawled backwards on all fours and disappeared inside.

"Can I have my breakfast, then?"

"Yeth."

It was awkward to get down on my knees while juggling everything in my hands, but somehow I managed. I shuffled along the floor and ducked to get under the clothes-pinned upper part of Erik's doorway. Because the sheets were light colored, it wasn't dark inside. I wasn't surprised to see Scout lying on a beach towel next to the legs of one of the chairs. Our old green sleeping bag was unrolled next to her, and it took up a good portion of the middle of the fort. A stack of six or seven books was in front of Scout's paws.

"Scout reading those books?" I asked.

"No. Thcout can't read." Erik looked at me like I was the dumbest person on Earth. So he didn't get my joke. That was okay.

The fort roof wasn't high enough for me to straighten, so I maneuvered onto one of the burgundy chair pads he had lined up perfectly on the floor. There were four pads in a row, so I took the second one from the door and kneeled on that. I let the cereal box slip from the crook of my arm to the floor, then I set the milk and bowl down as well.

"Thith ith my fort," Erik said as he settled onto the sleeping bag and picked up one of the books. "And Thcout ith my guard dog. She won't let monthterth in."

I opened the box of cereal and poured it into the bowl. "Have you had a problem with monsters?"

"No." Erik stroked Scout's paw. "Thcout thcareth them away. Thee'th my good dog."

"Scout's a great dog," I said. A quick image of last night's scare flashed through my mind. "We're lucky to have her."

He nodded and opened a big blue hardcover kids' book that I recognized.

"Is that *The Adventures of Robbie the Raindrop*?" I asked. Because he was so afraid of storms, Mom had bought it hoping that if he understood the cycle of a raindrop that it would help him also understand why there are thunderstorms.

He nodded again. "Robbie floatth up and makth a cloud. He'th not thcary. Cloudth aren't thcary."

I'm sure Mom had said that over and over when they'd read the book together.

"That's right. Clouds aren't scary." I took the cap off the jug and poured milk onto my cereal, filling the bowl to the brim. Scout shifted on her towel, and when I looked, drool dripped from her mouth. It probably was a tease for her to have me pouring food that sort of looked like dry dog food into a bowl. She knew better than to come near when we were eating, so I knew my breakfast was safe, but her sad look still made me feel guilty. I picked up the bowl and spoon and dug in, slurping the cereal and milk off the over-sized spoon I had chosen so I could eat more in one bite.

"There are cloudth today," Erik said. "There were lotth of Robbieth when I got up."

"Uh-huh," I mumbled through the next spoonful. I was glad I'd chosen the sweetened cereal.

"Do you want to learn about the thycle of a raindrop?" he asked.

"Okay." I wiped my mouth with the back of my hand to get rid of the milk that dribbled down my chin then slid the back of my hand across my t-shirt.

He slammed the book closed, got on his hands and knees and crawled to the fort opening.

I quickly swallowed the mouthful of cereal and milk. "Where ya going?"

He was already outside the fort. "I have to get paper tho I can draw for you." His bare feet pounded across the floor, and a minute later he was crawling back inside, several sheets of paper in one hand and a marker in the other. He settled back onto his spot started drawing.

"Firtht, Robbie ith in the othean but then he vaporateth."

I was going to correct him on the pronunciation of evaporate, but he plowed ahead. The depth of his details astounded me. He sounded like a genius using words that I was sure other six year olds wouldn't have a clue about. His pictures to go along with his explanations were amazing, too. When did my little brother get so smart? And when did he start drawing like *that*?

Every now and then he showed his drawings to Scout, too. She pushed her nose into the paper like she was really interested, and then he'd put it down and continue. While he talked, I looked around the inside of the fort and back at him. This was a cute scene. Why hadn't I ever done something like this with him before?

Then the truth hit me. I had always been so wrapped up in myself and what I was doing that I'd never taken the time to get to know Erik. I knew him, but over the last few weeks I'd learned things about him that I should have already known. It had always been easier to let everyone else deal with him because they were older and knew what to do.

Like a bulb had been clicked on, I saw Erik in a totally different light. I didn't really know many six year olds, but I was sure he was smarter than most. He was also kind, and honest, and compassionate, and sometimes even funny. On purpose. And he really loved Scout, and showed her his love like he couldn't show any of the rest of us.

I realized Erik had been continuing his lesson while I was daydreaming. I focused in on what he was saying, not because I really cared about the cycle of rain, but because I needed to care about Erik and what interested him in order to understand him. He was a cool little kid, and he was putting his trust in me. It showed last night when he clung to me after Scout was hit. He showed it again just now when he invited me into his fort. His world.

Warmth spread across my chest and up my neck. Because of my lack of understanding, or caring to understand, I now knew that I'd let him down. It shouldn't have taken this many years for me to get to know my brother.

That was changing right now. I would never let him down again.

After Erik taught me about the rain cycle, we laid on the floor in his fort with Scout. I lay on one side of her, stretched out with my hands clasped under my head, and he lay up against her belly. He hummed like he was happy and in another world, which he probably was. There were times when he'd get so deep into the world in his mind that no one could get him to hear, even if he was wide awake. But I liked that he sounded content. I felt like it was probably enough for him that I was with him and his dog, so I didn't talk.

I closed my eyes and let my mind wander. If anyone had asked me what I was thinking about, I couldn't have really told them because I was thinking about everything and nothing at once. I thought of the cops at Willow's, but I didn't want to start worrying again, so I thought of something else. Last night's homerun popped into my mind next. My friends back in Manhattan. That led to thinking about Randy, Tyler and Connor and wondering if we would end up hanging out after the season ended. Brock was a fleeting thought before I pushed him out and let the good times with Willow take over.

When the doorbell rang, my eyes flew open and I bolted up. So did Scout, and her ears were up and eyes alert.

"Who'th here?" Erik asked.

"I don't know." I scrambled up off the floor and crawled through the opening in his fort. Our great grandmother's antique mantel clock was perched on top of the rolltop desk, which was also passed down from her grandmother. A jolt careened along my nerves. It was already 9:30. I twisted around and stuck my head in through the opening. "Erik, I'm going to go see who's at the door, but you need to get dressed."

He didn't acknowledge me. He had his hands up in the air above his face, twisting his fingers in and out of each other like his fingers were one of those wire brainteaser puzzles.

The doorbell rang again. I'd deal with him after I checked to see who was at the door. I stood and hurried to the foyer. To be safe, I peered through the side light window first. My heart tripped into high speed when I saw the gray uniform. A sheriff. I yanked open the door and stared at him.

"Hi, are you Dylan?" His voice was deep. Scary deep.

I swallowed the huge pocket of air caught in my throat. "Yes."

"I'm Officer Titus from the Sheriff's Department. I was told that you're a friend of Willow Anderson."

Dread heated my body, and I could barely get my mouth to move. "Yes. Is she okay?"

"Well," he said, his eyes never wavering from mine, "we hope so. Her grandmother said you're a friend of hers, and we're trying to find her."

"Find her?" I blurted out.

He held up a hand. "She said she was staying at a friend's house last night, but she left there early and never returned home. Her grandmother suggested you may know where she went."

I shook my head and thought I'd throw up. How many times had Dad come home talking about these kinds of cases? And how often had he followed up with the grim outcome? Acid rose in my throat.

"All I know is she said she was at a friend's house last night. I don't really know her other friends. Is she in trouble?"

"Our focus right now is to locate her. A guy on the next road over called and reported that his horse was stolen and accused her. We're trying to put all of the pieces together to see if the two things are even connected. Our priority is to find her."

I clamped my mouth closed, struggling with the decision about what to tell him. Considering what I'd learned the week before, it wouldn't surprise me if she'd taken Lightning again. And maybe she'd run away because of Brock. But those were all guesses on my part. I considered telling him I was supposed to meet her in half an hour in the woods, but then maybe she wasn't even going to be there, and instead of him spending time looking for her somewhere else, he'd waste his time in the woods. Or maybe she had contacted me to meet her in the woods because she wanted me to help her in some way. If I brought the sheriffs, it would betray her trust.

Officer Titus scratched his temple like he was trying to be patient.

"I haven't seen her in a week," I finally said. That was the truth.

He tipped his head like he didn't believe me. "Didn't you say she told you she was at a friend's house?"

My insides froze. Was he trying to trap me? "She sent a text from her friend's phone," I blurted. "But then after that when I saw the police cars at their house, I sent a text to see if she was still at her friend's, but I didn't get an answer."

He pulled a small spiral notebook and pen from his pocket. "Can I get some information from you?"

He took down my name, our address, Mom and Dad's names and my cell phone number. He asked what time she'd sent the message. This all seemed like some weird dream. When he was done, he flipped the notebook closed and took out a business card and handed it to me.

"If you hear from her, or hear anything you think might help us find her, call that number." He pointed to a phone number below his name. I nodded and put the card in my pocket.

"Will do." Although I tried to sound cool, inside me everything was twisted in knots.

I watched him walk back to his cruiser and get in. He turned the car around and headed out of our driveway. As soon as he was on the road, I raced back inside. Erik hadn't moved from his fort. I got down on my hands and knees and crawled partway through the door.

"Erik, come on," I said more urgently. I was relieved when he rolled his head to look at me. "Let's take Scout for a walk," I said. Scout's ears perked up as soon as she heard the word walk, but she laid still. "Can you change out of your pajamas fast?"

Erik continued to stare at me but didn't move. I wanted to drag him out of there, but touching him would be a bad idea, so I thought fast. "If we go for a walk and you bring your treasure box, I bet we'll find something super special to put in it."

He popped up from the floor. "Like what?"

"I don't know," I said, backing out of the fort. "But I bet there's a secret treasure out there with your name on it."

"My name?" He scrambled to the opening. "Do they know how to thpell my name?"

I stood and turned to him as he was getting up. "Who needs to know how to spell your name?" Scout squeezed out between us.

"Whoever hath my treathure."

If I hadn't been so tense, I probably would have found that amusing. "Your name won't really be on it. I meant it would be a special treasure meant only for you."

"Oh," he said, and raced toward the stairs with Scout beside him.

"Put on jeans," I added as I followed him up the stairs. Who knew what we'd end up doing, and I wasn't chancing poison ivy for either of us.

Erik was already at the bottom of the stairs when I came down. Scout stood in front of the door, watching as he put on his sandals.

"You'll need to wear socks and sneakers. We're going into the woods."

He looked out the window above the open foyer. "There are cloudth. What if it rainth?"

"We're going to hope it doesn't, okay. Can you change your shoes?"

He pushed his sandals aside and crossed the hall to the foyer closet. "I'm wearing my bootth."

"Fine." Scout's leash hung on a hook just inside the closet, so I reached over Erik to get it while he slipped into the rubber, calf-length boots that he called his fireman boots.

As soon as Scout saw the leash she began prancing in place. Her tail wagged so hard her backend slipped on the shiny hard wood.

"Scout, sit," I ordered. She complied, and I snapped on the leash.

Erik reached for the end of her leash. "I'll take her. The'th my good dog."

I handed it to him and opened the front door. "Okay, let's go look for treasures."

Scout walked perfectly next to Erik as we started down the driveway. I had planned to walk down the side of the road, but thought better of it when I considered Erik. Instead, we veered toward the field on the other side of the ditch from the road. Weeds as high as Erik's waist scratched at my legs below my shorts, so I walked in front to protect him from the sharp stems.

My mind was on Willow and why she wanted to see me. If she apologized for not being honest, how would I respond? If that's not what she wanted, should I bring it up and get it out in the open? Was I prepared to end my relationship with her for good?

I looked across the field toward her grandmother's house. No, she was too close for comfort. Even if it meant we'd never go out, I needed some kind of closure that didn't leave me wondering about the "what if". As she had pointed out, I was the kind of person who cared what other people thought of me.

A drop of rain splattered against my cheek, and I snapped my head toward the sky. Thick, dark clouds swirled like demons with long, gnarled fingers. I looked over my shoulder and saw Erik ambling along, blessedly unaware of the possibility that the sky might open up any second. There was no way to know if those ugly clouds were only threatening or if they'd make good on their threat. Dried weeds crunched under our feet, weeds that would be happy to have the rain, but I prayed it would hold off even for an hour. I studied the clouds again, and concern gnawed at my gut.

"You doin' all right back there, bud?" I asked. If Erik said he was scared, then we'd turn around.

"Yeth."

I did a mental fist pump. I'd given him the option to back out and he said he was fine. That was good enough for me. We were almost down far enough in the field so I could see Willow's front door. Maybe if we were lucky she'd come out of her house as we were passing so we wouldn't have to go to the woods. I wasn't looking forward to going back to the cabin considering its proximity to the ravine, but Willow didn't know it gave me chills just to be that close to the edge. To her, it was nothing.

When we got almost to Granny Annie's house I led Erik along the edge of the field toward the woods, following a route Willow had taken me with Lightning. I didn't want to take the chance that Brock would see us. The dense bushes that separated the field from her grandmother's house were high enough to hide Erik, but I had to bend down to get below the top line. This route took me away from the familiar, but I was confident that I'd know how to get to the trail that led to the cabin.

I was on high alert for any noises coming from the direction of the house or barn. Every snap of a weed behind me jangled my nerves, not only because of Brock but because I wanted things to go right with Willow – whatever that meant.

A cool breeze picked up across the field, a scent of rain clinging to it. At the edge of the woods I reached for my phone in my pocket and checked for messages and the time. 9:55, and I noticed I only had one bar of signal.

"There it ith!" Erik yelled.

I almost jumped out of my sneakers. "What?"

He squatted, poking at something in front of Scout's nose on the ground. "Thith. I'm looking for my name."

I bent over and all I could see was an old snail shell. "That used to be a snail's home," I said. "I don't think your name will be on it, but if it feels special to you, then it's your treasure. Pick it up."

He flipped it a couple of more times. "It will fit in my treathure box."

"Then it's yours. But we have to get going, so put it in your box."

It was like he was in slow motion. He pulled up the little clasp on his treasure box. Then he lifted the top as if he thought something would spring out at him. It took every ounce of patience for me to not grab it from his hands, shove the snail shell into it and slap it shut.

I gritted my teeth but forced a smile. "Would you like me to help you?"

"No." He picked up the shell, and Scout's nose followed it until he had finally dropped the shell into the treasure box and re-secured the latch.

I looked at my phone. Two minutes wasted. "Okay, let's go."

When we entered the woods the air warmed without the breeze pushing cool air through it. We hiked along the path that I was sure led to the cabin. Tree branches draped over the path in places, looking like arms and fingers reaching out to get us. They reminded me of the trees along the yellow brick road in *The Wizard of Oz* that suddenly came to life and grabbed the characters. I hadn't seen the movie in years, and I was glad Erik had never seen it.

The leaves barely rustled, but other than a lone chipmunk, the woods were strangely quiet as if the forest life was waiting for something. Maybe it was the storm pressing in on everything.

I rolled my head to loosen the muscles around my neck and shoulders then shook my hands out in hopes of getting the edginess out of my body. Maybe Erik's fears were starting to rub off on me.

Thanks to the crunch of his and Scout's footsteps on the old leaves, it was easy to hear when he slowed to look into his treasure box. I stopped one time and turned to find him picking up the shell and examining it. "Be careful about opening that too much, Erik. You don't want any of your treasures to fall out."

He snapped it shut and walked up to meet me. "I don't want to loothe my treathureth."

"Then we'll have to be very careful." I chanced putting my arm across his shoulder and encouraged him to walk next to me. After a couple of minutes, parts of the grayed wood siding of the broken down cabin were visible between tree trunks. My pulse sped up.

"Do you want to show it to Willow? We're going to see her in just a minute."

Because he and Willow had become fast friends, I knew that would get him to move faster.

"Willow?"

"Yeah. She's meeting us at the cabin."

It worked. His strides lengthened and his head bobbed as he tried to see around the trees. I took the wide route off the path to the cabin in order to avoid going anywhere near the edge of the ravine. As soon as Erik saw the cabin, he darted off, with Scout right next to him.

"Willow!" he yelled. He ducked in and around the lower branches and twigs on the trees.

I took off after him so he couldn't get too much of a jump on me, but I wasn't worried. His target was the cabin and Willow, so he wouldn't go beyond it. But when he and Scout disappeared around the corner of the dilapidated building, my discomfort skyrocketed. I heard the echo of the thud of wood on wood, then Scout's muffled bark.

"Hey, Erik. Wait up," I yelled. I couldn't dodge the branches and twigs as well as he could, so it slowed me down. As I approached the side of the cabin, I could tell Scout's barks were coming from inside.

"My dog!" Erik's voice cut through the stillness with the shrill of panic.

"Erik!" I yelled. I skidded around the corner, almost losing my footing on some loose dirt.

Adrenaline stole my breath when I got to the front.

Scout was locked in the cabin.

And Brock held Erik under his arm like a football, and the edge of the ravine was only a few feet behind them.

CHAPTER FIFTEEN

Pandemonium: it was a "word of the day" from eighth grade English that now pounded like a lightning bolt against my brain. Erik's piercing screams and Scout barking and scratching at the inside of the cabin door shattered the stillness of the woods. Every centimeter of my body was tense, on edge, but Brock didn't seem fazed by Erik's flailing arms and legs or Scout going crazy barking and scratching or the fact that he was just a few feet from the edge of the ravine. And it went thousands of feet down. His stance, feet spread shoulder-width apart and his chest puffed out, oozed challenge.

All I wanted was to get Erik away from him.

"Let him go." I managed to keep my voice steady as I stared Brock down, willing him to not step back. I was no more than ten feet from him and Erik, but it might as well have been a football field.

Brock's stare drilled into me. "We have a score to settle."

Like a scene from a movie, a clap of thunder followed his words. Erik screamed louder and pressed his hands to his ears as he wiggled against

Brock's hold around his waist. The situation couldn't get any worse.

"That's cool," I said, afraid to take my eyes off him. "But it has nothing to do with Erik. Put him down, and then it will be just you and me."

I took a step toward them.

And Brock took a step back.

I sucked in a breath and froze in an awkward stance. He was crazy.

I wished help would suddenly appear. Then I glanced around. I'd been so distracted by how close Brock and Erik were to the edge of the ravine that it hadn't even registered that Willow was nowhere around.

I looked back at Brock. "Where's Willow?"

His answer was a ridiculous laugh. "Sucker."

My jaw clenched. I hated that he used the exact word from my thoughts last night to describe my decision to come to the cabin. And I'd been right.

I couldn't believe how gullible I'd been. "You sent that text."

His smile was so wide I swore I could count every tooth in his ugly face.

Spit gathered under my tongue. "You bast—"

The sound of shattering glass yanked Brock's and my attention toward the cabin where Scout's barks turned to a yelp then a cry. She had broken out a small corner of the old, cloudy window. She scratched on the intact glass, desperate to escape and get to Erik. I glanced toward the door. Brock had jammed something through the clasp of the lock to prevent it from opening. On the ground in front of it, Erik's little green metal treasure chest laid wide open, his treasures scattered like trash among the dirt and leaves.

My brain was on overload with the barking and howling, the screaming, the thunder, the scratching against the window. I hoped at any second I'd wake up and find this was a nightmare. But I could smell the dampness in the air, feel the heaviness of the impending rain and taste acrid fear rising in my throat. This horror was all too real.

I looked back at Brock and had to yell over all of the other noises. "I'll do whatever you want if you'll let Erik go."

Brock glared at me.

Erik's cries ripped my heart. My mind scrambled for a negotiation tool. "You want me to quit the team? Done. You want me to leave Willow alone. Done. You want to beat the crap out of me? Put Erik down, and I'll take you on."

"You turned my sister on me," Brock barked.

Stunned by the accusation, I grappled to make sense of it. "How do you figure?"

"You taught her karate."

My first instinct was to correct him, tell him it was Taekwondo, but reason shoved out my instinct. "I taught her how to protect herself."

His expression darkened. "She turned on me. Just like everyone else." Brock shuffled back another step closer to the edge of the ravine, and my heart flew to my throat.

"No!" I yelled, thrusting my hands in the air. "Are you nuts?" My paralyzed muscles wouldn't move my feet. I didn't have to see the drop off behind him for it to make me dizzy.

Lightning sizzled above us, and I ducked instinctively. The lightning was quickly followed by a deafening roll of thunder that shook my body. What if Erik's twisting caused Brock to lose his balance? Brock scowled at Erik like he was persistent mosquito.

With his attention averted, I lunged forward, wrapping my arms around Erik's waist just below his underarms and above where Brock held him. Brock pulled against me, but there was no way I was letting go of Erik now. Brock lurched to the side in an effort to break Erik from my grip, but when he did, his heel tangled in a root sticking up from the ground. His eyes popped open as wide as fifty cent pieces. He let go of Erik in an attempt to catch himself. At the same time, I threw my weight in the direction away from the ravine, and Erik and I rolled to the ground a safer distance away.

Brock fell backwards and swore as the line of tree saplings at the edge snapped under his weight. His hands flew in every direction in an attempt to grasp anything to break his fall. And then his flailing body disappeared over the edge. I pulled Erik's face against my chest to shield him from witnessing anything more, while I tucked my own head against the top of his head. Brock's explosive grunts mingled with crunching leaves and cracking branches. I wished I could block my ears from the rapid fire snapping and cracking of the thin, young tree trunks that sounded like they were breaking like toothpicks under his weight.

Then, abruptly, every noise in the woods stopped. Even Scout was oddly silent.

Brock's whole fall, or at least the part of it I could hear, lasted only a few long seconds. Erik whimpered into my shirt, his hands clamped against his chest. I knew I needed to move, to see if Brock was broken and bloodied at the bottom of the ravine, but fear of getting that close to the edge held me in place.

Erik shook, so I pulled him closer. Rain swooped in through the canopy of the trees, splattering humungous drops against the dry ground around us to create tiny dust explosions. There was a small rumble of thunder, but I didn't see lightning. Erik seemed beyond reacting.

I loosened my grip and turned his head to be sure he could get full breaths of air. His eyes were closed tight as if it would prevent him from experiencing all of this if he couldn't see it. I lifted my head to listen. Scout had resumed scratching at the door. And from the direction of the ravine, moans floated up.

Relief flowed through my veins. Somehow, Brock had survived that fall.

My mind raced. Help. I needed to get help. I released Erik and got up on my knees so I could reach my phone in my pocket. My hands shook so much that the phone kept slipping out of my fingers, but finally I managed to get enough of a grip to pull it out. Ground in dirt covered my thumb, so I slid my index finger across the screen to unlock it. My fingers trembled as I tried to dial 9-1-1. I waited for the ring, but it was silent. Finally I pulled the phone away from my ear and looked at the front. There wasn't even a hint of cell signal. A lump pressed into my throat. I looked toward the ravine. How long could Brock hang on while I found an area with cell service so I could call for help?

"Brock!" I called. Erik startled then closed his eyes and pulled his arms tight against his chest again. I trained my ear on the direction where Brock had fallen. At first I heard nothing, but then a faint moan floated up again. The sound was close enough to tell me that he hadn't fallen to the bottom, but that was all I could guess. Without actually seeing how far down he'd fallen and how badly he was hurt, I wouldn't know what to tell the rescuers. Fear spread like a cold wave through me. Nothing scared me more than extreme heights, and the ravine's drop-off was something from my worst nightmares. But I had to see if there was any way to help Brock before I left.

"Erik." I kept my voice soft and calm to avoid startling him again. "I need to check on Brock. You stay right here and wait. Okay?"

He whimpered, but I wasn't sure that he was actually responding. When I wiped the rain off his cheek, it created mud streaks that reminded me of Indian war paint. If we'd been little kids pretending, that would have been fun. But this was on the opposite end from the fun spectrum. I laid my hand on his shoulder, closed my eyes and swallowed hard. The rain soaked my back and hair, and now was making splotches on Erik's dark green t-shirt. The conditions weren't going to get better, so I had to do this now.

"I'll be right back," I whispered.

For the first few feet I crawled on all fours, stopping, then forcing myself to move forward in tiny increments. My heart hammered against my ribs and sweat popped out on my forehead and neck. Mud ground into my sweaty palms. I tried not to look toward the edge, but I also had to be aware of where it was. A few feet from it, I could see the snapped off saplings where Brock had fallen. I dropped to my belly and pulled myself along with my elbows, inches at a time, not moving forward until I knew the ground under me was solid.

Brock's moans grew louder, and at one point I heard a weak cry for help. I didn't dare call out to let him know I was coming. I worried it might rattle the ground and make it crumble under me.

Fear thrummed through every nerve, but I'd gotten this close, I had to keep going. I inched forward. Sticks and pebbles jabbed into my skin despite my t-shirt. I reached forward just as a tiny brown snake slithered from under a rock in front of me.

"Uh!" I yanked my arms back and waited until it disappeared, moving under a layer of dried leaves a couple of feet away.

I took a deep breath, closed my eyes and said a prayer before I opened them again and scooched forward. My arms were outstretched, and my fingers came to the edge. I stopped and let them lay there, feeling the nothingness at their tips. The nothingness that could drop thousands of feet. I fought the shudder that threatened.

Finally I pulled myself forward enough so my head was halfway over the side. I squinted, trying to see only as much as I had to. But it wasn't enough. I needed to move forward more. I reached out and grabbed onto a pine tree branch that stuck out close to the ground. With that anchoring me, I wiggled forward a bit more until my whole head and neck were hanging out in the openness. Fear robbed my breath. I felt like any second I could go over the edge, too. I wanted to call Brock's name, but I was afraid to move that much air in my lungs.

I forced myself to open my eyes all the way. When I saw the drop off, bile shot into my throat and I gagged. I closed my eyes again for just a moment then reopened them, directing my focus to the area just below me. I saw Brock about fifty feet down. His body was pressed against a narrow ledge of rock that barely sustained tree roots and dirt. One of his hands hung limply at his side, but the other clutched a root sticking out of the dirt. He was far enough away that I could barely make out some deep scratches on his face and arms.

"I'm going to go get help," I called to him. "Just hold on."

"No," he croaked. "Don't le-leave me. I c-can't hold on. My f-fingers are g-getting numb."

"I'll get someone who can help," I repeated. Bits of dirt moved under my forearms and tumbled in tiny avalanches down the side. I winced when some hit him in the face.

"You help," he said. "I c-can't wait. I'll die."

Lightning cracked through the clouds, followed by a long rumble of thunder that shook the ground. I scrambled back a few inches, convinced the ground would give way. I heard movement behind me, and then out of the corner of my eye, I saw a dark blur go past the cabin. Scout launched into frenzied barking again inside the cabin. Using my elbows, I pulled myself back a foot so I could turn to check on Erik.

He was gone.

I dug my hands and arms into the coarse dirt and leaves and scrambled backwards on my stomach until I could stand without the fear of slipping over the edge. I cut across the front of the cabin and around the corner. All I saw was tree after tree. I ran a few more feet and lurched to a stop. I didn't know where to run. Panic jolted my body. Erik would run away from the ravine, right? But how deep were these woods? Would he run into any wild animals?

I whirled in a circle, trying to think fast, when Scout's barking cut through my fog of panic. I raced back to the cabin door and grabbed the top and bottom of the piece of stick Brock had wedged in the clasp and yanked it, breaking it in half. Only the middle piece was still stuck. I scoured the ground for something to hit it out with and spotted a round, palm-sized stone. I grabbed it and used it like a hammer on the top of the stick until the dried wood splintered and fell out of the clasp. I hurled the door open and Scout shot past me. Her nose was to the ground, trying to pick up Erik's scent. She zigzagged along the front of the cabin, stopping at his treasure box and its contents.

I snagged her leash, afraid she would bolt away when she caught his scent. Her sniffing reminded me of a freight train as she focused and plowed her nose through the leaves. I pulled her in the direction where Erik had gone, hoping she'd have an easier time picking up his scent if there was only one line of it for her to follow.

"Help me!" Brock's faint cry was muffled by the rain that bounced off every leaf in the forest.

I turned toward his voice. There was nothing I could do for him. But I couldn't just leave him to think I was abandoning him. Scout was determined to pull in the opposite direction, but I yanked her a few feet closer to the ravine in hopes that Brock would be able to hear me.

"I'll get help," I yelled.

"I'm sl-slipping," he responded. "I c-can't hold on."

My throat tightened and I looked back and forth between the emptiness in the woods where Erik had disappeared to the open chasm a few feet away where Brock clung to a tree on a ledge.

Scout bounced at the end of the leash, determined to find Erik. And she was right. Erik was our priority. But how long could Brock hold on?

"I'll be back," I called down to Brock. Before I could change my mind, Scout jerked on the leash and dragged me around the front of the cabin and into the woods.

Despite the fact that I was in great physical shape, Scout pushed me to my limits. We lurched over downed trees, under low hanging pine branches and over rotted logs and rocky patches. A few minutes into her search, I was gasping for breath, wishing I could stop to pull in one lungful of air. But she was relentless and focused, so I hoped that meant she was onto his scent.

"Erik," I called, knowing if he was in hiding mode, he would never respond, but I had to try, especially since he was scared. "We're out here, Oops." I pulled in a breath. "Scout's looking for you. Come to your good dog."

Every inch of me was soaked, and water ran off Scout's fur. I suddenly realized there hadn't been thunder or lightning since the hardest of the rain started. Maybe if Erik was hiding he'd come out now.

Scout continued to pull me forward. I glanced behind me, wondering if I'd be able to find my way back. Even though it had seemed like we'd been running for a long time, in reality, it had probably only been four or five minutes. As soon as the concern came to mind, Scout stopped and lifted her nose in the air. I almost tumbled over her, but I caught myself just in time. She started circling in the area.

"Where's Erik, Scout? Where's your boy? Find him."

Her nose dropped back to the ground and she jerked me toward several logs that looked like they'd been cut and stacked as if someone had intended to come back and get them. There was a space between the ground and one of them, and Scout crouched at her shoulders and pushed her nose underneath. I was excited, thinking she'd found Erik until she backed out quickly and ran past the logs. But like before, she stopped. Her ears went up and she raced back toward the logs, but on the other side.

And that's when I saw the rubber boots sticking out. Scout tugged me in that direction and lay down next to Erik's legs. I dropped to my knees and looked under. He had wedged himself in so he was protected from the rain. I couldn't even imagine how he'd spotted this crevice in between the logs.

"Erik!" I was so relieved, I could have cried. I closed my eyes and lifted my head toward the sky. The rain raced down my sweaty face, leaving salty dribbles on my lips. I could finally catch my breath. I heard movement, and when I opened my eyes, Erik had shifted so he could wrap his arms around Scout's neck. I wanted to hug her, too. She'd done her job, but we couldn't waste any more time.

"Erik, we have to go back to the cabin. We have to help Brock."

He shook his head. Scout's tongue flicked at the dirt caked around Erik's ear.

"It's only rain now," I said. "It's okay. There's no more thunder and lightning. I'll keep you safe."

He pressed his cheek against Scout's face. "Thcout ith my good dog."

"Yes. And Scout wants us to help Brock. We have to get him help, Erik. I need you to come out so we can help him."

Erik's buried his face in Scout's fur, but I heard him say, "Brock ith bad."

I couldn't disagree. Erik was always honest.

"Yeah, he can be bad. But right now he's hurt and we have to get back to help him." I hoped it wasn't too late. When Erik didn't move, I took hold of Scout's leash and lightly tugged. "Scout, here." At first she resisted, but then she stood and shook the rain off her fur. I wasn't fast enough to cover my face, and the water that landed on around my nose smelled like dog. When Erik still didn't move, an idea hit me. "Erik, you dropped your treasure box. We have to go get it."

I was shocked when he squirmed his way out of his hiding spot. "Where ith it?"

"In front of the cabin. Hurry. Let's go get it."

"Okay." He jogged ahead of me like he knew where he was going while I held Scout's leash and she ran in front of me. The
direction seemed right. Erik had the best memory out of everyone in our family, but we'd only been in these woods two or three times.

A couple of minutes later, the cabin came into view, and once again, relief was my best friend. I knew Erik had one goal – to get to his treasure box. My goal was to see if Brock was still clinging to the ravine's ledge.

When we got in front of the cabin, Erik froze when he saw the contents of his box scattered. "My boxth," he said, his eyes wide.

"It's okay. I'll find your treasures." I kneeled down and started picking up everything I could find – an acorn, a tiny brown and black speckled feather, the snail shell, a nickel with a red stripe painted on it, and several little rocks of different shapes and textures that either were or weren't in the box before but were going in now. The most interesting thing was the small dangly purple earring that I recognized as the match to one that

Christina had been searching for about two months before we moved from Manhattan.

"My token," he said.

"What token?" I asked.

"My thubway token. My dad gave it to me."

Under normal circumstances, at this point I'd laugh at Erik's possessiveness of our dad, but there wasn't an ounce of amusement in any cell in my body. That token was the most important possession in his box because it represented the time Dad took us to a Yankees game. He had told Erik that if he held onto that token with the "Y" in the middle that it would help the Yankees win. And they did. From that point it became his most prized possession, along with the scraggly cat ear.

"I'll find it," I promised, although I was concerned that it would blend with the bronze color of the leaves. While I sifted through the debris, I listened for any noises from Brock, but there was nothing.

Suddenly Erik started jumping and flapping his arms. "There! There! There! I thee it."

At the same time I saw the corner of the token poking out from under some dirt. I snagged it and wiped it against my wet t-shirt, leaving a tiny line of mud that looked like a racing stripe across my chest. I put the token in the box and quickly closed the lid.

"Here," I said, and handed it to him. He took it but held it at arms' length like it disgusted him.

I straightened and pushed open the cabin door. "Erik, I want you and Scout to go in here so you're out of the rain. I have to check on Brock. Only come out if I ask you to come out, okay?"

He nodded and walked toward the cabin like Frankenstein with his arms and the box straight out in front of him. Probably for him, because there were bits of dirt on them, his treasures were ruined. I'd deal with that later. At least I'd found his token.

Scout stuck close to Erik's side and we went into the cabin. I hadn't been in the rundown shack since the day Willow had brought us, so I'd forgotten about the ropes and old knives left behind by hunters.

There were the ropes I'd noticed the first time we'd come in, but now I saw there were also ropes of different lengths and widths coiled under an old chair in the corner. I took what looked like the longest and strongest one off the wall, although none of them appeared to be in great condition.

"I'll be right back, Erik. You and Scout stay here," I repeated.

I looped the rope over my shoulder and walked as close as I dared to the edge before I finally had to drop to my knees and crawl the rest of the way.

"Brock!" I yelled before I looked. "Brock, can you hear me?"

"Help me." His voice was scratchy and weak.

"I'm going to throw a rope down to you. Tie it around your waist to hold you in case you get tired."

"C-can't," he called back.

He was wrong. He'd have to do this. Still on my hands and knees, I backed away from the edge and then stood up and jogged to a big tree that had probably been growing for decades. I wrapped the rope around the tree and made a bowline like my dad had taught me, then unraveled the rest of the rope back toward the edge of the ravine. Like before, when I got closer to the edge, I dropped to my hands and knees and continued the rest of the way on all fours. When I was a about a yard away, I laid on my stomach and snake crawled to the edge. I couldn't look out over the ravine again; I had to keep my eyes focused on solid ground, but then I came to the point where I had no choice but to look over the edge.

The top of Brock's head was the first thing I saw. "Hey, I'm throwing down the rope now. Tie it around you."

I saw a bit of movement from him as he tried to look up. The small tree he held onto swayed with his weight. "I c-can't hold on anymore." The tone of his voice rose, so I knew he was scared.

"Yes you can." I started feeding the rope over the edge. It caught on little trees and rocks, forcing me to snap it free, but then that caused dirt and pebbles to roll down onto Brock's head. "Grab the rope," I yelled when it dangled next to him.

"C-can't let go," Brock said back. "I th-think I b-broke my arm." His voice didn't have its usual strength. "I'm tired." His head rolled back, throwing him a bit off balance, but he jerked himself back toward the little tree. "C-can't hold on. Letting go."

"No!" I yelled. "You can't." I managed to take my eyes off him and look to the landscape below. If he let go, he'd be dead. There was almost nothing to stop him from going all the way down.

I wanted to run for help, but I was afraid to leave him for that long without him being secured with the rope. It was obvious that he was too injured and too tired to help himself. I rolled up onto my hip and pulled my phone out of my pocket, praying that I'd miraculously suddenly have a cell signal. There was nothing. I turned it off and back on again in case that helped. But a minute later, I had a wet phone and no signal. I shoved it back in my pocket and looked over the edge again.

A shiver shot through me. I had one option. I had to get down to Brock and tie the rope around him before I could go for help. My heart kicked into high speed. Getting stuck on top of the roller coaster was nothing compared to what I was considering doing. I owed Brock nothing. And I definitely didn't owe him my life – which I was thinking about risking to help him.

I laid my head on my wet, muddy arms for a moment and instantly thought of Willow. Her life would be better without him. As soon as the thought came into my mind, I was disgusted with myself. She wouldn't want her brother to die. She'd want him to get help. He was her twin. Somewhere inside him there had to be the same goodness that she had. I picked up my head and looked down toward Brock who was now looking up at me with a vacant stare that told me he was putting his life in my hands. I pounded my fist on the ground, angry to be put in this situation. I hated heights, but I'd suck it up. I had to do this.

"Hold on, Brock. I'm coming down," I called.

I moved away from the edge then ran back into the cabin. Erik sat on the worn wooden floor with Scout next to him, her head in his lap. He held his box in one hand but the fingers of his other hand were rubbing the top of Scout's head. Her eyes darted between watching me and watching Erik.

While I took another rope from the wall, I said, "I'm going to help Brock. I don't want you to go anywhere near the edge, do you understand?" My stomach flip-flopped when I said my plan out loud. When it was only a thought in my head, it wasn't so real. Now, I'd said it, and I was getting the rope to do it. This was real, and I couldn't believe I was serious about following through.

Erik nodded and started to hum. It was a sure sign that the idea made him uncomfortable, but I wasn't sure he was fully aware of the danger.

I ran to a tree next to the one where I'd tied the rope for Brock so that our two ropes would be side by side. His lay loose against the trunk and ran across the ground and over the edge of the ravine. Once I tied the bowline knot for my rope, I tugged on it several times, first close up to the tree, and then at different intervals as I backed away. The rope was old, but it looked strong.

I walked as close to the edge as I dared, and then took the other end of the rope and tied it around my waist, making sure the loop would be just long enough to get me down to what I thought was Brock's level on the ledge but not much farther than that. It wasn't ideal, but I was pretty sure it would hold me if I slipped. I moved closer to the edge then turned with my back to the ravine and tugged hard on the rope again. The huge knot in my chest made it hard to take a full breath.

Finally, I laid down face first with my feet toward the edge, tugged on the rope one more time and worked my way backwards so I'd be going over feet first with the front of my body against solid ground.

As soon as my feet hung suspended in the air, I froze. Once I moved closer to the edge, there was nothing to stop me from falling all the way down if this rope didn't hold. I closed my eyes and said a little prayer. What I was about to do was totally insane, but I was Brock's only chance. If he was right, and he couldn't hold on much longer, then leaving to get help would be useless.

I sucked in a ragged breath, grasped the rope as tight as I could and inched my way back. My ankles hung over the edge. Then my knees. My legs were stiff but I continued to work my way back. When my hips reached the edge and I could feel there was nothing solid under the bottom half of my body, my heart banged so hard in my chest that I could barely breathe. My next move would put me completely over the edge.

I prayed the knot and rope were strong enough to keep me from plummeting to the bottom of the ravine.

CHAPTER SIXTEEN

My feet and legs banged against the crumbling wall of dirt as I dropped over the edge. A current of fear shot through every fiber of my body, and I panicked. I jammed the toes of my sneakers into the side of the ravine, trying to get a hold on anything to keep from slipping, but all I accomplished was pushing loose dirt and leaves into a mini avalanche that bounced off trees growing out of the side like they were hanging on for dear life, too. My fingers gripped the rope so tight that my knuckles already hurt. I quit kicking and tried to press myself against the side. The only thing that kept me from losing my mind was knowing I'd tied the rope around my waist so I wouldn't fall too far if I slipped.

I took a deep breath then slowly looked down to get my bearings in relation to where Brock was. I guessed he was about thirty or forty feet below me. At any moment my heart would probably explode out of my chest, but I was committed to getting the end of the other rope wrapped around him before I went back up. Which couldn't happen soon enough.

The rope burned my fingers as I inched my way down. I groaned as coarse fibers dug into my skin like tiny tacks. There was no doubt I'd have nasty rope burns and multiple cuts before I was through. Despite my best efforts, with each step against the dirt, more debris rolled down, some of it hitting Brock.

"Sorry," I called through gritted teeth. My hands and arms tingled from tension and being in the air over my head in a tight grip. An added problem was the rope was slippery from the rain, so I had to hold on tighter. Instead of looking down, I kept my eyes up so I couldn't see what our fate could be. The trees at the top hovered over us like guards watching. If only they could reach down and pull us up!

The minutes ticked by as I inched my way down. There was no room for a misstep. Even though my arms ached, I had no choice but to continue to work my way down until I saw Brock out of my peripheral vision. Just a few more feet and I could settle on the same outcropping of ledge that he was on and catch my breath.

The closer I got, the more I moved my feet around in an attempt to find footing. When I finally hit the hard surface, I loosened my grip until my feet were flat. There wasn't much to stand on – at the most maybe twenty four inches of depth. I took a minute to steady myself and then experimented with letting go of the rope. My muscles screamed for a break, but I was afraid to let go completely.

I was side by side with Brock. His face was whiter than a brand new baseball. Rain cascaded off his dark hair and dribbled across his bloodshot eyes. He stared at me, but I got the sense he wasn't really seeing me. With one hand he held onto a sapling that was bending toward him. His other hand was pressed against his stomach. I couldn't see much of it, but what I could see made my stomach roll. His hand hung limply at an odd, unnatural angle from his wrist.

I nodded toward his hand. "Looks broken."

At first he stared at me like he didn't understand what I'd said. But then his vacant expression clued me in that he was probably in shock. He started to move his hand then jerked and shrieked, making a sound no teenaged guy should ever make.

"Don't move it," I ordered. The last thing I needed was for him to be in so much pain that he let go of the little tree. Or passed out. It was obvious he wouldn't be able to help me put the rope around his waist.

I clung to my rope with my left hand and reached out to grab his rope with my right. There was way more rope than I needed, but I decided I could probably loop it around him two or three times just to be safe.

"I d-don't w-want to f-fall." His teeth chattered and the words were slurred like he didn't have the strength to talk right. The tough guy I'd known for the last month was gone.

"Then work with me. We need to get this rope around you. Lean out a little." When he did, there was just enough room between the wall of earth and his body for me to feed the rope through. It was awkward trying to tie him with only my free hand, but I had a death grip on my lifeline with the other hand, and there was no way I had the guts to let go even though it was tied around my waist. Brock's rope needed to be tight enough so if he slipped it wouldn't come up over his head.

I stopped abruptly when I realized I had no choice but to let go of my rope completely in order to tie his into a knot. Pain twisted his face into an odd expression. My throat tightened and I realized it was because I felt sorry for him, yet powerless to do anything about what he was going through. I couldn't believe after everything we'd been through in the last few weeks that here I was on a ledge trying to save his life at the risk of mine. This was all too crazy to be real.

Then his last comment before he had fallen popped into my head. *"She turned on me. Just like everyone else."* What did he mean by that? Who *was* everyone else?

"I c-can't h-hold on," he said, then sagged against me and the wall of dirt.

"Brock!" I yelled. "Hey, you all right?"

His chin dropped against his chest and his hand came off the sapling he'd been holding.

"No! What are you doing?" I slammed him against the wall of the ravine with my free arm, which caused one of my feet to slip dangerously close to the edge. Still keeping my arm against him, I plastered myself against the wall.

"Brock! Open your eyes!"

His body was limp, and the only thing keeping him from falling was the rope around his waist and my arm holding him against the wall of dirt. I gulped back fear. We were stuck.

"Whatcha doin'?" Erik's voice carried out over the ravine.

Was I hearing things? It was difficult, but I angled my head to look up. My heart skipped a beat when I saw him standing at the edge, one hand holding a tree and the other hanging with his hand on Scout's shoulder.

"Erik, get away from the edge," I yelled. He didn't move because he'd never had a real sense of personal danger. One step and he would tumble – no, plummet to the bottom.

"I'll pull your rope," he said matter-of-factly.

"No! Don't touch the rope." I glanced at Brock's, wondering if it would support both of us if Erik started messing with the one tied to me. "You can't help."

I scanned the landscape above and below me. There were no options for escape. Going down was out. One wrong step and I'd be going straight down – not to mention I didn't have enough rope to reach to the bottom. And, at this point, I didn't have the strength to go back up, either. I glanced at Brock. And I couldn't abandon him.

A lump slammed into my throat, blocking my breath. The reality of our predicament stole any optimism. How long would it take for someone to find us? Who would even know where to look?

Willow. But she didn't know we were here. I wanted to check my phone for signal, but there was no way I would let go of my rope again, and I couldn't take my arm off Brock. Even if I could, if I didn't have signal up in the open, there definitely wouldn't be signal here. The only positive in any of this was the rain had let up as quickly as it began. Besides the pounding of my heart, all I could hear was the birds that had started singing from the surrounding trees. They sounded happy. I was scared beyond belief.

"I'm hungry," Erik called down. "I'm going home."

I stiffened and looked up. "What? No!"

"I want macaroni and cheethe."

"Right now you need to get away from the edge. We'll go and get some when I get out of here," I promised. But I realized how ridiculous that was. I needed help. Brock and I were trapped. I looked back at Brock. He opened his eyes, but the dazed look was scary. I'd give anything to be able to call 9-1-1.

I turned my attention back to Erik. *I* couldn't call 9-1-1, but Erik could back at our house. With his memory, he'd have no trouble finding his way out of the woods. It would also mean that he'd have to show any rescuers how to get back to find us, but it was a chance I'd have to take. Erik was our only hope for being saved.

"Erik," I yelled. His head popped back over the side and the familiar pang of panic shot through me. "Erik, do you think you and Scout could find your way back home?"

"Yeth," he replied. It was moments like this, when he sounded like every other six year old boy in the world, that I could forget for a moment his struggle with autism.

"Listen carefully," I yelled. "Take Scout and go home. As soon as you get there, dial 9-1-1. You remember how Mom and Dad taught you?"

"Yeth. For emergenthees."

"This *is* an emergency. Run home and dial 9-1-1, and when someone answers, tell them there's someone hurt. A policeman, like Dad, will come to our house, and you'll have to show them how to get back here. Can you do that?"

He didn't answer but disappeared from the edge. I could hear his voice because he was shouting, "9-1-1. 9-1-1. 9-1-1." The sound grew fainter until the woods were silent again, except for the birds. They resumed their chirping as soon as he was gone.

There was no way I could relax, but at least now there was a shred of hope. Pressed against the side of the ravine and holding Brock in place, I said a prayer that Erik would follow through.

I pushed my arm against Brock and shook him a little. "Brock. You hangin' in there?"

He rolled his eyes toward me, looking helpless and vulnerable. I understood the feeling. All we could do was hope we could hold on until someone found us. I needed a distraction. Several ideas whirled through my mind, but I settled on naming every pro baseball player I could think of. To make it more distracting, my goal was to do it in alphabetical

order. "Andy Petit," I said out loud, figuring Brock could use the distraction, too. I stopped and thought. Should I alphabetize by first name or last name? Last name. "Hank Aaron. Jim Abbott." I concentrated hard, hoping help would come way before I got to Gregg Zaun.

I had just passed Alex Rodriguez in what I thought was the correct order when I thought I heard someone calling my name from above. I looked up but didn't see anyone.

"Hey! We're down here." I hated that my body jerked when I yelled, because even that small amount of movement felt like it could make me fall.

"Dylan?" The voice was faint, but it sounded like Willow. "Dylan, where are you?"

"Down here," I yelled. "Follow the ropes."

Several seconds later, Willow appeared above us on her hands and knees. "Oh, no!" she said, her eyes wide. "What happened?"

"Brock tripped and fell over the edge. I came down on the rope, but now we're stuck. He's hurt pretty badly, his arm and his leg, so I can't let go of him. I sent Erik back to our house to call for help because my phone doesn't have signal. Did you see him?"

She shook her head. "No. I came from the other side of the woods. How long has he been gone?"

"I don't know," I said. "I only know I made it to Rodriguez. Erik was my only hope."

"What? Did you hit your head? You're talking crazy."

I didn't want to take the time to explain. "No, I'm okay, but Brock's hurt pretty bad. Can you go and see if Erik called?" I hated to send her away, but there wasn't anything she could do here, either, and at least then I'd know for sure help was on the way.

"I have Lightning," she said. "We'll be fast. Just hold on."

My mind buzzed. She had taken the horse after all.

"Okay," I managed to choke out.

A few seconds later I heard her whoop like she did to get Lightning to run fast. I could faintly hear the pounding of his hooves. Then, like before, there was only Brock and me.

I leaned my forehead against the dirt and closed my eyes. Disappointment crowded past my fear. So the sheriff had been right. I'd really wanted Willow to prove them all wrong.

Brock moaned and moved against my arm. I opened my eyes then tightened my muscles even more to hold him in place.

"Hang on. Help is on the way."

Brock's eyes fluttered open and he stared at me like he was thinking hard. "You're an ass," he mumbled.

Rage turned my vision to red. "You're an ass," I countered. "You'd probably be dead now if it weren't for me. I was an idiot to come down here to help you because now I could die, too."

"Yeah." His lips curved into a ridiculous smile, and I wondered if he even knew he was talking, let alone what he was saying. "Th-that's why y-you're an ass." He grimaced then continued. "I'm n-not worth saving."

I was so shocked, all I could do was stare at him. His eyes suddenly looked more alert.

"Y-you're lu-ucky, Westcott." He started to move his arm. "Ow!" He slammed his eyes shut and his face twisted. Based on the angle of his wrist, I couldn't even imagine the pain he was experiencing. Now it was swollen into a grotesque shape and turning purple.

I wanted to try and distract him. "Why am I lucky?"

He drew in a couple of ragged breaths. "Nobody ever gave up on you."

"Who gave up on you?" This conversation was surreal. We were literally clinging on the edge of life and death and Brock decided it was time for a buddy chat. But, if it kept him conscious, I'd talk. Finally, the first aid course Mom and Dad had forced me to take when I was twelve was paying off. I knew enough to keep him talking in case he had a concussion. We didn't have anything else to do, anyway.

"Who gave up on you?" I repeated.

"My d-dad." He winced. "My mom. They left us." He closed his eyes and moaned. When he reopened them, they were watery like he was going to cry. I didn't know whether it was physical or emotional pain the tears.

"Willow told me your mom died. She didn't leave you."

"She quit," he mumbled.

I wondered if he meant her heart stopped beating, or she quit fighting a disease.

"What do you mean she quit?"

"Killed herself."

A shiver shot through my body. I hadn't expected that answer, and there was nothing for me to say in response. *I'm sorry* sounded weird given the bitterness in his voice. I wondered why Willow had kept that detail to herself. I hoped someday she'd feel it was safe to talk about it with me.

I decided to focus Brock on what he did have instead of what he'd lost.

"You have Granny Annie," I argued. "And Willow."

He shook his head. "We're s-so messed u-up. I h-hate myself. I hate my life." He pushed back against my arm like he was trying to move away from the solid wall in front of us. I countered his effort.

"Then change," I said.

He quit pushing and laid his cheek against the dirt. His shoulders sagged. "I don't know how."

"Me either." But in my mind, I figured a good place to start would be by treating Willow better.

The birds started to tweet louder like this was all a good Disney movie. And the absurdity of it almost made me laugh.

The minutes seemed like hours, and I was beginning to question if I had imagined Erik and Willow going for help. Brock didn't say another word, but at least he was keeping his eyes open now, staring at me. Every now and then he moaned, but I'd seen no more hints of tears.

I was wondering how long we had actually been down here on this ledge, perched hundreds of feet above the death trap below, when I thought I heard a siren far off. I tried to block out all other sounds and focus on that. Was that siren for us – someone coming to get us out of here?

"Dylan!"

Now I knew I was hallucinating because that was Dad's voice.

"Dad?" I yelled so loud my voice echoed from the ravine walls.

"Dylan. Brock. Hang on."

I heard him again, and it sounded like his voice was coming from above. I looked up and was shocked to see him looking down. My body relaxed just the slightest bit. Was he really here?

"Dad! What are you doing here?"

"I came up to make sure everyone was okay after what happened last night with Erik."

I couldn't comprehend the passage of time. Last night seemed so long ago.

"Are you hurt?" he asked.

"I'm not, but Brock is. I think he broke his arm and maybe even his leg."

"The ropes rescue team is on the way," Dad said.

"Where are Erik and Scout?" I asked.

He motioned behind him with a nod of his head. "They're here with Anne."

"Erik's okay?"

"Yes, he's fine. I had just gotten home when he came out of the house. He said he had called 9-1-1."

I was surprised by the surge of pride that pushed out a bit of the terror I'd been dealing with. "I knew he could do it."

"He'd do anything for you – for any of us," Dad said.

I looked at Brock. He was right. I did have it all. Then that reminded me of all he had left – Willow and Granny Annie.

"Did you see Willow?" I called toward the top.

"She's waiting for the rescue team out by the road. Are these ropes tied around you?"

"Yes. I put one around Brock and one around me."

While we'd been talking, the sound of the sirens had gotten closer and then stopped. I hoped that meant the rescue team would be here soon. Willow would know the fastest way into the woods.

Dad yelled, "I hear the fire trucks getting close. Hang tight."

"Like I have a choice?" I would have laughed, but this was far from funny.

Dad scrunched up his face. "Yeah, sorry. Bad choice of words."

Having this conversation made me feel a little normal, which was a relief. My muscles all ached, and at times, trembled with fatigue. Help was almost here. I could hold on.

I looked back at Brock. His eyes were still open.

"We're getting out of here soon," I told him.

He nodded and licked his lips. "I'm thirsty."

"Me, too. I'll race you to the top."

"Hmph." It seemed to be the best response he could give. At least he was still in a condition to respond.

Dad had tried to distract us by talking about anything except our predicament, and I realized now it had been a while since we'd first heard the sirens. I had no idea how much time passed before

I finally heard other voices up above. I couldn't make out what the new voices were saying, but I could tell there were lots of people. Dad was still near the edge, and his voice was the clearest as he relayed to them what I'd told him about Brock's arm and leg.

Three new faces appeared at the top.

"Damn! This ain't gonna be easy," I heard a man say.

"Dylan and Brock," another guy said, "I'm Will Burke with the fire department. The ropes rescue team is on the way and should be here soon. The important thing is for you to stay calm and move as little as possible."

I didn't know where he thought we were going to move to, but I figured I wouldn't point that out to someone coming to save my life.

"Okay."

"So only one of you is hurt?"

"Yes," I answered.

He continued to ask me about our condition and how we ended up down here. Then, he disappeared from the top of the ravine, but Dad always stayed where I could see him. Even though we were so far apart, there was some comfort in knowing that he was there. When the ropes guy wasn't there, Dad gave me updates about what was happening. He had distracted me enough that before I knew it I saw two people standing at the top with some kind of harnesses looped all over their bodies. I glanced down at my crude attempt to secure us with ropes. It was amazing that either one of us was still here to be rescued.

"Coming down," a woman called. "Keep your head down in case dirt or rocks fall."

Despite her directive, I continued to look up. Unlike the way I went over the side, she and the guy came over like they were stepping into a bathtub. There was no hesitation on their part. Their descent was smooth, and very little dirt came off the sides as they leaned back and dropped like spiders on a silky web. I couldn't tell if they were controlling the ropes or if it was the people up above. The woman was coming straight down, but the guy was bringing some type of big equipment with him.

The woman came on my side. Her curly brown hair hung below the back of her red helmet. There were belts and harnesses attached all over her, and then hooked to the belt were tools and a couple of white helmets.

"Stop!" she yelled toward the top when her feet hit the ledge next to me. The ropes attached to her stopped moving, and she turned to me. While she talked I could see her assessing our situation, including how I'd secured us.

"I'm Jesse and my partner is Tim. Bet you're ready to get out of here," she said.

"You have no idea." I tipped my head toward Brock. "Brock's hurt. Take him first."

"That's cavalier of you," she said. "But, we'll take care of him after I get you secured. He's going up in the Stokes basket." I figured a Stokes basket was the long wire thing the other rescuer, Tim, was maneuvering between him and the wall of the ravine as he descended.

The way Jesse moved around, as if she wasn't concerned about falling, gave me the chills. She positioned herself behind me so if I lost my balance, she would be there to stop me. "First things first," she continued. I glanced under my arm and could see her unsnapping one of the helmets. "Let me get this on you."

She set the white helmet on my head and snapped the chin strap before I had a chance to consider how to do it one handed. "Now, I'm going to change out your securing rope with an appropriate rescue rope."

While she switched ropes on me, I watched the guy settle into place next to Brock. To me it looked awkward because the basket was so long, but he didn't seem bothered.

"Okay, grab onto my rope," she directed.

I struggled to open my hand because my fingers were cramped from holding onto my rope so tight for so long. Finally I worked the muscles enough so that, despite the ache, I could switch my grip to the rope Jesse had just put on me.

She tugged once more on the ropes she'd just clicked onto me. "I'm going over to help my partner and your buddy."

She took a couple of steps sideways until she was next to Brock.

"I put these ropes around us in case we slipped," I said, nodding my head toward the one around Brock's waist. "I didn't know what else to do."

"You did fine," she said. "You worked with what you had." She and Tim collaborated to put ropes on Brock. Each snap of metal to metal actually helped me relax. Finally, I wasn't scared that one of us would make a misstep and end up dead at the bottom. She and Tim worked in sync without talking to each other, each knowing exactly what to do. Instead, she continued her conversation with me.

"I know it's too late now, but you should have called for help instead of taking the rescue into your own hands. You got lucky. And, it would have been easier to only have to rescue one person."

I couldn't get defensive about the reprimand, because she was right. But I did what I had to do. "I didn't have cell signal, so I couldn't call for help. Brock was slipping and said he couldn't hold on anymore. I had to do something."

She turned and looked at me, kindness sparkling in her eyes. "Then he's very lucky to call you friend."

A snort would have been a perfect response to Jesse's comment, but I decided to 'take the high road', as Mom and Dad always said, and simply said, "Yeah, I guess."

For the first time since Jesse and Tim had reached our level,
Brock looked at me. His cheek was swollen and bruising, so I wasn't surprised to see him wince when he raised his eyebrows in response to her comments. I had no idea what that meant, but at least he didn't give me his usual middle finger salute.

Tim was next to Brock but suspended since there wasn't enough room for him and the long body basket he had. He and Jesse started talking to each other. I strained to hear what they were saying, but their voices were too soft to make out the words. I wondered if that was on purpose. The muffled voices up above mingled with what sounded like the beating of a helicopter's rotors somewhere in the distance. I focused on the sound of the helicopter when I realized it was getting closer. I pictured it hovering over us and dropping one of those long lines that they used to pluck victims out of the ocean. This was feeling more like an action adventure movie with every passing second.

"Is that helicopter coming to get us?" I asked.

"Not exactly," Tim said. "It's the medical helicopter. It's like a flying ambulance." He nodded toward Brock, and I got his point.

Which really scared me. I wondered if they were afraid Brock might die.

"I'm going to stabilize his arm," Jesse said, "then we'll get him in the basket." She leaned around Brock. "Hey, buddy. How're you doing?"

Brock grunted in response. He stared at me like he thought we were still the only two here. Tim took something from off the basket and handed it to Jesse.

"Brock," Jesse said, "I have to stabilize your arm with a vacuum splint and sling. I know it's going to be uncomfortable, but trust me, it will save you a lot of pain when we have to move you."

Brock's voice sounded like a croak when he answered, "Okay."

Jesse's body blocked my view of what was happening, but whatever it was, Brock came to life.

He let out a yelp and arched his back, pushing away from the wall. Jesse threw her knee against his legs and Tim put his arm across his back, holding him onto the ledge.

"Easy does it, pal," she said. "I'm sorry this hurts, but we have to do it. Yell all you want if it helps, but you've gotta hold still."

She worked fast, but Brock's screams echoed off the ravine walls. Tim moved in as soon as Jesse was done with the splint and sling, and between the two of them, they were able to lay Brock into the basket. Their hands flew over straps and ties as he fought against them.

Tim put his arm across the basket. "Chill big guy. I haven't lost anyone yet, and I don't plan to change that record with you."

At that moment, the helicopter came into view, flying right above us. It made a wide arc then moved out of sight past the trees. Tim tugged on the ropes tied to the basket.

"Let's get him outta here," he said to Jesse. He turned his attention to the top. "Rescuers ready with the Stokes. Haul team, haul slowly," he yelled.

From above us I heard a chorus of voices.

"Ready on belay?" a deep voice yelled.

"Belay on," was the response from someone else.

While Jesse moved back next to me, I looked up to see where those voices were coming from. I could see another helmeted rescuer lying on his stomach at the edge, watching us below, but whoever the men were calling to, they were obviously not near the edge.

"Haul team ready?" the deep voice called.

"Haul team ready."

"Haul slow," he ordered.

"Haul slow."

Tim and the basket with Brock started to inch up the side.

Jesse walked along the ledge, her ropes taut over our heads, and positioned herself behind me again. "Sounds like the helicopter landed. We had to get your friend out of here first so he can be treated as soon as possible," she said. "You and I are climbing up together."

I wanted to get out of here, but it was tough to concentrate on me.

"Is Brock going to die?" I asked.

"He's in rough shape, but he's young. He'll be fine," Jesse answered.

I glanced up to see how Tim was doing with Brock in the basket. He used his feet to keep him and the basket away from any little trees that were sticking out. They were moving at a slow and steady pace. I couldn't make out the conversations from above, but at one point when I looked to the top, I saw Dad kneeling on the edge and looking over. When he gave me a thumbs up, I assumed it was to boost my confidence. I returned the thumbs up, but my knees and hands were still shaking.

I'd been so distracted by the helicopter and Tim and Brock's ascent that I had forgotten Jesse was still securing me. When she started clicking snaps, she had my attention again. "That does it," she said. "You ready for this?"

I'd actually begun to think I was safe on this ledge, and the idea of moving off it shattered my confidence. "What if the ropes break with both of us on it?" I asked.

"Won't happen," Jesse said from behind. She tugged on the straps attached to me; I assumed to double check them. "Believe me, I don't want to end up at the bottom any more than you do."

A lump filled my throat. Didn't this kind of drama only happen in movies?

"What do I have to do?" I asked.

"Just trust me, Dylan. Relax and hold on to the rope as they hoist us up. We're going to walk up the side. This is almost over." She tugged on the rope then looked to the top. I looked up, too. Tim and Brock had already been pulled to safety. "Rescuer ready," she yelled.

The straps tightened around my legs and waist. I wanted to close my eyes but couldn't. When my feet lifted from the ledge, I started praying. Jesse must have felt my body tense, because she put her arms around me.

"You can count on the crew up above. They're pros." Pride was evident in her voice, and somehow, that calmed me. "Imagine you're Spiderman going up the side. Just keep your feet moving."

"I hated that movie," I said, but I chose not to tell her that it was because I had to close my eyes every time the camera showed a shot of the super hero from a high angle. Maybe if I survived this, I'd be able to watch that movie without cringing.

The rope inched us toward the top like we were in slow motion. It was hard to not dig my feet into the side of the ravine and try to pull myself up faster. I finally believed I was going to make it out of this alive.

We were less than fifteen feet from the top when suddenly we stopped moving.

CHAPTER SEVENTEEN

Panic raced across my chest and down my arms.

"What's going on? Why aren't we moving?"

Jesse put her hand on my shoulder. "Just relax. I'm sure we'll be ascending again any second."

No sooner had she said that than there was a slight tug on the rope and we were once again going up. And less than a minute later, we were hauled onto firm ground. My legs were rubbery, and I found it difficult to stand while two men moved in to help Jesse remove the harness and ropes that had secured us.

"Thank the Lord," I heard Granny Annie say, but I couldn't see beyond the rescue workers surrounding me. After a minute, the two men stepped away and I could see what was happening around us. Dad moved in closer to Jesse and me, and beyond him at the far side of the cabin I saw Erik with Granny Annie and Willow. Granny Annie had one hand on Willow's arm like she was holding her back. My mother was there, too, on her knees next to Scout, but I couldn't see what she was doing.

I looked toward a group of people gathered around the Stokes basket that held Brock. Three of them were dressed in matching blue cargo pants and white shirts with patches on them. I assumed they were medical personnel. I looked for an ambulance or some kind of rescue vehicle, but all I saw was a John Deere Gator, a four wheeled off-road vehicle like my grandfather kept on his small farm for hauling barrels of water and mulch for my grandmother's gardens.

"You okay?" Dad asked. His hands were shoved in his pockets and his shoulders were squared, telling me that it was taking all his self-control to keep from stepping in and making the process of unhooking me go faster.

"Yeah. Just some scratches." I glanced at my hands. They were pretty chewed up from the rope, but the blood was already dried. I looked over my shoulder toward the ravine and shuddered. Even though I had just been brought back up it, I couldn't wrap my head around the reality that I had purposely gone over the edge. And I'd done it for someone who had been nothing but a nightmare in my life for the last month. "Is Brock going to be okay?"

Dad shrugged. "The medical team went right to work on him." He used his thumb to point over his shoulder. "The helicopter landed out in the clearing. He's getting the attention he needs."

I swallowed hard. "A helicopter is serious." Brock and I weren't buddies, but I wouldn't wish something this bad on anyone.

Jesse spoke as she pulled the last strap from me. "It's protocol considering the prolonged extrication and the fact that we're not sure if he lost consciousness or not."

As soon as I was free, Dad pulled me into a bear hug. I grabbed him back, relieved to be safe. Relieved to have him home.

I looked toward Erik. His attention was fixed on something inside his treasure box. "Did Erik really call 9-1-1?"

"Yes. He was too excited to give them information, but they had our address from the enhanced system. I got there just as they called back to verify that it was a real emergency call. Then Willow showed up on her horse and had the details to give the dispatcher."

I smiled, and my chest tightened. "Yeah, I sent her. But, Erik did it. Really, he did."

Dad put his arm across my shoulders. "Yes, he did. Even if Willow or I hadn't shown up, Erik had at least called for help. I'm convinced he would have shown the rescuers where to find you. I'm proud of him." He squeezed my shoulders. "And you." His voice was tight, and when I looked up at him, moisture hovered on his eyelids. He was the toughest man I knew, and for some reason, this reaction made him seem even stronger to me.

A strange warmth washed over me. "Erik's a real hero," I said.

Dad squeezed my shoulder again as we walked toward the cabin. He swiped the back of his calloused hand across his eyes and cleared his throat a couple of times but didn't say anything.

I guessed maybe I had said it all.

There was so much happening around us that I didn't know where to look first. One of the women from the medical team approached us. Her brown hair was pulled back into a braid and bounced against her white uniform shirt. Light blue latex gloves covered her hands.

"How ya doing?" she asked.

"I'm okay," I said.

"I'm Melinda. I'm an E.M.T. with the Keuka Shores Fire Department. Can I check you over real quick to make sure?"

I shrugged. "Yeah, I guess."

She put her gloved hands along the side of my neck and gently moved her fingers against my muscles. "Anything hurt here?"

"Nope," I said, ignoring how much all of my muscles, not just my neck, were aching even though I was starting to relax.

She took hold of my hands, which were completely filthy on top and turned them over. She lifted her eyebrows when she saw how raw they were. "Well, let's get these hands cleaned up."

She continued to hold one of my hands and led me like I was a little kid toward the Gator where a big medical bag was unzipped and all of the medical supplies were in view. She grabbed gauze and a bottle that I assumed was some kind of disinfectant and dabbed and wiped my palms. The liquid was warm, but every cut and tear in my skin stung when she touched it. When she finished, she studied my hands for a few seconds then let go.

"I can't do much about all that dirt and mud on the back of your hands, but at least your palms are cleaned and disinfected," she said.

"Thanks," I said. "I'll wash them when I get home."

She looked up at Dad. "You're taking him to have a thorough exam at the hospital or urgent care, I hope."

He nodded. "Yes, ma'am."

"Good."

Our attention was suddenly drawn to the people working on Brock as they lifted the basket onto the back of the Gator. A firefighter jumped into the driver's seat while the three other medical people and one of the rope rescuers each took a corner of the basket to hold it in place.

"Ready," one of the guys in the back called. The motor revved to life and the driver steered the Gator toward the path that led out of the woods.

Mom looked up at Granny Annie and said something that I couldn't hear over the engine noise. Then Granny Annie nodded and followed the Gator, leaving Willow with Erik, Mom and Scout. The ropes rescuers were breaking down equipment and packing everything back into special canvas bags. They were talking among themselves, but it was clear that they all knew exactly what to do and they worked efficiently together.

I had no idea how Brock and I would have gotten off the side of the ravine without them – or if we would have safely. I moved away from Dad and approached the rescuers. When they realized I was there, they all stopped and turned toward me, each seemingly frozen holding a piece of rescue equipment.

"I just realized I didn't thank all of you," I said, focusing first on Jesse and Tim, and then taking in the other five. "What you did was amazing. Thank you for saving our lives."

Tim let go of the bag he was holding and stepped forward, his hand extended to shake mine. "You're welcome. After what you did today, maybe you should join our team in the future."

"Uh, no thanks." I laughed and extended my hand in return, then pulled it back as soon as I remembered the cuts and blisters underneath and saw how grungy it was on top. "Sorry, my hand's disgusting and to be honest," I turned my hand over to show him my palms, "it would probably kill if anyone touched my hands right now."

He lifted his hand to my shoulder instead. "You earned that dirt and those chewed up palms."

I laughed. "Yeah, well, I'm still going to pass on joining your team."

He smiled. "Understood. Good luck to you and your buddy."

I nodded. "Thanks." I didn't see any point in telling them that Brock wasn't my friend.

Out of my peripheral vision I saw Mom approaching. I turned and started toward her wide open arms, and she wrapped me into her warm hug. Her cheek vibrated against my jaw when she said, "You could have told me when I left this morning that you had plans to audition for an action adventure movie."

"Yeah, believe me, that was not in my plans," I said.

We parted, but she still held my arms.

"What were you doing out here?"

I looked past her at Willow, whose sad expression tugged at my gut. "A sheriff came to our house this morning asking if I knew where Willow was. I thought maybe she'd be out here. Instead I found Brock."

"Yeah, the sheriff. Anne filled me in while we were waiting for the rescuers to bring you up. There's a lot going on in their family."

I glanced toward Willow, thinking about the bruises I knew were hidden by her jeans and long-sleeved t-shirt.

"Yeah," I said, "they aren't as lucky as we are."

Mom smiled. "In so many ways." She dropped her hands from my arms and went to hug Dad.

"I'll be glad when we're all here together for good."

"Just a few more weeks," he responded.

I heard something snap on the ground behind me and turned to see Willow coming toward me with Erik and Scout next to her. Her attention was totally fixed on me.

"Can I talk to you?" she asked.

"Yeah."

She tipped her head toward the woods away from the ravine. "Over there."

I glanced toward Mom and Dad then back at her. "Okay."

I was shocked when she took my tender hand and led me away. Her fingers were hot, like she was nervous. The woods were eerily quiet until the rotors of the helicopter started beating the air. She took us far enough away so we couldn't be heard, then stopped, let go of my hand and turned toward me.

"I'll totally understand if you'll never talk to me again, but I had to tell you that I'm sorry."

I stared at her, not knowing what to say.

"All of this is my fault. I got scared when Social Services came to our house yesterday. Apparently my dad wants us to go live with him. He told the social services people that Granny Annie isn't fit to take care of us and that she abuses us."

I stiffened. "What? That's crazy!"

"I know you can't understand it because your family is so perfect —"

I interrupted her. "My family is far from perfect."

"It's not messed up like mine," she said. "But even if mine is messed up, I don't want to leave. Granny Annie does the best she can with us." The helicopter sound got even louder, and she turned in that direction for a second. "I was wearing shorts and a tank top when the social workers showed up." She turned back toward me. "They saw the bruises and thought Granny was doing things to me because of what my father said."

"But it's Brock," I said.

"I know." She gave me one of those looks of exasperation that she's so good at. "But they don't know that and thought I was covering for her. And I know you can't understand it, but I don't want them to take Brock away either. We only have each other."

This time I took her hands. "But he hurts you. It doesn't matter that he's your brother. It's wrong. You shouldn't have to put up with it."

"I don't know what to do, and I don't think Granny Annie knows, either."

I looked toward my parents. I should have said something to them the first time Willow told me what Brock was doing to her. I wanted to kick myself for being so stupid and thinking it was better to keep quiet. I'd failed in the friend department.

She looked in the direction of the helicopter that we couldn't see from here. "Maybe Brock will be different now. Maybe this scared him."

As if on cue, the intensity of the beating of the helicopter's blades increased. I wanted to say, 'If he lives,' but I trusted Jesse when she had told me he would.

"He needs help, Willow. He's not going to suddenly change."

She dropped her chin and stared at the ground. For a minute we stood that way, then tears rolled down her cheeks. "I'm scared, Dylan. I'm scared because Brock's hurt so bad. I'm scared we'll have to leave Granny Annie. I'm scared because I just don't know what to do."

I wrapped my arms around her and hugged her. Her body started to shake and she cried harder.

She sniffled then continued. "I-I ruined it with you. I'm in trouble because I took Lightning. I make stupid decisions."

When she took a breath between her sobs, I finally said, "Are you through taking the blame for everything?" She shrugged, but her face was buried against my shoulder, where her hot tears soaked through my shirt to my skin. "If Granny Annie doesn't know how to help you then ask my parents for help. My mom's a great listener, and I swear she knows everything." I kind of laughed, hoping to make this not so serious. "But don't tell her I said she knows everything. And, heck, my dad's a cop. He's seen it all. Probably he'd know what to do, too."

Willow hiccupped a little like she was trying to catch her breath and stop crying. "I hope so. I've felt so lost since my mom died."

I slid one of my hands up her back to the nape of her neck and massaged her tense muscles. After a moment, I felt her relax. The ends of her chopped off hair danced against my skin, reminding me of what she'd been through just since I'd moved to Keuka Shores – and this was nothing new.

Willow tightened her arms around my waist. "I'm glad you're my friend, Dylan."

I leaned back so I could look into her eyes. "Hey, what happened to O'Dylan?"

Her face was soaked with tears, but she smiled. "Guess we're growing up."

"Wow! That was fast." It was my turn to smile. As much as I wanted to be angry about everything that had happened, when I looked into her sad blue eyes this close, everything inside me melted. "I need to know something, though," I said.

"What?"

"If you didn't send the text, how did you know to come out here?"

Willow squirmed out of my hug, but she caught my hand and held it. "Brock is friends with my friend Lexi's brother. Lexi left me a voicemail and told me she found texts to you on her phone that she hadn't sent. When she saw what it said, she knew that Brock had taken her phone and done it. My phone was off all night to save power, so I didn't get the message until this morning."

"Were you at her house last night?"

She shook her head. "No, I was going to stay at Chelsea's, but then everything else happened with the social workers and I took off."

"Wow! What a mixed up mess," I said.

It sounded like the helicopter was preparing to lift off. We turned in that direction even we couldn't see through all of the leaves. Because it was so loud, we didn't hear Mom, Dad and Erik coming down the path in our direction. Dad carried Scout against his chest like a baby, and she hooked her front paws over his shoulder.

I tightened my grip on Willow's hand and this time I led her toward my parents and the path. "Why are you carrying Scout?" I shouted.

Mom pointed to some gauze on Scout's paw and cupped her other hand around her mouth to shout back. "She cut her foot. The medics let me borrow saline and alcohol to clean it out, so I don't want her to walk on it again until we can properly treat it."

"Did she cut herself on the window in the cabin?" I asked.

Mom nodded and yelled back, "Apparently. There was a good amount of blood in there."

I felt bad that I'd made Scout run through the woods looking for Erik earlier, and I realized I hadn't even told Mom and Dad she'd done her job like she was supposed to.

"Scout's a hero just like Erik," I said, looking first at Mom and Dad, and then to Erik to see his reaction. His blank stare told me that the compliment was going over his head, but it didn't matter. I knew, and feeling pride for him for the second time in one day made me glow inside.

Maybe Willow was right. I wasn't thinking like a kid anymore.

We followed Mom, Dad and Erik down the path. No one was talking because the helicopter drowned everything out. We were almost to the end of the path and to the clearing when two sheriffs approached. Through the leaves I could see the helicopter slowly lifting off the ground. The leaves on the trees strained against the artificial wind it kicked up. We were far enough away that very little debris flew toward us, but we turned our backs for a moment anyway just to give everything a chance to settle again. The higher the helicopter went, the less pressure on our ears. I turned around in time to see it switch from going straight up to flying forward. I stared, still trying to comprehend that Brock was in it and that we had both survived going over the edge of the ravine.

The sheriffs stopped and waited for us to reach them. One rested his hand on the top of the gun in his holster, something I'd seen Dad do so casually that it might as well have been a squirt gun. The second one pushed his gray hat back off his forehead and spread his feet like he meant business, something else I'd seen Dad do plenty of times.

"Willow Anderson with you?" the first guy asked.

"Yes," Dad answered.

Willow tightened her grip on my hand. I glanced at her and realized the color really does drain from people's faces when they're scared. I squeezed back to reassure her, and we stepped around Mom and Dad.

"I'm Willow," she said.

I kept my attention on her, unable to imagine what she was feeling. She ran her tongue along her lower lip, and it was then that I saw her lip trembling.

"You need to come with us," the hat cop announced. They didn't look mean or angry, just official. The other sheriff picked up the microphone to his two-way radio and turned away from us.

"Yates dispatch, this is 1M-12. We're out with the juvenile female now," he said.

A scratchy reply answered. "1M-12, Yates dispatch copies that."

Willow's body stiffened and she shot a terrified look at me then my parents. She turned back toward the sheriffs. "Where's my grandmother?"

"She's heading up to Rochester to meet your brother at the hospital, but we need to talk with you."

Mom stepped next to Willow. "If Willow wants, can I stay with her since her grandmother can't?"

Willow dropped my hand and whirled toward Mom, relief returning some color to her face. "Yes." She sounded breathless like she couldn't get enough air.

Hat cop shrugged one shoulder. "We were going to have one of the social workers meet us, but if she wants you there, too, I think given the circumstances, it's prob'ly a good idea."

The other officer stepped forward. "Where's the horse?"

I'd forgotten that Willow had ridden in on Lightning when she found Brock and me over the side of the ravine.

"In our barn," she said. Her expression changed, and the old, defiant Willow reappeared. "But he can't go back to Mr. Zurlik. He doesn't take care of him. I'm the one who makes sure Lightning's hooves get trimmed. I'm the one who makes sure there's enough food and water for him." She emphasized each point by tapping herself in the middle of her chest. "I'm the one who cleans the cuts after Mr. Zurlik hits him with a pitch fork."

Both sheriffs tensed and looked at each other, then back at Willow. "Are you accusing him of animal cruelty?" the hat cop asked.

"Yes."

I spun toward Mom. That explained the scars we'd seen on Lightning the first time Willow had ridden him to our house to have Mom treat his leg wound. Mom's lips were in a straight tight line and she shook her head, most likely annoyed with herself for not questioning Willow that day.

The hand on holster sheriff squinted like it hurt his brain to deal with this complicated case. "Then we'll take a look when we get back there, and if you're right, we'll have that taken care of, but it doesn't absolve you of guilt. We were advised of the situation with you harboring the wild animals, too. You've gotta learn that there are proper channels to follow if there's a concern."

"The animals trust me."

"Doesn't matter, young lady. The law is the law," he said. "We have a whole laundry list of issues to clean up, but right now our biggest concerns are to straighten out your disappearance last night and to let your neighbor decide if he wants to press charges. Let's go." He swept his hand in front of him to indicate to Mom and Willow to walk ahead.

I wished I could do something, but I knew this was something Willow had to answer for on her own. She and Mom stepped past the sheriffs and started toward Willow's house. We followed, too, but everyone was quiet other than the two sheriffs chatting. When we got out into the clearing, the medical crew was gathered around the Gator. A couple of them turned and looked in our direction, but other than that, they paid little attention to us.

It only took us ten minutes to cross through the weedy clearing and reach Willow's house.

Along the way we passed two oversized pick up trucks parked in the field and two fire engines on the path next to the barn.

Willow headed for the barn.

"Lightning's in here," she said. She pushed the huge barn doors to the side. Willow and the police disappeared inside, but Mom stopped and came back to us.

"See if my father will take Scout into the clinic," she said as she lifted Scout's bandaged paw. "I'd like them to give this a good cleaning and dress it. They can't stitch up the cuts on her pads, but we don't want them to get infected."

"Okay," Dad said.

Then Mom knelt in front of Erik. "Scout needs you to be brave and help take care of her. She's had a tough couple of days. Can you do that?"

Erik looked up at Scout, who covered most of Dad's front. As if Scout sensed a need, she turned toward Erik then struggled to get out of Dad's arms.

"Easy girl," Dad said, but she kept pushing against him.

Erik raised his hand to rest it on her back. She settled down instantly and relaxed against Dad's chest.

"Thcout'th my good dog. My friend," Erik said.

Mom smiled. "Yes, she is. We're very lucky to have her."

Erik flexed his fingers in her fur. "I love her," he said softly.

At the same instant, Mom, Dad and I looked at each other.

Love? Had Erik verbally expressed an emotion other than fear or anger?

Mom's eyes filled with tears, Dad's Adams apple bobbed in his throat and I knew my eyes were wide with disbelief. I took a deep breath and fought the strong emotions swirling inside. Once again we were reminded of the power of this connection between my special little brother and his special dog.

Scout wasn't changing the quality of just Erik's life; her effect on him was making a difference in all of our lives. I never imagined I'd ever feel such gratitude for a dog.

I also never imagined I'd ever develop a brotherly connection to Erik.

But in this moment, I knew over the last few weeks that the seed had been planted, and now its roots were digging deep into my heart.

Erik suddenly understood love.

And I suddenly understood how much I loved him.

CHAPTER EIGHTEEN

I stopped raking the small pile of leaves from last fall that the previous owner had left under the deck and leaned on the rake handle. Despite the clouds that blocked the full effects of the sun, sweat covered nearly every inch of my body. I removed the work gloves I'd put on to protect my hands and took my cell phone from my pocket to check the time.

This had been five of the longest hours of my life. Patience had never been my strength, but it seemed like it had been days rather than hours since Willow had been taken away by the sheriffs and Brock taken to the hospital. Mom had texted Dad a couple of times to say she was still with Willow, but there were no details. The not knowing was making me crazy.

I glanced toward Dad on the other side of the deck. He held the hedge trimmers sideways as he shaped the top of a shrub to match its counterpart next to me.

"Dad, can I talk to you about something?" I yelled so he could hear me over the buzz of the trimmers.

He took his finger off the power trigger and let the trimmers down until they hung at his side. His

forehead, what I could see under the bill of his
navy blue NYPD baseball cap, wrinkled with
concern. "You okay? Need a break?"

My ears felt like they were stuffed with cotton
after the sudden end of the monotonous noise. It
took a minute for my hearing to adjust so that his
voice and the birds' chirping didn't sound
muffled.

"No, I'm okay."

He didn't look convinced. The emergency
room doctor had cleared me. Just some bruises and
scrapes and probably pretty tired muscles later, but
otherwise he agreed I was fine. But, for the last
hour, I saw Dad checking on me every few
minutes when he thought I wasn't noticing. He'd
wanted me to chill out in the house while he was
outside working, but I was too jittery to sit around.
Despite his objections, I insisted on helping with
the yard work.

"I need advice," I said.

He pointed to the chairs on the deck. "Wanna
sit?"

"No, I'm good." I tossed the gloves onto the
deck stairs and shifted so I could look down the
road toward Granny Annie's house. "It's about
Willow."

"Okay," he said. Dad used his free hand to
push his cap up off his sweaty forehead. The bill
stuck straight up in the air like it was pointing at
something.

I loosely wrung my bandaged hands around the
top of the rake, struggling for the right words.
Dad's attention shifted momentarily toward Erik
and Scout on a bed sheet spread under the big
maple tree near the swingset. Scout was stretched
out next to him, her front paws, one of them

bandaged, resting against Erik's leg, her tongue hanging out as she panted despite the shade.

"Willow needs help," I said.

He squinted and looked down the road then back at me. "That's why your mother's with her."

"No, I'm not talking about today. I'm talking about every day. Brock is hurting her."

Dad scowled. "Hurting her how?" Dad's job was to protect people, so I knew this set off alarms in his mind.

I hesitated for a moment, concerned that I'd be breaking Willow's trust by giving specifics, but then realized a real friend wouldn't keep a secret that was putting her in danger.

"He's purposely tripping her. Hitting her with things like sticks and rocks. She told me he even pushed her down the stairs one time."

Dad's eyes narrowed, a sure sign he was shifting into police officer mode, but he stayed quiet while I rambled on.

"She has bruises all over her arms and legs. That's why the social workers think her grandmother is doing something. But
Willow told me that ever since their mother died and their dad moved away and started a new family that Brock has been really messed up."

Dad wiped his hand across the dribbles of sweat rolling into his eyebrows and whistled softly. "That is quite a mess. Too bad you didn't say something sooner."

"I promised Willow I wouldn't." My palms felt hot against the rake handle. "At the time it had seemed like the right decision."

"There're times when breaking a promise is also the right thing to do." There was no hint of judgment in his voice, only compassion.

I took a deep breath; it felt like the first one I'd taken since Brock had fallen over the edge of the ravine. "I thought I could
handle it on my own, and she wanted to deal with it herself, too." I shrugged one shoulder and added, "I even taught her self-defense moves from my Taekwondo class. She wanted a way to fight back."

Dad squinted one eye, which meant he didn't agree. "What do you think your Sabum would have to say about that?"

My martial arts instructor's face popped into my head, and I knew what he'd say, but this situation seemed different. "He hasn't seen what Brock's been doing to her. All of the bruises."

Dad looked up toward the sky like he was thinking. "I believe he said something like, without proper training and practice, a little knowledge of the martial arts could be more dangerous than none at all because in the case of a bully, it might worsen the situation."

His retelling sounded pretty accurate.

"I know, but —"

Dad's cell phone rang in the pocket of his shorts, interrupting my comment. He set the trimmers on the ground then pulled the phone out and glanced at it. "It's your mother." He swiped the keypad then answered. I tightened my grip on the rake and leaned closer as if that would help me hear her.

"Hi, honey," he said. He listened for a minute, sometimes shaking his head or nodding. "Erik seems to be doing fine at this point," he said. "He's playing under the tree. So far I'm not seeing any signs of stress from him."

There was another short stretch while Mom talked, then Dad said, "Hold on. Let me put you on speakerphone so Dylan can hear, too." He pressed a button then held the phone between us. "Okay, go ahead."

I could tell Mom was on the Bluetooth in her car because the air conditioner created extra white noise. "Willow and I are on our way to Rochester. Brock just got out of surgery. He had a compound fracture of his forearm. His ankle is also broken, but that didn't require surgery."

"So he's going to be okay?" I asked.

"Yes, he should be fine," she answered.

"What about Willow?" I knew she could hear me. "What did the sheriffs say?"

The airspace was filled with soft crackling because nothing was being said. Then Willow spoke up.

"I'm not going to be a jailbird, O'Dylan, if that's what you're worried about." Her sassy reply made me smile.

"That's good." I wanted to pick up on her light-hearted response, but this didn't seem like something to joke about.

"And Lightning is probably going to be taken from Mr. Zurlik's farm. I think they believe me that everything I did was to help him."

"But does that mean you'll never see Lightning again?" I knew how much she loved the horse, and I felt bad that she might not get to see or ride him anymore.

"I think I will, but all I care is that he's taken care of. If it can't be by me, I just want to know he's okay and treated right. I want him loved."

My heart swelled for her. That statement was proof that, first and foremost, her concern was for the well-being of all of the animals. Maybe how she had gone about it was wrong, but it really wasn't about her.

"I can't wait to see you when you get home," I said.

I heard her pull in a deep breath and hold it. I pictured her nibbling on her lower lip as I waited for her to respond.

"Are you okay?" I asked.

There was a bit of awkward silence, and finally she said, "I'm going to be gone for a while."

Panic slammed into me. "Gone? Where?" I wanted to climb through the phone and be with her. See her. Hold her. Get all of the answers now.

"I'm not really sure yet," she said. Her voice trailed off.

Mom spoke up at that point. "The social workers are helping place Willow in a safe home until all of this gets straightened out."

"She can stay with us," I blurted out. "She'll be safe at our house."

Dad smiled and shook his head, but Mom was the one who jumped in and responded. "It's a nice thought, Dylan, but that wouldn't work. I'm at work all day."

It didn't take a genius to figure out what she was implying,
and I realized that my suggestion was ridiculous. I was reacting with my heart not my head. But all I wanted was for Willow's life to be better.

I moved my face closer to the phone as if that would get me closer to Willow. "Willow, you have to tell the sheriffs or somebody who can help what Brock's been doing. If you don't, I will."

Dad clamped his hand on my shoulder. I realized that even though I had asked for his advice, he hadn't had time to give me any. But this showed me I'd known what to do all along.

"I talked with the social workers," she said. "They're going to get us into counseling so we can get back together as a family."

Get back together as a family? I tried to imagine *wanting* to be around Brock. And couldn't. Maybe he really had become a mean person since the problems with his parents so I never got to see a good side of him, but it was hard to imagine him ever being likeable.

Then I thought of my own family. I knew most people couldn't imagine wanting to be around Erik, either. And I was ashamed to admit, even to myself, that that had been me, too. I never thought I'd see the day when I'd be anything but embarrassed by some of the things he said and did. But, I'd learned a lot about my younger brother in the last month, things I hadn't taken the time to learn before. Now there were plenty of times I did like being with him. It was as if Willow had introduced me to my brother.

We were all quiet for a moment, then Mom said, "Don't wait up for me. We may be quite late. The authorities are working on Willow's temporary placement, so after she sees Brock, I'm taking her wherever she'll be staying tonight."

"Okay," Dad said. "But I do have to head back to the city tomorrow morning so I'm there for my afternoon shift."

Even though I knew it was inevitable, hearing Dad say he was leaving again so soon was disappointing.

"Todd," Mom said to Dad, "can you take me off speaker?"

"Sure." He flicked his attention to me for a second then pressed the button to make the call private. When he turned his back and walked away, my stomach knotted. I figured there were lots of reasons that Mom might want to talk with him privately, but privacy usually meant serious.

I leaned the rake against the side of the deck and wandered to where Erik and Scout were on the lawn. I dropped down on my knees on the edge of the sheet and winced when I landed on spots that were scraped up and sore from going down the side of the ravine. Scout rolled her eyes to look at me and thumped her tail a couple of times, but she looked like that was all the energy she could exert.

Erik had brought out his treasure box and he had many of the items from it laid on the sheet. I kept a safe distance from his treasures, but his attention was focused on the old subway token in his left hand. He hummed just loud enough for me to hear him, but not loud enough for me to distinguish whether it was a song or just random noise. Then I noticed he was rubbing the worn stuffed cat ear against his leg with his right hand. Despite the fact that on the outside he didn't seem to be affected by the frightening situation today, this one action suggested otherwise.

"Hey, Erik, your treasures are pretty cool." He didn't respond, but that didn't stop me. I wanted him to know I was interested in what he was doing. "So, which one is your favorite?"

He didn't stop humming, but he turned and looked at his collection. I hadn't noticed before that the treasures seemed to be arranged by color this time. I figured the bronze subway token came from the group with an old rusted bolt, a bent and scratched dog tag, a marble that had mostly brown zigzagging through it and an ornamental "S" hook that had scroll designs. Finally Erik held the token out toward me.

"My dad gave me thith. Ith good luck. It hath a 'Y' on it." That's what Dad had told him when he gave Erik the token, and obviously Erik now applied the token bringing good luck to everything.

When I reached out to take it, Erik snatched his hand back. "No. Thith ith thpethial. It'th magic."

I felt like a jerk for trying to intrude on his private space, but I was determined to connect with him and reassure him that everything in his world was okay.

"Wow!" I said. "You're lucky. I wish I had a magic token."

That must have seemed like a threat, because he squeezed his hand into a tight fist so I couldn't see the token anymore.

"I won't take it," I promised. "That's yours, and I would never take anything that wasn't mine." My mind flashed to Willow and Lightning. I wondered what kind of desperation drove someone to feel they had to save everything, even if it meant taking something that didn't belong to them. Then I thought about her broken family, and my mind wandered to a moment of fantasizing. If Erik's coin really was magic, I'd use it to fix Willow's life.

The thought made me smile. Maybe I did understand her need to try and make things better for the animals after all.

"Dylan?" Dad called from behind me.

I shifted on the sheet. He was coming across the lawn, his hand holding the phone was extended. "Willow wants to talk to you."

My heart rate jumped. I scrambled up, ignoring my sore muscles. When I took the phone, I repeated what Dad had just done – I turned and walked away for privacy.

"Hey. What's up?"

"I wanted to thank you again for what you did today." Her voice was muffled a little, so I guessed she was trying to keep this conversation as private as possible considering Mom was sitting right next to her. I imagined her with her face turned toward the car door window and her hand cupped over her mouth. "You didn't have to risk your life today."

I stopped walking at the corner of the house.

"It was the right thing to do. You're my friend. He's your brother." The truth was, I wanted her to be more than just my friend, but who knew what the future held with today's turn of events.

But I'd wait for her. I'd learn to be patient.

"I don't deserve your friendship," she said even more quietly.

I gripped the phone harder, wishing we were face to face. "Friendship isn't about only the good times, Willow. We both made mistakes."

Willow laughed. "As Granny Annie would say, mine were doozies."

"And as my grandmother would say, it's okay to make mistakes as long as you learn from them."

Willow sniffled, her typical attempt at toughness apparently crumbling. "If you stick with me Dylan, I promise I'll never let you down again. I need you."

A dull ache radiated through my chest. "I'll be here when you come home, Willow. You can depend on me. Always."

"You did it!"

Her leap from subdued to enthusiastic confused me.

"Did what?"

"I said I'd wait until you asked me in a romantic way to be your girlfriend. Is that what you just did?"

I stopped pacing and froze. Finally, I said, "In my mind, you've been my girlfriend since our first kiss, Willow."

"Really?" Her voice squeaked a little at the end, and I thought she might be crying.

"Really," I said. "And I promise I'll make our relationship official in person as long as *you* promise to not meet some other guy while you're away."

The sniffling on the other end of the phone was undeniable. I hoped it was happy crying.

"Deal?" I asked.

"Deal," she whispered.

I listened to her ragged breaths. I had no idea what else to say, but I didn't want to hang up. I resumed pacing up and down the driveway. And waited. Even in the silence I still felt connected. After a minute I heard Mom say something in the background.

"We're pulling into the hospital now," Willow said. "I have to go. Hopefully I'll see you soon, O'Dylan."

I loved that she had used her nickname for me again.

I hesitated, tempted to say 'I love you', but I stopped myself before I blurted it out. The first time she ever heard those words from me, I wanted her to be in front of me so I could punctuate them with a kiss and hug. I wouldn't cheapen them in a quick hang up phone conversation.

Instead, I said, "Call me when you can. I'll miss you."

"I'll miss, you, too. Have fun with your friends. Bye."

I stopped pacing again. Have fun with my friends? What did that mean?

I hit the end button and stared at the phone. Maybe we were all so tired that we weren't making sense anymore. At least talking with her, knowing that she was okay, settled my stomach a little. Now I'd start counting the days until we could be together again.

I returned to the yard. Dad was lying on the sheet next to Erik and talking with him, so I took him his phone.

"I'm going up to my room for a while. I'm more tired than I thought."

Dad nodded. "Maybe you'd like to pack your suitcase while you're there."

I had to be overtired, because now Dad wasn't making sense either. "For what?"

"Your mom and I think you've earned a break. Would you like to go back with me tomorrow and spend a couple of weeks in the city now in addition to later in the summer?"

"Are you serious?" Excitement shot through me. Two weeks back with my friends in the old neighborhood? It's all I'd
wanted since we'd moved up here. The craziness of the day became a blur of unreality. Reality was waiting for me in Manhattan.

Dad smiled. "Yeah, I'm serious. But we have to be out of here by 6 a.m., so you need to pack tonight."

I wanted to holler "hallelujah" but opted for the mature response and kept my thrill in check. Still, it bubbled like boiling water inside me. "I'll pack now." I turned to go to the house but stopped and pivoted back toward the blanket. Erik looked frozen in place, staring at me. His fingers aggressively worked the cat ear.

"What about Erik? Who's going to watch him?" It was just another sign of how much I'd changed since moving here. In the city, I wouldn't have concerned myself with that.

"Your mother and I will work that out."

For a moment I wondered why, if it was that easy to take me out of the equation now, I'd had to leave the city in the first place. But I'd just been given a free pass so I wasn't going to ask questions that might cause Mom and Dad to rethink the offer. I glanced at Erik. His expression, or lack of it, didn't give me any clues about what he was thinking.

At some point while I was on the phone he had set down his token. He must have noticed that I looked at it, because suddenly he snatched it and folded it in his small hand, hiding it behind the cat ear. Maybe he was thinking what crossed my mind: that token just might be magical if suddenly I'd been given this opportunity.

I started toward the house again, but stopped one more time and turned around.

"I can't go. What about the baseball team?"

"Who pitched before you got on the team?"

"Zach." Then I smiled. Zach wouldn't be happy about Brock being hurt, but he'd be happy to have his pitching spot again. It actually felt like I'd be doing him a favor. "Yeah, Zach can do it. I'll call Coach Gordon to let him know I'll be gone. I'd only miss one game since the week after next we drew a bye, but it wouldn't be right to just ditch the team, especially now that Brock's out."

"I'm sure the coach will understand," Dad said.

"Yeah, I think you're right. This is great! Thanks, Dad," I said, and hurried into the house.

I patted down the pile of clothes in my suitcase, tucking in my gray Yankees t-shirt as a back-up in case my blue one got dirty. On my bed was the list of the things I definitely didn't want to forget. My baseball glove, laptop, swimming trunks, phone and charger. The really important things. While I was picking through the clothes that were strewn on the floor, I folded and put away the clothes that weren't going with me and put the ones I was taking in the suitcase.

My back was to the door, and I was zipping the suitcase when I heard shuffling behind me. I glanced over my shoulder. Erik and Scout stood in the doorway, a folded piece of paper dangling from Erik's hand.

"Hey, Oops, what's up?" I turned back to the suitcase and finished pulling the zipper around.

Erik came up next to me and held out the paper. "Thith ith for you."

When I took the folded piece of printer paper, he slipped out the door before I could ask him what it was. I looked down at it.

On the front was a picture of a kid I assumed was supposed to be me. I was holding a baseball bat, and my glove was on my other hand. I looked pretty tall and skinny in the picture, so my dark green baseball jersey with the big white 18 and the team name, Chargers, on it looked like a tent. The cleats on my feet were black with three white stripes on each side. He'd even drawn in my signature green laces. I was stunned to realize he'd noticed those details about my uniform from my old team, when I'd always thought he was oblivious to anything important in my world. The baseball hat he'd drawn was way bigger than my head, but he'd probably made it bigger in order to fit on the words "Best Brother".

A lump jumped to my throat. I didn't feel like the best brother, but it made me happy to think he'd written that. I opened the homemade card and inside was a picture that I assumed represented Erik, Scout and me standing on the dock at the pond in the woods. Erik's hand was on Scout, and my hand was on Erik's shoulder. Scout held a lime green tennis ball in her mouth and he'd drawn in water dripping from it.

The amount of detail he had in this drawing, too, was amazing. The shape of the pond was accurate, as well as the bushes and trees. While I was studying it, I noticed there was something in my right hand in the picture. I brought the drawing closer and could see a small round object with a "Y" in the middle of it.

His subway token. Even though he wouldn't let me touch it in real life, in the picture, he'd put it in *my* hand, not his. It was then that I noticed another tiny detail that I would have missed if I had only looked quickly.

Tiny tears were drawn just below his and Scout's eyes.

Emotion. He couldn't show it appropriately in real life, but in a picture he could. I looked to see if he was still in my room, but the doorway was empty. And surprisingly, my heart suddenly felt empty, too. More than a month ago, my reaction probably would have been different, but now I knew that I would miss Erik, and Scout, just as much as I'd miss Willow for the two weeks I'd be gone. I couldn't believe how lucky I felt that my world had become so complicated. I pretended the moisture in my eyes was from humidity.

I unzipped my suitcase and carefully laid Erik's drawing on top of my clothes then re-zipped it before carrying it over and setting it next to my door. Now I felt like I was taking a little of Erik with me. I smiled. That feeling was fantastic.

Overwhelmed by the conflicting emotions, I got ready for bed. Morning couldn't come fast enough.

My eyes fluttered open as I struggled to adjust them to the morning sunlight. I'd purposely left my shade up and curtains open to make it easier to wake up so early. The birds sang their little hearts out and, in the distance, Einstein screamed like he had in our tree the first time I'd met Willow. At least this time he wasn't outside my window, but thanks to him, she was the first person I thought about for the day. I hoped her night away from home was okay.

When I started to roll over to look at my clock, every muscle in my body burned in protest. I massaged my neck, hoping the tension was only temporary. Even my ankles and wrists pulsed with pain. I kicked off the sheet and rotated the joints, wincing with each muscular roll. I couldn't believe the difference a day made. Yesterday I was a teenager and today my body felt like it belonged to an old man. And then I thought of Brock, and my pain was put in perspective. I couldn't imagine the agony he was probably experiencing.

I'd slept well all night so I hadn't heard anything. I assumed Mom was home, but I'd never heard her come in. I climbed out of bed and hobbled to the shower, hoping hot water would loosen my muscles the rest of the way.

Erik's bedroom door was open, and as I passed I saw Scout curled up at the end of his bed. She lifted her head when I walked by, but there was no way she was leaving him. I was still amazed at how quickly Scout had adopted him as *her* boy.

I rushed through my shower because I couldn't wait to get on the road, get to the city and see my friends. It seemed a lifetime ago that we'd hung out. Texting, phone calls and social media definitely weren't the same as being face to face.

I was lacing my sneakers when Dad stepped into my room.

"Heard you up. This must be one for the record books. It's not even noon." I had a reputation for sleeping late when I could, but I knew if I wasn't ready, Dad would have to leave without me. I wasn't taking that chance.

"I'm all set. Have to grab my baseball duffle out of the garage then I'm ready to go." I tugged on the laces to make sure they were tight then stood. "When did Mom get home?"

"Around midnight." He picked up my suitcase from next to the door. "I'll take this out to the car."

I grabbed my cell phone off the nightstand. "What did she say about Willow and Brock?"

"Brock will be in the hospital a couple of days, and Willow has been placed with a friend's family. Apparently they're a registered foster family and were willing to have her stay with them until everything gets straightened out."

I was flooded with relief. "I'm glad she's not with strangers."

"Me, too," Dad said. I followed him out of my room. Erik was coming out of his room at the same time and halted suddenly in the hallway. His hair stuck out in a million directions and his eyes were as wide as quarters.

"You're leaving me and Thcout?"

There was that huge lump in my throat again. His drawing with the tears popped into my mind. I went to him and kneeled so we were at eye level, even though it was doubtful that he would look at me.

"Yeah, but I'll be back before you know it, and we'll play with your trucks. We can make a fort in the dining room again, too. And we'll take Scout to the pond to go swimming." At the mention of her name, Scout opened her mouth like she was smiling and her tail wagged.

I didn't know what else to do, so I held my hand up. "High five me, Oops. I'm going to miss you."

He didn't lift his hand, and instead, dropped his chin and stared at the floor. A little knot tugged at my stomach. I let my hand down slowly and got up in spite of my protesting muscles. "You're a good brother, Erik. I'll be back soon. You'll see. I'll bring you another treasure from Manhattan."

Even though he didn't acknowledge me or my offer, I couldn't believe how hard it was to turn my back and walk down the stairs. I knew as soon as we got on the road I'd be so excited to get to the city to see my friends that this wouldn't bother me anymore. Or at least I hoped that would be the case.

Dad went out the front door, leaving it wide open, and Mom met me at the bottom of the stairs.

She smiled when she saw me. "How are you feeling this morning? I want to give you a hug, but I'm worried I'll hurt you if I do."

I put my arms up. "Hug away. Really, I'm fine, Mom."

She held me loosely, like she still wasn't convinced. "You've earned this trip to the city, Dylan. I think it will be good for you to get away from all of this and just be yourself for a couple of weeks."

I let go of her and stepped back. "Thanks. I'm psyched, but I'll probably drive you nuts checking in with texts."

Her eyes misted over. "That's okay. But this will all be here when you come back. Try to put it out of your mind and enjoy your friends. This is what you've been asking for since we moved here."

"Yeah, I know." I glanced toward the kitchen because I couldn't handle the emotion etched on her face. "Did Dad say if I should grab something to eat?"

She cleared her throat, but her voice still came out raspy. "You're eating on the way."
She looked up at Erik. "Come on, Erik. Bring Scout and you can say goodbye to Dylan and Dad outside."

He sat down on the top step and Scout sat next to him. He didn't have to say anything for us to get his message.

"Okay, I'll be right back in," she said, then she walked out onto the front steps and I followed.

Before closing the door, I glanced up at the top of the stairs. Erik and Scout sat there, watching us. My throat tightened and it impossible to get enough air to say good-bye, so I waved instead. As expected, there was no response from Erik.

As we walked along the sidewalk to the car, my legs felt like they were made of concrete. Dad slammed the trunk closed then came around to wrap Mom in a hug. I slid into the passenger seat and closed the door, eager to get going. Because it was early morning, it was still cool inside, and I was thankful for that because, for some reason, I'd broken out in a sweat.

A moment later Dad slipped into the driver's seat and put the key into the ignition. "You excited?" he asked as he started the engine.

I nodded. "Yep." By the afternoon, I'd be hanging with my friends. What wasn't exciting about that?

He shifted the car into drive and started to pull out of the driveway when Mom banged on the window. "Hold on a second."

Dad braked and I opened my door. I hadn't noticed that Erik and Scout had come out of the house until Erik stepped around her, holding out his hand toward me. The rising sun glinted off the metal token between his fingers.

"Take thith with you tho the magic will bring you back," he said.

The tiny lump that had been in my throat before became a full-fledged blockage, and I couldn't catch a breath.

I opened my palm and he dropped his treasure into it. I stared at it, surprised by the gesture. Except, when I thought about it, this was just like in the picture he'd drawn. He must have decided last night that he was giving it to me for the trip. Erik took a step back, and a hint of a smile lifted his cheeks.

It hurt my throat to swallow, but I did it so I could get enough air to say, "Thanks."

Dad cleared his throat. "Well, we better hit the road."

"Be safe," Mom said before she pushed the door shut again and waved.

I watched Erik take hold of Scout's collar and pull her away from the driveway.

I squeezed the token in my palm until the round edges pressed into the tender spots and forced me to loosen my grip. Erik had never included me in his world before.

Then I realized I also had never included him in mine until we moved here and was forced to. I had to look away from him and Scout. I never imagined leaving Erik would be so hard.

"Ready?" Dad asked.

Unable to speak, I nodded.

Dad stepped on the gas and the car continued forward. I stared straight ahead until we reached the end of the driveway. Even though there was no traffic, Dad turned on his signal light and the clicking sound filled the heavy silence in the car.

Just before we pulled into the road, I couldn't help myself - I glanced in the side rearview mirror. Erik had run out into the driveway and he and Scout were following our car. Mom was beside him to keep him from running into the street, but his attention was fixed on us.

Dad must have looked in his mirror, too, because suddenly he said, "I miss that little guy when I'm in New York."

I tried to focus on the moment. Dad eased the car into the road and accelerated. Finally, we were on our way.

I opened my palm and stared at the token. Erik believed the magic of the token would bring me back. My jaw tightened. I'd only be gone for two weeks. For a moment I considered that. I wasn't sure if he even understood the concept of two weeks.

But I did. And the reality slammed me in the chest.

I reached over and grabbed Dad's arm. "Dad, stop!"

His right foot jerked toward the brake. "What's wrong?"

"I have to go back," I said.

He glanced over at me as he slowed the car to a stop. "Did you forget something?"

I looked in the mirror again. Erik was waving so hard I thought his little arm would fly off. "No, I remembered something."

He narrowed his eyes. "Are you okay?"

"Oh, yeah. I'm more than okay."

I unbuckled my seatbelt, grabbed the door handle and shoved open the door.

"Dylan, what are you doing? I'll back up."

"I don't have time, Dad." I jumped from the car but turned back to quickly explain. "I'm not going to the city. I'm staying here."

"What about being with your old friends? It's all you've wanted."

"I know. That's what I thought. But now isn't the right time. I have to stay here."

His forehead wrinkled. "You sure?"

I took a deep breath, and when I let it out, I couldn't fight the smile that joined it.

"Oh, yeah. I'm sure."

I slammed the door shut and jogged back toward our driveway.

Mom glanced between me and the car, confusion creasing her face. "What's wrong?"

"I can't do it," I said as I passed her.

"Do what?"

But I didn't answer. I wanted to show her not tell her.

"Erik, look," I said as I approached him. "You were right." I held the token out in front of me and stopped in front of him. My fingers shook. "Your treasure *is* magic." I bent so we were face to face, but he averted his eyes to the token.

"The treathure brought you back to me and Thcout?"

I moved to get my face in front of his, but he continued to avoid eye contact.

"Yes, it did. And I'm going to stay right here with you, because you and Scout and I are a team. We belong together."

When he reached out to touch the coin, instead of releasing it, I held it. Our fingertips touched, but he didn't withdraw from the contact as he typically would. The warmth of his skin shot right to my insides. I felt happier than I ever had in my life. My face heated as I fought the swell of emotion that was taking over.

"I want to be with you and Scout this summer, Erik."

He pressed his cheek to the side of Scout's head, and Scout turned and flicked her tongue against his chin. He giggled and rolled his head away from her, but she was relentless.

"Thcout ith my good dog," he said.

"I know," I answered, trying to keep my emotions in check. "You're lucky."

Erik shifted his focus back to the token and our fingers. "And you are my betht brother."

I choked a little and my eyes welled up. "And you're *my* best brother, Erik."

Even though I knew it was risky, I swept him into a hug, hoping the contact wouldn't cause him to have a meltdown. At first he stood stiffly, leaving the hugging to me.

But then his small arms slowly slid around my waist. At the same time, fireworks exploded inside me. I never realized how important a hug could be until this moment.

He allowed only a few seconds of contact before he pulled away. I was disappointed to have the moment over so fast, but I felt lucky that he had allowed it all.

Then suddenly, the most amazing thing happened - he lifted his gaze and stared straight into my eyes.

And we really connected for the first time ever.

For at least this moment, we'd broken the barrier of his autism, and it was a better feeling than the grand slam homerun from two nights before. Every fiber in my body sizzled.

Without breaking our eye contact, he whispered, "Thith ith the betht thummer ever."

With that simple statement, the dam broke. Tears streaked down my face, but I didn't care.

I held up the token and smiled. "You know what? You're right, Erik. This *is* the best summer ever."

AUTHOR'S MESSAGE

This novel only scratches the surface of topics that could be explored further. While this is a work of fiction, and I wrote it to entertain readers, but the storyline deals with serious issues.

Intolerance toward anyone who seems "different" runs rampant through our world. For those who are involved in the daily struggle of living with autism, this intolerance and lack of understanding is frustrating, at best, and hurtful at worst. There are many ranges of autism on the spectrum, and in some cases, it's not as easy to recognize the person has challenges. During my 26 year career teaching middle school, I taught several students on the autism spectrum, and at the college level I worked one on one with students with autism. Regardless of age or where they fall on the spectrum, that all have the same desire in common – to be treated like everyone else and to be successful. Members of my extended family and friends have children with autism. Their daily struggle to create a "normal" world can't be fully appreciated by those fortunate enough to not have those challenges. Education and tolerance are the key to understanding how to help those with autism enjoy acceptance and a fulfilling life. For more information about autism, I've included links in the front of the book to some of the Internet sites I found of value in my research. I'd love for this book to be a catalyst for change.

I included the storyline of Scout, the assistance dog, because through my research I've learned how these well-trained dogs can have a positive impact for those who need them. I focused on assistance dogs for people with autism, but there are resources for those with physical and emotional disabilities to also bring an assistance dog into their lives. For those with Post Traumatic Stress Disorder (PTSD), and people with physical limitations and disabilities, these dogs can change their lives. There are many excellent organizations that help connect those in need with a trained animal.

Because I was a middle school teacher for so long, the issue of bullying has always been in the forefront for me. I hope for those who read this book who are being bullied that they will realize they're not the ones with the problem; it's those who are bullying who have a problem. If you're the victim of bullying, please seek help. No one deserves to be bullied by anyone – another kid or an adult. If you're a witness to bullying in any form, it's important to speak up and support the person on the receiving end of the bullying. Take their side and help empower them. Together we can take away the bullies' power.

Finally, there are two more points I'd like to make. First, training of assistance dogs should only be done by professionals who have been educated in the process. Not every dog is the right fit for this type of service, regardless of its breed. Leave the training to professionals. The same is true for rehabilitating animals. As well-intentioned as we may be, this should be left to professionals who have been well-trained to care properly for these animals to give them the best chance for survival. They also know when rehabilitation isn't in the best interest of the animal, and this is important.

Thank you for reading *Over the Edge*. I hope you'll visit my website or "like" my Facebook page. I love hearing from readers.

ABOUT THE AUTHOR

Besides writing books, Laurie Gifford Adams is a multi-published freelance writer. She taught English in Connecticut before moving back to the Finger Lakes of western New York where she grew up. Because she loves kids and animals, she will continue to give them starring roles in her books.

Made in the USA
San Bernardino, CA
07 July 2014